Winning
THE
Gentleman

Books by Kristi Ann Hunter

HAWTHORNE HOUSE

A Lady of Esteem: A HAWTHORNE HOUSE Novella

A Noble Masquerade

An Elegant Façade

An Uncommon Courtship

An Inconvenient Beauty

HAVEN MANOR

A Search for Refuge: A HAVEN MANOR Novella

A Defense of Honor

Legacy of Love: A HAVEN MANOR Novella from The Christmas Heirloom Novella Collection

A Return of Devotion

A Pursuit of Home

HEARTS ON THE HEATH

Vying for the Viscount

Winning the Gentleman

HEARTS *on the* HEATH

Winning
THE
Gentleman

KRISTI ANN HUNTER

BETHANYHOUSE
a division of Baker Publishing Group
Minneapolis, Minnesota

© 2021 by Kristi L. Hunter

Published by Bethany House Publishers
11400 Hampshire Avenue South
Bloomington, Minnesota 55438
www.bethanyhouse.com

Bethany House Publishers is a division of
Baker Publishing Group, Grand Rapids, Michigan

Printed in the United States of America

Library of Congress Cataloging-in-Publication Data
Names: Hunter, Kristi Ann, author.
Title: Winning the gentleman / Kristi Ann Hunter.
Description: Minneapolis, Minnesota: Bethany House, a division of Baker
    Publishing Group, [2021] | Series: Hearts on the heath
Identifiers: LCCN 2020046866 | ISBN 9780764235269 (trade paperback) | ISBN
    9780764238154 (casebound) | ISBN 9781493429950 (ebook)
Classification: LCC PS3608.U5935 W56 2021 | DDC 813/.6—dc23
LC record available at https://lccn.loc.gov/2020046866

Scripture quotations are from the King James Version of the Bible.

This is a work of fiction. Names, characters, incidents, and dialogues are products of the author's imagination and are not to be construed as real. Any resemblance to actual events or persons, living or dead, is entirely coincidental.

Cover design by LOOK Design Studio

Author is represented by Natasha Kern Literary Agency.

21 22 23 24 25 26 27   7 6 5 4 3 2 1

To the Provider of New Dreams
1 Peter 1:3–4

And to Jacob,
for helping me see that where
I came from doesn't
dictate where I'll go.

Author's Note

You won't find Sophia Fitzroy if you look up the first female jockey in history, because she is fictional. If you look hard enough, though, you'll find Alicia Thornton.

Mrs. Thornton ran two races in 1804, one as a personal challenge and one against a professional jockey. Both of them caused quite an uproar. Though her story inspired mine, that is where the similarities end. The rest of Sophia's experiences and skills are pieced together from the lives of other remarkable equestrian women of the early nineteenth century.

Today's female jockeys don't owe a great debt to Mrs. Thornton, since it would be well over a hundred years before the sport acknowledged another woman in any official capacity, but the question isn't always *did* it happen but *could* it have happened. And that is what makes history so very interesting.

One

After twenty-two years, Aaron Whitworth should have been aware of his closest friend's idiocy. Yet it had never crossed his mind Oliver could do something so utterly foolish.

One could argue the man had saved Aaron's sanity, if not his life, during their school days, but sometime in the years since boyhood, the heir to the Earl of Trenting had lost his mind. Befriending Aaron hadn't been the wisest decision, though, so it was possible Oliver's penchant for making poor choices, or at least rash ones, had always been present.

Aaron clamped his teeth together to avoid saying anything he might later regret. Yanking memories of better times to the front of his mind, he forced his voice to remain even. "You did what?"

"Accepted a challenge. That *is* what men of the turf do." Oliver lifted his chin as his gaze slid from Aaron's and dropped to the horse patiently awaiting its rider.

Aaron frowned at the reins in his hand. He'd been moments away from mounting, ready to make the ride to the Stourbridge Fair in Cambridge and approve an order of saddles one of the sellers planned to deliver after the fair.

Dawn was stabbing its first streaks of light into a clear sky.

9

Oliver's cook had prepared him a breakfast of cold meat, cheese, and bread to eat as he rode. Aaron's horse, Shadow, had been energetic on the short ride from his cottage to Oliver's stable, assuring an enjoyable journey to the next town.

The promise of the morning paled in the aftermath of his friend's blunder.

Aaron sighed and draped Shadow's reins over a hook on the wall of the stable. Ever since Oliver had gotten betrothed to the daughter of one of Newmarket's prominent horse breeders, he'd been determined to participate in the interests he would one day inherit.

Starting with the racing stable.

Unfortunately, though Oliver was a solid, loyal friend, his knowledge of property and business was little more than conceptual. He seemed to know he'd made a mistake this time, even if he didn't realize the enormity of it.

Aaron spoke slowly, weighing every word before allowing it to cross his lips. "Yes, men of the turf—and please don't use that term again—arrange and accept challenges." He paused. "It is customary, however, to only enter a challenge when one has a jockey to ride his horse."

Oliver shifted his weight and cleared his throat, slowly sliding his gaze back to Aaron's. "We don't have a jockey?"

"Not since I fired him four days ago, no." It should have been done weeks, if not months, before, but Aaron had put it off because finding a good jockey who was willing to work for him was difficult. He had high demands on the skill of the rider, the care of the horses, and the character of the man.

Because Aaron's reputation was less than ideal, he often had to settle for two out of three. Since he wasn't about to let the animals pay the price, he'd been forced to give way on character. Hughes had been a lout, but he rode well and never hurt the horses.

At least, he didn't when he was sober.

"Why did we fire him?" Oliver asked.

And that unwavering loyalty was why Aaron would always put up with Oliver's naïveté.

"He was enjoying his gin so much he thought the horses should have a nip as well and poured two bottles into the water trough." Risking his own health and reputation was bad enough, but endangering the horses was unacceptable.

"Don't we employ more than one jockey?" Oliver asked.

"Your other two took horses to a race in Yorkshire and have been delayed returning," Aaron said. "Right now, I'm just hoping they're here in time for the first of the October Meetings."

"What about Hudson's jockeys?"

Hudson, Viscount of Stildon, owned the other stable Aaron managed, though Hudson had been absent from the area until a month ago. They'd moved from employer and employee to friends faster than Aaron would have thought possible, and he wasn't sure he fully trusted the relationship or the way it had changed his life.

Still, if the situation were dire enough, Aaron could probably stomach asking a favor of him.

Maybe.

Fortunately, that wasn't an option. "One went to visit his ailing mother and isn't due back for at least another week. The other stepped wrong dismounting yesterday and turned his ankle."

Oliver ran a hand through his hair, making the light brown strands stick up at odd angles. "Equinox has no jockey."

The quiet statement cut through Aaron's control, and a groan escaped as he dropped his head back to look at the lightening sky. "Why would you agree to a challenge without asking me? Especially since we've several races on the books already with the upcoming October Meetings."

"Davers was rather adamant."

Aaron's head jerked hard enough to strain the muscles in his shoulder. The challenge was with Lord Davers? Aaron's relationship with the Newmarket horse owners was tenuous but decent.

Except with Davers. The other man had never liked that Aaron was allowed to sully his presence simply because he had an excellent touch with horses and a few decent connections.

Oliver knew that. Why would he have anything to do with—

"And Brimsbane was there," Oliver admitted with a sigh, once again shifting his gaze to avoid looking Aaron in the eye.

For as long as Aaron had known Oliver, the man had gotten on well with everyone. Now, for a reason even Oliver probably didn't know, he had formed a one-sided rivalry with his future brother-in-law.

With a sigh, Aaron reached out and buried his hand in Shadow's mane, drawing comfort from the warmth of the horse's neck. "You have the girl's affection, her father's agreement, and a wedding date set in a month. What does it matter if her brother thinks you a cod's head?"

Oliver snapped his attention back to Aaron and frowned. "Brimsbane thinks me a cod's head?"

No, but Aaron was on the verge of it. "To my knowledge, Brimsbane doesn't think of you at all beyond your ability to make Lady Rebecca happy. You've known the chap for years."

"I know." Oliver began to pace, the dressing gown he'd been wearing when he rushed from the house to catch Aaron flapping about his knees. Pacing was a sure sign his grip on practical reality was sliding into panic based on some illogical conclusion only he could understand. "Did you see him at the training yards last week?"

"Brimsbane?" Why were they still talking about him? The challenge with Davers was far more pressing. They had one day to find a solution.

Aaron took a deep breath and counted to three. Oliver wouldn't move back to the original conversation until this new one was completed. "Yes, I saw him. When he's in town, he checks his horses' training at least twice a week."

"Exactly." Oliver swung his arms wide as he continued to pace.

Aaron waited, but nothing more came. "Exactly what?"

"Brimsbane knows his horses." Oliver stopped and pointed at Aaron. "Did you know he asked me why my horses ran without blankets, and I didn't even know what he was talking about?"

"I don't care for sweating the horses." Aaron lifted one shoulder and let it drop. "Wearing a winter traveling coat doesn't make a man faster. Why would a horse be any different?"

Many of the methods he used on the horses in his charge were different from the normal ones, and both the stables he managed— including Oliver's father's—had shown increased success because of it. The care of horses and advancements in their training had long been a passion of Aaron's.

Despite his closeness with Aaron, Oliver attended very few races and never expressed interest in his father's racing stable. Before he'd fallen in love with the daughter of an avid horseman, Oliver had cared only that his horse looked good and was fit enough to carry him wherever he wanted to go.

Perhaps it was love that had finally sent Oliver over the edge of reasonableness. It had certainly wreaked havoc in Aaron's life, and he wasn't even the one experiencing it, thank goodness.

Aaron didn't have anything to offer a woman. At best he dallied on the fringes of polite society. At worst he was an outcast. Far better for Aaron to keep his circle of friends small and tight so his situation affected as few people as possible.

If only those few people would stop falling in love and expanding the circle. Each and every one of them had gone through a period of acting a complete fool because of their love-addled brains.

None had recovered from the malady with sanity intact.

"Forget about Brimsbane, at least for the moment." *Hopefully forever.* "Let's discuss the agreement with Davers."

Oliver winced and blew out a long breath before relaying to Aaron the details of the challenge. "Might he agree to a postponement?"

"Oh, most assuredly," Aaron said dryly, "but not before ensuring that everyone in Cambridgeshire, Suffolk, and Essex knew you'd reneged."

It was possible that had been Davers's plan all along. The man had a history of trying to tap a weakness in Aaron's employers in order to mar Aaron's reputation. If Oliver canceled the challenge, everyone would assume it was because Aaron didn't think he could win. He'd tried to fire Hughes quietly, but if Davers somehow knew Aaron had no jockey . . .

Regardless of the method or motivation, Aaron's carefully and strategically cultivated reputation was in danger. The small foundation he'd managed to build himself would crack. One crack would lead to another, and in little time at all, he'd become exactly what his father had told him he would be: nothing.

Aaron couldn't—wouldn't—tell Oliver that. He never admitted his fears aloud to anyone. Ever.

Besides, guilt would wrack the man if he knew Aaron's concerns, and he might try to correct the disaster with an even more foolish decision. Oliver and Graham, the viscount who made up the third member of their boyhood trio, had sacrificed enough for Aaron as it was. Their friendship had inspired him to hope. He wouldn't repay them by inspiring worry—or worse, pity.

Oliver ran his hand through his hair and resumed pacing. "We have to run the race."

"Yes." Knowing he couldn't stop what had already been set in motion, Aaron turned his mind to potential solutions. Newmarket was the heart of English racing. Jockeys abounded in the area.

Unfortunately, he couldn't think of anyone who met even his two essential criteria and would be willing to ride for him this close to the October Meetings. Jockeys worked closely with their horses, and the decent ones had all been hired long ago. They wouldn't want to jeopardize those positions by agreeing to run for Aaron. Though superb, his reputation was fragile, and no one wanted to be the jockey at the helm when the ship finally crashed.

Either God thought Aaron needed another lesson in perseverance, or the world wanted him to remember his proper place—or rather his lack of one.

Existential issues notwithstanding, tomorrow morning Aaron would be expected on the Heath with a horse and rider at the starting post.

He sighed. "I suppose we could use a groom." It would likely mean losing the challenge. Aaron's stomach burned. He'd lost his share of official races, of course, but he'd never lost a personal challenge.

Mostly because he never accepted one he didn't know he could win.

And while a loss would undermine his reputation, missing the race altogether would destroy it.

"The grooms are all excellent riders." Oliver smiled, unsurprisingly unaware that anything aside from the money wagered might be lost during this race.

"You know I wouldn't hire a man who didn't ride well or treat a horse correctly," Aaron grumbled. That didn't make them good jockeys, though. Stable work tended to require stronger, larger men, which wasn't the ideal build for a jockey.

Oliver's smile fell, and he resumed pacing. "A loss won't look good to Brimsbane or Lord Gliddon."

Aaron narrowed his eyes at his friend. "I do hope once you're married you give more concern to how your wife feels about you instead of her brother and father. I didn't haul your lovesick foolish self from London to court the earl."

"Rebecca loves me." Oliver frowned.

"Precisely." The calmness Aaron held with an iron grip shattered, and he stepped forward to grip his friend by the shoulders and give him a slight shake. "She loves you. Since the betrothal has been announced and you aren't going to live with Lord and Lady Gliddon after the wedding, what are you worried about?"

"You don't understand." Oliver shook his head and looked away.

No, Aaron would never understand. He'd seen caring families and had, at times, craved one of his own, but in his experience, family was nothing but shameful responsibility. His father considered him an example to hold before his real son to show that choices had ramifications.

"Explain it to me, then." Aaron's voice was hard, not because he was frustrated with Oliver but because there were going to be consequences, possibly dire ones, and Aaron intended to take the brunt of them. Graham and Oliver were the only people who had ever chosen to be in Aaron's life despite his less than noble beginnings. The least he could do was protect Oliver in return.

"I love Rebecca," Oliver said softly as he broke away from Aaron and paced again.

"We established that."

"I didn't propose in London."

"As I'm well aware." Aaron had only visited London a few times during the Season, but he'd seen how Lady Rebecca's popularity had paralyzed his friend, despite the indications that she reciprocated his feelings.

"You had to drag me here from London and kick me in the backside to act before I lost her." Oliver shoved his hand through his hair again.

"Again, I am aware."

"Yes, well—" Oliver cleared his throat—"so are they."

Aaron frowned. "Is she—"

"No," Oliver cut in sharply before sighing. "She understands. Lord Gliddon . . . well . . . I don't believe he'd have given his blessing if Rebecca hadn't forced him to. I don't think he likes me."

"Everyone likes you, Oliver."

"That doesn't mean he respects me."

The truth of that statement silenced Aaron. Lady Rebecca saw the man's faults as well as his virtues and loved him anyway, but to someone who didn't take the time to get to know him, Oliver could look something of a cake.

"I thought if I took an interest in the stable, won a few races, that would be something Lord Gliddon could appreciate."

Aaron clenched his jaw to keep the words in his head from rushing through his mouth. If Oliver had enlisted Aaron's help, it would have been simple to teach him the right things to say and do to appear a proper horseman. But what was done was done.

"Don't worry," Aaron said, swallowing hard to keep the burn in his stomach from crawling up his throat. "I'll find another rider." Somewhere.

Oliver's shoulders lost their tension, and he smiled, obviously content that Aaron would handle everything.

Before Aaron said something to crush his friend's ease, he mounted Shadow and pointed the horse toward Cambridge. While he wouldn't be spending the day leisurely strolling through the fair, he still had to make the final arrangements on his order.

Besides, there wasn't a better place to ponder a problem than on the back of a horse. By the time he returned to Newmarket, he'd have a plan in mind, if not in place.

As the horse walked by the Heath, Aaron looked over the expanse of grass that had been his restoration. Hopefully it wouldn't soon be the site of his humiliation as well.

Two

Though the solution didn't materialize as Aaron rode through the countryside, a sense of desperation did. Unfortunately, the ideas of desperate men are risky. They might pay out in the end, but more often than not, they caused more problems.

Somewhere between stabling Shadow at one of the temporary liveries and meeting with the saddle maker, Aaron convinced himself that his absurd idea was one of the good ones.

What if his solution was hiding among the stalls of horse breeders and tack salesmen? What if he hired a complete unknown as a jockey? All he needed was someone of small stature with a good seat and the proper respect for horses, someone who didn't fear the rush of wind as an animal in its prime surged at a gallop across the Heath.

Even if he lost, it would look better than putting a groom on Equinox's back. At least then people could only question the race and not Aaron's ability to manage and staff the stable.

The entire idea was ludicrous, though. How was he to go about testing a man's abilities in the crowded confines of a fair? One could barely walk at a decent pace, much less ride.

With more attention on his musings than his surroundings, he didn't realize he'd wandered into the edge of a crowd until he'd been swallowed by it. *Oohs* and *aahs* filled the air as the people pressed against the rickety fence of a traveling show.

He looked up just in time to see a horse performing moves he'd never known horses could do. Startlingly white to the point of glowing, the horse captivated Aaron as it pranced around the performance area, mane and tail flowing behind. Surely anyone who could make a horse do that could encourage one to run fast along a course.

His gaze tracked to the rider. His hopes plummeted even as his attention sharpened. Blond hair streamed down her back and across her shoulders. Her green gown, with long, wide sleeves and panels of sheer fabric floating about the skirt, shimmered in the morning sun. On the back of the horse, she appeared to be flying.

This wasn't the solution to his problems, but he was intrigued enough to keep watching. It looked like a dance as the horse performed a series of intricate steps before running in a circle while the faerie stood on its back.

Aaron knew that excellent female riders existed—he even counted one among his small circle of acquaintances—but he'd never seen one ride like that.

A man stood to the side recounting some story that was likely meant to give meaning to the moves, but it was nothing but noise to Aaron's ears.

Such a beautiful horse needed no additional story to be admired. The rider's overdone gown and abundance of hair detracted from the beauty as far as Aaron was concerned. They were a distraction he narrowed his eyes to remove.

Though he wouldn't discount the lady's skill in being able to stay atop the horse's back, he could see no signal from the rider to guide the horse. Likely the animal had been taught the routine by someone else and performed it so often that it would go through the motions, rider or no.

Murmurs of delight swelled through the crowd as the white horse knelt and the faerie dismounted to bestow a rose upon one of the boys crowded close to the fence. She climbed back on the horse, and the pair departed while the storyteller crossed in front of the crowd with a basket on a stick, collecting coins from the awed observers.

Aaron stepped away. There would be more shows today, perhaps even two or three. Well-trained horses and skilled riders should be rewarded, but he wanted to see the entire show before depositing his coins.

In the meantime, there were plenty of stalls in which he could have horse-related conversations and seek out someone ready to be molded into an excellent jockey, or at least an adequate one.

His hopes faded as he finished perusing the second full row of stalls without a single prospect. He'd circled back to the performance area, so he secured a position near the front but far to the right. Tales of the faerie queen must have spread, because several boys were already clustered near the center of the fence.

Though the traveling group had likely been here for days, it still drew a large crowd, and Aaron's expectations grew. He glanced over the variety of people, stopping on a little boy edging his way into the crowd at the opposite end of the fence from Aaron.

Aaron had been that little boy staying carefully out of everyone's way. Before his father had swooped in with a sense of responsibility and sent Aaron off to school, there'd been no fancy clothes or quality horseflesh. Aaron's admiration for the animals had been fed by traveling shows such as this one.

They'd been his escape.

The performers didn't care if he'd ruined his mother's life or his father considered him the embodiment of sin's consequences. They didn't call him names or pretend he didn't exist. They gave him the same show they gave everyone else.

Aaron took note of the boy's height and what he was wearing so he could find him after the show and create some sort of errand that would earn the boy a coin.

The show began, and Aaron frowned. It was obvious why the

faerie queen came out last, despite the uninspiring story supposedly being all about her. Other riders, dressed as wood nymphs and sitting atop brown horses, did little more than avoid falling, confirming his suspicions that the horse trainer should be receiving the applause. To the untrained eye, the display was fabulous, but even though Aaron hadn't a clue how to make a horse walk with his forelegs high and stiff, he knew what it looked like to give a horse a command.

A few acrobats were mingled into the show, but soon the faerie queen made her entrance, eventually reaching the point where he'd begun watching the first time.

The horse paused for the others to clear the area, then, instead of moving forward, reared up until it was standing tall on its back legs. The crowd gasped and cheered while Aaron's gaze flew to the rider's face. A grim frown flashed across her mouth and then the horse was back on the ground. Moments later, the routine continued as if nothing had happened.

Obviously, the faerie's skills far surpassed those of the other performers. Still, she had to be relying on the horse's knowledge of the routine, considering she often knelt upon the horse's back, with one leg draping down the animal's side.

Was the trainer here? Perhaps behind the wall that had been erected as a backdrop for the performance? Aaron wanted to meet him. Had he trained the horses with a firm, caring hand instead of fear and pain? Was he short in stature himself, allowing him to easily train horses for female riders?

Perhaps God had a miracle for Aaron after all.

Once more the horse knelt and the faerie queen dismounted. The cluster of boys called out and pressed closer to the fence, rocking it until Aaron feared it might topple.

She stepped forward, shimmering from her head to her hem. Even her skin caught the light, covered in some sort of powder that gave it an unnatural glow and kept him from getting a clear look at her features.

A tightness squeezed Aaron's chest as the faerie veered away from the center and walked toward the boy in the ill-fitting coat at the end of the fence. She extended the rose toward the lad, and a hush fell over the crowd, followed by a swell of displeased murmurs.

Aaron couldn't help but direct a nod of respect toward the performer, though she couldn't see him. She'd known who was enthralled by the show and who simply wanted to be entertained. That boy would cherish the flower until it turned to dust.

Soon the rider disappeared behind the wall. Aaron dropped two coins into the passing basket and cut through the crowd in search of the little boy. He was still on the far side of the area, clutching his rose to his chest while two boys in pristine tiny cravats stared him down.

Aaron knew that scenario as well.

He ignored the glowering boys and stepped up to the grim-looking lad. "Do you like horses?"

Eyes wide, the boy nodded. "Yes, sir."

Aaron gave a sharp nod in return and pulled two more coins from his pocket. "My horse is stabled at the end of this row. His name is Shadow. He's a chestnut with a white face and white socks on all four legs. Do you know what that means?"

The boy nodded and flicked a glance down at the coins before meeting Aaron's eyes once more. "Yes, sir."

"Shadow doesn't always do well in strange, noisy places." Surely God wouldn't care all that much about such a harmless lie. "I'd like you to purchase him a treat, whatever you feel appropriate, and check on him for me. You can keep whatever you don't spend."

The boy pried one hand from the stem of the rose and slowly reached out to accept the coins. His fist closed tight and tucked up against his chest once more, a hint of fear edging into his face.

Aaron cut a look at the boys hovering nearby and tightened his jaw. He may not bear the name or the title, but there was aristocratic blood in his veins, and he could make himself look powerful and intimidating to those who didn't know any better.

"If you have any trouble," Aaron said slowly, "let me know."
The boys scattered.

"Thank you, sir. I'll make sure your horse is in fine shape." The coins disappeared into a pocket.

After receiving a final nod of approval from Aaron, the boy ran off to enjoy the rest of what might very well be the best day he'd ever had in his life.

Aaron stayed in the shadows of the show's ramshackle construction, edging around the enclosure to see the makeshift paddock and dressing area behind the rickety wall. Positioned on the end of the row, the lot extended far back, keeping Aaron from getting too close to the horses, unless he wanted to step fully into the blocked-off area.

In the farthest corner of the space, a short man with a shock of bright red hair brushed down the horses from the show. The faerie queen stood nearby, the green gown looking gaudy and cheap now that it lay motionless.

As the man talked, he gestured to the horse's foreleg, then swept his hand out in a wide motion. Were they discussing that moment when the horse had reared?

The faerie nodded before patting the horse on the neck and moving away toward a wagon positioned to hold up part of the dividing wall.

Aaron kept his attention fixed on the white Andalusian he would have given a few teeth to get his hands on. He might even be willing to suffer bodily harm for a closer look. He'd heard about the horses and seen them in paintings, but this was the first he'd glimpsed in person. The Andalusian was as glorious as reputation claimed, though how it ended up in a traveling show and not the stable of a duke, Aaron couldn't begin to guess.

The red-haired man led the horse in a circle, slowing each time they passed the corral. With each circle, that moment grew slower and slower, until the man was bringing the horse to a stop before continuing on. After three successful stops and starts, the man pulled something from his pocket and fed it to the animal before getting an affectionate nudge in the chest in return.

The trainer was on the smaller side, though not as short as most jockeys. He was wiry. Thin. He wouldn't slow a racehorse down overmuch.

"You, boy!" The show's narrator, wearing a tailored coat and an attitude of superiority, stalked across the lot to the horseman. Most likely he was the circus owner. Aaron couldn't hear the conversation, but from the sharp arm gestures and the angry expression, it was easy to see he wasn't happy.

Through it all the red-haired man calmly stroked the neck of the white horse. The angry man stomped away, mustache trembling with displeasure. "And be quick about it, or I'll dock your pay."

The horseman didn't react, which meant he'd probably heard that threat before. Even if the man didn't make a good long-term jockey, there was always room in Aaron's stable for one who didn't allow his circumstances to affect his care of the horses. He hadn't been in either show, so it wasn't a love of performing keeping him here. Aaron could offer him a better life.

The white horse was led into a fenced area already containing two draft horses and the brown horses from the show. Despite the beratement, the trainer didn't rush his care of the animals, keeping his movements measured and easy until he finished. Only when he'd stepped out of the enclosure did he hustle off to take care of the requested business.

Everyone in Newmarket would think Aaron's scheme mad. Teaching a horse to perform in such a way required considerable riding ability—ability that should be transferable, at least for a challenge race.

Aaron couldn't pursue the idea without pondering it over, at least a little. Another rash decision would only make the situation worse. If it still seemed sound after the next show, he would act upon it.

Maybe.

Instead of joining the crowd for the next show, he circled around to the boundary of the back lot to watch the preparation of the horses.

The red-haired man stood by, the faerie queen at his side, as one of the brown horses pranced through the routine riderless. Aaron smirked at this final proof that he'd been right. The nymphs could have been sandbags for all the difference it would have made. The white horse had performed far more intricate steps, so the faerie was at least a superior rider, a distinction that didn't matter to Aaron, though standing on a running horse was a very impressive trick.

The show concluded, and once more Aaron waited for the crowds to disperse. Would the trainer have a break soon? Could he catch him away from the circus?

"He no sell," a thickly accented voice said from his left. Aaron turned to see one of the performers from the show. This close, he could tell she was far older than she'd appeared during the play.

"I beg your pardon?" Aaron asked.

"White horse. He no sell."

"I don't want the horse." It was an understandable assumption, as they likely received multiple offers a day for the mesmerizing beast.

"Why you stare, then? Scare children."

Considering these people made a living by being stared at and he couldn't see anyone in the enclosure who could pass for less than fifteen, Aaron discounted the woman's claim. Even so, the moment had come to go for the whole hog or throw up the sponge.

"I wish to speak to the horse trainer."

"No allowed out here."

Aaron frowned. The man wasn't allowed to leave the paddock? What sort of hold did the circus owner have on him?

"I give message but no come out."

He was supposed to conduct business via this woman, whom

he could barely understand and who didn't speak proper English? Apparently so, unless he wanted to abandon the idea. The thought turned his stomach. "I wish to offer him a job riding my horses." Aaron cleared his throat. "My racehorses."

"You offer job to horse trainer?" The woman's mouth lifted at the corners.

"Yes," Aaron said slowly, eyes narrowing at the woman. "The one with red hair."

The woman nodded, her small smile evident now. "Fitzroy. You offer riding job to horse trainer Fitzroy with red hair."

Aaron rolled the name around in his mind. *Fitzroy* sounded a lot like *You, boy.* Perhaps that had been what the circus owner yelled earlier. "Yes."

More nodding. "I go tell." The foreign woman stepped around the wagon and out of sight before calling out. The red-haired man finished checking a horse's hoof and then moved toward the wagon, joining her out of Aaron's sight.

When she returned to Aaron, she carried a small travel desk. "Lose job if go with you. Want promise. Want written offer."

The man was smart. Another point in favor of Aaron's decision. That this man would be leaving his livelihood created a heavy sense of responsibility. Aaron would find something for the man to do. Besides, Newmarket was a horse town and close enough to London to draw plenty of aristocratic ladies who would like fancy stepping horses. He'd be able to earn at least as much as he did with the circus. Aaron slid a piece of paper from the desk's opening and selected a quill from the holder.

Now that Aaron had decided on the ridiculous idea, he gave it his total commitment.

What terms would be convincing enough? One month employment, to be extended if things went well. Food and board and the same wage Aaron had paid his previous jockey. He included the date and time of the challenge race, ensuring there would be no confusion as to when the job needed to start.

The scribblings hardly made for a professional contract, but it would do.

"Write for red-haired horse trainer."

Aaron paused, quill poised over the paper. "Why don't I simply write his name?"

"You said hire red-haired horse trainer."

Aaron gave the woman his most intimidating stare, sensing she wasn't being honest with him. He and his friends had fobbed one off on each other enough times for him to know how to get around it.

At the top of the paper he wrote, *Offer for red-haired horse trainer of Notley's Equine Circus by the name of Fitzroy,* then signed at the bottom. That should take care of whatever trickery the woman intended.

She took the desk and the paper and disappeared behind the wagon again. Aaron was starting to sweat by the time she returned, paper in hand and a grin on her face.

He took the offered paper covered with unfamiliar handwriting. His terms had been copied to the paper with *S. Fitzroy* scrawled across the bottom.

"Keep copy," the lady said thickly.

A sudden urge to rip the pseudo contract to shreds burned through him, but it would mean nothing since the trainer had wisely retained the one Aaron had written. He looked toward the wagon, expecting to see the trainer waving or giving some other indication that he was excited about the job, but only the faerie's head was poked around the corner, watching him with wide, curious eyes.

Aaron gave her a polite nod and folded the paper before sliding it into his coat pocket and stepping away to blend into the crowd. Really, what was the risk? He'd resigned himself to a likely loss anyway. Nothing worse could happen.

Three

Sophia Fitzroy's heart pounded hard enough to knock her wig askew, but she didn't look in the mirror to ensure her red hair remained fully hidden by the heavy, itchy blond curls. Even though the reflection would bear little resemblance to her true self, she couldn't face it yet. Makeup and powder could transform her into the ethereal faerie queen, but it would do nothing for the guilt pinching underneath her skin.

Despite the stabbing pain in the back of her throat and the swirl of anxiety in her stomach, she went through the motions of preparing for the next show. As long as she didn't look herself in the eye, she could pretend the man in the burgundy coat had known whom he was hiring.

The peek she'd taken at him as Margaret had gone to deliver Sophia's acceptance had nearly made her run after the woman and rip the paper to shreds. What she'd assumed would be a slovenly, down-on-his-luck horse trainer with more paunch than hair was a fine gentleman with neatly tamed dark curls and a trim physique who could definitely handle the horses he apparently wanted a rider for.

"Fitzroy! If those horses aren't ready in five minutes, I'll dock your pay."

Sophia winced at Mr. Notley's threat. Jonas already worked for nearly free. If the owner docked his pay any further, her brother would be paying him to work.

The rekindled anger burned away some of her blooming guilt. Yes, Jonas no longer rode in the show, but he was far from useless. He still saw to the care of the horses and completed every non-performing duty he'd had before the accident left him injured and unable to ride.

It was the show that made money, though, so in Mr. Notley's eyes Jonas wasn't earning anything. He didn't care that the accident cost Jonas far more than he'd ever gained from the circus. Didn't care that it had been Mr. Notley's insistence that they travel despite the weather that had allowed the accident to occur in the first place. Didn't care that the way he continued to pile extra jobs on Jonas's shoulders was preventing her brother from healing.

She and Jonas had scraped together enough money to pay for a physician's examination, and the diagnosis had been simple— a broken coccyx. The only known remedy was rest, something that was difficult to find when one lived and worked in a traveling circus.

Sophia pulled the paper out of her pocket and unfolded it. After hundreds of prayers, God had finally answered. One month. For one month she would have steady income, a place to stay, and food to eat. Somehow, she would find a way to share it all with Jonas, and maybe, just maybe, it would be enough.

Please, God, let it be enough.

"Are you ready, faerie queen?"

Her twin brother gave her a lopsided grin that she couldn't help but return. A sense of peace wormed its way through her uneasiness. She could do this. For him. For them. They had no one else in the world but each other. How many times had Jonas sacrificed in the past six years, making choices simply so they could stay together?

Now it was her turn. All she had to do was abandon common sense in order to believe the job offer was meant for her. One month and then they would have a little bit of money and a wealth of new opportunities.

A white horse head popped over Jonas's shoulder, dragging a long, silky mane across his face. He spit the strands from his mouth and gave the horse's nose an affectionate stroke. "Your magical steed awaits."

Sophia shook her head as she climbed atop the costume trunk. The heavily embroidered panels of her skirt swirled about her legs as she shifted them to the side and mounted the horse in one efficient movement. It took Sophia a moment to shift herself into the proper position on the horse's bare back, but soon another layer of peace smothered her trepidation.

The back of a horse was the only place she knew she belonged. Even if her father hadn't pulled her up into the saddle with him before she could walk, she liked to think she'd have eventually found her way to the majestic animals. They were in her blood.

Jonas handed her the thin reins. "I walked her through a full halt like you asked. She shouldn't rear up this time. The *passage* looked rough in the performance, though. Not that anyone else would notice."

"I think it's because I'm kneeling on one leg when we do it," she murmured, wishing, not for the first time, that the abilities of the horse and its meticulous training didn't have to be enhanced by grand schemes on her part.

"That sleeve is big enough to hide a whip," Jonas said, giving the long tail of her wide sleeve a flick. "Perhaps you can replace the other leg aid that way."

"Maybe." She sighed and fingered the panels of the embroidered skirt. "Or if I re-drape the skirt, I could ease my leg down farther."

Jonas nodded. "There should be more space in the next village, and you can work with her. I can use the longe as well, make sure she understands the adjusted command."

"Hmm." Sophia nudged the horse into a walk and guided her to the end of the wall. It didn't matter if the next village had a large open area. With this new job, they wouldn't need it.

The idea made her giddy.

How many times had she sat at the end of the dividing wall, listening to the crowd enjoying moves she'd trained other horses to do and pleading with God to somehow make this the last time she would have to go out and perform?

Countless. At least, she'd stopped counting long ago, instead giving all her focus to that prayer in that moment.

This time, her prayer was different. Thin wisps of gratitude stuttered through her mind. Would God want her thanks? Could she really claim this was the miracle she'd been asking Him for when she was practically lying to obtain it?

What was done couldn't be changed. Not showing up tomorrow would leave the man without a rider for his race. For now, she would just be grateful. If things went poorly, she could work them out with God then.

She would hardly be the first person of faith to do something foolish and then pray for a fix.

Knowing that she was still on the front end of that foolishness eroded some of the peace she'd been feeling moments before.

A glance over her shoulder revealed Jonas braced against the small dressing table. Deep breaths made his chest rise and fall slowly. Pain and exhaustion twisted his face into a tight grimace.

Pressing her mouth into a stern line, Sophia adjusted her hold on the reins until they were taut enough to create a proper connection with her horse and pasted a smile on her face. One more show. One more evening. Then they would make their escape, running into the dark to find a new life that suited them all.

AARON'S UNEASE GREW with every mile he put between him and his new employee. What if the man didn't show tomorrow morning? What if he couldn't ride? He *had* been using a lead. At the time, Aaron had seen it as deference to the fact that the horse was carrying a rider in all the shows, but what if it wasn't?

What had Aaron been thinking to hire a man he hadn't even spoken with? What if he didn't speak English? What if he didn't speak at all? Every breath brought a new question to mind that he should have asked while at the fair.

No matter what, he'd still find the man a job. His acceptance of Aaron's offer meant the trainer was as desperate as Aaron was— maybe even more so. If he wanted out of the circus life that badly, Aaron would help him.

That didn't *have* to involve a race, though.

Aaron urged Shadow to move faster down the road. If he could get to Lord Davers tonight, he just might be able to avoid the challenge entirely. It was a long shot, but he had to try.

Back in Newmarket, he stopped by Oliver's stable to arrange for one of the stable boys to see to Shadow. Aaron usually did it himself, but he didn't have time if he wanted to stop the challenge.

Three-quarters of a mile down a rutted road behind Oliver's stable sat Aaron's small cottage. A two-stall stable of nearly the same size sat behind it. Aaron loosened Shadow's girth and made sure the water bucket was full before going into his house to change. The stable boy would see to everything else.

Fortunately, Aaron knew where Davers was likely to be this evening.

Unfortunately, it wasn't somewhere Aaron would be particularly welcome. Yes, he'd received an invitation, but no one— especially not the hostess—expected him to use it. That was assuming Aaron could even find it. He normally tossed them out as soon as they arrived.

Which was why he didn't have a set of true evening clothes in his cottage. He kept his formal clothing in London, where he did—on exceedingly rare occasions—use one of the elaborately written cards that came his way in order to appease his father, the Marquis of Lindbury.

He pulled out his best ensemble, one of the two he wore to church on Sundays, and splashed some water into a basin so he could wash off the road dust.

The sun was dipping into the trees as he departed and strode toward the center of town. At least the card party was close enough to walk to. Not having to stable his horse at the gathering allowed for a quieter entrance and a hastier exit.

With any luck, he'd be in and out in half an hour. As much as he wanted to slip in the back, see to his business, and glide out again with no one the wiser, he knew better. Coming through the front door would mitigate some of the murmurs about whether he'd been invited.

Instead there would be gasps at his audacity in showing up in the first place.

He showed the footman the card he'd pulled from a pile of paper on his hearth and then bypassed the receiving line. Just because he wasn't going to slink in didn't mean he wanted to endure the false greetings and tight smiles of his hosts.

All the doors of the ground-floor rooms had been thrown open and guests milled about, talking and preening and seeking the best position to show off their new fashions. A ballroom would have been more convenient. It was far easier to find someone when there was only one room to search instead of several.

He finally found Davers in the drawing room, standing near a cold fireplace. Two men and two women stood with the baron. Approximately four more people than Aaron would have preferred. Rather than attempt to infiltrate the group, Aaron positioned himself in a corner, waiting for them to naturally disperse. He would catch Davers before he entered a new conversation.

"Whitworth?"

Aaron turned his head to acknowledge the speaker and gave a nod of greeting. "Mead."

Mr. Theophilus Mead was the embodiment of everything Aaron despised about society. The man mistreated his horses, relied on his father's money and reputation, and was a terrible rider to boot. Yet *he* was welcome here, while Aaron was not.

"What are you doing here?" Mead asked with his customary sneer and a tilt of his chin that made it appear he'd smelled something foul. Given how often his face bore such an expression, one could surmise it was he who was creating the odor.

"I'm meeting someone."

Mead glanced around the room. "Here?" He chuckled. "Who is it? I'll save them the effort of slowly killing their social suitability and aid them with a quick blow."

Aaron fought the urge to roll his eyes. It was true he wasn't desirable company, but one conversation with him wasn't enough to ruin a man's value. A woman's, perhaps, but not a man's—at least not in Newmarket, where there was a high probability their conversation was about horses.

"Whitworth?"

Weren't corners supposed to be hidden, out-of-the-way places? Aaron might be slightly taller than the average man, but he wasn't a giant. He turned his head to greet the newcomer and relaxed when he saw Hudson, Viscount Stildon. Miss Bianca Snowley, the only woman Aaron had ever voluntarily befriended, was at his side. Unsurprising, since the two had been inseparable since they started courting.

Aaron gave a nod, reminding himself this was a formal setting and he couldn't use his friends' given names. "Stildon. Miss Snowley."

Hudson shifted until Bianca was on his other side, placing her between him and Aaron and away from Mr. Mead, who'd tried to court Bianca before Hudson had come along. If the nasty look he was sending the lady's way was any indication, he wasn't happy she'd chosen another.

"Have you greeted Mrs. Turner yet?" Mead asked, eyes wide in an overblown attempt to look casual. "I can send her your way if you need to pay your respects. Wouldn't want to be rude and ruin her gathering."

"No," Aaron said tightly. "I wouldn't. Rather why I'm standing in this corner."

"One would wonder why you came at all." Mead cut a look across the room at Davers. "You couldn't possibly be nerv—"

"Apollo had a good workout today," Hudson cut in. "He looks in fine shape for the October Meetings."

Aaron nodded, welcoming a topic he could comfortably converse on. "He's been getting better and better. He should peak at the perfect time."

Mead frowned. "I'm introducing a new horse at the first meeting."

Aaron winced as the man's voice grew louder. Was he trying to draw everyone's attention to Aaron's presence? Probably. And it was working. Several heads had turned his way, including Lord Brimsbane's.

He stepped into the circle to address Mead. "That's rather odd timing, isn't it?"

"I wanted his first run to be on my home turf."

Aaron bit his lip to keep from laughing at the idea that Mead somehow ruled the Heath. The truth was his father had enough money to run a stable barely decent enough to keep him in the Newmarket social mix. They only ever ran the smaller races, and no one took them seriously.

With three other horsemen in the circle and a woman who rode better than most other men in the room, the conversation flowed freely without any input from Aaron. He slid to the side, his shoulder moving behind Bianca's, allowing Brimsbane to ease farther into the circle.

Three more subtle shifts and the viscount had unconsciously moved to block Aaron from the conversation.

Only Bianca noticed, and she threw Aaron a frown.

He gave her a quick grin and shrugged one shoulder. He wasn't here to talk horses, at least not with these men. Nor were they intent on talking to him. Even Hudson hadn't noticed Aaron's departure from the grouping, though Aaron didn't think any worse of him for that.

Mr. Mead's voice rose again, drawing Lord Davers's notice. His glance connected with Aaron's, and his mouth turned up at the corners in a smirk. Like a cat. Right before it knocked over the milk pitcher.

"Whitworth," he said, in a voice just loud enough to carry across the room.

Silence fell over the area for the space of a breath, followed by the low hum of conversations moving from general gossip to discussing someone present in the room. They were far from discreet, and normally Aaron could have made his own amusement by casually asking each and every one what they were talking about, but he had another goal this evening, one that making a nuisance of himself wouldn't help.

Aaron crossed the room, ignoring the young lady who darted out of the drawing room, nearly hitting the doorframe because she refused to take her eyes off him. As if he might do something thrilling, like make a scene or throw a punch. Aaron knew better. Acting the perfect gentleman that he'd worked so hard to become was far more powerful. It made people uncomfortable, made them question their world, made them angry that he would dare to fit in on the surface when they all knew he didn't under the skin.

Normally he reserved showings like this for London, where they were far more effective at strengthening his resolve to cling to the respectability he'd gripped with the tips of his fingernails.

Lord Davers's companions shifted to allow Aaron into their midst, eyes darting to and fro so they wouldn't miss a moment of the interaction.

Aaron nodded his greetings and waited for Davers to speak.

The man swirled the amber liquid in his glass before taking a slow sip, eyes fixed on Aaron the entire time. "I had no idea Mrs. Turner had issued you an invitation."

The poor woman was going to get quite the interrogation

tomorrow about including him on the guest list, despite the fact that most society matrons in Newmarket and London did the same, on the off chance his father might ask them if they were following his wishes.

"I wished for a bit of company this evening," Aaron said, refusing to defend himself or pull the card from his pocket as proof. "As this seems to be where everyone has gathered tonight, I came here." It was hardly everyone, but as far as Davers was concerned, it might as well be. *Everyone* was a very loosely defined term among the elite.

An older woman rushed into the room, mouth pressed into a thin line. People stepped out of her way, causing a commotion Aaron caught out of the corner of his eye. She gave him a look of near fear before grabbing the arm of a young lady in Davers's circle and hustling her away.

Aaron didn't even know the young lady's name.

"Getting in your last moments of glory before you lose your streak tomorrow?" Davers grinned, trampling any hope Aaron had of convincing him to at least delay the challenge.

"Many a greater horse than yours has tried to end my challenge streak," Aaron said, unwilling to give Davers the satisfaction of slinking away. At least he hadn't made his request yet.

"Ah, but I'd place a wager that my jockey is finer than yours."

Yes, Davers had known exactly what he was doing.

Aaron had put himself, his friends, and his hostess through an uncomfortable evening for no reason.

If there was one thing he'd learned in his years on the edge of society, it was that the appearance of confidence was almost as good as possessing it. "I think you'll find my jockey sufficient to the task."

Davers's grin faltered. "You do have a reputation for hiring a certain quality of rider."

Aaron nodded but said nothing. He wasn't entering into a discussion about reputations with a man who wanted to wreck the only one Aaron had that wasn't tainted.

One of the other gentlemen in the group cleared his throat. "I heard your jockey was making a scene in the tavern this afternoon."

"Hughes doesn't have much discretion when he picks up the bottle," Aaron said. "Since I fired him, that is no longer my problem."

Everyone in the circle blinked, surprised that Aaron had stated the facts with such bluntness. It was a simple tactic that always threw everyone off guard long enough for Aaron to step away without appearing rude. He did so now, walking farther into the house instead of heading straight for the front door. Let them think he intended to stay at the party. No one needed to know that he would soon be causing a ruckus among the servants as he exited through the kitchen.

A few gasps and squeals, and a dozen questioning looks later, Aaron was walking through the house's back gardens and making his way to his cottage.

He poked his head into the small stable to check on Shadow and then entered his home. One room, divided into areas that suited all his needs. Situated as he was on a shielded corner of Oliver's family estate, he never received visitors, keeping his tiny abode secure and safe. The door closed behind him, and he wrenched his cravat loose, breathing easily for the first time in over an hour.

Moving around the small space, shucking the trappings of polite society and making himself a truly awful cup of tea, Aaron's muscles relaxed one by one. No more pretending was required of him tonight. Here, he was finally where he belonged. Alone.

Four

For two years Sophia's life had been the circus and the fairs and amusements that surrounded it. Noisy. Crowded. She'd learned long ago how to sleep through the drunken revelries. Tonight, though, she lay on her straw pallet, listening for the world to quiet so she could slip away.

Jonas told her to sleep since she was riding a race in the morning, promising to wake her when it was time to go, but rest was nowhere to be found. She forced herself to close her eyes, drifting off for snatches of time here and there, but never truly easing into sleep. It was almost a relief when Jonas touched her shoulder, summoning her into the darkest part of the night.

No one but Notley was going to care about their departure, but that didn't stop her from jumping at every noise and peering at every shadow. The eerie quiet scraped across her skin, joining her guilty conscience in slicing her nerves to ribbons.

Rhiannon plodded along between Sophia and Jonas, everything the twins owned in the world strapped to her saddle. Two pots wrapped in a thin blanket to keep them from clanging were draped off one side of the saddle, while the longe and other training tools hung off the other. Two small bags were strapped to the seat. Altogether, it was a lighter load than when the horse carried Sophia.

Pitiful, really, that it was all the siblings could claim after twenty-three years on this earth, but it made fleeing in the middle of the night somewhat easier.

Sophia glanced at Jonas, who was barely visible in the starlight as they walked steadily through the quiet marketplace. "You've scarcely said a word since I told you about the job." What little he'd uttered had been in relation to their departure. He didn't want to risk an outcry either, so they'd made this plan to creep away in the middle of the night. It also allowed them plenty of time to walk from Cambridge to Newmarket. Who knew how long that would take?

"Say something," she hissed.

He turned her direction, eyebrows lifting slowly, and she knew what was coming before he even opened his mouth to say, "Something."

She rolled her eyes to the dark sky. It would be a relief if his ability to crack a joke meant he was embracing this gamble, but the truth was Jonas was capable of being ornery no matter his mood. She bit her lip and dropped her gaze to the path in front of them. Should she push him for more? Try to convince him the idea had merit?

They reached the far end of the marketplace. Soon they'd be leaving the fair, the city, and their old lives behind them. The circus was scheduled to move on today, and she'd rather be far away when Mr. Notley learned he was moving on without them. While he wouldn't delay the departure, he was sure to be loud about his displeasure.

The scent of food and animals gave way to the freshness of trees and fading cookfires. The space between the buildings grew. Soon they were at the edge of Cambridge, well on their way to Newmarket and new opportunities.

Jonas waited to speak until they'd rounded a bend in the road and a copse of trees hid the last vestiges of the town from sight. "I do believe this is a bad idea."

The idea went beyond bad and into the realm of terrible, but it had been the only opportunity to come their way in years. Jonas seemed to thrive no matter where he was, but Sophia knew life could be much better.

There had to be a way for it to get better.

"We don't have a choice," Sophia said, crossing her arms to hug her middle. "The surgeon said your only treatment is rest. Constantly traveling, suffering the seat of a wagon or a horse, or walking miles upon miles is not rest. It's been months and you still can't bear to sit down."

Jonas sighed and looked at Sophia before giving his head a small shake. "We don't know if that surgeon had any idea what he was talking about. It's possible I'll never heal."

Sophia straightened her spine and stared into the deep darkness of the countryside. "It won't hurt to try resting for a few weeks."

Even the suggestion that Jonas might have to live in pain forever made her eyes burn. If rest wasn't what he needed . . . if that would never be enough . . . She shook her head, refusing to entertain the option. "It's not as if I'm asking you to try medication sold by that quack at the fair. Lying down is perfectly normal."

He didn't say anything, and she rushed on, trying to convince him—and maybe herself—that this was going to be a good turn of events. "It isn't a new activity. You already lie down every day. Walking isn't a bother until you've been on your feet for a long time, so now you can spend a month alternating a little walking with lying about."

Jonas leaned down and snapped a flower from its stem but continued walking.

Sophia continued talking. "We can even take one of our bags and fashion you a pillow of sorts. Maybe stuff it with grass or—"

The taste of dirt and leaves and who even knew what else hit her tongue as the soft petals of the flower were smushed into her mouth, bringing an abrupt halt to her rambling. Spitting the flower out, she frowned at her brother but fell silent.

Jonas kept walking, his mouth pressed into a grim line. She

knew that look. He was thinking, and nothing would make him talk before he was ready.

Often he came to a conclusion that made Sophia feel foolish, but in this case she knew he'd ultimately see things her way. If God hadn't wanted them to take this chance, potentially less than honorable though it may be, He could have provided something else during their years of praying for relief.

Jonas sighed. "Tell me again what you'll be doing?"

Sophia rolled her shoulders back and tucked her chin down. "Riding horses."

"And to think I was worried."

"Jonas."

"Sophia."

Sophia repeated the story, leaving out any question of the offer's authenticity. The man *had* nodded at her. She ran one hand down Rhiannon's neck and twined her fingers in the soft mane. "The job comes with food and board, so even though the wages aren't high, we can save most or possibly even all of it while you heal. It should be enough to support us while we search for other employment."

"May I see the paper?"

She bit her lip. "Why?"

Jonas turned his expressionless stare her way. "Originally because I was curious and there seems to be enough moonlight on this patch of road to read it, but now it's because I'm guessing there's something you aren't telling me."

With a sigh, Sophia pulled the paper from her pocket and handed it over. After several moments, Jonas passed it back to her. "He's expecting me."

There was no censure in his voice, but the frank statement sent a wave of guilt crashing through Sophia. "I believe so, yes."

"Instead it will be you."

She bit her lip again, intent on staying quiet and letting him think. Instead she blurted out, "You can't ride. You cringe every time you sit on a horse. Riding in the wagon leaves you in a cold sweat. I know he's expecting you, but I can do the job while you can't."

Jonas threw another flower at her, his threat clear enough to have her snapping her mouth shut with a click of teeth.

"We have to be smart about this. It's best if he doesn't see me at all." He glanced at the horse. "Or Rhiannon. I don't want you walking around with a valuable horse unprotected."

The blow to Sophia's plans cracked her resolve. Why hadn't she considered that lodgings for *her* wouldn't include a space for Jonas or her horse? "What will you do?"

He shrugged. "We'll find a place to hide. This is English country-side. There's bound to be a set of ruins or an abandoned cottage somewhere out there. We've done it before. The bigger question is, what are you going to do if he won't let you work?"

"I have a contract."

"Signed under false pretenses."

Sophia frowned. "He hired the red-haired horse trainer named Fitzroy. That's me." He would let her work. Any man who hired someone the way he did was desperate.

"I'm not denying that your skill with horses far surpasses my own," Jonas said slowly, as if explaining to a child why she had to be careful of sharp hooves. "The man was deceived, though, and all you have is a piece of paper to cash in against his honor. If he has none, there's nothing you can do. It's not as if we've the funds to hire a solicitor."

No, they didn't have the funds. They didn't have their father's riding school, didn't have their family home, didn't even have family, since what distant relatives they could claim had declared them old enough to be on their own when Mother died. They'd left Ireland when the man they'd been working for accused them of theft in order to disguise his gambling losses. For the past six years it had been them against the world.

For the past five, it had felt like they were losing. This time she was going to win.

"All I need is a chance. He's too desperate not to use me. I'll show him what I can do, and he'll keep me on. Maybe even past one month. With two months' wages, we could really start over."

Jonas probably saw a dozen additional problems, but Sophia pressed on before he could state them. They'd all be hypothetical anyway. "I must say I'm quite looking forward to riding in a capacity that doesn't require I wear a wig or billow my skirts about. Not being able to work with Rhiannon every day will be disappointing, but you can use the longe to keep her exercised. I'm sure there will be times I can come out to see you and ride her and—"

Jonas reached under Rhiannon's neck and pinched Sophia's lips together. "Sophia."

"Yes?" The word came out muffled from her closed mouth.

"You're rambling." He released his hold.

She sighed. "I know."

"What are you worried about?"

So many things, none of which she could give voice to. Saying them aloud made them real. "I don't like the idea of you with nowhere to stay."

Jonas laughed. "You do remember where I slept last night, right? And the hundreds of nights before that? Rhiannon and I will be better off, even if we camp down in the middle of the woods somewhere. Food may be difficult, but we'll manage."

The mention of food made Sophia's stomach grumble, and she pressed a hand to her middle. The sky had lightened enough that she could clearly make out the countryside and its lack of taverns and food stalls. Why hadn't she thought to procure something for breakfast?

Jonas grinned at her, reached up into one of the bags strapped to Rhiannon, and pulled out two small rolls.

"What's this?" Sophia asked even as she accepted the bread and took a large bite.

"One of the vendors had a few of these left when he was shutting down last night. Sold them to me cheap." Jonas took a bite of his own roll and then leaned down to see her past Rhiannon's bobbing head. "Now, what's really bothering you?"

Sophia swallowed the bread that now felt solid in her throat despite her careful chewing. "What if I'm not a good jockey?"

Jonas sighed. "Sophia, you're the best rider I know. Better than I was before the accident. Probably better than Father ever was."

She winced. It seemed somewhat sacrilegious for Jonas to say such a thing about a dead man. "We don't know what Father was like when he was young."

"Maybe not, but I know what you're like now. There isn't a horse alive you can't ride."

"What I do—what Father taught us—those things aren't anything like racing. What if my skills aren't enough?" Now that the fear was out in the open, Sophia couldn't seem to pull it back in.

With a laugh, Jonas reached over and shoved at her shoulder. "You stand on a galloping horse four times a day and now you're worried about sitting on one?"

Sophia grunted a response, her breath coming easier the farther they got from Cambridge. "You're right. I can do this. Once I win this challenge, he'll be inclined to keep me on despite the circumstances." She refused to say he'd been tricked, because then she'd have to say she'd been tricked too, and the very fact that she was thinking such thoughts meant she'd known what Margaret was doing from the beginning and gone along with it.

Maybe even encouraged it.

"Why do you suppose Margaret did that?" she asked softly.

"Because she knows we've been taken advantage of? Because she hates Mr. Notley and thinks this will make him lose money? Maybe she thinks her daughter can do what you do." He sighed. "To be honest, it doesn't matter."

Jonas was right. What mattered was that a window of hope had opened through unexpected means and Sophia was going to crawl through it.

"If I'm good enough," she whispered, "other people will hire me. This is the beginning, Jonas. This is what will create the foundation for us to reestablish Father's school."

Jonas grunted but said nothing. Did he also feel the danger of speaking their real dream too loudly?

Neither of them had a watch, so they weren't sure of the time, but the rising sun gave them a good idea. The increasing number of homes and the distant estates indicated they were nearing Newmarket. The Heath, her destination, had to be close.

Jonas pried the reins from Sophia's fingers and then pressed her bag into her arms. "I'll take her. You'll want your bag with you since it will be a day or two before we can meet up."

Reality hit her hard in the middle, and she hugged her bag closer. How long had it been since they'd spent a full day apart—much less two?

Her brother's callused hand covered hers and squeezed. "It's going to be all right, Soph. God promised to never fail us nor forsake us." He gave a twisted grin and a one-shouldered shrug. "Since Israel got that promise, besmirched though it was, what we're doing isn't going to send Him running."

That Jonas had said *we* gave her some comfort. They might be apart, but that didn't mean they weren't still in this together. "How will I find you?"

Jonas looked around and then pointed to a knoll with a cluster of trees. "I'll meet you there tomorrow. I'll head that direction to find a place, then return in the morning and hide in those trees. If things go badly this morning, you can stay there until I find you. If they go well, you meet me there as soon as you can. I'll go every day until I see you."

Sophia swallowed. As always, Jonas had constructed a plan that saw to all the flaws she'd been in too much of a hurry to consider. From here, she was going to be on her own, though.

Jonas wrapped his arm around her and pulled her into a tight hug before giving her one last nod and leaving the road to cut across the fields still wet with morning dew.

She would not cry. If she was going to claim this job, she had to be tough. Resilient. Mr. Whitworth wasn't going to like that she was female. Others might not like it either. Some didn't even care for a woman performing in the circus. Were racehorse owners likely to be more inclined to accept female riders?

She didn't need anyone's approval, though, only their money.

Wiping her hands against the rough fabric of her skirt, she shifted her bag so that it rode more easily on her shoulder and walked on. Fabric bunched around her legs as her loose trousers rubbed and clung to the fabric of the overlying skirt. It wasn't an outfit made for walking, but she didn't think there would be time or a place for her to change before the race. This outfit allowed her to ride astride with modesty. Riding sidesaddle at length wasn't always comfortable. She doubted it was the best way to race, either.

She felt every wisp of breeze, heard every twitch and rustle in the grass. As she approached the Heath, a trembling worked from her knees upward, making her stumble as she left the road. The Heath was beautiful, but the small gathering coming into view held her attention and kept her from taking in the full expanse.

In the distance were several clusters of people. Some were standing, others were seated in open carriages. A scattering of men on horseback trickled toward her across the expanse and ended at a grouping of two horses and three men, one of whom held the reins of a sleek black horse with one hand and his pocket watch in the other. His clothing was crisp, though his hair bore the disarray that comes from spending a great deal of time without a hat on while atop a horse.

The coat was blue today instead of burgundy, but it was the same man who had been to the circus the day before. Sophia's gut tightened. She'd been so focused on riding the horse and keeping the job that she'd forgotten about facing the man.

His glance flicked often toward the road and then to the distant spectators. Twice he passed over her. She could tell herself it was because he didn't recognize her without a wig, but how many redheaded women were wandering about the Heath?

It was too late to back out now.

She strode forward, trying to pretend it was just like the circus show. Confidence wasn't necessary, but the appearance of it was.

"Mr. Whitworth?" The words came out slightly raspy but strong, lightly touched with the Irish lilt of her childhood.

He frowned down at her. "Yes?"

"I am your new jockey."

Five

"My new . . ." Aaron's voice trailed off as he took in the woman before him.

Bold red hair caught and reflected the sun as the wind pulled at the strands that had come loose from the bun at the nape of her neck. Clothing that had seen better days and certainly hadn't been designed with an eye for fashion covered a body that was the perfect size for a jockey. He frowned as he took in her pale face and confident expression.

In another time and another place, he'd have taken a few moments to analyze the way her green eyes seemed to punch him in the gut, but here on the Heath, with Davers standing a few feet away, such an indulgence wasn't an option. He had to get this woman—whoever she was—out of the way and decide what to do about the non-arrival of his new—

He blinked down at the woman. How had she known he had hired a new jockey? "You're the faerie."

Her chin lifted another notch. Much farther and she'd be forced to look at the sky instead of him. "Yes."

"I didn't hire you." Had she been a man, he might have. Her riding was impressive. "I hired an Irish horse trainer with red hair."

She pointed to her head. "Red. And I can thicken my accent if that makes me more palatable."

By the end of that statement, the light brogue she'd started with had thickened until it was barely understandable. Despite the way everything was unraveling right before his eyes, he wanted to laugh. "No one is doubting your heritage."

"I am also the horse trainer." She inclined her head and pulled a paper from her pocket. "Sophia Fitzroy. For one month I will ride your horses in exchange for food, lodging, and a weekly salary."

Aaron wrapped his fingers tighter around the reins, afraid Equinox might be the only thing keeping him standing. "There was a man. . . ."

She shrugged. "He just sees to the horses. Does a few things here and there to keep them sharp. I do the training."

The sense of foreboding he'd had coming home from Cambridge churned through him until dread ran through his veins. "I can't put you on this horse," he choked out.

She glanced around. "Without a mounting block available, I'm afraid you'll have to."

The entirely inappropriate desire to laugh speared through him again, quickly doused by the dismay that grew as his mind settled on the facts of the situation.

Davers approached, his strut recognizable even at the corner of Aaron's vision. "You don't mean to ride the beast yourself, do you, Whitworth? Seems a foolish way to attain your first loss." He looked Miss Fitzroy over. "And in front of your lady too. It seems you've finally realized your own worth."

The insult rolled over him and stabbed the woman. Her eyes widened, and fire flushed across her pale cheeks. He had learned long ago to ignore the men who thought their birth made them better. A woman working with the circus should have as well, but perhaps the avoidance of people's scorn was why she'd stayed tucked away behind that wagon.

He swallowed. Working as a traveling performer might not be a respectable job, but it was a living. One she'd left because he'd offered a better option.

What would she do if he sent her away? He could find her work.

His friends owned estates all over the country. There'd be a space for a maid somewhere in one of them.

That didn't solve the immediate problems of Davers looking at her like she was a bug on his shoe and him standing beside a riderless horse.

Aaron growled and jerked his chin in Miss Fitzroy's direction. "She's my new jockey."

Davers's mouth dropped open. "You can't be serious."

Oh, how he wished he wasn't. "Completely."

The woman's entire body seemed to vibrate, and the tiniest of smiles touched the side of her lips and the corners of her eyes.

At least one of them was happy. Aaron was soon going to have to help this woman onto one of the fastest horses in the world with a saddle that was most definitely not designed to be ridden aside and allow her to run across four miles of Heath. That was a far larger expanse than the performance area of the circus.

It was enough to make his stomach threaten to return his breakfast.

"Unacceptable," Davers snapped.

Aaron pulled upon years of experience to adopt a position that appeared bored. "You surrender, then?"

"I do no such thing. I'll not allow you to make a mockery of this sport," Davers sneered. "One week. I'll give Farnsworth one week to make this right—preferably by firing you and ridding us all of the embarrassment of your presence. Mark my words, Whitworth, you will regret this."

He already did.

At least now he had a week to find another jockey. And a job for Miss Fitzroy. And an explanation for Oliver.

Actually, he had only moments to determine what to say to Oliver. The men who'd been lingering near the start post had rushed to share the news with the crowd waiting to see the finish, and that crowd was now on the move. Riders, walkers, and carriages took a very slow, circuitous route away from the course, and onlookers craned their necks to watch Davers walk away from Aaron and Miss Fitzroy.

Aaron kept his narrowed gaze on the woman before him, as if he could somehow extract her confidence that way.

He wanted her as uncomfortable as he was.

As the noise lessened to the point that a few birds could be heard among the mingled conversations, his ploy seemed to work. The stiffness seeped from her shoulders, and she caught her lip in her teeth. Small, white, the left front one just a little crooked.

Once more he felt kicked in the gut. Significant words were going to be sent God's way when Aaron got to his cottage to-night. His simple, straightforward life was gone, crushed beneath the delicate heel of a faerie who was apparently a Delilah in disguise.

He pointed a finger at her. "Explain."

"Explain what?"

"Everything."

She pressed her lips together and swallowed, the jerk of her throat visible in her pale neck. "You hired me to ride your horses. I accepted the offer." She swallowed again. "Left my job to do so."

Forget having words with God—that always proved a futile effort anyway. Aaron was going to blister Oliver's ears. This was his fault. He'd been the one to put Aaron in such a desperate position that he'd done something rash. When had he ever made such a significant action without a great deal of forethought?

He groaned and moved one hand to the neck of the racehorse pawing the ground beside him. Equinox was getting restless, not understanding why they were standing at the beginning of the course instead of barreling down it.

With a slip of a woman on his back.

A woman who would be jobless and homeless if he sent her away now.

That seemed a rather more significant problem than the maintaining of his professional reputation, though the fact that he'd just introduced her to Davers as his jockey might do more damage than a loss or even a forfeiture would have.

The dark cloud of anger was nearly tangible in his body. The sensation had been a common one growing up, and he knew it was best to stay still and let it work its way through before he spoke or acted.

He wasn't certain whom the sharp emotion was even aimed at. Himself, certainly, for doing something so utterly irresponsible. Oliver. Davers. The foreign woman who had tricked him. The tiny woman who had accepted. Maybe he could just be angry at all women. His life had run smoothly until his friends had brought females into it.

Clearly, women were going to plague his life until he lost his mind.

He'd thought the anger had been coursing beneath his skin, but it must have shown on his face, because the defiant demeanor of the redhead in front of him faded. She licked her lips and crossed her arms across her middle, the strap of a half-empty threadbare sack falling to hook on her elbow. One leg started shaking, making her skirt ripple as her eyes flitted back and forth from his face to his hands.

Did she think he meant her harm? Was she afraid? Yes, he indulged in fencing and boxing as forms of exercise, but he hadn't engaged in anything that could harm another human since he'd been fourteen. He didn't want her here, but that didn't mean he would hurt her.

She couldn't know that, though.

No, she knew life wasn't always as kind to the defenseless as it should be. She knew a paltry rose that would die within a day could mean the world to a dirty-faced little boy in ragged second-hand clothes.

He took a deep breath and buried his hand in Equinox's mane, this time for his own comfort instead of the horse's. When he spoke, his voice was calm, though to his ears it sounded even more ominous. "I apologize for the misunderstanding. You are an excellent rider. I'm sure the circus will take you back."

She frowned. "Mr. Notley doesn't give second chances. Even if he did, I'm not sure where the company went. They were to travel north this morning."

If Aaron hadn't known how completely unpredictable and abnormal his own behavior had been, he'd have thought this entire business a swindler's setup. At best, it was a case of extreme naïveté that depended upon the honor of a man who had acted far from sane.

At worst, it was a crime of opportunity.

Since the woman before him appeared to have most of her wits, he was leaning toward the latter. "Perhaps you and the foreign lady should have thought through the risks before tricking me."

Brows that were slightly darker than the red of her hair pulled together in a frown. "Foreign lady?"

"The woman who took you the contract."

She blinked. "Margaret is from Kent."

He'd been more addlepated than he'd realized to have accepted the lack of proper communication because of a thick, false accent. That didn't absolve her from her part of the trickery. "And you didn't think my offer strange enough to require validating it yourself?"

"Notley doesn't like the faerie queen seen outside of the show," she said, crossing her arms. "Besides, Margaret said you'd explicitly stated whom you wanted to hire and she'd verified it with you. I suppose we were both desperate enough to believe her."

Aaron plowed a hand through his hair. He didn't like thinking of her as desperate, though the fact that all her earthly possessions were likely inside the single bag hanging from her elbow underlined the truth of her status. The chances of her having any means by which to support herself until she found a new job were slim.

That, at least, he could fix. He'd promised her work for a month. He could pay her the salary she would have earned. It would support her until she found a position. "I'll pay you."

Her frown deepened. "Of course you will. There's a salary stipulation in the contract, along with food and lodging for the length of my employment."

"I mean I'll pay you for the entire month now." It grated at him to give any sort of concession when he knew he'd been tricked, even if it hadn't been by her. The idea of her wandering off all alone with nowhere to go and no money for her future grated worse. "Then you can do whatever you'd planned on doing a month from now."

Her eyes darted away from his for the first time since she'd approached him. She took in the horse, the Heath, and the surrounding spectators, who were stretching their necks to catch a word of this conversation. She shifted the bag until it was once more secure on her shoulder, bit her lip, then tilted her chin up once more. "No."

"No?" His eyebrows shot up. Of all the responses he'd expected, a flat *no* hadn't even been on the list.

"No. I want more than money."

So, this *was* a swindle. The knowledge that he was indeed being taken for a ride by this woman somehow eased his anger. He wouldn't be the first man to stumble because of an attractive female. Granted, it hadn't been her appearance that had caused his initial idiocy—that wig and dress had been awful—but it had played a part in his handling of this morning.

"What do you want?" he asked, already prepared to decline it and send her on her way. He'd like to say with nothing, but he knew he'd give her at least a week's wages. Swindler or not, he had to be able to look himself in the mirror tomorrow.

"Riding for you gives me a chance to show people what I can do. I want to make a name for myself as a horsewoman and not a performer. If I can ride your racehorses, people will respect my abilities. I'll be taken seriously enough to train horses and riders again."

Once more she'd managed to throw him sideways. Of all the

things he'd been expecting, a chance to prove herself wasn't on the list. Despite his irritation, he had to give her a grudging dollop of respect. "You intend to trade my reputation for your own? Ruin me in an attempt to make a name for yourself?"

"I won't ruin you if I win."

She could ruin him simply by existing. If he allowed her to race, people would doubt his discernment. If it got around that he made an offer of employment and didn't follow through, his honor would be questioned. "And if you don't win?"

More nervous lip licking. Her lips were going to fall off if she kept doing that. "If I don't win . . ." She cleared her throat and straightened her shoulders. "The day I don't win, I'll quit. You can pay me for whatever time I've worked and I'll move on."

Her confidence impressed him even as it made everything more difficult. His name meant less than nothing away from the turf. While his bank account was healthy, he had no legacy. He didn't have family connections relying on him to make things better for the next generation. He had only today and his reputation as a horseman and stable manager.

And that reputation was about to be damaged. Because whether she said anything or not, whether the rest of Newmarket learned the details or not, whether he'd been tricked or not, he couldn't go back on his word and still consider himself a gentleman.

He was racing against Davers again in a week, but it was possible he could find someone else she could race quietly before then. In the meantime, he would suggest other places of employment more respectable for a woman on her own. This entire debacle could be over in a matter of days.

"If you lose, you'll drop your claim to employment as my jockey?"

She licked her lips and took another deep breath before giving a decisive nod. "Yes."

"Then we have a deal."

And he had an entirely new host of problems.

He offered his hand as he would to any man he was making a business deal with, but the slight hand that grasped his in return was most decidedly feminine. His calluses caught against hers, but the hand itself was slim. Though the grip was strong, the bones were delicate. This woman was turning everything he thought he knew about females topsy-turvy.

And he had a suspicion it was only the beginning.

Six

Sophia's heart threatened to drop right through her feet and puddle into her boots.

Despite the assurances she'd given Jonas, she'd been terrified that she'd be spending the day hiding in those trees, waiting for her brother to return and find they were without jobs, homes, or direction.

Her stomach grumbled through the sudden rush of relief, making her aware that the roll she'd eaten before the sun rose wasn't enough to sustain her for the day. She pressed a hand to her middle and breathed out a prayer of gratitude. Granted, she hadn't assured herself any work beyond a week—or even a day if he could arrange another race that quickly. But for today at least, she could provide for her tiny family, and there was a chance—a small chance, but a chance nonetheless—that she'd be able to do more.

A thin man with a neat, full beard approached, brows lowered and arms crossed over his chest. "What's the meaning of this, Whitworth?"

Mr. Whitworth extended the reins of the sleek racehorse to the newcomer. "I've hired a new jockey." The man's green-grey eyes cut in Sophia's direction and speared her clean through. "Temporarily."

The thin man shook his head and stroked the horse's neck.

"Have you lost your mind, Whitworth? A girl in the yard? What is she going to do there?"

Sophia drew herself up to her full height, slight though it was, and lifted her chin. At three and twenty, she was not a girl, though stating that wouldn't help her situation. She bit her tongue to hold in the retort.

"Ride," Mr. Whitworth said flatly, "just as Hughes did. That is the position I promised her, and I'm a man of my word."

His word had been for a month's employment, and he'd already gone back on that. Pointing *that* out would likely get her sent away completely, so she swallowed the comment with assistance from the pinched pain of nipping her own tongue again.

At this rate she'd have a hole in her tongue by nightfall.

A sigh gathered in her chest, and she clenched her teeth to keep from letting it out. She didn't do well with silence. If she needed to keep her thoughts from escaping through her mouth for the duration of her employment, it might be a good thing it was to be temporary. It would take a miracle to keep her thoughts inside for an entire month. Given the dubitable merit of her recent requests, it was probably best to refrain from asking anything else of God at the moment. Her tongue was simply going to have to toughen up.

"They aren't going to like it," the man continued, talking to Mr. Whitworth as if Sophia weren't there.

Mr. Whitworth's gaze, however, stayed fixed upon hers. "That I even contemplated such an experiment will give them fodder for months. They'll thank me for handing them the weakness they've been looking for."

Sophia didn't know who *they* were, but she knew what it was like to be ridiculed. What had he claimed earlier? That she was trading his reputation to make a name for herself? She'd thought he was simply being dramatic, but what if it were true? She twisted her fingers together, wishing she could take all she'd learned today and go back to yesterday and discuss it with Jonas.

Such a pity time only moved forward.

The thin man grunted and shook his head again. "I'll see you tomorrow. I hope you have a plan by then."

He led the horse away, leaving Sophia and Mr. Whitworth staring at each other, a situation made far more awkward without the horse as part of the picture.

Mr. Whitworth shoved his hand through his hair and shifted his weight to one foot. "What am I going to do with you?"

"I thought we'd agreed I was going to ride." She bit her tongue in reaction to the blurted statement. The pain was too late to be of any benefit.

His eyes cut toward her and his mouth pulled into a slight frown. "Unless you intend to sleep in the stall with Equinox and share his feed, that isn't the answer to my question."

Oh. Right. He wouldn't be able to place her wherever he normally housed his jockeys. Another issue she hadn't considered.

"Have you been reading Wollstonecraft in your spare time, Mr. Whitworth, or have you always harbored this heretofore hidden need to buck tradition?" A sweet, smooth, feminine voice drifted from behind Sophia's shoulder, and she twisted her head to see a couple approaching them.

She was everything a lady should be. Dark hair that maintained its careful styling despite being out of doors, pale skin, and a dress cut to skim across the grass as she walked. Her arm was linked with that of an equally polished gentleman. Only the disheveled light brown hair kept him from presenting perfection.

Standing in front of Mr. Whitworth had made Sophia feel shabby enough, but the approaching couple made her catalog every mend and patch in her clothing. None were easily visible, but even the slightest level of scrutiny would reveal them.

Mr. Whitworth evened his weight, crossed his arms over his chest, and lifted one eyebrow, once more looking as if he were in complete control of the situation. "Unless you have recently procured a copy of Wollstonecraft's work for Oliver's library, I fear such writings are not available to me."

A small idyllic smile graced the woman's face. "Father would never approve of my reading such a book."

"Meaning you've already hidden your copy among Oliver's volumes." Something that might have been a smile twitched at the edges of his mouth, but Sophia blinked and the hint of humor was gone.

The man escorting the dark-haired woman tensed visibly at the exchange, losing the indulgent smile he'd been wearing moments before. He looked at the woman, then at Sophia, and finally at Mr. Whitworth. "You could have warned me."

"Actually, I couldn't have," Mr. Whitworth grumbled, but his voice was too low to interrupt the other man, who continued speaking.

"Everyone is asking me why I would agree to this." He glanced over his shoulder to where a few nosy busybodies still lingered.

"Why indeed," Mr. Whitworth said with a narrowed look in Sophia's direction. He sighed, and the accusatory look dropped from his face. "I'm afraid more than one misunderstanding has led to this moment. The result is that Miss Fitzroy is, indeed, your new jockey." He paused, eyes locking with hers once more. "For now."

Sophia licked her lips and swallowed. Would he even give her a chance to win? No matter how good a rider she was, if he placed her on a slow animal, there was nothing she could do to win.

"The more immediate problem," he said, "is where to put her for the night."

She didn't like the implication that she represented more than one problem, each of which would have to be dealt with in a certain order, but even she had to acknowledge that the housing he'd promised was made infinitely more difficult by her skirt.

Irritation kept her from feeling too sorry for him, though. Three people had approached since they'd reached an agreement, and not once had the man seen fit to introduce her. She hadn't the slightest idea who was talking to her—or rather who was talking *about* her. Granted, everyone in the immediate vicinity was likely talking about her, but it would be nice to know who was doing so within her hearing.

"She can't bunk with the grooms," the man said, shoving his hand through his hair, displaying how it had gotten disheveled in the first place. "The maids?"

"I think not," the dark-haired woman said. "You've a bachelor's residence and she isn't a servant. It isn't proper."

"Neither is riding a racehorse," Mr. Whitworth added.

"Well, then, it isn't proper for Oliver."

Sophia wrapped one arm over her middle and forced her chin up.

The woman's expression was respectful, despite her dismissive words. "She can stay with me."

"What?" both men asked at the same time.

"Not *with* me, exactly, but there's no issue with her staying in the maids' rooms at my family's house."

"We race against your father," Mr. Whitworth said. "Housing our jockey with him doesn't seem right."

"She will be riding for the man who is soon to be my husband, and I should be part of his success," the lady answered, maintaining her perfect smile the entire time.

Sophia tilted her head. Was the lady's face painted to hold such a consistent expression? She'd met people with impressive makeup talents, but none that could produce a look that real.

"I haven't a better solution," said the man with her, who Sophia assumed was the soon-to-be-married Oliver.

She really wished someone would make introductions. More than that, though, she wanted her lodgings settled. Obviously she couldn't sneak Jonas and Rhiannon into maids' quarters, but if she were eating from the same house as this fine lady, even the remainders of the family's meal would likely be enough for her to split with her brother. "I won't be any trouble. All I need is a bed and a meal." Her stomach grumbled again. It was embarrassing, but if it convinced them she needed a large meal, all the better. There would be more to share with Jonas.

"It's settled, then," the lady said, her expression still serene, if a little strained about the mouth.

"Where are your other bags?" Oliver asked. "I'll send a man to fetch them."

Hot embarrassment surged from where the bag pressed against Sophia's shoulder up her neck and across her face. Likely she was as red as her hair. Maybe more so. There'd been a time when she'd traveled with a trunk of her own. Sometimes even two.

That seemed a lifetime ago.

"No bags." She swallowed hard as the woman's perfect smile finally drooped into a look of pity.

Sophia fought against indulging in such an emotion for herself. Her situation would appear dire to these people, but things were looking somewhat better at the moment. She had to remember that.

Unfortunately, she didn't know how to navigate out of the pity-inducing moment with any sort of grace. Fortunately, she was adept at verbally blundering about. Awkward was better than pitiful. "Since *Mr. Whitworth* has not seen fit to properly introduce us, perhaps we could do the honors ourselves?" She pressed a hand flat to her chest. "Miss Sophia Fitzroy."

The lady's eyes widened, but her smile returned. "Lady Rebecca, daughter of the Earl of Gliddon."

Oh dear, she was a real lady. Sophia had thought her simply a member of the gentry. Nobility had visited the circus show, but Sophia hadn't interacted with anyone of rank since her father's school fell into decline.

If Lady Rebecca noticed the sudden discomfort, she didn't acknowledge it. "Allow me to present my fiancé, Lord Farnsworth, heir to the Earl of Trenting."

And the man who could negate any agreement Mr. Whitworth had made. Wasn't he the owner of the horses?

Sophia dropped into a curtsy. If he hadn't decided to send her away yet, she wasn't going to give him a reason to. "My lord, my lady."

Lord Farnsworth drove his hand through his hair again. "Yes." He looked down at Lady Rebecca. "Right." He turned his head toward Mr. Whitworth. "Well. I suppose you can . . . make arrangements, then take her to Meadowland Park."

Mr. Whitworth smoothed his dark brown curls into place before looking to Lady Rebecca. "Which door?"

Sophia's cheeks flamed even as she saw the appropriateness of such a question.

"The kitchen door would be safest," Lady Rebecca said, her smile drooping for an instant before sliding back into place.

"Safe is relative at the moment," Mr. Whitworth said, once again locking eyes with Sophia.

As much as she didn't want to give him the final word, she couldn't think of what to say that wasn't nonsensical, even in her head. Knowing her, she was two breaths away from blurting it all out anyway. She bit her tongue once more to keep the words in. She truly was going to wear a hole in the thing.

Seven

Oliver and Lady Rebecca walked away, and Aaron had to stop himself from calling them back.

When was the last time he'd been alone with a woman? Even the ones he'd come to think of as friends and watched over with brother-like indulgence never went anywhere with only him. Their husbands, friends, or family were always in attendance.

There was nothing wrong with Aaron standing alone with the new jockey. They were both Oliver's employees, at least for the moment. A handful of people were still scattered around the Heath, unabashedly keeping the pair in their line of sight.

Still, it felt improper. Calling Oliver back wouldn't change anything, either. He could do nothing but stand there since Aaron had all the decision-making rights in the stead of the owner.

And Aaron wasn't about to get Lord Trenting involved. The earl ignored Aaron and the stable for the most part. As long as the horses were winning and enhancing his social standing, he'd let Aaron do as he liked. It was best for everyone if it stayed that way.

Aaron glanced at Oliver's retreating back. He'd have to find Oliver tonight and ask him not to write to his father about the day's events. It would take time for the social gossip to make its way to the earl. Hopefully, Aaron could have this entire mess sorted by then.

"Apologies, but was I supposed to go with them?" The feminine

Irish brogue fell softly on his ears, and he was already coming to loathe the sensation. Not only did it remind him of his dilemma, but when he wasn't braced against it, it seemed to roll from his ears to shiver down his back.

Aaron shook his head and gave his attention back to the woman in front of him. "No. We need to discuss . . ." What? They'd already hashed out how they'd gotten into this mess, and he refused to indulge his growing curiosity about her. "A plan. For training. I assume you've never raced before?"

"Not officially, no." She shook her head. "I've ridden many a fast horse, though. You won't have to teach me how to stay in the saddle, if that's what worries you."

"Have you ever been to Newmarket?"

She shook her head again. "Mr. Notley always plays the Stourbridge Fair. We stay long enough to pull the Newmarket crowd. He doesn't do much else in this area."

"How long have you been in the circus?" He pinched himself on the leg. What happened to not asking her any questions? He didn't want to know more about her, despite the protective urge that threadbare bag inspired.

"Two years." She crossed her arms across her waist.

She looked as if she might say more, so he whirled away and started walking toward where he'd tied Shadow. There was a scramble of boots on grass before she fell into step beside him. He reached over and lifted the bag from her shoulder without comment. The weight of it barely pulled on his arm as he slung the strap into place.

"I can carry my own bag." She did a funny little hop-step to keep up with his longer stride.

His jaw tightened as he adjusted his pace accordingly. "You shouldn't have to if an unburdened gentleman is present."

"I . . . oh." She paused. "Thank you. I usually have to carry my own things."

Despite his adjusted stride, she slowly fell behind, doing that odd skip-run every five or six paces to keep up with him. Aaron's own step faltered as it suddenly occurred to him that she'd arrived on foot. She'd *walked* from Cambridge this morning. Or she'd walked the night before and slept . . . who even knew where?

He couldn't now make her walk all over Newmarket. He'd have to find her a mount.

He didn't have many options, and Hudson's stable was the closest. Part of Aaron wanted to throw her onto Shadow's saddle so she didn't even have to walk that far.

Her head bobbed in the corner of his vision as she did her catch-up step once more. As he adjusted his pace again, she continued talking.

"—not around the circus, at least, so I haven't experience with many. Gentlemen, that is, or at least ones who are unencumbered. There are some good men at fairs and such, but they're usually carrying things about already. So am I, for that matter. No one sits around when the circus is moving."

Why was she blathering on about the lack of gentlemen in the circus?

"We all have to earn our keep, you know."

Was Aaron supposed to respond to any of this? Evidently not, since she didn't pause her monologue. She'd said more words in this short walk than he normally said in a day.

Besides, he didn't know the first thing about men in the circus, and he could hardly tell her his thoughts and misgivings on taking her to Hawksworth to borrow a horse. Hudson might have been at the race to witness the debacle firsthand, and if not, someone had likely gone by to tell him about it. The viscount was going to have questions, and Aaron didn't want to answer them—at least not today.

"I hope you don't think that makes me less of a lady. Though I suppose I can't really lay claim to that, since I'm hardly highborn. My parents—"

"Do you ever stop talking?" The last thing Aaron wanted to

discuss with her was his parentage. Normally he openly acknowledged his illegitimacy, mostly because it made people uncomfortable and gave him a momentary advantage, but he had a feeling
that if Miss Fitzroy knew his true social standing, he'd lose what
little leverage he had in convincing her she didn't want to work
for him.

"I talk when I'm nervous," she said with a sigh.

"That seems a bad habit."

She licked her lips. "It covers an awkward silence rather nicely."

Was she truly that naïve? Didn't people who lived as she did
harden themselves to the ways in which the world could take advantage of them? "Jabbering on makes it difficult to keep a secret."

She shrugged. "I haven't many secrets."

Meaning she did have some. Curiosity crawled up Aaron's
throat, but he swallowed the questions back down. Her invasion
of his life had already made him more aware of her than he liked.
All he really needed to know was what marketable skills she had
other than riding. He wouldn't break his agreement or toss her out
on her ear, but if she were to find other employment, he'd happily
be the gentleman and let her renege on the contract.

"I'm not often nervous," she continued. "I find it helps to put
myself in situations where I know what I'm doing. It's the wondering what is going to happen that disconcerts me." She let out
a short laugh. "Admittedly, I often talk a great deal anyway. It's
only that I have trouble stopping when I'm nervous."

He would not smile. He simply would not. He would hold on to
the irritation he'd felt when he first realized what a muddle she'd
created. That should be enough to keep him from being charmed
by her guileless ramblings. "Does that mean you'll be yammering
to the horse if you race?"

"*When* I race, everything will be fine. I can't imagine being
nervous on the back of a horse. It's people I don't always know
what to do with."

How well Aaron could relate to that sentiment. It was why he'd made his life on the Heath. Here, people were predictable—as much as they ever were—and horses ruled the day.

He should have kept to his intention not to ask any questions, though. The moment he had, he'd found something they had in common. If putting her on the back of a horse would stop the talking, he was going to have to rethink his decision not to place her on Shadow as they walked the rest of the way to Hawksworth.

"We had a lot of different people in the circus, but they always—oh, I say! Is that your horse? He's lovely."

Shadow stood tied to a post next to one of the weigh-in houses, chewing on a mouthful of grass. The chestnut thoroughbred had been on the weaker side when he'd been born, and the large white markings on his legs and face had made him less desirable as a racer, but Aaron had seen his potential. Though he'd never officially raced the animal, he'd timed his rides through the courses and knew the horse could have held his own in his prime.

Miss Fitzroy rushed to the horse and ran her hand gently along the stallion's neck. The horse sniffed at her skirts but didn't shy away.

Aaron untied Shadow and led him toward Hawksworth. "We'll borrow a horse for you, and then I'll show you around the area."

She looked around. "Is the stable I'll be working from near here?"

"No." He wasn't going to say more, but he could *feel* her expectant stare. "There are training yards that hold the racehorses. The stables are for breeding and pleasure riding."

"So, we're going to Lord Farnsworth's stable?"

"No," he said on a near groan. He was so accustomed to everyone knowing his situation that he had forgotten to explain it. "I manage two stables. Lord Stildon's is closer."

Blessed silence fell between them, but it was short-lived.

"Don't the owners get mad at you if one of them beats the other?"

Until recently, both owners hadn't cared much one way or the other. The previous Lord Stildon had been too old and sick to go to the races, and Lord Trenting only cared that Aaron didn't operate the stable at too much of a loss. "They trust me to run their horses to the best advantage. I never purposely set someone up to lose."

Her question poked at a growing unease he'd been trying to ignore. The new Lord Stildon was far more interested in his stable and horses, and the races in two weeks would be the first time he'd had a horse run against one of Oliver's since taking control of the estate.

Aaron was fairly certain Hudson wasn't going to be a problem. At least, not as much of a problem as Oliver's new need to impress his future father-in-law.

"Do you ever pair them to give one an advantage?" Miss Fitzroy's head cocked to the side, and a small frown pinched at her mouth.

The urge to smooth away the wrinkle that formed between her eyebrows had him clenching his hand harder around the reins. "What do you mean?"

"Say you have two equally good horses and two lesser ones. Do you make the good ones race each other, or do you pair them each with a lesser one in order to increase the chances that each gets a win?"

The fact that Aaron had, in fact, done just that more than once inspired an itch between his shoulders. He fought the urge to squirm under the weight of that direct green stare. "Like I said, neither owner has any complaints."

She nodded. "So, you play the game well. I'm glad. I'm happy for the work either way, but it's always better to have an employer smart enough to work his advantages."

Was this how other people felt when Aaron spoke with blunt honesty? No wonder they seemed stunned.

He'd never understood why the tactic worked so well until Miss Fitzroy's ramblings set him back on his heels. How was one to know what to do when the other person didn't react as anticipated?

As his companion rattled on about his horse, the view, and seemingly anything else that popped into her head, Aaron led her onto Hawksworth land. They passed the shell of the old farm stable that had been abandoned when the surrounding lands were changed into pasture and then reached the paddocks. Aaron opened the gate and turned his mind to the possible reactions that awaited him at the stable.

If word hadn't yet reached Hudson, and if Bianca wasn't visiting the stable, he might be able to borrow a horse and leave without a confrontation. If he were creative, he could put off the meeting for several days. Hopefully until Miss Fitzroy was on a path toward a new livelihood.

"All this belongs to one stable?" Miss Fitzroy asked quietly, her energy subdued as she took in the expanse of grass, trees, and fences.

"Yes. Hawksworth belongs to Viscount Stildon. He has other land as well, being worked by tenant farmers. This area is all for the horses, though."

"Oh." She fell quiet as the stable and house came into view.

The sudden quiet he'd wished for only moments ago now set him on edge. If incessant talking meant she was nervous, what did silence mean? The removal of her voice allowed the noises of the surrounding area to press into his ears, emphasizing the sudden change.

Any hope of getting away from the stable unscathed faded as Bianca stepped through the open stable door and onto the gravel drive to meet them, calling "He's here" over her shoulder.

Hudson emerged and moved to her side while three grooms filled the door, all staring with unapologetic curiosity.

"After all your huffing and puffing about not letting me on one of the thoroughbreds, you hire a female jockey?" Bianca crossed her arms and glared at Aaron.

Aaron refrained from wincing, but only just. Bianca lived at the neighboring estate and had been riding the pleasure horses at

Hawksworth since before Aaron had taken over the management. The head groom had never let her on the thoroughbreds, even the ones that were no longer racing, and Aaron had always been in adamant agreement.

"I'm borrowing a horse for Miss Fitzroy," he said, hoping that he could keep this encounter short.

"Perhaps Midas?" Bianca asked with an oversweet smile that was obviously fake, though her eyes glittered with mirth. "He's spirited enough for a decent female rider."

This time Aaron couldn't hide the wince. He'd said that very thing to Bianca before when she'd asked to ride one of the retired racehorses. The friendship that had grown between the two of them meant Bianca was going to tease him mercilessly the moment he allowed Miss Fitzroy onto the back of a racehorse.

He couldn't resist the urge to get in a dig or two first. "You aren't mistress of this house yet, you know."

"It's only a matter of time." She huffed and stuck her nose in the air, trying her best to look put out, but the twitch of her lips ruined the effect.

Hudson had been giving Aaron a hard look, but his gaze softened as he turned it to Bianca. "Does that mean your father is ready for me to ask for your hand?"

Bianca gave up her irritated pretense and sighed, meeting the viscount's soft gaze with one of her own. "No. It feels like he's going to make me wait forever."

Aaron hadn't orchestrated the distraction, but he'd take it. He looped Shadow's reins on the fence and then stepped around the couple to speak to the grooms. "Saddle Poseidon."

The grey had been an excellent racer a few years ago and was one of Aaron's favorite mounts at Hawksworth. It would give him a good idea of whether Miss Fitzroy could actually handle a powerful horse. The ride might even frighten her into quitting.

He bit back the urge to have one of the more temperamental horses saddled instead.

The couple behind him didn't remain distracted for as long as he'd have liked, and he and Miss Fitzroy were soon face-to-face with them again. While Bianca seemed to find the entire situation amusing, Hudson's expression was far more concerned.

"When did you hire her?" he asked in a low voice.

"This morning." Yesterday he'd offered a job to a man who apparently didn't exist.

Hudson's eyes widened.

Aaron took a deep breath. How could he explain the situation without telling the entire story? Leave out any piece of it—including Oliver's growing insecurities—and Aaron appeared an utter madman.

One of the grooms, Miles, led Poseidon and a trail of other grooms onto the drive.

"We'll discuss this later," Hudson said.

Aaron had no doubt that they would. If Hudson hadn't been considering managing his own stable and pushing Aaron out of the position before, he probably was now.

"We put Miss Snowley's saddle on him," Miles said. "It's the only sidesaddle we have."

"Oh, I can ride astride," Miss Fitzroy said, lifting part of her skirt to reveal what she wore underneath.

Not a word was said by the people amassed in front of the stable. Even the birds seemed shocked into silence.

Aaron stared at a woman's legs for the first time he could remember. Despite the lifted skirt, he wasn't taking in strong calves or a delicately turned ankle. No, beneath that ill-falling skirt, Miss Fitzroy was wearing trousers.

Eight

"Trousers?" Miss Snowley surged across the drive, eyes locked on the wide-leg trousers Sophia wore beneath her skirt. "I've never seen anything like it."

A burning sensation started at Sophia's hairline, crept over her ears, and slid down her cheeks. She hated when she blushed. Jonas would tease that it looked like her hair was bleeding into her face.

Miss Snowley was bent nearly double now, her hands wrapped in the fabric of her proper pinned-up riding skirt. "You ride astride in these?" Her eyes flew up to meet Sophia's. "Is it easier to control the horse that way?"

"Sometimes?" Sophia hated that the answer came out like a question, hated that even more heat flooded her face.

"All the prattling you did on the walk here, and this is what embarrasses you?" Mr. Whitworth shook his head and looked past her shoulder. "Put your skirt down. Simply putting you on a racehorse is scandalous enough. I'll not add your riding astride to the mix."

Gracious, he intended for her to run harum-scarum across the Heath in a sidesaddle? She could do it. The thought of everything that could go wrong made her knees shake, but she could do it. She smoothed her skirt, lifted her chin, and walked over to the grey horse. His back wasn't nearly as wide as Rhiannon's and was at

74

least a hand higher. The nostrils flaring in his thin face implied an energy she'd not handled before.

She swallowed hard. "I'll need a leg up, please."

This was one reason why she often rode astride. It was nearly impossible to mount a sidesaddle on one's own without a block to stand on, because there was no way to resettle the saddle once she was atop the animal.

If she put too much weight in the stirrup while racing . . . no, she wouldn't consider that. Dwelling on the potential problems would have her quitting before Mr. Whitworth could find a reason to fire her.

Everyone was still for a moment, and then Mr. Whitworth stepped forward, joined his fingers, and lowered them for her use. It wasn't until she'd placed her foot in his hands and pushed up that she saw a mounting block a few feet away on the horse's other side.

The burn in her cheeks continued as she settled in the saddle and arranged her skirts. The wide leg of her trousers was still visible, and the skirt didn't flow like a proper riding habit, but that couldn't be helped. This was the best riding outfit she owned.

She gathered the reins and looked down at Mr. Whitworth. There was a peculiar expression on his face, one that might have been admiration if she didn't know he already considered her a thorn in his side.

And wasn't that a shame? It would have been nice to talk with a handsome man who respected horses and her abilities with them. Jonas never talked down to her, often even deferred to her when it came to equine knowledge, but it just wasn't the same.

Mr. Whitworth swung up into his saddle and secured her small bag to the back of it. Lord Stildon crossed to stand at the horse's side and speak in low murmurs.

"Don't you need a chaperon?" Miss Snowley asked. "I could mount up, perhaps even ride—"

"As we are both employees of Lord Trenting and will be out in the open for the entirety of this ride," Mr. Whitworth said, cutting off both Miss Snowley and Lord Stildon, "a chaperon will not be necessary."

Miss Snowley sighed.

Lord Stildon crossed his arms.

Sophia shifted in her saddle and looked away. Was this why Mr. Whitworth had said she would ruin him? If she cost him this job . . . no, she wouldn't. She would win, she would show people what she was capable of, and she would make these men glad they had taken a chance on her.

If only they gave her time to do that. She cut her eyes to see the end of a hushed conversation between Lord Stildon and Mr. Whitworth. He was frowning as he nudged his horse forward. Had he already lost his position?

"Come along," he said, turning the horse from the stable and crossing the paddock to return to the Heath.

Sophia sent her horse after him, enjoying the steady gait of the grey and resisting the urge to encourage him to hold his head higher.

"Is everything well with your position?" she asked as she pulled her horse alongside his.

"Your concern for my position is somewhat late," he said with a lift of his eyebrow. His glance barely skimmed her face before he nudged his horse forward to see to the gate that would let them out of the fenced paddock.

She rode Poseidon through the opening. "You alone extended the job offer. How was I to know you would answer to someone else for the decision?"

"Fair." He gave a nod as he closed the gate but didn't look at her. Nor did he say anything else as he turned and rode on.

That was okay. She didn't *need* him to talk to her. He was providing her with a chance to demonstrate her abilities, a place to stay, money for the future, and, hopefully, enough food for both her and Jonas.

Expecting him to converse with her was asking too much.

The silence was nearly unbearable, and there were dozens of things she could have happily commented on. She'd ridden across miles and miles of countryside in the past two years, but the Heath was more marvelous than any of it. Perhaps it was because hope rolled across the expanse along with the sea of grass.

Everything looked bright, new, and fascinating. Even the horse beneath her, with movements that were far different from Rhiannon's, was giving her a sense of newness.

The last time she could remember feeling like this was standing in the bow of the boat that had taken them from Ireland to England. Despite the turmoil they'd left behind, she'd thought that this country would bring bright new opportunities.

She'd been wrong then. She wouldn't be wrong this time.

This time, she would create those opportunities instead of simply looking for them.

"Let's see what you've got, then."

Sophia jerked in the saddle, startling the horse beneath her into a rapid sidestep. She'd entirely forgotten about her companion as she'd watched a cluster of horses run along a distant ridge. "Pardon?"

He nodded toward a low, shadowy building in the distance. "That weigh house. Let's see who gets there first."

A race. He was proposing a race.

Her hands gripped the reins tighter, and the horse shook his head. She'd come here to do this—had expected to be racing this morning—but she still felt woefully unprepared for the moment.

Mr. Whitworth's stoic face didn't ease her sudden nerves. He didn't intend to count this as her trial race, did he? That would certainly be a handy loophole. They'd ridden no faster than a brisk walk so far, and despite his claims, the horse she was on might be slower than a mule.

She could call him on it, but his honor was the only thing keeping her here. She would simply have to focus on winning. And pray that God kept him honest.

Both would be preferable.

"Who will call the start?" She shifted her weight, squeezing her right leg tightly against the pommel to ensure she didn't end up in the mud the moment Poseidon started running.

"I'll give you the advantage." Mr. Whitworth lined up his horse beside hers, face devoid of any telling expression. "When you're ready."

She took a deep breath, resettled her seat, and called the start, nudging the horse with her foot as she yelled.

Wind filled her face and hair, whipping pins from their moorings and pulling tears from her eyes. Poseidon surged forward, legs eating up the ground at a pace Sophia had never experienced. His head bobbed with the rhythm of his stride, pulling against the tight hold she had on the reins and forcing her to hold them looser than she did when working with Rhiannon.

His smooth, supple movements didn't prevent little tremors from passing through her body each time a hoof impacted the ground.

It was glorious.

She glanced to and fro across the ground in front of them, searching for obstacles or more advantageous pathways. A blur loomed to her left, creeping into the corner of her vision. Mr. Whitworth's mount was close, but he hadn't yet pulled ahead.

Afraid to push her foot deeper into the stirrup and knock the saddle aside, she shifted her hip and gripped the pommel tighter. She leaned forward and molded herself to the back of the animal as much as possible, focusing on moving with him—even breathing with him.

The weigh house loomed larger, becoming a building instead of a blur. Almost there. Did the horse have any more? Was there a last surge of effort in those muscles that could push them to victory?

If there was, she didn't know how to find it. Train a horse to step elegantly and follow nearly invisible commands from talented riders? She was confident she could stand with the best of them. Urge an already galloping horse to go faster? She hadn't a clue.

Mr. Whitworth did, though. As they approached the building, the haze at the edge of her vision turned into a horse and rider. He passed the edge of the weigh house with Sophia and Poseidon right on his tail but most definitely behind.

They eased the horses down slowly, until both were plodding along, sides heaving, heads slightly drooped.

She'd lost the impromptu race, but what did that mean? She was proud of her first run. Had she done well enough to impress him?

What if she saw disappointment when she turned to look at him? What if his mouth was pressed into a thin line and his face was covered in resignation, knowing she was going to lose the race and take both of their reputations down with her?

She knew she didn't exactly belong here, but she desperately wanted the reason to be because she was female and not because she lacked ability. Her riding skills were all she had. If he wasn't impressed with those . . .

Mr. Whitworth cleared his throat and pulled his horse in front of hers before stopping.

Poseidon stopped as well, giving Sophia no choice but to look up into Mr. Whitworth's stony visage.

His expression seemed much the same as it had when he'd grudgingly agreed to honor her employment, but there was something different about it now, something she couldn't put into words. Maybe it was wishful thinking on her part, but despite the fact that the man clearly knew how to keep his emotions a secret from his face, she thought maybe, just maybe, he wasn't quite so resentful of her presence.

Or was he?

She dearly hoped he learned how to speak at some point in this endeavor. She also hoped she'd become immune to the urge to squirm under his quiet, steady gaze. The way he seemed to know things just by looking at her, as if he could see beneath the surface, made her feel vulnerable.

Clearing her throat, she looked over her shoulder at the stretch of land they'd just run across. "I've never done anything like that before." As she swung her face back toward Mr. Whitworth, she couldn't suppress a wide grin. "It was incredible."

His eyes softened at the corners. If she hadn't been staring at him, trying to read him the way he seemed to be reading her, she'd have missed it.

He nodded and turned his horse to start walking again. This time he kept up a running, if dry, commentary. They rode past the training yards that bordered the Heath, with their small stables and individual training rings. He pointed out landmarks as the horses plodded closer to the town. Grass gave way to lanes and buildings. Taller roofs indicating the main street of town could be seen to her left.

When there were no more horse-related areas to indicate, he lapsed into silence.

Sophia soon broke it. "I've never been to Newmarket."

"This will be a new experience for you, then."

Her subtle attempt to get him talking about what they were passing or the unique idiosyncrasies of the town hadn't worked, and she bit her tongue to keep from asking directly. The man was her employer, not her friend. He'd offered a job, not a holiday.

A couple of people tipped their hats in his direction, their speculative eyes taking in both the lathered horses and Sophia, but he offered no introductions or explanations.

They rode in silence down a street leading out of town. The homes couldn't hold her interest without tales of the people who lived within them, so she gave her attention to the man at her side. He rode the horse as if he'd been born in the saddle, with an easy grace that she couldn't help but admire.

He was handsome too, though Sophia had to admit it wouldn't be hard to surpass most of the men she'd been in contact with over the past two years. Traveling performers weren't well known for their cleanliness. When they had to choose between adequate sleep and another futile fight against the collected road dust, it wasn't much of a battle.

They turned off the road and onto a drive that cut through a tree-dotted lawn to a large estate house. Was this where she was to be staying? She'd never set foot in a home so grand, not even the servants' quarters.

Mr. Whitworth rode past the house, though, and down to a stable tucked away from the house behind a large walled garden. Three stable boys rushed out to greet them.

Sophia kicked her foot free of the stirrup and mentally measured the distance to the ground. More than once she'd jumped down from a sidesaddle on her own, but from the back of this grey beast, the ground looked very far away indeed. Self-sufficiency was a good quality, but turning an ankle wouldn't help her cause.

If she turned fully sideways before making the drop, she'd be able to land evenly on both feet, thereby preventing injury. She unhooked her right leg from the pommel and gathered the reins loosely in her hand.

"Are you intending to jump from the back of that horse?"

Her head jerked up, and she nearly tumbled from her new precarious position in the saddle. His face was incredulous as she scrambled to adjust her weight. "I was considering it, yes."

"No."

She froze, still twisted to cling to the pommel. "I beg your pardon?"

Instead of answering, he stepped up to the horse and lifted his arms to snag her about the waist. Her attempts not to squeal left her squeaking like a mouse as he lowered her to the ground. His grip remained firm as she found her footing; then he stepped back as if nothing had happened.

Her heart pounded as if she were right back in that race across the Heath. It was a ridiculous reaction. Men had been lifting women down from horses for ages. Jonas performed the task nearly every day. Perhaps that was the problem. She couldn't remember the last time she'd been assisted from a horse by anyone other than her brother. Having an enigmatic gentleman do the honors would undoubtedly elicit a different response.

He gave the stable boys instructions on caring for Poseidon and returning him to Hawksworth. Shadow was walked over to the side of the stable and given a bucket of water.

Horses taken care of, Mr. Whitworth turned to Sophia. "Meadowland Park is perhaps three miles west of here. Are your legs sufficiently rested, or have you need of another horse?"

She grinned and gave a short burst of laughter. "If you think riding a galloping horse sidesaddle will rest your legs, you've clearly never experienced it."

His eyebrows lifted slightly. "Clearly."

Did the man pay to rent words from one of the Cambridge professors?

"Yes. Well." She cleared her throat. "This would be an excellent opportunity to tell me I did well on my first run. In case you were wondering."

"You lost."

She frowned. "Not by much. Admit it. There's not as much to teach me as you thought there would be."

"You didn't fall off. That's good."

Was he joking? She truly hoped that was meant as a teasing remark and not an indication that her ability to hold on to a horse was the only redeeming thing about that ride.

"Do you require a horse to go to Meadowland Park?"

Her legs ached—her entire body ached, if she was being honest—but she wasn't about to ask for a concession or appear less than capable for a single moment. "I, er, no."

He gave a sharp nod and walked to his horse. She followed, because what else was she going to do? He unhooked her bag from the saddle and handed it over before taking the reins from the stable boy. "Geoffrey here will show you the way."

Geoffrey was trying—and failing—to follow Mr. Whitworth's

emotionless example. The slack jaw as he stared at the place where her trousers were visible beneath her wrinkled and twisted skirt revealed the moment was too much for his restraint.

Leather creaked and buckles jangled as Mr. Whitworth took the reins of his horse and led him farther down the path. Past the stable, the lane became rutted, narrow, and overgrown. What was down that way? He called over his shoulder, "Pay attention to the way. I expect you in the training yard at nine tomorrow morning."

It was the sort of statement one would say to an employee, so why did it feel so rude? And why did his departure leave her suddenly feeling alone and abandoned?

Nine

Geoffrey shifted his weight, feet sliding about in tiny circles in the dirt. He coughed and nodded at the lane that she'd come in on. "If you're ready, er, miss?"

No, she wasn't ready, but when was the last time anything in her life had cared whether she was prepared?

"Yes. Of course."

He gave her a nod of acknowledgment before silently leading the way around the edge of town to another estate.

If she'd thought the earlier house grand, it was nothing compared to this one. Her mouth dried as it came into view, the wings stretching far enough that one would wish for a horse if tasked with circling the building. Perhaps they'd only gone two miles since they'd left Mr. Whitworth and it was another mile around to the kitchen door.

Perhaps she was losing her mind.

The boy led her to a door and then stood a bit to the side as she lifted her hand to knock. He shifted his weight as they waited for an answer. "Will that be all, miss?"

She smiled to acknowledge his attempt at good manners. It didn't cost anything for a person to be polite, despite what her new employer seemed to think. She dismissed him and turned back to face the door just as it swung open.

A woman wearing an apron, mobcap, and deep frown looked Sophia up and down. "The rider, I'm assuming?"

"Yes, ma'am," Sophia said quietly. It shouldn't be exhausting to be scrutinized, considering how little effort it required for her to stand there and be stared at, but she could perform a dozen circus shows and not feel this drained.

Particularly since the woman in front of her obviously found something lacking. When was the last time she'd seen such disdain on a person's face?

"This way." The woman turned and Sophia scrambled after her, following her up stairs that seemed interminable. Finally, she flung open a door to a room near the top of the house.

"The maids' rooms line this corridor. Don't disturb the other women's sleep or work. You get two meals a day—a breakfast tray and a dinner tray. They'll come up at Cook's convenience. You can eat it then or eat it cold."

"I, er, yes." Sophia fisted her hands to keep from dancing at the prospect of a solid roof, a real room, and two prepared meals a day. The woman didn't seem the type to appreciate such celebrations.

Sophia stepped into the room and turned to thank the woman, only to see her back as she moved toward the stairs. Sophia eased the door shut and took in her temporary home.

A small bed complete with pillow, linens, and a blanket sat against the wall under a sloping roof. Beside it sat a plain washstand with a pitcher and basin at the ready. A wooden chair stood next to a small chest of drawers. A line of hooks graced the cheery but faded yellow wall beside the door. Her knees gave way and she slid down the door to sit on the floor.

It would have seemed simple and bare to her when she'd been a child, but now? Luxury.

Knees still weak, she crawled across the floor and onto the bed, every muscle relaxing as she sank into the mattress. Guilt made her exhaustion heavier as she contemplated what Jonas was doing at that moment. Whatever it was, it didn't include a bed, a private room, and the promise of a cooked meal.

She would make it better for them both, though. A sudden rush of excitement smoothed over her guilt, dread, worry, and even her aching body. She'd done it. The first step was completed. This was going to work. A new and better life would be theirs.

She drifted into a hazy state that wasn't quite a nap but certainly wasn't awake. The arrival of a maid with her dinner tray interrupted her doze, and she had no idea how much time had passed. Possibly quite a while, given the pinch of disapproval in the maid's face as she took in Sophia lying atop the bedcovers in her clothes. Sophia winced. Her boots were even still on her feet.

The maid didn't wait for an explanation, not that Sophia had any good one to give. It didn't matter. One look at the laden tray and the maid was the last thing on her mind.

It was a large bowl of stew that contained more meat and vegetables than water. She gobbled it down, glad that no one was around to witness the unladylike enthusiasm. Not wanting to cause any more work than necessary, she returned the tray to the kitchen herself and then slipped quietly back up to her room.

With her stomach fuller than it had been in years, she undressed and crawled back into bed.

Sleep didn't come as easily this time. Every creak of the house and whisper of wind against the window startled her awake until trying to sleep left her more exhausted than staying up all night.

The unfamiliar night noises shifted slowly to the scrapes and rumbles of a wakening house. Grateful that she could now rise without guilt, she climbed from the bed and donned her second-best riding outfit. One could also call it her worst riding ensemble, since she only possessed two, but that seemed a disservice to the trusty garment.

Unfortunately, her morning preparations didn't take a great deal of time. The world outside the window was still dark, and she had nothing to do but wait for the sun to rise and the promised breakfast tray to be delivered.

She settled into the lone chair. It would have been simpler—and given her something to do—if she could go below and obtain the food herself, but the woman who'd shown her to this room had been very particular.

There was nothing to do but watch the sky lighten with the edges of a new day's sun. As she sat in the hard chair with her head propped against the window, she once more fell into a hazy doze.

A short perfunctory knock was followed by the opening of the door, and Sophia jerked back to wakefulness. The chair beneath her tipped, coming to rest against the foot of the bed, leaving her at an awkward angle, looking up at a wide-eyed maid. It wasn't the same one from the night before, but Sophia guessed the two would compare experiences at some point. She wasn't going to come out favorably.

Scrambling out of the angled chair was not an easy or elegant feat, and by the time Sophia had regained her composure, the maid had deposited the tray on the chest of drawers and departed.

Aromas she hadn't enjoyed in ages filled the room, and Sophia's stomach clenched in anticipation. Last night's stew had been more than enjoyable, but this . . . Her eyes widened and her mouth watered.

Bread—fresh bread, not the day-old loaves the bakers sold her at a discount—sat beside a bowl of porridge and a plate piled with meat and eggs. Likely the meat was from the day before, but Sophia didn't care. What little meat she normally ate was scraps of leftover tavern fare tucked into a pastry, so the spread on the tray was sheer delicacy.

There was more than enough for Jonas to eat as well, if she could find a way to transport it. A bowl of porridge couldn't be wrapped in a cloth and shoved into a sack like a meat pie could, but there had to be something she could do.

She would have to check the clock in the kitchen, but she should have time to go by the knoll where Jonas said he would be waiting before she went to the training yard. After she ate her portion, she scraped the remaining porridge to the side of the bowl and laid the meat and eggs in the other half. The food wouldn't stay separate on the journey, but Jonas wouldn't care. He'd be as excited about the jumbled-up fare as she'd been about the prettily laid out tray. Turning the plate over, she set it on the bowl and then tied the napkin around both to secure them.

If she carried it carefully, it shouldn't spill too much.

Returning the tray to the kitchen herself would be easy enough, but if anyone saw her leaving with her bundled dishes, they'd have questions.

Her two changes of clothes now hung from the wall pegs, leaving her bag nearly empty. She dumped what contents remained onto the bed. Her father's horse training manuals, the miniature of her family, and a small wooden box that had once held a set of jewelry were all quickly transferred to the top drawer of the chest. They didn't even fill it halfway.

Gently, she laid the covered bowl in the bottom of the bag.

Frowning, she experimented with lifting the sides. As soon as she put the strap on her shoulder, the food would fall sideways and spill. It needed support. She pulled a sheet from the bed and coiled it in the bag as a nest for her brother's meal.

Satisfied that it was as secure as could be, she laid the bread atop the bowl and secured the flap of the knapsack. For extra protection, she curled her arm beneath the bundle. Just imagining Jonas's reaction put a smile on her face.

She turned to leave the room, but her body froze as her fingers landed on the latch. Looking over her shoulder at the small chest of drawers, her breath hitched. Those mementos hadn't been far from her side in years. She hadn't even left them in the wagon at the circus, instead choosing to store them with the grooming tools and Rhiannon's tack.

She had no reason to distrust the staff here, but those she'd met hadn't cared much for her presence. Quickly she stepped back over to the drawers and tucked her few belongings into the bag as well. She would leave them in Jonas's care until this was over.

Bag under one arm and tray carefully balanced in the other, Sophia eased down the steps to the kitchen. The rooms had been nearly empty when she'd gone down the night before, but this morning there would be plenty of people about. Any of them could notice that her tray was absent of its dishes. Lady Rebecca's offer of a place to stay would be rescinded if Sophia caused a ruckus.

Fortunately, the morning seemed busy enough that no one cared what she was doing. It was easy to slip the tray among the others in the scullery and escape out the kitchen door.

She took off at a brisk pace. The trees where she was to meet Jonas were a long walk from Meadowland Park, but, fortunately, they were close to the training yard. She should have enough time.

If Jonas was there.

What if he wasn't? What if something terrible had happened? What if someone had found him? The horrid possibilities were enough to make Sophia want to give up her room in Lady Rebecca's home and sleep with Jonas under the stars, because at least then she'd know where he was.

Jonas stepped from the trees as she approached, sending a spiral of relief to her lungs and allowing her to breathe easy once more. Only the bowl and plate digging into her side kept her from running to him. She'd made it this far without spilling his breakfast. She could make it five more steps.

He wrapped his arms around her, and she buried her nose into his shirt. He smelled of dirt and grass and horse. To some it would be off-putting, but to her, it was familiar and comforting.

After a few moments, she pulled back. "Where's Rhiannon?"

"In the cottage I found a little north of here. It's been long abandoned. Half of it is fallen down, but I've managed to fashion a sort of stall on one side and arranged a few scraps of furniture on the other. The area is overgrown, so I have to be careful coming and going, but there's a few trees about and it's not far from water. It will do for a while."

Sophia nodded and then knelt to lower her knapsack to the ground, biting her lip as she opened it. "I brought food."

Jonas's stomach rumbled as she removed the bowl and plate. His gaze lifted from the food and narrowed at Sophia. "This isn't all you got, was it?"

She shook her head. "I ate. I promise. If I ate any more, I'd be sick."

He nodded, shoved a piece of ham into his mouth, and re-wrapped the bowl. He took her knapsack. "Can you come see the cottage now?"

She shook her head. "I'm not sure what time it is, and I don't want to be late."

He nodded. "I'll be back here this afternoon. If you can't come, I'll find a way to bring a map with me tomorrow morning."

Sophia licked her lips and pressed them together to keep from crying. This had seemed like such a perfect idea yesterday morning, but it wasn't an exciting adventure. It was terrifying.

"Soph?" Jonas reached out one hand and nudged her chin up.

"What?" she whispered.

"Be strong and courageous."

It was a quote Jonas used frequently. While she might have their father's training manuals, Jonas had his Bible. They'd made a great team over the years, Jonas seeing to the siblings' faith and Sophia to their livelihood. She couldn't rest on Jonas's faith now, though. She had to be strong and courageous on her own and had to trust that God was with *her* and not just with *them*.

"Be strong and courageous," she repeated before giving him one final nod and fleeing down the lane.

Ten

"I don't know about this, Whitworth." Mr. Barley, the horse and jockey trainer Aaron had been working with, ran a finger across his nose and gave Equinox a narrow look.

Theirs was an interesting relationship, with Aaron filling the shoes of the owner while not having the actual status. It often forced Aaron to exude more confidence than he felt to maintain his authority.

Though he couldn't verbally agree with Barley, Aaron wasn't sure about it either. Yet it was the decision he'd made, so it was what they would move forward with.

Not that he would be sad should Miss Fitzroy decide not to appear today. If she walked away from the agreement, Aaron's honor would remain intact. While there were some who wouldn't consider breaking an agreement with a woman as a lapse of honor, Aaron did. Those he cared about most would agree.

That didn't mean he wouldn't breathe a sigh of relief if he never saw the feisty redhead again.

At least, that was what he kept telling himself.

He ran a hand down the black thoroughbred's neck. "Consider it an experiment, Barley. A temporary alternative training method."

"I've added more than enough of your alternative methods, thank you." One side of the older man's mouth quirked up as he shook his head. "You've made some strange suggestions over the years, but this . . . I just don't know that it's worth giving it a shake."

Aaron was constantly researching and questioning, challenging the established ways of horse training, and some of the ideas he'd brought to the trainer had been short-lived, as they proved themselves inferior to the accepted way of doing things. Sometimes he proposed a truly mad idea just to see if the other man would go along with it.

Even he wouldn't have come up with this, though.

"A woman," Barley said with a shake of his head, followed by a deep sigh. "Is she even capable of controlling this beast?"

"She nearly beat me on Poseidon yesterday." Aaron had been impressed. He also had to give more merit to the circus show now that he knew she was the trainer. Miss Fitzroy was at least good enough to safely manage a challenge race. Would she win?

Maybe.

Something still felt off about her arrival in Newmarket, but he'd learned long ago to trust facts over feelings. The fact was she had the best seat of any woman he'd ever seen on the back of a horse. If there was some other trickery waiting to befall him, it didn't have to do with her ability to ride.

Mr. Barley sighed. "I don't know. . . ."

"If she can't handle the horse, she'll have to give up the position." Aaron ran his hand down the horse's neck again, feeling the jerk of the ready muscles beneath the skin.

The idea that she might fail sent a surge of conflicting thoughts through him. If she couldn't ride the horse, his issue would return to the far simpler matter of needing to quickly find a new jockey. But she would be left without a means of providing for herself. What would she do? A few days ago she hadn't been his problem, but now he couldn't pretend he wasn't connected to her next steps.

A dull throb started at the nape of his neck and spread through his mind in the wake of the bouncing thoughts. Did he want her to be as good as she claimed? As much as he detested the idea of a female jockey, the fact was that with the challenge only delayed a week, she was currently his best chance of winning it.

Heavy silence fell over the training yard, followed by the low buzz of people from nearby yards who'd come to watch and were really bad at whispering.

His new jockey had arrived.

Aaron slid his watch from his pocket and gave it a quick look. Seven minutes early. A grudging approval tipped the scale more in her favor.

He turned. Once again, the bold expression on her delicate features slammed into his gut and her dramatic coloring stole his breath. She was in another strange riding ensemble consisting of skirt and trousers. If the other women in Newmarket started wearing trousers instead of proper riding habits, their angry fathers and husbands would create far bigger problems than gossiping stable boys.

These garments had obviously seen a great deal more wear than yesterday's, if the patches and stains were anything to go by. She would hardly be the first person to wear less-than-pristine clothing to accomplish the dirty work of dealing with horses, but it still bothered him.

"Good morning," Miss Fitzroy greeted in her soft voice and slight accent.

Aaron could easily understand why horses responded to it.

She came to a stop in front of the men, glancing over them briefly before gazing at the horse, consuming him from ears to tail and down to the hooves.

It was an action he had to approve of. He was halfway to liking this woman, and he couldn't allow that. He had more than enough friends in his circle, more than enough people connected to his name and reputation. He did not need another.

He could, however, offer her the respect she deserved. The rest of her story might be suspicious, but it was obvious she knew horses.

That didn't ease his trepidations about putting her on one and sending her flying across the Heath. "You did well enough on

Poseidon yesterday, but he's no longer racing." He gave Equinox a steady pat on the neck and the horse lightly tossed his head. "Equinox is in prime condition."

She moved about the horse, inspecting him from all angles, running her hand along his withers and forelegs. She murmured nonsensical croons to the horse as she stroked his nose and offered her flattened palm for the horse to nuzzle.

Barley crossed his arms over his chest, clearly disgruntled that she was doing everything they would expect a good jockey to do the first time he met a new horse.

While the trainer's displeasure was somewhat amusing, his new jockey's competence squashed Aaron's small hope of resolving this situation easily and quietly. He blew out a breath and cast his eyes heavenward. *Dear God, what did I do to deserve this?*

He'd thought he and the Almighty had a decent agreement. Aaron didn't ask God for miracles, and the Deity didn't make Aaron's life any more difficult than it already was. Somewhere along the way, that deal had faltered.

It *had* been a while since Aaron had visited the people and places that reminded him of the delicateness of his position in life. Was this God's way of reminding him not to get too comfortable? Not to start thinking too much of his life simply because his longtime chums had attained wives with enough connections to fill a society column?

It wasn't until Miss Fitzroy was checking the stirrup that Aaron noticed the horse wore his normal saddle instead of the sidesaddle Aaron had sent over early this morning.

Aaron frowned and stepped forward, ready to signal to a stable boy to have the issue corrected, but before he could say a word, Miss Fitzroy grasped the saddle and lifted her leg, the skirt falling away to reveal the wide-leg trousers beneath. She slid her foot into the stirrup, a move that required she bend her knee clear to her chest. After a single small bounce on her right leg, she pushed herself up and swung smoothly into the saddle.

As Barley coughed and sputtered, Miss Fitzroy quickly and efficiently adjusted her skirts until they covered her trousers to the knee, as if she'd done this a thousand times before.

Obviously, she hadn't been lying about being able to ride astride. "I can't let you ride about in trousers," Aaron said with a sigh, stepping up to the horse and preparing to help her dismount, though the ease with which she'd gotten up there indicated she could probably get down without a problem.

"Riding without fabric between my skin and the saddle doesn't sound the least bit comfortable." She looked down at her leg, drawing Aaron's attention in the same direction. "Besides, I rather think trousers are far preferable to showing a great deal of leg."

He did not need to think about her skin or her bare leg or any other part of her person. A flush worked its way up his neck when he wasn't entirely successful at avoiding imagining what her leg would look like. "You could wear a habit."

"I don't own one," she said softly, shifting in the saddle. "Besides, I don't think that would adequately cover my legs without a sidesaddle."

"Yes. I sent one down this morning. They apparently forgot to use it."

Mr. Barley turned to the stable and beckoned for the stable boy, carefully avoiding meeting Aaron's gaze. Clearly the trainer had his own plan to rid himself of having to work with a woman.

It had failed to embarrass her, but the fact that Aaron had discussed this issue with her yesterday and she'd still been challenged with it certainly embarrassed him.

He did not like being embarrassed.

Miss Fitzroy kicked her feet free of the stirrups and dropped to the ground, Aaron extending his arms awkwardly to attempt to catch her. She sighed and looked up at him, trapped between him and the dark horse. "Like it or not, Mr. Whitworth, for the time being we are partners of a sort."

"We are not partners," Aaron ground out, looking down into

eyes as green as the grass on the Heath. "You are my employee." He swallowed. "For now."

He never asked his friends for favors, but he just might have to give in on this one and request they help him find her new employment.

The prospect twisted his stomach until he thought he might be ill.

An awkward silence covered the yard as the horse was saddled again. Since mounting blocks weren't a training stable necessity, Aaron had to step forward to assist her into the sidesaddle. Her foot landed in his hands. Just like the day before, he could feel her bones through the thin, worn leather. It was a reminder that he could not simply turn her away.

Nor could he buy her a proper riding habit or boots. If he arranged new clothing for her, the whispers and rumors would turn cruel and any hope of her obtaining proper employment in this area would wither and die. He'd never bought a jockey a pair of boots before. He couldn't start now.

Once she was settled, she gathered the reins and looked down at him. "What now?"

"Now we see if you can learn how to guide Equinox through his paces in a way that keeps you on course while obtaining the maximum speed. Yesterday it would have been enough for you to hold on and not die. Now we have a week to try for something better."

Mr. Barley grunted. "Let's get on with it, then. Yard's not getting any less crowded. The onlookers want to see what you've gotten us into."

The trainer was no longer attempting to hide his derision at the circumstances, and Aaron chanced a look up at his jockey to see how she was taking it.

Her chin was a notch higher and the lines of her neck were strained, as if her teeth were clamped together. She was the picture of determined defiance, and blast it all, but it just made her look prettier.

Eleven

Sophia had been on the back of a horse since before she could walk. She knew how they moved, how to communicate with them, how to assess different temperaments.

It was the racing of them that left her weak in the knees.

Of course, that sensation could also be attributed to the ache that radiated from her bent leg up to the middle of her back from the effort required to sit aside while the horse ran as if hounds were nipping at his heels.

Equinox was taller, faster, and all-in-all far more terrifying than the grey thoroughbred from the day before.

Not that she would tell anyone.

After an hour of experiencing how the horse would jump into a gallop at the start of the race and attempting to learn how to change her reins and leg commands to communicate with a horse incredibly focused on moving with such speed, she was grateful for the way her skirt fabric never lay quite right over her trousers. It prevented anyone from seeing the way her legs trembled when she dismounted.

Unfortunately, she had nothing to disguise her tongue.

"That was more difficult than I anticipated," she blurted out as she braced her feet on solid ground.

There was no immediate response. Perhaps she'd said it low enough that no one other than the horse had heard?

She glanced sideways at Mr. Barley's stunned face. Mr. Whitworth's expression was so blank that it had to be deliberate.

They'd heard.

She lifted her chin, folded one hand around the reins, and buried the other in Equinox's mane. "All told, I think I did sufficiently well."

Mr. Barley grunted.

Mr. Whitworth said nothing.

The stable lad who appeared to collect the horse avoided her eyes entirely.

She curled her hand tighter around the reins, hoping the bite of leather into her palm would remind her to keep her mouth shut.

It didn't work.

"I didn't fall out of the saddle, which is a feat you might not fully appreciate, given you've likely never ridden aside. Fortunately, the saddle didn't slip. I admit that was somewhat of a concern."

Stop talking, Sophia.

"There were several onlookers, I'm sure you noticed. Some were impressed. One man remarked on my fine seat."

Mr. Barley spluttered, Mr. Whitworth blushed, and Sophia realized the man's comment hadn't necessarily been complimentary. Heat spread over her cheeks, and she cursed her fair skin and lack of makeup.

The stable boy tried to tug the reins from her hand, but Sophia thought she'd be better off biting the leather than relinquishing it. Anything to stop herself from talking.

"I need the horse, miss," the lad said quietly.

Sophia's cheeks flamed more as she pried her fingers loose and crossed her arms over her chest. Forcing herself to meet Mr. Whitworth's gaze, she asked, "What else will I be doing today?"

Mr. Barley took the cap off his head and banged it twice against his leg before slapping it back atop his thinning hair. "Same time tomorrow will do fine."

Mr. Whitworth didn't contradict the trainer, though Sophia

wished he would. Her days were going to be incredibly long if she had no tasks aside from these hours of learning, but she wouldn't push him for permission to haul feed or muck stalls.

Couldn't he say *something*, though? A word of praise or even censure would give her a sense of where she stood.

It shouldn't matter, so long as he didn't fire her, but it did. She was drawn to this man. Something about the quiet in his eyes and the way there seemed to be so much more going on in his head than he let on.

She wanted him to approve of her.

Complaining or staring at him in a silent battle she was doomed to lose was more likely to antagonize him than impress him, so she gave a single nod and left the yard.

Every eye was on her as she departed. She knew the difference between looks filled with awe and admiration and those heavy with speculation and suspicion. She was most definitely experiencing the latter.

Because those watching would expect her to go into town, she headed that direction. Hopefully the streets of Newmarket would be busy enough she could lose herself among the people and find a way to circle back to the trees to await Jonas.

No such luck.

She was nearly as infamous in town as she'd been in the training yard. People pointed and stared, preventing her from slipping down a side street or hiding in an alcove. Some women crossed the street to avoid her. Some men leered in such a way that she crossed the street to avoid them.

What was she supposed to do? She didn't know anyone in town or have any possessions or property to see to. Even if she had any money, she wouldn't spend it on frivolous shopping. When was the last time she'd had five minutes with nothing to do, much less five hours?

On the premise of adjusting her shoe, she stepped into a small alley and leaned against the side of a building to observe the other people. What were they doing with their afternoon?

Several men went in and out of the area taverns. Women strolled about, looking in shop windows and occasionally stepping inside. Curiosity almost propelled her to choose a pair of women walking arm in arm and follow them simply to see what ladies of leisure did with their day. Instead, she eased farther and farther into the alley until no one from the main street could see her, then worked her way behind buildings until she was back outside of town and headed toward the meeting spot.

Jonas might not return for hours, but her only other option was to go to her attic room, lie on the bed, and stare at the ceiling. She'd rather watch the clouds go by while she dreamed of the riding school she would one day have.

AARON'S LIFE COULD be divided into two sections by one very distinct moment in time—the day he'd met Oliver and Graham.

Before them, his life had certainly been simpler, though devoid of much joy. After them, things had gotten both better and more complicated. To survive, he'd broken his new life into different realities. It had taken him a while to determine where everything went, but several years ago, he'd settled into a comfortable division.

Each reality had its own rules, its own connections, and its own ramifications. If he carefully managed how much time he spent in each reality, his life remained in balance. He didn't entertain illusions of grandeur or start thinking he could attain that which was never meant to be his. Nor did he fall into the doldrums of melancholy and self-loathing, or worse, self-pity.

But those lines were blurring now, and the balance was slipping away. Oliver's interest in the horses was making their friendship bleed into Aaron's professional life. Not to mention the fact that Aaron's relationship with his newest employer, Hudson, was far from the strict professionalism he'd anticipated.

Because of that friendship, he'd agreed to open the gate to his family life, such as it was. Of all the walls coming down around him, this one terrified him the most.

Hudson wasn't happy about Miss Fitzroy's employment, and really, Aaron didn't blame him. Hudson was furiously working to earn the respect of Newmarket's racing populace, and attaching his name, even distantly, to a potential scandal wouldn't help matters.

There was one other thing he desperately wanted, and though Aaron had promised to attempt to get it for him, he hadn't done anything about it yet. Perhaps if he got things in motion, his friend would be pleased enough to overlook Aaron's misstep.

Even better if Aaron could work out a deal that didn't cost Hudson a small fortune.

That was a long shot, given what he was after, but he'd still gone ahead and sent a message to Lord Rigsby yesterday afternoon.

Now Aaron had to put the last of his guiding life principles aside and meet with the one man he'd spent most of his life avoiding.

Until a few weeks ago, it had been at least a decade since he'd exchanged more than a nod of greeting with his legitimate half brother and four years since he'd done even that. Their recent encounter on the Heath had surprised them both.

They'd done little more than lay eyes on each other before Aaron departed the area, assuming he knew the sort of man his half brother was. Now he had to question his entire opinion of the man.

Aaron had left the particulars of this meeting up to Lord Rigsby. Instead of choosing his own stable or home, or even an elegant club or restaurant, the man had selected tea in a private dining room at an inn in a nearby village.

It should have been the least threatening place possible.

Instead, a sense of dread made the walk from the stable yard to the inn seem to take hours.

The inn wasn't busy. In another week or so it would be filled to the rafters as people came into the area for the October Meetings and surrounding festivities. The current stillness brought a welcomed sense of privacy. Aaron usually took great care to keep his name out of conversations, but there were far too many for him to control at the moment. He didn't need any more.

Locating the private dining room was simple.

Walking through the door not quite as much.

After a deep breath, he pushed through the portal to find Lord Rigsby sitting at the small dining table, a tea service at his elbow and a book open in front of him. He set the book aside and stood as Aaron entered the room. As Aaron hadn't yet moved past seeing Rigsby as the dismissive lad he'd been in school, the show of respect caught him off guard.

"Whitworth."

Aaron swallowed. "Rigsby."

Even though he referred to all his close friends by their given names, dropping the honorific *Lord* from the front of this man's name felt daring and wrong.

Perhaps because, had Aaron been legitimate, the title would have been his.

"Tea?" The man gestured to the pot but didn't offer to pour.

As one who managed his life by reading the unspoken social cues in a room, Aaron had to appreciate Rigsby's attempt to put them on something resembling equal footing. Perhaps this meeting would go well after all.

All Aaron had to do was strike a deal that Hudson would be ecstatically happy to receive and he could go another four years without seeing his half brother.

Aaron moved to the table and fixed a cup of tea before filling a plate from the selection of sandwiches and scones on the tray.

"Shall we discuss the horse or our history first?" Rigsby lifted his teacup and sat back in his chair, taking a small sip before cradling the cup in both hands.

Taking up his own cup, Aaron mirrored the position. Despite

the relaxed appearance, it was a move of power, an indication to the other party that one wasn't at all concerned about the outcome of the discussion. Aaron didn't know about Rigsby, but his lack of concern was an utter lie. "Have you anything pertinent to add to the history?"

There weren't a great many shared moments between the two men, but Aaron could clearly recall the first one.

Rigsby had been a scrawny little boy standing at his father's side in Aaron's mother's broken-down little cottage. Their father delivered a lecture on a man's responsibility to account for his mistakes—with Aaron as the primary example.

It wasn't the sort of meeting fast friendships were made from.

Rigsby didn't break eye contact, though he didn't seem focused on Aaron anymore. "He told me stories, you know."

Aaron set his tea down, afraid whatever Rigsby said next might cause him to bobble the cup and appear less than stable. He didn't want to think about the man who'd barely known Aaron or his mother sharing tales. "What about?"

"You."

Good thing he'd set the cup down. "Me?"

Rigsby nodded and leaned forward to put his tea down and push it away. "Most mentioned how my veins held the proper mix of aristocratic blood, so I should be able to accomplish more than his accidental by-blow."

It was a difficult idea to digest, the marquis using his illegitimate son as a measurement against his legitimate one. "I thought I was the ultimate example of the consequences of straying from the correct path."

That was what Lord Lindbury had said to Rigsby that day. Aaron had stood there, unable to leave as they blocked the only door, and memorized every word he hurled.

Rigsby shrugged. "I think you're his favorite example for everything wrong in life, whether it's his own shortcomings or mine."

"Makes one wonder why he acknowledged me in the first place."

The macabre grin the other man offered sent a shiver across Aaron's shoulders. "Because the soul is strengthened by being bludgeoned with guilt and the reminder of our own imperfections."

Aaron blinked. "He said that?"

Rigsby gave a mirthless laugh. "No. A priest did." He shrugged. "Well, those weren't his exact words, but that was how I interpreted them."

"How old were you?"

"Twelve."

Aaron's tumultuous upbringing was suddenly looking far better. Many of life's avenues weren't open to him, but for the most part he had turned into a sane, healthy, complete gentleman. "I'm beginning to think I may have gotten the better raising of the two of us."

"I think I made it out alive. My mother . . ." Rigsby shifted in his seat. "My mother sees things differently."

Discussing their shared wastrel of a father bothered Aaron far less than he'd expected it to, but addressing their different maternal experiences destroyed the small sense of ease they'd created. Social discomfort might often be to Aaron's advantage, but in this particular case, he didn't want it.

He cleared his throat and took another sip of tea. "Perhaps we should discuss the horse instead."

Rigsby nodded. "It's not as if we can change the history."

"Do you intend to tell him?" Aaron didn't identify whom he meant by the word *him*. He had a feeling the word would always have a certain understanding between the two of them.

Rigsby frowned. "I haven't even told him my plans to race horses, much less race them in Newmarket. Unless I end up in the scandal sheets, he doesn't seek me out beyond our quarterly account reviews."

Everything Aaron thought he knew about Rigsby was melting in the face of this meeting. Why had he believed the marquis would somehow become an exemplary father to his legitimate children? Aaron shouldn't have been surprised that the son didn't fit neatly into the same box as the father. The rest of his life was in upheaval. Why not this as well?

He shoved a hand through his hair and leaned forward to brace his forearms on the table. Despite the softening of his thoughts toward the man he'd spent most of his life despising, Aaron couldn't lower his guard. Their agreement hadn't been set yet, and there was a good chance it wasn't going to be a simple exchange of money for services. That was the way Aaron's life had been going of late.

"Shall we talk business?" Aaron asked.

Rigsby leaned forward. "As I understand it, you want my horse, Sunset's Pride, to cover one of Lord Stildon's mares."

Aaron nodded stiffly. It sounded as if Rigsby wanted to make this deal with Aaron instead of Hudson.

"I'm amenable."

Yet again, it was time for Aaron to plunge in on a ludicrous idea or toss the entire consideration aside. "Stildon isn't pleased with me right now." That was putting it mildly. "I'd like to come to an agreement that alters that."

Rigsby leaned back. "I can think of an exchange that won't cost your employer a penny."

Aaron's jaw clenched. The lack of fee was certainly good news. Whatever replaced it wouldn't be.

"Instead of money," Rigsby continued, "I'd like you to do me a favor."

That was what Aaron had been afraid of.

Twelve

Jonas met Sophia at the trees and showed her the way to the cottage he'd found.

With a large portion of roof fallen in and a wild tangle of brush and grass extending from a nearby grouping of trees, there was no question as to whether or not the place had long been abandoned. She dearly hoped it looked better on the inside than the outside, but that would wait until she returned with their dinner.

As much as she wanted to see Rhiannon and share every detail of her day with Jonas, she didn't want to chance missing the tray, so she took her knapsack and returned to her little attic room and waited.

And waited.

And waited.

By the time the tray was delivered by a hesitant and harried-looking housemaid, Sophia was desperate for both the food and a chance to get away from her own thoughts. All they seemed able to do was bounce between guilt that Jonas didn't have the same comforts she did, terror that she'd fail, and irritation that thinking of her job always slid to thoughts of Mr. Whitworth and how she couldn't remember the last time a handsome man had been nice to her.

She jammed all the food together on a single plate before covering it with the other and wrapping the entire makeshift container in a pillowcase before lowering it gently into her sack. A glance at the bed had her biting her lip and carefully arranging the blanket to hide the bareness. She would have to remember to bring all the linens back with her tonight, along with the dishes.

There was no good way to carry the tea, so she gulped it down before creeping down the stairs to carefully deposit her tray with the dishes awaiting cleaning. She hoped her heart didn't damage her throat with its thumping as she jumped at every noise. She *knew* she had been invited and had every right to be there, but she didn't *feel* welcome. Everything about the situation felt wrong.

The pressure eased from her chest with every step she took away from the grand house. All the stress and newness of her day's experiences had left a strange pall over her entire being.

She didn't have to worry about any of that for the rest of the evening. The fresh air filled her lungs and stretched right down to her toes, making every step lighter and easier.

No one seemed to pay her any attention as she walked into the countryside, avoiding the main streets and carefully retracing the path she'd taken earlier. As she passed the final landmark—a tree that had twisted into a curve and now grew along the ground—the shabby abandoned cottage came into view.

It couldn't be any worse than sleeping beneath the wagon or with the horses. Even some of the dilapidated inns they'd stayed in weren't much better. Still, by the time she picked her way through the overgrowth, the lightness brought about by her walk was once more buried under a mountain of indecision and guilt.

"Jonas?" She knocked on a door lying crooked in its frame, only the top hinge remaining. "Are you there?"

The leather hinge creaked as the door swung slowly inward. Jonas leaned one shoulder on the doorpost. "I thought about making a visit to the local duke, but they say he's rarely in residence, so I decided I might as well stay here and wait for you."

Sophia rolled her eyes and pushed past him to get a look at his temporary home.

The corner that no longer had a roof to support had crumbled into a pile of rubble, but the rest of the structure appeared sound. A scattering of shabby furniture had been pulled into the corner farthest from the exposed portion. The table had certainly seen better days, but it didn't fall when she gave it a little push before setting her knapsack atop it.

That morning's dishes were stacked in one corner, while Jonas's Bible, a hoof-pick, and a small pile of twigs sat in the middle.

A single wall divided the interior, though part of it had fallen victim to the elements. It was little more than waist high in spots and stopped several feet shy of the other wall. Rhiannon poked her head over one of the low sections, greeting Sophia with an enthusiastic nod and whinny.

While Jonas unpacked the food, Sophia walked carefully into the crumbling side of the cottage. Most of the floor had been cleared of debris to give the horse adequate space.

Sophia indulged herself and the animal with a good, long hug. As she scratched the mare behind the ears, she gave the area a closer look. What she'd thought was a haphazard pile of wood and stone looked deliberate upon closer inspection. "What are you doing over there?"

Jonas poked his head over the low wall to see where she was indicating. "I'm building a stall." He turned an accusing glare on the horse. "She keeps to her space fine when I'm here, but as soon as I leave, she likes to wander. I'm fashioning a stall to put her in while I'm gone to get water or gather firewood."

Her throat clogged with a hard rock of emotion as she nodded. She'd seen Jonas briefly a few hours earlier. How could she miss them as much as she did?

"We couldn't talk much earlier. Did you ride today?" Jonas leaned against the wall, plate of food in hand. It was difficult to eat with gentlemanly manners while standing in a collapsing building, but he was trying.

"Yes, I rode today." She'd done well enough not to embarrass herself, but was it good enough to win? She was terrified that everything would be over in a week and all this effort would have been in vain.

"Soph."

She ran a hand through Rhiannon's mane. "Yes?"

"How did it go?"

"We went fast, and I didn't fall off."

"Given those are the objectives, I'd say you did well, then." He shrugged. "Better than going slow and landing in the mud, anyway."

Sophia gave the horse one last pat before moving to the other side of the cottage to collect her own plate. Two broken chairs were piled in the corner, but a third sat at the table. She gave it a test before lowering herself onto it.

"Did we do the right thing, Jonas?"

He watched her for a moment before setting his empty plate down and nudging her portion closer to her. Then he picked up the hoof-pick and crossed to one of the wooden support beams. He dug the tip into the wood. "Unless you've come up with a way to undo the days, that's a useless question." He paused in his efforts and looked at her. "And if you had such a power, I'd like to think you'd have used it to keep Prancer from ever stepping on that loose ground and sliding into the ravine."

Sophia contemplated throwing her bread at the bothersome man, but she wouldn't waste food. How could he joke about that? Fresh pain stabbed through her chest at the memory of those horrible moments. The screams the pounding rain could not drown out. Jonas lying in the mud where his horse had thrown him before tumbling down the side of the ravine. The pain on his face as he tried to stand and go to his horse.

She set her bread gently on the plate. It would be several moments before she could swallow anything. "I thought we didn't discuss how things could have been."

"Sorry, Soph," Jonas said with a shrug and a smile that said he was apologetic, but not completely. "You started it." He turned back to the beam and dug at it once more with the pick.

He had a point. He always had a point. Brothers were infuriating.

She rose and crossed the room to look over his shoulder as the fading evening sunlight streamed through a windowless hole in the wall. "What are you doing?"

"Engraving Rhiannon." He gave her a quick grin. "She's by far the most picturesque subject in this place."

Despite the roughness of the wood and the crudeness of the tool, the lines of the majestic horse could be seen in the beam. Jonas shifted his grip to the end of the pick and made a series of tiny movements to create the mane. "I've always been curious about how they make the etchings in the magazines. I've been practicing carving away the extra instead of the picture itself."

"It's lovely." Sophia meant it, truly she did, but was he saying he wanted to work as an artist? If Jonas wasn't working with her, was there any chance of her dreams of training horses and riders coming true? No matter what she'd told Mr. Whitworth about making a name for herself, she knew that no one would actually hire her. On her own, the best she could hope for would be the chance to teach a few ladies here and there. She'd never re-create the glory that had been her father's riding school. If there was a man they could appear to hire, though, she had a chance.

Jonas looked up at the partial roof of his temporary abode. "Maybe I can indulge in a few art supplies after we take care of attaining a real roof. Until then"—he shrugged—"I'll practice."

"At least you'll leave the place looking better than when you found it." Sophia could spy other carvings scattered about the room. "It will be the best-looking decrepit cottage in Newmarket. Maybe in all England."

Jonas's gaze made the same track around the room hers had. "I like to think of it as a sort of reverse vandalism."

Sophia smiled, and it was probably the first real smile to cross her face since they'd left the circus. No matter what, Jonas would ensure they maintained a good attitude and counted their blessings.

"It's getting dark."

His slight smile faded, and the lines around his mouth deepened for a moment before he reached an arm over to wrap her in a hug. "Wish I could walk you back. Or send you on Rhiannon."

"We both know I'd lose this job in a moment if they knew you existed. And before you suggest racing the horse yourself, let me tell you that you wouldn't make it a mile before you toppled off in pain. My backside is sore, and I don't have anything broken."

His frown eased as he gave a short laugh. That she could alleviate some of his stress buoyed her spirits. They were a team. They would get through this together.

"Stay safe," Jonas said.

"I will." Sophia gathered up the dishes and bed linens, gave Rhiannon another scratch behind the ears, and slipped out the door, making sure it was carefully balanced in the doorframe behind her.

The sky was growing darker, so she cut through the center of town on her way back to her lodgings. The housekeeper already didn't like her. Traipsing in after sundown would only give the woman a reason to get Sophia's invitation revoked.

Town was different in the evening. Raucous voices burst forth when anyone opened an alehouse door, while carriages driven by liveried servants rolled down the street. It no longer felt like a place where everyone went about their own business. Instead there seemed to be a joined rhythm of those who had found and claimed their space in this community.

Would she have experienced something like this if life had gone differently? She knew she wasn't supposed to dwell on what might have been, but with nothing but her own thoughts for company, it was difficult not to wonder. Had her father not pretended he wasn't having money issues . . . Had he not fallen ill . . . Had Mother lived longer . . . Had Sophia and Jonas been just a little older so they could keep the business going . . .

And then, of course, there were the people who had tried to take advantage of them and the ones who had succeeded. The decision to keep their personal horses instead of sell them, to leave the difficulties in Ireland, to join the circus when Mr. Notley invited them.

So many times when life could have gone a different direction. All those paths were now lost to her. Would they have been better than the one she was on?

A loud burst of laughter made her jump sideways and tuck herself against a building. She shook her head and walked on. Searching the past would uncover nothing of present value.

One day, she would belong again. Maybe not here, but somewhere like it. Someday, perhaps even someday soon, she'd walk through a town and know she was home.

Thirteen

As if meeting with Rigsby hadn't blurred the lines of Aaron's life enough, Oliver had seen him returning and convinced him to accept a mutual friend's invitation for dinner. Agreeing to go was simpler than explaining how his afternoon interactions had left him undesirous of company.

Aaron was acquiring far too many friends. There were no orderly divisions in his life anymore, no boundaries to help him remember who he was supposed to be at any given moment.

People all over the world relied upon different parts of their personality in different situations. It was the way the world worked.

Just then, Aaron didn't know who he was supposed to be.

His professional friend Hudson was standing with his close friend Oliver, and both of them were talking to a man who had forced his way into Aaron's circle even though he was never supposed to be anything other than a business connection.

His life had become a crazy mess of unpredictability.

Oliver and Hudson laughed as Trent nearly fell on his face attempting to use a contraption his brother-in-law had recently sent from London. He'd called it a dandy horse, and the idea seemed to be that a man was to sit upon a seat affixed to two wheels by a plank. When the man ran, the wheels would allow him to go farther with each step.

Calling that ridiculous thing a horse was insulting to animals.

Why would someone want to balance on two wheels that couldn't give you warning about holes or jump over ditches? A horse had four legs, eyes, and a mind of its own to help you get where you wanted to go safely.

His friends weren't hurting anyone, except possibly themselves given the way Hudson toppled into the grass, so Aaron left them alone.

He considered leaving. He could return to his cottage and spend the evening alone, reading or writing or contemplating the follies of other humans. It was what he usually did.

The only problem was, if he left, what would he do with the baby?

Trent's daughter, Caroline, was sitting in his lap, and Aaron wasn't entirely sure how it had happened. After arriving with Oliver, Aaron had found himself a chair on the terrace instead of joining in the so-called entertainment. It kept him away from Hudson as well, thus putting off the conversation he didn't want to have at all and particularly didn't want to have with witnesses.

His out-of-the-way seat had been the perfect solution.

Until the nanny needed to step inside and Trent had somehow convinced Aaron to watch the child. Although Aaron had to admit that Trent's plopping the baby against his chest and running back to play with his new toy was an effective method of convincing.

Now she looked up at him, all big green eyes and dark hair. He'd decided long ago not to have children, not to put the difficulties of navigating his life onto a wife and son, or, worse, a daughter. Looking down at the child in his lap, he felt the loss of that decision.

What was it with green-eyed women mucking with his sanity lately? Though, Caroline's eyes were a different shade from Miss Fitzroy's, whose eyes resembled grass in the noon sun.

An ear-splitting squeal emerged from her open, smiling mouth. A collection of sharp-looking teeth made a sporadic appearance, while two pudgy hands clapped repeatedly. Sometimes they only connected by two fingers, sometimes the hands missed each other entirely. Aaron couldn't begin to guess the rules of the strange game, but the child seemed to like it.

Then her smile faded.

Her hands stopped moving.

Those green eyes slid into a wrinkled squint.

A thin whimper replaced the giggling squeals.

What was happening? What was she going to do? If she made a sudden movement, would she topple to the stone pavers? He tightened his grip to ensure she didn't fall.

Apparently, he tightened it a little too much. A new noise erupted, but not from the girl's mouth. A soggy wail even louder and sharper than her earlier giggles followed. Aaron tried to curve his body into a protective cage to ensure his now-clammy hands didn't suddenly lose their grip. Frantically, he searched the veranda for assistance. Hadn't the nanny said she'd only be gone a moment?

He jiggled his leg up and down. Riding a horse gave him comfort. Maybe something similar would help the baby.

It didn't.

He tried cooing at her like he'd seen Trent do. He shifted the way he was holding her. He even tried to scare the crying out of her. Everything he did only made things worse.

Much like his life at the moment.

Trent laughed as he climbed the wide steps to the veranda, scooped the girl from Aaron's lap, and cuddled her against his chest. She screamed even louder, making Aaron feel a little less like a failure. How did such a loud sound come from such a tiny person? Her focus stayed on Aaron as huge tears dripped onto her father's shoulder.

Murmuring in a low voice and patting the child on the back, Trent disappeared into the house, presumably to find the nanny, although Aaron didn't care much what he did as long as the screaming went with him.

"Makes you want to have one of your own, doesn't it?" Oliver watched the door Trent and Caroline had disappeared through with a dazed expression on his face.

Hudson gave a short laugh. "I believe I'll focus on getting married first."

"Well. Yes. That first." Oliver grinned down at Aaron. "It will be fun to see if you panic like that when it's your daughter screaming."

"Since Aaron has no intention of entering into matrimony, I doubt we'll find out," Hudson said, having no idea that he'd just revealed a secret Aaron had never intended to tell Oliver.

He'd never intended to tell anyone. A moment of weakness and the desire to keep his new friend from doing something foolish had led him to make the confession to Hudson a few weeks ago. He'd never informed the man it was a secret, so he couldn't be angry at him for repeating it among friends.

"Unless a certain lady jockey has recently changed that thought?" Hudson crossed his arms and lifted his eyebrows above a glare that pinned Aaron to his chair.

Now Aaron could be angry at his friend.

It was safer, though, to keep the discussion on children. If he thought too much about green eyes, red hair, and a small, stubborn chin, he might find himself blushing. Then he'd truly never hear the end of it.

He rose and walked toward the abandoned dandy horse. If the heat from his neck decided to spread up to his ears, it would be harder to see if he was in motion. "I believe there will be plenty of small humans among the rest of you for me to play uncle to."

Given that he couldn't see any of his friends relegating their children to the nursery and schoolroom until they were fully formed and ready to disappoint their parents, there would probably be many more instances of children being shoved into his arms in the future. Eventually he would be comfortable with it. He'd be able to dote upon them and not feel the loss in the slightest.

"You've been quiet this evening," Hudson said as he poured himself a glass of lemonade.

"As if one could get a word in with the way you three talk," Aaron grumbled, working to sound far more put out than he truly was. He certainly didn't want to admit he'd been comparing a child's eye color to that of a lady.

Oliver laughed and took a drink from his own glass. "More likely, he's been contemplating this jockey debacle."

"Hmm, yes," Hudson said. "I'd like to know more about that myself."

"It's entirely Oliver's fault," Aaron said, keeping his face carefully turned toward the contraption and away from the other men. The seat on wheels was even more ludicrous up close, but scrutinizing it was better than discussing Miss Fitzroy. He held on to the seat and rolled it back and forth. He wasn't quite desperate enough to mount the thing. Yet.

Oliver chuckled and dropped into the chair Aaron had vacated. "I'm not the person who signed a contract with a circus performer without meeting him." He chuckled again. "Or her, in this case."

Hudson stepped down to the bottom stair and leaned against the stone pillar. "That must have been quite the performance."

His voice was hard enough to let Aaron know all had not yet been forgiven. Aaron didn't want to discuss Rigsby in front of Oliver, but hopefully a discussion tomorrow would soften Hudson's opinion.

Since he had to say something, he said, "It was an impressive performance. The horses were knowledgeably trained and well cared for. I hired the trainer."

Seeing her ride today, he'd had to grudgingly admit she was as good as she'd claimed. Instead of simply hanging on and yelling for the horse to go faster, she'd adjusted her seat, experimented with the horse's response to tapping her crop in different places, and not only implemented every correction Aaron or Mr. Barley gave but also enhanced it.

She'd earned his admiration and ignited his curiosity, but he wasn't in a position to do anything about either one. If he complimented her, she'd think he wanted her to stay. If he asked her about the work she'd done, she'd think he wanted to get to know her.

And while he might feel a burden of responsibility toward her, that didn't mean he wanted to keep her in his life. Once she was better situated, he could—*would*—forget about her. He couldn't allow her to start feeling at home in his stable.

He certainly couldn't allow himself to enjoy seeing her there.

"Is he always this quiet?" Hudson turned to Oliver. "You've known him far longer than I. Does it mean anything? Perhaps remorse for not thinking through the ramifications of this choice?"

Obviously Aaron had been right to attempt to limit his friendships. Hudson and Oliver wouldn't have met if it hadn't been for Aaron. Even Trent wouldn't have become connected if Aaron hadn't started working at Hudson's stable and brought the business connection along.

Was he getting lazy about keeping the parts of his life separate, or were people simply hammering their way in?

For so long, his only personal connections had been to Graham and Oliver. Then Oliver's sister had needed help, and Aaron had extended his care to her.

Then Graham had gotten married, and Aaron could hardly ignore his closest friend's wife. Said wife had friends and issues of her own, and somehow Aaron had found himself stepping in there as well.

And that was the crack that had started it all. It wasn't very gentlemanly to blame a woman, but Aaron needed this whole debacle to be someone's fault, and Graham's wife, Kit, wasn't here to protest.

He could blame Oliver as well, since Aaron had only opened a personal connection with Hudson to keep him away from Lady Rebecca until Oliver stopped making a muck of that situation. In the process, he'd discovered he liked and respected the man, and now there seemed to be no end to the stream of people flowing into his life.

Next time he saw Kit, he was definitely going to frown at her.

"I don't think he's listening," Oliver said.

Aaron blinked. He'd missed the entire conversation. "What did you say?"

Hudson sighed. "I was lamenting the damage this is going to do to my reputation. I know she's not riding for my stable, but I'm still connected to you."

Yes, he was—for now. This was the problem with friends. Aaron didn't need the money, but he didn't want to lose his job. Without the work running two stables required, he didn't know what he'd do with himself.

Unfortunately, he couldn't look at this as simply a business decision. There were relationships involved, and Aaron would rather make himself uncomfortable than put Oliver in the middle.

He sighed. "I had a meeting with Lord Rigsby."

"You did?" Oliver asked in obvious surprise.

Hudson was far more interested in the meeting's results. "What did he say?"

"You're getting your foal."

And it was only going to cost Aaron a little bit of time and a lifetime of peace. Rigsby was going to be in his life for the foreseeable future, and he hadn't yet decided how he felt about it.

"He's gone quiet again," Hudson said. "And though I'm happy to hear you've made arrangements with Rigsby, that doesn't ease all my concerns."

"He'll talk more when Graham gets here," Oliver said.

"Graham is coming?" Aaron wrapped a hand around the handlebar. It wasn't that he didn't want to see his friend. He'd never turn down a chance to see Graham, but he'd rather have this jockey business cleared up first.

"He'd already planned to attend the wedding, of course." Oliver tipped his glass back and drank the rest of his lemonade. "I sent him a note about recent developments, so I expect he'll arrive sooner if he can."

Aaron relaxed. Graham and Kit traveled a great deal, so correspondence always had to go through his solicitor. It could take weeks for Oliver's letter to reach the other man. "Any idea where he and Kit are traveling now?"

"No, but last I heard they were planning to stay in the southern area for a while, so it shouldn't take long for my letter to reach him."

All the more reason for Aaron not to let this jockey problem linger. Miss Fitzroy needed a new livelihood and she needed one now. It bothered him far less for Oliver to see his faults than for Graham to witness them. He was somewhat in awe of Graham, though it would thoroughly embarrass them both if he admitted it out loud. He admired the way Graham was investing in becoming the man he wanted to be as he waited the hopefully long time for his father to die and pass on the earldom. Aaron didn't think he would ever have such a sense of direction.

"At least tell me she's not going to be an embarrassment," Hudson said with a sigh, holding on to the topic of Miss Fitzroy. "She seemed to have a good seat when you brought her by Hawksworth, but that doesn't mean she can race."

"She can race." Aaron could have elaborated, told them she was better than adequate, that she was smart and adaptable, and that his belief she would lose the race was waning, but he was accustomed to keeping his thoughts to himself. Though this affected the others in this conversation, he couldn't find the words to share.

"Does that mean she's doing well enough to win, or good enough that you're afraid she won't lose?" Oliver asked.

Apparently he didn't have to find the words after all. When had Oliver become so perceptive? Aaron narrowed his eyes at the other man. "Which do you want it to be?"

Oliver shrugged. "I'm not sure. Lord Gliddon keeps sending messages. It will be easy enough to avoid him for a few days, but my continued dodging will soon become conspicuous. I doubt he approves, but I'd rather not confirm it."

Did Gliddon not know he was housing the controversial jockey? Aaron wasn't going to ask. He did not want to feel honor bound to find her new lodging.

Hudson shook his head. "As entertaining as it is to watch you squirm, Whitworth, I'm concerned. Davers can stir up a lot of trouble in a week." He rubbed a hand down his face. "Bianca is talking too. She says there's no reason for her not to be allowed to ride the thoroughbreds at a full gallop now."

Hudson's betrothed was an avid horsewoman, but Miss Fitzroy on the back of one of those volatile beasts was nerve-racking enough. He couldn't take responsibility for Bianca too. "Tell her she can do that when she can stand on a galloping horse."

Both men blinked. "Miss Fitzroy can do that?" Hudson asked.

"Circus," Aaron muttered.

Trent stepped back out on the terrace, his wife, daughter, and nanny trailing behind. "Adelaide, I think I've learned how to ride this apparatus."

"I don't care how good you are, our daughter isn't getting on," his wife responded.

Trent demonstrated his ability to run while sitting on the plank, and talk of another dinner party arose. They hadn't even eaten tonight's dinner and the group was discussing gathering for another one—only Adelaide insisted more ladies be invited next time.

Social plans and gossip swirled around, replacing the earlier uncomfortable conversation and giving Aaron an entirely different feeling of discomfort.

He didn't begrudge his friends their happiness, but there was no denying they seemed to be leaving him behind. Long ago, he'd accepted that domestic bliss would never be his, but he hoped that as his friends found theirs, there'd still be a place for him on the fringe.

Fourteen

Aaron arrived at the training yard early the next morning intent on settling himself with the familiar surroundings of horses. The smell of animal and leather, the shouts of trainers, the dust and grime that made all who worked among the racehorses equal. If he could absorb enough of that, he would remain focused when his new jockey arrived.

His plan had one problem.

She was already there.

He heard her before he saw her. It wasn't difficult, given that only two of the boxes in the stable were occupied and Sweet Fleet was such a quiet, sedate animal Aaron wasn't sure they could train the horse to race at all. The stillness allowed Miss Fitzroy's ramblings to drift through the dim building.

"Not the least bit burnt. How do you think they know when to take it out of the fire?"

What was she talking about?

"I guess it's like anything else. If you pay enough attention, you can learn the nuances of anything, including properly cooked toast."

Aaron frowned. Properly cooked toast?

"I've never given much attention to cooking." Aaron couldn't see her, but he could imagine those slim shoulders shrugging in the short space of silence. "Horses are far more interesting than toast."

It was a ridiculous statement, but Aaron had to agree.

She came into view, visible through the bars that made up the top portion of the stall walls. One hand worked rhythmic circles over Equinox's dark coat while the other soothingly stroked the stallion's neck. Everything about the horse looked utterly relaxed, despite the constant jabbering.

She'd moved on to marmalade. Yesterday's orange was apparently far better than today's prune offering.

Once again, Aaron couldn't fault her opinion.

"I'll eat them both, mind you. I haven't had marmalade in so long it's a wonder I've a preference at all, but there's something delightful about orange marmalade."

"The peels from an orange candy better than those from a prune."

Stone-cold silence descended on the stable. Miss Fitzroy froze, blinking those green eyes his direction. "Well," she said slowly, "I suppose that's true."

The horse shifted, nudging the woman to remind her to keep combing. She resumed the circles, and the horse gave a sigh of appreciation.

"I've never thought much about candying the peels. I don't think I knew that's what it was called." She paused. "I'm still not sure what that means."

Aaron knew the term and the idea but not well enough to explain it.

"I'm not much good in the kitchen," she continued as she finished combing the horse and gave him a pat on the neck. "I did well enough in the scullery when I got demoted at the house I worked in for a while."

Don't ask, don't ask, don't ask. "What were you before?"

"Upstairs maid. I wasn't good at it."

"I wouldn't think dusting is all that different from brushing a horse," Aaron said dismissively. Knowing she'd worked as a maid before sparked a flicker of hope. "Have you considered working in a house again?"

"I'll do it before I starve."

She said the answer so simply that it took Aaron a moment to realize what she'd said. How could he respond to that? "Let's saddle the horses. Today I'll teach you how to do a brush run."

"You're going out with me? It will be nice to see a proper example."

"I'm not a jockey." He went to saddle Sweet Fleet and sent the stable boy to prepare Equinox.

All too soon it was just the two of them, walking the horses out of the yard.

He tried to keep everything focused on the animals. It was easy enough on the short bursts when the horses had to run, usually up the berms and dykes on the Heath, but during the walking portions, the woman insisted on talking.

Somewhere around the third or fourth set, he found himself replying. Probably because the topic turned to horses.

"You wouldn't think that riding one type of horse would be different from another, but it is. They're trained to move differently," she said.

"Could you teach a racehorse the steps you did in the circus?"

She lit up at his interest. "I could eventually, but it would require a good deal of work. I'd have to reteach him how to move." She tilted her head and bit her lip.

Aaron looked away. He never noticed women's lips or hands or anything about them. Most of the time he only noticed they were women long enough to give a polite nod and then avoid them.

"I wonder what it would look like," she continued. "They normally take such long strides that they might be even better at certain maneuvers."

"Do you miss the horse from the circus? That was a fine animal. I don't think I've ever seen one like it."

Her gaze dropped to the ground. "There aren't many Andalusians in England. That one came from a farm in Ireland. It was bred from horses the owner brought from Spain."

"That explains why the story followed an Irish faerie."

As much as Aaron hated the incessant chatter, the sudden silence was somehow worse. Or maybe it was the way her shoulders slumped and she folded the reins through her fingers.

Should he just keep riding? Make her shift behind him so they could form a proper string? With only two horses to run, it had seemed silly to line them up like they normally did, but this was what happened when he didn't stay with proper procedures.

"The first horse I fell in love with was in a traveling show," Aaron said. "It wasn't an Andalusian, but I think the rider had similar training. He'd been in the military. He made the horse do this strange jump every time someone put money in the hat. To a little boy, it looked like the animal could fly."

Aaron hadn't meant to speak, and he certainly hadn't meant to tell that story. He didn't talk about his past, as a rule, and he definitely didn't talk about his childhood. Not even with Oliver and Graham. As far as they were concerned, he'd dropped out of the sky as a ten-year-old with a scandal and a benefactor.

"Horses always look like they should break," she responded. "Thin legs and big bodies that do the most marvelous things. It shouldn't work, and yet it does. And they do everything with grace and beauty. It's entrancing."

Aaron worked with a lot of men who loved horses. They breathed them, bled them, and he'd never heard any of them voice their obsession that way.

"Now we'll run them up that hill." Aaron pointed to their left. It wasn't his normal route, and turning now would make their brush run series at least a mile short, but it would end this conversation, and right now, that was far more important.

THERE'D BEEN A certain consistency in Sophia's life for the past two years—performing the same show with the same people, continually moving on, meeting a plethora of strangers at every stop. Somehow the familiarity of constant change had been more comfortable than the regularity she now lived.

Each day was essentially the same. Rise with the scullery maids, dress, wait for the tray that, thankfully, came around early, and then scuttle off to Jonas's cottage. Sometimes he was still asleep when she arrived, but even if he was awake, she didn't linger, just left the knapsack on the table and departed.

Then it was off to the stable for hours of work before wandering back to the house to collect her dinner. Back to the cottage, where she would visit with Jonas until the sun started to sink beneath the trees, then once more across town to climb into the same bed she'd slept in for five nights running.

Everything was the same. Well, except for Mr. Whitworth. He'd trained her the first two days, but now he left it to Mr. Barley, and she never knew when she would see him or what mood he'd be in. He was often stoic, occasionally frowned, and even more rarely smiled. Mr. Barley's attitude was changeable as well, though his seemed to move steadily downhill.

She didn't know if they feared she was going to take a tumble or worried the judgmental onlookers would start doing more than mumbling.

She did know that her head didn't miss donning that horrid wig every day, her stomach didn't miss being hungry, and not a single part of her missed arguing every day about receiving her full wages. Mr. Whitworth had said she'd be paid on Saturdays, and yesterday she'd received her money promptly and without requiring even a subtle hint from her.

There was money in her bag to take to Jonas today. Actual money.

If there was a downside, it was not being able to ride Rhiannon or stay with Jonas and look up at the stars. Well, that and having to deal with the way her insides tumbled over each other every time she saw Mr. Whitworth. Or sometimes when she didn't see him. Or when she saw him and then he left.

Yesterday she'd gone on another brush run, though this time she'd been added to the back of the line for another stable Mr. Barley worked with. Every movement she'd made had been scrutinized, and she'd bitten her cheek until it felt bruised and tender to keep from speaking the entire time.

Then she'd had to do another set of starting trials in the afternoon because she was to have today off. She'd told Jonas they would get to spend the whole day together, but he insisted she attend church first. It was important that people see her, that she not arouse suspicion.

Life was a delicate balance right now, and it wouldn't take much for it to come tumbling down.

She lay looking up at the ceiling, having woken even earlier than usual. In an hour or two, she would rise, dress in her one good dress, and go to church. She wasn't expecting much of the service, but Jonas was rarely wrong with his advice.

He seemed better already. It hadn't even been a full week yet and the rest was doing wonders for him. He could even sit for short periods, using a pile of leaves and grass as padding. She had to keep this job, this room, and the food that went with it so she could provide him more time.

It would be best if she could find her way back to sleep. Even though she wouldn't ride today, there was a lot of walking in front of her. The thin leather of her boots was paying the price for walking the miles to and from Jonas's cottage every day.

With a sigh, Sophia closed her eyes and willed her body to relax. In her mind, she rode Rhiannon and counted the jumps as they charged through the fields of Ireland. When she reached triple digits, she gave up and returned to staring at the ceiling. Ireland wasn't big enough to get her to sleep, apparently.

If only it had been big enough to provide her a home.

Fifteen

She managed to doze until the movement of the waking maids signaled it was time for her to rise as well.

She reached for her riding dress before remembering it was Sunday. Just shifting the fabric of her practice gown sent a stench into the air. Frowning, she held it up to her nose. One inhale almost sent her cross-eyed. She'd have to ask someone where the washroom was.

And if she was allowed to use it.

At least she had another dress—a proper dress—for church this morning. She washed as best she could with the basin of water and dressed. Then she bent to press her face beneath her arm and sniffed. There were certainly times she'd smelled better, but at least people would be able to sit next to her during the service.

As for tomorrow, when she'd have to put that practice gown on again, well, she would just have to hope that the odor of the horses disguised the residual smell of her clothing.

At the cottage, Jonas was still sleeping, stretched out on the pallet he'd made from grass and a blanket. He seemed to be getting his best sleep in months, thanks to the lack of excruciating pain.

She gently set her bag on the table, noting the surface had obtained several more carvings. At least Jonas had found something to entertain himself.

As much as she wanted to see his friendly face, she crept out again without waking him. They would have the entire afternoon together.

Sophia sat in the back of the church, sliding all the way down one of the narrow benches and trying to hide in the corner. Despite doing everything she could not to draw notice, it felt as if every eye in the building was upon her. Whatever was said, whatever was sung, she missed it all as she focused on preventing the encroaching numbness from overtaking her and making her a permanent fixture of the wooden bench.

The few times she managed to look up from her toes, there would inevitably be another set of eyes to meet, and no matter whose they were, they were not filled with the sort of admiration that would help her attain work after Mr. Whitworth let her go.

She could only hope and—she glanced at the altar behind the droning rector—perhaps pray that her race would change a few minds.

The moment the service finished, she retreated to Jonas's cottage, taking a long, circuitous route to ensure no one followed her. Her presence was already somewhat incendiary. Discovery of her secret brother might get her run out of town.

At the cottage, she found Rhiannon munching on a pile of grass and hay scraps while Jonas lay across the horse's back on his stomach, methodically braiding the long, silky mane into an intricate design.

"Interesting way to pass the time," Sophia said with a giggle.

Jonas grinned back. "It's not as if you can bring me a book with my next meal." He nodded to the neat stack of dishes on the table. "That's as close as I'd like to come to stealing, thank you."

Guilt stabbed Sophia. She, at least, got to be out and about riding during the day. "Did you see the money? I can take a portion. Buy you a book." She looked around at the cottage in the full sunlight, noticing Jonas had practiced engraving on most of the non-rotten surfaces. "Maybe a notebook and a pencil?"

"No." Jonas rolled off the back of the horse and landed on

his feet. "We'll need that money later." He shoved the long, thin fingers of one hand through his red hair, leaving a dirty streak through the middle.

"It must be hard, being here," Sophia said softly.

"I don't know." Jonas shrugged. "I get to spend my days hiding a horse, finding ways to feed a horse, cleaning up after a horse."

"Giving the horse a new look." Sophia stepped forward and ran a hand over the intricately twisted braids.

His returning grin was weak and then it faded entirely. "What I hate is you being out there without me."

Despite being the younger twin by a few minutes, Jonas had always looked out for Sophia. Even when they were children, he'd been the one to remind her it was time to go in and eat when she became too preoccupied with the horses. She pressed a hand to her stomach. Now it was her turn to care for him.

"You spend your days taking care of this beast, then?" Sophia ran a hand down the horse's neck.

Jonas shrugged. "I sleep a lot too. I stand until I can't anymore, then I lie down. Inevitably I fall asleep. Sometimes I wake up in the night and take her out and exercise her on the longe." He sent a crooked grin her way. "I took her for a walk like a dog once. Let me know if you hear tales of a ghost horse roaming the fields."

Given that no one talked to her about much of anything, she wasn't likely to hear such rumors.

She lifted one hand to run along the horse's back. As always, the soft hair and warm animal gave her a sense of calm. "I wish I could ride you, girl. We could prance through the Heath and show those racehorses a thing or two."

"You'll be on her again soon." Jonas wrapped an arm around her shoulder and gave a squeeze. "Remember to have patience."

"You always had more than I did."

"Good thing I'm the one stuck in a broken house with a horse, then, isn't it?"

The statement was meant to be a joke, and his tone almost

achieved its normal joviality, but there was an underlying bitterness to it.

Or perhaps that was Sophia's own feelings lingering in her ears.

Jonas gave her another squeeze and returned to his side of the wall.

"How is the stall working?" Sophia asked, more to change the subject than out of real curiosity.

"It keeps her in place. I hate not being able to take her out during the day, but I can't risk it. Alone, I don't inspire much curiosity. If I were with her, though . . ." He shrugged again. "I don't go out often, but unless I want to start breaking into barns, it takes a while to find enough tall grass or hay scraps to feed her."

"It's just for a few more weeks," she said, though she wasn't sure which of them she was trying to convince. "A few more weeks and we'll be together. You'll be better. I'll have other job offers. We'll start a riding school and horse farm, just like we had before."

Jonas looked at her, his face unreadable. Sophia's chest started to heave, then her chin began to quiver. She clenched her teeth together to keep the vibrations from becoming tears. She had to hold on to this dream, because if she lost it, she didn't know what she would do.

Jonas leaned one shoulder against the side of the opening between the two rooms. "Are you safe, Soph? Really, truly safe?" He looked down at the ground and then back up at her. "I'm trying not to worry, reading all the passages where God talks about holding us in His hands, but . . ." He sighed. "The circus world accepted a female rider, but racing, well, I just can't imagine it being the same."

"They've been rather supportive," she said. If one took a lack of negative comments as encouragement. Everyone had shifted to glaring silently instead, but Jonas didn't need to know that part. Sophia would win them over before Jonas met them. She would.

Jonas pressed his lips into a thin line. He knew she was lying,

and he knew that she knew he knew she was lying, but still he nodded, allowing both of them to believe the comfort of the untruth.

"Come over here," Jonas said, nodding his head toward the
table. "You attended service today, but I didn't. How about we do
our own study like we did when we were traveling?"

Sophia nodded. While she'd physically been to church, she
hadn't gained any spiritual insight there. Bible study with her
brother would do her good.

He led them through a passage from the book of Matthew
about not fearing. Then they put Rhiannon in her makeshift stall
and went for a walk together around the cottage. A close call with
another strolling couple was enough to send them scurrying back
inside for the remainder of the afternoon.

When it was time for Sophia to return to Meadowland Park
to get their dinner, she was grateful for the excuse to leave. After
one afternoon stuck in that cottage, she was unbelievably restless,
desperate for something to do. How did Jonas manage?

She returned with their evening meal, but the camaraderie was
stilted. It was obvious Jonas detested having to rely on her for
everything, even though he didn't say it out loud. It was a shift for
them both, but what else could they do? Revealing his presence
in town would prove to Mr. Whitworth that he'd been tricked.

It was only delaying his anger, because Jonas would join her
once she had a more secure position. The man was hardly all smiles
and grins now, but his stoic impassiveness was better than having
him frown at her in blatant displeasure.

Or worse, ignore her entirely.

In a mere week she'd become fascinated by him. He wanted to
appear simple to the world, but she could tell he wasn't. There were
too many questions, too many secrets. Every time she thought she
had him figured out, he would say or do something unexpected,
and she was right back where she started.

He probably didn't mean to be fascinating, but since she
couldn't stop staring in his direction anyway, she might as well

think about him. Sometimes she thought about him even when she wasn't looking at him.

KNOWING THAT JONAS had planned to take the horse out at midnight, she wasn't surprised to find him asleep when she took him breakfast the next morning. She arrived even earlier than normal, so she took her time strolling to the training yard. She wanted to see the Heath without any horses on it.

To her surprise, it was already bustling.

There were a few strings of blanketed horses darting about under eagle-eyed trainers, but there were also gentlemen dotting the landscape. Some rode leisurely, while others participated in impromptu races of their own making. The entire expanse looked alive, rolling and shifting under the hooves of all the horses. Here the men and the horses and the land all blended together.

She'd never seen the like, but something about it reminded her of home, of her childhood. How many times had she sat in the hayloft or on the fence and watched her father's horses? Watched him train rider and animal to work as one?

It had been a long time since she'd allowed herself to remember those years, a long time since she'd mourned the loss of what she'd thought would always be there. Mostly she dreamt of re-creating it. That was far less painful than remembering it was gone.

Sixteen

Miss Fitzroy stomped up the lane toward Oliver's stable, sending a surge of thoughts through Aaron's head. A storm of emotions tripped over themselves as well, but he didn't know how to identify them or what to do with them, so he ignored them.

He'd barely seen her since he'd accompanied her on brush runs, and he'd convinced himself that he'd imagined the pull he felt to her.

He hadn't.

Despite his own irritation, he grinned at the outward expression of hers. Was she miffed that he'd sent a note beckoning her to him? Or was it because he'd made her walk from Meadowland Park to the training yards and then halfway back again to Oliver's?

Neither act was very gentlemanly, but he was in such upheaval about her that he'd had to do something. Barley threatened to quit if Aaron left him to deal with this nonsense alone one more day, so Aaron had to take over today's training, and he'd needed to do it as far away from speculative eyes as possible.

There'd be no stopping the stories after tomorrow, though. Was he truly going to put a woman on a thoroughbred stallion and let her race?

Yes, he was. Whether he liked it or not, the woman had won his respect. She had ridden long, hard hours. She walked across

Newmarket daily without complaint. She wasn't afraid to do the dirty work of caring for the horses or tack, though he'd hired an extra boy for the stable to do most of that for her.

What he needed was to find her another job. He'd started going to local taverns for dinner each night, hoping to overhear something that might spark an idea. For the first twenty minutes, he had to endure snide comments and accusatory glares. When he gave no response, people changed to ignoring him and he was able to listen in on their conversations. None had given him any clue of what to do with her.

Not that a tavern was the best place to find a job for a lady, but what else could he do? He had no knowledge of her non-equestrian abilities. If she even had any. The story about the scullery didn't seem promising.

Miss Fitzroy finally reached him, and her chin jutted up as she looked him in the eye. Her hands opened and closed at her sides as if she didn't know what to do with them—or rather as if stopping herself from doing what she wanted to with them.

He was thankful. She had strong arms from all the riding. A punch from her might hurt.

"Is there a reason to have me wait around the yard for half an hour?"

She was mad about waiting? Not about all the walking? He hid his surprise and amusement at her pique. "Apologies. I didn't make these plans until last evening."

"You could have sent the note to me instead of Mr. Barley."

Aaron led her to where the horses were tied up. "Do you honestly want me sending you a communication at Meadowland Park?" Aaron still wasn't positive Lord Gliddon knew Miss Fitzroy was residing under his roof. Questions about her treatment at the estate welled in his throat, but he kept them silent. What he didn't know about he wouldn't feel compelled to fix.

Miss Fitzroy looked away from Aaron. "No, that would not have been the best."

He approached the side of the horse he had for Miss Fitzroy only to find she was no longer next to him. He turned to find her scowling at the horses.

"I don't suppose that's your mount for the day."

"No." Aaron nodded to his chestnut thoroughbred. "Surely you recognize Shadow."

"Indeed I do. I do not, however, recognize that horse."

Aaron turned back to the mare to hide his grin. Scarecrow was an excellent horse, but by no means was she a racehorse. "I need to show you the course you'll be running. We can't put you on it, but we can ride near enough to see it. I also need to see to a few things around the area. You can take the chance to see the countryside."

He positioned himself at Scarecrow's side and cupped his hands, ready to help her mount.

"And we can't look at racecourses on the backs of racehorses?" she grumbled as she slid her foot into his hands.

Her bones pressed through the thin leather into his palm. Was it even less substantial than it had been a week ago? Instinctively, his grip tightened, and the lack of substance beneath his fingers sent guilt spearing through him. Of course her boots were thinner. She walked clear across town daily in less-than-adequate footwear.

Could he buy her boots and be able to convince anyone that it was part of her uniform? Just giving her the silk shirt in Lord Trenting's colors made him uncomfortable. A man didn't provide clothing for a woman unless she was his mistress.

Even if he could find a way to make it a uniform and thereby respectable, *he* would know that he'd only done it because he cared that her shoes were as thin as his stockings.

And because he'd spent far too much time thinking about what their rides would be like if he were a man who could indulge in a flirtation or even something more.

Once she was settled in the sidesaddle, her skirts draped oddly over her trousers, Aaron moved quickly to his own horse and mounted with a single smooth move.

He took them south, away from the Heath and racecourses, away from the prying eyes and the judgmental glares.

"I don't know my way around just yet, but I do know this isn't the way to the racecourses."

"No. I have a few things to look into for a . . . friend." Referring to Rigsby in such a way made the word feel thick in his mouth. Was his half brother a friend? He certainly wasn't the foe Aaron had always thought him to be. They rode in silence for a long while, leaving Oliver's estate behind and riding toward a section of land that was rumored to be made available for purchase soon.

Rigsby wanted land in the area to set up his own home and stable, but he wanted to do it quietly so word wouldn't get back to his father until the deed was done. No one would suspect Aaron was working with Rigsby, so he was the perfect scout. Aaron hadn't told Hudson this was Rigsby's request instead of a stud fee, even though he'd shared that the two had come to a deal that wouldn't cost Hudson anything yet still would give him access to one of the finest horses in the world.

The news had appeased Hudson somewhat, but Aaron still didn't know how he felt about it. He'd agreed, though, so he would find his half brother a good piece of property.

"What made you decide to manage racehorses?"

Aaron jumped at Miss Fitzroy's question. He'd almost forgotten she was there. No, that wasn't quite right. He'd done his best to forget she was there, because whenever he thought about riding beside her, that urge for something more niggled at his toes.

"I don't only manage the racehorses. I manage the entire stable. Personal mounts, active racers, breeding."

She blew out an exasperated sigh. "Very well. What made you decide to manage all the horse concerns of other men?"

Apparently belittling her knowledge didn't anger her enough to stop the talking. "What made you decide to work in a circus?"

"Oh no." She shook her head, grinning at him in a way that made him jerk his head to face forward again. "I asked you first."

How much should he tell her? It was common knowledge in Newmarket, indeed throughout most of England's upper class, that Aaron was illegitimate. It had been a defining quality of his life, and for the most part, he'd come to terms with it.

If she considered him an outcast, like she was, she might think they had something in common. She might think they had a connection. She might even start thinking he wanted to keep her around.

He didn't. He wanted her gone. Safe, of course, but most definitely gone.

"Horses were the only subject I liked in school." He'd enjoyed riding and learning about horses from the grooms and instructors far more than he had the classes with their smirking students and ostracizing teachers. "I took care of the horses when my friends and I traveled."

More to the point, he had made sure Oliver and Graham properly cared for their horses. He'd enjoyed his role of equine caretaker, telling the others what to do. Both of his friends were going to be peers one day, with seats in the House of Lords and positions of societal power. Aaron, whose highest possible rank was that of somewhat disreputable gentleman, had taken the opportunity to be in charge when it had arisen.

"One of those friends was Oliver—er, Lord Farnsworth. That's who you're riding for." Aaron shifted his reins to one hand so he could wipe his suddenly sweaty palm on his breeches. "His father gave me the job of managing his horses a few years ago. I've done well enough with it that I was entrusted with another stable."

Miss Fitzroy nodded. "A younger son having to make his way in the world, I take it."

A burning sensation crawled up Aaron's throat. He was the eldest, but it didn't matter. He was still the one making his own way in the world without even the advantages younger sons could claim.

"I'm afraid my, er, father didn't have much to leave me in the way of a fortune." The misleading words scraped across his tongue.

Why did he feel the need to revert to subtle statements and veiled remarks, implying something other than the truth without telling an outright lie? He'd been boldly claiming his true condition for months now and enjoying the freedom it brought. Was he trying to prevent a connection with this woman or trying to impress her? His muscles tightened at the implications, sending the well-trained Shadow leaping into a sudden short run.

The house on the portion of land came into view, so Aaron steered them down the other side and back toward the Heath. His only job was to determine the potential of the land. "We'll go this way and show you the duke's course. That's the four miles you'll be running tomorrow."

A leisurely tour through the countryside had been a bad idea. It was time to change the course of both their ride and their conversation. He needed a plan to get Miss Fitzroy out of his life, and for that he needed information. "Were you raised a traveling performer?"

She shook her head. "My father was a horse trainer. I lived at his side, learning his tricks and how to read a horse. That was all I wanted to do with my life. When he died, my brother and I tried to keep the business going, but no one trusted us. We were too young, not even eighteen. They didn't think we could do what my father had done." She gave a short shrug of one shoulder. "Like you, I took the skills I had and made the best of them."

The woman had found a commonality between them after all. That she had a brother was news, though. How could a man worth the name allow his sister to join a traveling company, no matter how dire the circumstances? "Where is your brother now?"

She glanced away from him, looking over the expanse of Heath that was emptying as the strings of racehorses returned to their yards. "The last time I saw him he was sleeping in an abandoned cottage that was half fallen in."

Well. Perhaps the traveling company *had* been the best option. Aaron couldn't imagine being that desperate. His life had been hard, yes, but he'd never had to worry about shelter or food. The allowance his father gave him could easily see to his needs. It had been in a meager fashion, but he'd been taken care of.

Some would say he wasn't living much above meager now, but he was doing it by choice. If he surrounded himself with the trappings of a successful gentleman, it would hurt all the more when his true destiny ripped it all away.

Forgetting where he'd come from would be a crushing emotional error.

"I'm assuming, since you left the circus, that isn't how you want to support yourself. You mentioned making a name in the race?"

She nodded, a splash of color riding in her cheeks and stirring his own blood once more. "I want to rebuild my father's school. Not on the same scale, but the essence of it. Training riders to work as one with their horses. Training horses to be exquisite equine athletes. It's all I know, really—all I ever wanted, even as a child."

How was he supposed to find her a different job given that information? "You've no other skills?"

She tilted her head and looked at him. "Not really. Why do you ask?"

The gentle way her eyes looked at him and the clearness of her gaze punched through him. They both needed to remember what was really going on here. "The race is tomorrow," he said gruffly, shifting in his saddle. "We need to determine where you're going to go after you lose."

Seventeen

Sophia wanted to fume over Mr. Whitworth's assumption, but the flash of anger quickly cooled into a core of determination. Everything she knew about horses, riding, and life was going into that saddle with her, and she would win that race.

Mr. Whitworth dragged his hand across his face. "Racing isn't really what you want to do. You just said as much."

That feeling of camaraderie she'd been relishing moments before crept back in, softening the edge of her frustration. "No, it isn't."

"It is, however, what I want to do." He sighed, and the next words crackled as he spoke them, as if the truth were clawing its way out whether he wanted it to or not. "The longer you race for me, the harder my job becomes."

Sophia bit her lip. She didn't want to make his life harder. But if she didn't do something to prove she was more than capable when it came to horses, she'd never be trusted as a trainer. Was she willing to ruin someone else's life to make her own better?

Mr. Whitworth's circumstances might not be as simple and easy as they appeared. Did she just want that to be true because the alternative would prove he wasn't the gentleman she thought he was? "Is this ride about lulling me into lowering my guard? Are you hoping I'll give up my dreams because I feel sorry for you?"

If her words cut him, it didn't show. He merely glanced her

way with lifted eyebrows. "You think me a far more devious man than I am."

"I think you want me to believe we have similarities that don't exist."

He coughed. "I beg your pardon?"

"What have you truly told me today? That you want to race horses and have since you were in school. You've left plenty of gaps for me to fill in as I wish, and I did." Sophia snapped her teeth shut with a click. Her tongue had run away with her all her life, but not until she'd met this man had it constantly said things that left her vulnerable and embarrassed.

Mr. Whitworth cleared his throat. "Are you complaining that I revealed too much or too little?"

Her mouth dropped open. How could he even pretend to have said too much? He'd barely said anything. She needed to take a page from his book and speak as few words as humanly possible. "My apologies."

"What are you apologizing for?"

Apparently, economy of words was a talent she didn't yet possess. "I am apologizing for hearing things you didn't say."

He stared at her, incredulous. She winced at how ridiculous that sounded.

"So, your ears run away with you like your mouth does?"

She wanted to be angry at the question until she realized it was somewhat true. "I believe," she said, unwilling to leave him with whatever interpretation had boiled down to that impression, "that I don't possess any great ability to interpret unspoken communication. My life has been full of strangers for the past two years. I could make any assumptions I wished, and they were never challenged. I'm afraid it's become a habit."

She fidgeted in the saddle and had to grab for the mane to avoid taking a tumble. Falling off a pleasure horse that was going only slightly faster than a plod would make this the worst embarrassment of her life.

"There were always interesting people along the fence of the show," she continued. "Creating stories for them helped me feel less alone. I could pretend I had a new friend or made someone happy or calmed an anxious child."

"I thought your tongue didn't get away from you when you were on horseback."

"It usually doesn't." Sophia chanced a quick glance at him. "This isn't a particularly challenging ride, though. At this pace, it's rather like a rocking chair."

Where was Jonas when she needed him? If he could just clap his hand over her mouth right now, that would be excellent. She would have to do it herself, but she could hardly chomp down on one of the leather reins. Instead, she ducked her head and bit the material at the neck of her dress.

She really needed to wash this outfit.

A low chuckle rose from her companion, and she lifted her head to see him shaking his as he looked over the countryside.

Wondering what he was thinking to have prompted actual laughter had her silent the rest of the ride. He seemed at ease with the quiet, but Sophia was anything but.

What was he thinking of her?

Why did she even care?

The point of this whole endeavor was to gain a measure of respect from the horse-loving people of Newmarket. Mr. Whitworth's opinion was her only available gauge of success. If he didn't think much of her, she was doomed.

Lord Farnsworth's stable came into view, and Mr. Whitworth's easy, relaxed seat suddenly became stiff, making him jostle in the saddle with every change of the horse's weight.

Sophia followed his gaze and found a man waiting beside a fine thoroughbred. In the past few days she had ridden what she assumed were some very fine racehorses, but she would truly love a chance to get on the back of that animal and charge across an empty field.

143

It would probably feel like flying.

Since that was unlikely to happen, she would simply enjoy how the man's presence had a profound effect on the heretofore unflappable Mr. Whitworth. Even when they'd been negotiating for her job, he hadn't seemed this tense, and definitely not this grim.

Two groomsmen came out, looking furtively between the two men and carefully avoiding meeting anyone's eyes.

Awkwardness grew as one groom helped Sophia dismount.

Tension increased as the horses were led away.

Anyone with their wits about them would know the men wanted to be alone, but Sophia wasn't going anywhere. She needed to know what was going on here. Her ability to read people's mannerisms and facial expressions might be questionable, but she was confident in her ability to determine status. The stranger's clothes indicated polite society.

Very polite society.

The men watched each other, giving occasional glances in her direction. If one of them asked her to leave, she would. She was stubborn, not rude.

Mr. Whitworth sighed and gave the newcomer a slight nod. "Rigsby."

"Whitworth."

Sophia waited, but no introduction was forthcoming. She gave a slight bob of a curtsy in the new man's direction. "Allow me to introduce myself. I am Miss Fitzroy."

A small smile tugged at the corner of the other man's mouth. "I am aware of who you are, Miss Fitzroy." He sent a polite nod in her direction. "I am Lord Rigsby."

Silence fell, and Sophia curled her hands into fists in an attempt to stay as still as the two men. It was uncanny, their ability not to move. She chanced a look at Mr. Whitworth, only to find him staring at her, brow twisted into a perplexed frown.

She refused to be affected by it. She needed to do anything necessary—within reason—to start a new life for herself and her brother. If that meant standing still as a statue and keeping her mouth shut, so be it.

Finally, Mr. Whitworth sighed. "What can I do for you, Rigsby?"

"I've been summoned to London by our—my father." Lord Rigsby cleared his throat. "If we want to finish the arrangements before I leave, we need to do so today."

"The marquis always has the worst timing," Mr. Whitworth muttered. "Most things are in place, so it shouldn't be a problem. Stildon should have received the papers today. We can meet at Hawksworth in an hour. I'm still collecting the information you requested."

Lord Rigsby nodded in agreement before mounting his horse and turning toward the lane. He looked from Mr. Whitworth to Sophia, an unspoken question in his single raised eyebrow. "A pleasure to meet you, Miss Fitzroy." He pinched the edge of his hat as he gave her a nod. "It is nice to know I am not the only one who makes Whitworth uncomfortable."

As the man rode away, Sophia couldn't help feeling she'd just learned something significant. The expression on Mr. Whitworth's face confirmed the suspicion.

Now if only she knew what it was.

She raked her mind back through every moment of the interaction, every nuance, every stated word.

Every stumbled-over word.

Her mouth dropped open on a gasp. If Lord Rigsby's father was a marquis, all his male children would bear the honorific of *Lord*, and though he'd tried to cover it, Lord Rigsby had almost said *our father*.

Her eyes widened in realization. That sense of connection, that idea of camaraderie hadn't come from nowhere. He may have made something of his life, but he also knew what it was to be on the outside.

Wonder as well as respect tinged her voice as she looked up at him and whispered, "Why, Mr. Whitworth, you're illegitimate."

JUST WHEN AARON had been beginning to like his half brother, something happened to make him disgusted with the fellow. Though this was as much his own fault as it was Rigsby's.

As he'd feared, the knowledge of his own brand of social ostracism had given Miss Fitzroy the idea that the distance between them was not as great as it had originally appeared. Aaron did not need that distance shortened. If anything, he needed to make the gap wider.

Her whispered conclusion contained no judgment, but there'd been a tone of conspiratorial reverence he could not encourage. Anyone in town could confirm it, so denying the claim wasn't an option. Ignoring it, however, was. "The race is tomorrow. Be in the training yard early."

She nodded in the direction Rigsby had ridden. "Is he older or younger?"

"Younger," Aaron answered before he could stop himself. He'd informed people of his birth many times in recent years, and local gossip had done it for him everywhere else. Never before had someone had the gumption to ask for more details.

He braced himself for what came next—because with Miss Fitzroy something was always going to get said next. He'd come to terms with his situation, as there'd been no other choice. That didn't mean he wanted to talk about it.

She blinked at him a few times. "That's why you're letting me do this, isn't it? Because you know what it feels like."

Oh no, she was not making him into some sort of . . . of . . . whatever she was trying to make him. He placed his hands on his hips in denial. "The only reason you are riding tomorrow is because, regardless of my birth, I am too much of a gentleman to go back on my word."

Miss Fitzroy mocked him by mimicking his stance. "Many a man claims the name of gentleman yet does not honor his promises."

He would not ask how she knew that. He. Would. Not. "Then perhaps he is not a true gentleman."

146

"Or perhaps he doesn't understand how much a promise can mean to someone who is desperate."

Aaron did not want to think about Miss Fitzroy as desperate, though she clearly was. He'd seen this dress every day except for race day and Sunday. Her shoes were as thin as paper. There was no doubt she had few means.

Nor was there doubt that he needed to keep that distance between them. Her dream of someone seeing her ride and asking her to train his horses was never going to become reality. Her connection to Lord Farnsworth was keeping her safe at the moment, but what about later? The sooner she was permanently situated somewhere safe, the better.

"I'll help you find other employment."

She stuck her chin up another notch and stepped closer until Aaron could see the variations of green in her eyes. "I'm going to win that race."

"And then what?" Aaron rubbed his hand across the back of his neck. It was a toss-up whether his frustration was with her, the situation, or his reaction to both. He wanted to send her away, wanted to pull her close and kiss her, wanted to shake her until she gave up this fool's errand. "We have established that I am aware of what it takes to find a way in this world when it gives you minimal encouragement to even keep breathing. I know how to fight for success." He swallowed and felt like he was opening his own coffin as he said, "I also know when something is a lost cause. Let me help you."

The fight seemed to drain out of her as she stepped back and lowered her chin. The space should have allowed him to breathe better, but it didn't. It only made him nervous about why she'd suddenly backed down.

"I appreciate your intentions." She lifted her head and straightened her shoulders. "I believe you are sincere in your offer."

She delivered the line as if she expected him to take the observation as a compliment of high order. What sort of life had she led before now to find sincerity anything other than her due? He wasn't insulted by her disbelief, knowing it came from being forced to develop a healthy mistrust of others, but he didn't want her to turn down his offer of help.

Aaron didn't rescue people. He'd never had a passion for the dark horse. For most of his life he'd *been* the dark horse. He funded other people's projects and dallied upon the fringes of them, but he'd never offered personal help before.

Maybe it was because his life was changing and all the comfort and security he'd carefully built was in danger, but he wanted to know he'd done something that mattered. He needed to do more, needed to pass along the gift of acceptance his friends had given him. They would never know, but he would, and he needed to know he was worthy of a place in their lives.

If Miss Fitzroy knew he was considering her something of a charity, she'd likely kick him as hard as he was considering kicking himself.

"You can't be my jockey forever," he said calmly, needing to rid himself of this unsettled feeling that kept him from remembering where he belonged in the world.

"We agreed to one month of employment as long as I'm winning," she said softly. "In one month, I'll take my wages and will no longer be your problem."

"You're not my problem." Not anymore. She'd just become his concern.

"Your inconvenience, then."

Aaron couldn't deny that. She was certainly still an inconvenience. "Even if you make a name as a jockey, it won't make people hire you on for anything else."

"These men have daughters. Wives. They may want to obtain skills like mine. Or perhaps they want horses they can show off. I am a good trainer, Mr. Whitworth."

"How will they know what you can do after seeing you run in a straight line?"

She glanced at the ground for a moment. When her head rose, her eyes were overly bright, and her smile fake and brittle. "You have a meeting to get to with your brother. I wouldn't want to keep you."

Before he could say another word, she was gone, nearly running down the lane to escape him. In a single morning the woman had gone from an inconvenience to a project to a mystery he was determined to get to the bottom of.

Eighteen

Knowing the next day would decide her fate, Sophia couldn't sleep. She lay staring at the ceiling as the house grew quiet around her. She did everything she could to keep her thoughts on the verses Jonas had read after dinner. He'd prayed over her and then told her to go get some rest.

He forgot to tell sleep to come to bed as well.

Her mind was already racing with all the possibilities. What could go wrong, what could go right. It left her dizzy. What she needed was to clear her head and start the process over. Maybe she could confuse her body into going to sleep.

She rose and put on the better of her riding gowns. She'd finally washed the practice gown, and it lay draped over the chair, drying. Sneaking out of a sleeping house was easy, and soon she was roaming the grounds, drawn to the stable and the comforting familiarity of the smells and sounds of horses.

Her intention had been to just walk by, maybe pet a horse or two if they were awake, but she wasn't met by the quiet hum of a stable at night. Instead, there was a bang, followed by a shuffle, and the snuffles and grunts of a discontent horse.

Sophia crept into the stable, keeping an eye out for any grooms coming to investigate. In a large box stall was a very tall, very unhappy horse. He circled the box, then pawed at the ground before shoving his side against the wall.

Poor thing. She'd seen a colicky horse before. It was too dark to see if the straw along the bottom of the box was clean, but it was obvious the horse was in distress. A coiled rope hung on a hook nearby, so she grabbed it to use as a lead to take the horse outside.

The grooms lived above the stable, but the noise didn't seem to have woken them. There was no need for them to rise when Sophia was already awake. Her restlessness might as well be of some benefit. She took the horse to an open space on the side of the stable away from the house and started walking in circles.

The first fifteen minutes were exhausting as the animal kept trying to stop and lower himself to the ground. Each time she'd poke and prod and pull until the horse started walking again. Eventually, he was walking smoothly, plodding along without complaint as they circled and circled the little area. The drowsiness that had been eluding Sophia chose that moment to appear, and she laid her head against the horse's neck as they walked, allowing her eyes to drift partly closed.

Finally, the horse found some relief, and Sophia led the animal back into the stable, stumbling over her own feet in her sleepy state. She sat in the corner of the horse's stall. She would wait a few moments to ensure the horse was okay, then return to bed. Her new friend gave her a brief nuzzle before settling in to enjoy the rest of the night himself.

More banging against the stall startled her awake, but this time it wasn't the horse. Whatever had cracked against the wood had done so inches from her head.

A very well-dressed, very angry man stood in the stall with her and the horse. The door behind him was open, and three wide-eyed stable boys filled the gap.

"You!" The man pointed his horse whip at her, likely what he'd hit the wall with a few moments before. "What are you doing in my stable?"

"I, er, sleeping?" Sophia rubbed a hand over her face, willing her brain to wake enough to extricate her from this situation.

"You're that woman jockey, aren't you? Was this your plan?" the man continued. "You distract us with your nonsense and then plot to steal our horses? You'll not be making off with Hezekiah!"

The man turned so quickly his still-extended whip made a whizzing sound as it slashed through the air. "Fetch the magistrate!"

That got Sophia moving. Thankful she was already dressed, she sprang from the corner, ignoring the tingling sensation in her legs, and pushed past the stunned stable boys.

There would be no breakfast this morning, no visit to Jonas. She would find a place to hide until it was time to run the race. She couldn't leave Mr. Whitworth without a jockey, even if it appeared he might be correct in his assessment of her chances of changing people's minds.

After that, she would go to her brother and they could decide what to do.

If they had to start all over again, so be it. At least they'd be together.

HAD THIS BEEN any other race day, Aaron would be preparing the horse with the calm born of easy confidence. It hadn't rained in over a week, so the track would be exactly the way Equinox preferred. The sun was rising in a clear sky, so the racers would have no trouble seeing the course. All Miss Fitzroy's training the past week had gone better than he'd expected. Hudson's deep frowns had softened to speculative scowls after signing the papers with Rigsby the day before. He'd even been excited enough not to push for more information on Aaron's part of the exchange.

So why was he feeling so unsettled?

Oliver stood beside him in the training yard, waiting for Barley and a stable boy to prepare Equinox. After several quiet minutes, he turned to Aaron and asked, "Are we hoping to win today or not?"

That was the question, wasn't it? And likely the source of his agitation. If Miss Fitzroy won, his challenge record would remain untainted and Oliver would be a thousand pounds richer. Convincing her to allow him to help her find another line of work would be more difficult, though.

If she didn't win . . . well, his situation didn't improve much. He still had to hope the other horses and jockeys made it back in time for the October Meeting, still had to find someone to ride Equinox, and still had to figure out where Miss Fitzroy could work. His only gain would be that she could no longer refuse to find a new position.

"Why don't we wait and see?" Aaron shrugged. "We'll act as if whatever outcome we get is the one we wanted."

Oliver nodded and gave a good-natured chuckle. "You can't lose with that plan."

Or it was the plan of a man who'd seen losing as inevitable. One way or another, he was going to be worse off. Still, there wasn't any point in speculating when neither option was good. He may as well want what he got.

Besides, he was too busy sorting through everything he knew about his little jockey. He couldn't keep his mind off her, so he would make the obsession useful. Something was pressuring him, something he hadn't quite put together. Her determination to be a jockey wasn't fitting with what he knew—or thought he knew—about her.

If only he could put a finger on why it didn't fit.

The object of his thoughts strode into the paddock. She was dressed in the same outfit she'd worn on her first day, with the silk shirt in Lord Trenting's colors pulled over the top and tied at the waist to keep it from flopping about her legs. Barley must have given her the shirt as she came through the stable. Was it really only a week ago that he'd seen those wide-leg trousers for the first time?

He took in her face and frowned. While he'd grown accustomed to receiving a wide range of expressions from her, be it a tight-lipped smile accompanied by nervous lip licking, or impudent chatter and a head tilt of utter confidence, he'd never seen her look terrified. Her eyes were wide, her skin stark white against the red of her tousled hair. It had been pulled back into a low bun at some point, but then it had been thoroughly mussed. There was even a piece of straw sticking out of one side.

The reality of what she was about to do must have finally hit her this morning. Though that didn't explain the straw.

She reached him just as Equinox was being led from the stable. He plucked the straw from her hair before helping her mount. There was nothing he could do about her fear now. They were both just going to have to see this through and deal with the consequences after.

Normally Aaron would have appreciated the fact that she'd yet to say a word, but instead he found it worrisome. Her fingers were gripping the reins hard enough to turn the knuckles white, and Equinox shifted restlessly as he absorbed her tension.

Aaron stepped closer to her side and laid a calming hand on the horse's neck. He couldn't reach any part of her aside from her legs, so he simply gave her what he hoped was an encouraging smile. "Take a deep breath. You're ready."

She blinked down at him but still said nothing. Then she closed her eyes and took a deep, slow inhale that seemed to expand every part of her body. As she deflated, her grip loosened and her spine relaxed. She opened her eyes to stare at the horizon and leaned forward to pat the horse on the neck.

That was as good as it was going to get.

They headed toward the starting pole. A scattering of people on horseback lined the second half of the course, ready to race alongside the track and see all the action. In the distance, a large crowd gathered near the finish post.

Had everyone in Newmarket come out to see the race? It was as crowded as a meeting day. Carriages lined the small hill, while people on foot scattered down the slope. Even the duke's stand had people in it. The small building was too far away to see faces clearly, but use of the stand had been granted to Lord Gliddon when the duke was away, so the man in the bright green waistcoat was likely him.

Aaron sent up a prayer of thanks that the first set of banns had been read this past Sunday. Even if Lord Gliddon's opinion of his future son-in-law dipped because of this debacle, he couldn't stop the wedding without creating an even larger scandal.

Aaron rolled his shoulders. He didn't care much what Lord Gliddon thought, aside from the fact that his opinion had a good chance of reaching the ears of Oliver's father. While the wedding was safe from an earl's displeasure, Aaron's job was not.

Lord Davers was already at the start with his horse, jockey, and trainer. He sneered at Aaron and Oliver but didn't even acknowledge Miss Fitzroy. Since that effort required him to avoid not just a person but an entire horse, it was an impressive, if annoying, feat.

Knowing Davers, he wasn't going to stop with unspoken slights. Words were going to be said. Unkind ones veiled with a sheen of propriety that would keep him from having to apologize later.

Aaron could take the insults, and he imagined Miss Fitzroy had heard worse, but Oliver was a socializing member of the community. The less direct unpleasantness he had to hear from the other aristocrat, the easier he would find it to smile at him later in a ballroom.

"We can take it from here, Oliver. Why don't you join your future wife in the stand so you get a good view?" Aaron assumed Lady Rebecca had come with her father. Even if she didn't care much for racing, she wouldn't miss this.

When Oliver didn't immediately agree, Aaron turned to see him watching Aaron with an expression Aaron couldn't quite read. Given their mixed company, Aaron couldn't ask him what he was thinking. Finally, Oliver gave a swift nod, remounted his horse, and rode away.

Miss Fitzroy cleared her throat. Though she still looked a bit wild about the eyes, her posture had returned to its normal fluidity in the saddle. Her abnormal demeanor was jarring, but at least her skill seemed the same.

"I look forward to breaking your record," Lord Davers said.

"You have been seeking a way to distinguish yourself for a while," Aaron returned, knowing he shouldn't reply at all but wanting to get in one last comment while he still had some claim to rightful arrogance.

After today he would be known as the stable manager who was either foolish enough to have a female jockey, desperate enough to recruit a female jockey, or stupid enough to allow a female jockey.

None of those were descriptions he particularly wanted attached to his name. Win or lose, his reputation was taking a hit.

As the horses lined up, Aaron took care to position Miss Fitzroy so that her whip hand was free. Sitting aside as she was, switching hands was not an option. Davers's rider could press in on the right side and prevent her from being able to maneuver the horse as well. If he pressed in from the left, he could knock her off balance or jostle the saddle enough to send her tumbling.

All the horrible possibilities sent a burning sensation climbing up his throat, and a stabbing ache formed in the back of his head. He wasn't going to breathe properly until Miss Fitzroy's feet were on the ground again.

The count was made, the gun was fired, and the horses took off.

Just as he always did once the riders were safely away, Aaron mounted Shadow and cut across the Heath to the finish post. The racers would follow the curve of the course, covering twice the distance he had to.

Instead of dismounting and joining the onlookers, he stayed in the saddle, ready to run interference if it became necessary to remove Miss Fitzroy from the premises quickly.

Would winning or losing require them to depart faster? Maybe they should make a run for it either way.

He couldn't see who was in the lead, though the roar of the crowd told him they'd rounded the corner. It was so loud the noise covered the pounding of hooves until the horses were in the final stretch of the track.

They were close—far closer than most people had likely expected—but neither had a clear advantage.

He avoided blinking until his eyes grew dry and his vision unfocused. Every muscle in his body drew tight, and Shadow leapt forward at the squeeze of Aaron's legs. He settled the horse and forced his legs to relax, though the rest of him remained tight and stiff. They were nearly to the finish.

As Aaron had feared, the other jockey was riding his horse close to Equinox, pressing in on Miss Fitzroy's legs. She had shifted her weight and leaned low over the horse's neck, practically turning herself into an equine neck scarf. It wasn't pretty, but she was hanging on.

More importantly, she wasn't losing.

In that instant, Aaron knew he didn't want her to. She was good. She deserved to win.

Though her whip was free, Davers's horse was far too close for her to get in a good kick to urge Equinox faster. As they got close enough to see the details of their faces, he noticed that while she'd been silent for the preparation, she was anything but in the race, vocally urging her horse to run faster.

Aaron winced. Dirt, grass, and who knew what else would be flying into her face right now. She'd be tasting grit for days.

Whatever she was shouting meant something to Equinox, because he gave a final surge of speed and finished the race with nearly his full body in front of the other horse.

Proving she was not a fool, Miss Fitzroy kept right on going, encouraging the horse to continue at a run as the encroaching crowd tried to block her in. People had to jump backward to avoid being trampled by the horse they'd hoped to intercept.

Aaron moved Shadow into her line of vision, keeping away from the edge of the crowd so she would have room to maneuver. Once free of the people, she slowed the horse and trotted to Aaron's side. Her triumphant smile revealed that she did, indeed, have dirt in her teeth.

But she also had the win.

Aaron hadn't been sure how he'd feel in this moment, but the unmistakable pride welling in his chest was unexpected.

Perhaps he had a soft spot for the dark horse after all.

Nineteen

She'd won. She'd actually won.

And she'd done it without resorting to the underhanded methods of the other jockey. Anyone looking for true horsemanship would have been impressed with her skills.

Even she'd been impressed. Despite the practice runs of the past week, she hadn't known she could ride like that, could urge a horse to pull out a little more speed, could think about the next few feet of a course that was flying by much too quickly.

She should be happy. This was what she'd needed to secure her future for a few more weeks, wasn't it? At least it assured her employment. A place to live might be in question.

The debacle of that morning put a pall over any sense of security her win had provided. She assumed the man who'd found her was Lady Rebecca's father, and he had definitely not been happy to see her. If he wanted to, he could cause a heap of trouble for her.

Unfortunately, she hadn't a clue how to keep it from happening. Just hoping the man wouldn't raise a ruckus and her win would make him more amenable to her presence didn't seem a proactive solution.

At least her most precious belongings were safe at the cottage. Losing her clothing and the knapsack would be a hardship, but those things were replaceable. It would mean less money to start over, though.

She gripped the reins until her hands shook. It wasn't fair. She should be happy right now, celebrating the fact that she'd done what no one—including herself, if she was honest—had thought she could do. Instead she was terrified that an angry lord was going to show up at the training yard and insist Mr. Whitworth get rid of her. Firing her wouldn't be a matter of misplaced honor then, but of self-preservation, and she wouldn't fault him for it.

She snuck a glance at Mr. Whitworth riding beside her as they returned to the training yard. He wasn't smiling. Nor was he frowning. In fact, his face appeared devoid of any emotion whatsoever. She swallowed hard and faced forward again.

"You did well." Mr. Whitworth's voice was deep, steady, and as emotionless as his face. "It was a good race."

"Thank you." Her breath came a little easier as they guided the horses into the paddock beside the small stable. Just knowing she'd impressed him helped her embrace the accomplishment. It was a simple statement, but in their brief acquaintanceship he'd shown himself to be a man who didn't lie.

Jonas never lied either, but he did tend to phrase things so as not to hurt her feelings. Mr. Whitworth's blunt honesty gave the compliment that much more significance.

She could not allow herself to become accustomed to receiving his commendations.

The noise of the crowd they'd left behind lessened as the people dispersed from the course. Some would be returning to town. Others would be coming toward the training yards, either to see to their own horses or say what they hadn't been able to when she ran away from the finish post.

This was the moment of truth. If they were impressed, her dream of opening a training school might work. If they were still disgusted with the idea of a female jockey, all was for naught. No matter how many times she won, it wouldn't change the minds of those who'd already set themselves against her.

She kicked her foot free of the stirrup and shifted in the saddle, preparing to jump down to the ground. It was only as she pushed herself away from the horse that she realized Mr. Whitworth had dismounted and come around to assist her down.

A squeal left her mouth as she slammed into his chest, and his arms wrapped around her as he stumbled back several steps.

He regained stable footing but didn't immediately put her down. They stayed that way—her nose pressed into his shoulder, arms awkwardly pinned to her side by the strong press of his—until one of the horses nudged its nose into the space beside hers.

Mr. Whitworth lowered her to the ground with one arm while the other pushed the horse away. Once she was back on her feet, his grip loosened, though his hand remained on her back. She looked up at him. He'd assisted her on and off horses several times in the past week, but never had he been this close.

Sophia, who frequently had to use some form of physical impairment to stop herself from talking, couldn't find a single word.

She heard the growing rumble of a potentially discontent crowd that certainly wouldn't take her seriously if they discovered her in Mr. Whitworth's embrace, staring up into his dark eyes and wondering how long they would have to stand like this before he either pushed her away or kissed her.

What a disconcerting idea. Did she *want* Mr. Whitworth to kiss her?

She dropped her gaze to his coat, searching for a loose string or a speck of dirt to focus on as she stepped away. The man was irritatingly free of visible flaw.

Of course he was. No seam of his would dare to unravel.

She took another step back and his arm fell away. The stable boy must have gone to watch the race and hadn't made it back yet, because no one emerged to collect the horse. Grateful for something to do and an excuse to get away from the approaching horde, Sophia collected Equinox by the reins and retreated into the stable, careful not to look back at Mr. Whitworth.

WHAT . . .

Aaron tried to form a full question, but he couldn't get his mind past the first word. What had just happened? What had he *wanted* to happen? What was he going to do about it?

And once he got past all the *what* questions, the *why* ones would be coming along behind.

He shook his head and stepped over to Shadow to gather the horse's reins. For lack of a better idea, he led the horse into the stable.

Following Miss Fitzroy.

He'd acknowledged to himself that he found her pretty and admired her spirit and athletic ability. He could have said the same about Bianca, though, and he'd never once thought of kissing her. Just imagining such a scenario was unsettling enough to clear part of the fog from his head.

He still didn't know what to make of that moment with Miss Fitzroy, but he needed to at least pretend it meant nothing. Despite his realization that he wanted her to win, he hadn't forgotten that her victory came with repercussions.

Before, she'd been a novelty. Now she was a threat. And some of the men on their way back from the course weren't going to take kindly to that altered status.

Shadow had spent a good part of the morning standing around, so he needed nothing more than water and a loosened girth. Equinox's dark coat had been marred with streaks of lather, though. The stable boy was surely hustling his way back, but there was no reason for the horse to wait when Aaron could start the process.

The last thing he expected to find when he stepped into the grooming area was Equinox already in the rack chains being scraped down by his little jockey.

If he allowed her to say one word about that moment in the paddock, she would find a way to utter forty-two. Maybe more. Perhaps if he didn't break the silence, she wouldn't either. He gave her a nod and went to work on the other side of the horse.

A low wall separated the rack chains from the rest of the stable, so Aaron could easily see when Oliver stepped inside, a frowning Lord Gliddon at his side.

Aaron kept working, thankful that the sudden tension in the room had chased the last of the emotional fog from his brain. He moved the comb in hard, tight circles. He thought best when he was working, but he couldn't get a good grasp on his thoughts with all the little distractions around him.

The way Miss Fitzroy's shoulders were curving in as she hid behind the horse's haunches.

The way Lord Gliddon, a usually amiable if self-important sort of fellow, was nearly red in the face.

The way Oliver frowned in return and neatly blocked the man from charging farther into the stable.

The way Lady Rebecca stomped up to her fiancé's side as upset as Aaron had ever seen her. There was no sign of the serene smile that had seemed permanently affixed to her face.

"Where is she?" Lord Gliddon sputtered.

Miss Fitzroy tucked herself closer to the horse. Aaron took a step sideways. He was fairly certain the horse and the partial wall would block Lord Gliddon's view of her skirt, but he wasn't taking a chance. Not until he knew what was going on.

"Oliver," Lady Rebecca said in a chilly voice, "kindly tell my father that if he persists in this nonsense, I'll have you collect me in a carriage and we'll elope to Scotland."

Oliver sighed. "I don't think that will be—"

"You'll do no such thing!" Lord Gliddon turned toward his daughter, but Oliver adjusted to block him.

"Why don't we all calm down?" Oliver extended one hand toward Lord Gliddon and took Lady Rebecca's hand in the other. "This is simply a misunderstanding."

"A misunderstanding? All week the Jockey Club has grumbled about this female jockey. She just won a registered challenge race. Does she have to go in the books now? There's talk of revoking

Mr. Barley's license over this. If they learn she's been staying in my house, they will not view that as a *misunderstanding*."

Spittle flew from Lord Gliddon's mouth as he ground out that last word. Oliver winced. Lady Rebecca stuck her nose farther in the air.

Aaron looked over the horse at Miss Fitzroy, who had gone entirely pale beneath her red hair. Was she going to faint? That would certainly lend more drama to this moment.

Lord Gliddon pointed at Aaron. "You know what they're saying about you, don't you?"

"Lord Gliddon," Oliver said in a low, warning tone.

"Let him speak," Aaron said, his voice calm, his eyes still glued to Miss Fitzroy's. "I'll hear it eventually."

"It's complimentary, if you look at it a certain way," Oliver mused.

"It's not a compliment at all," Lord Gliddon ranted. "He's trying to bring down the established powers in Newmarket. Some say you've been crafting this plan for years."

Aaron paused his combing motions and half turned to stare at the earl with incredulity. "Years? Have I supposedly been lying in wait for a woman who could ride well enough to challenge the status quo?" He shook his head. "I could have put Miss Bianca Snowley on a thoroughbred and had one of their own shake things up if I'd been of that mind."

He studiously avoided Miss Fitzroy's gaze as he went back to caring for the horse. That people truly thought he would endanger a woman for a social statement burned a hole in his gut. His gentlemanly demeanor and business acumen should have spoken for themselves, but angry people rarely thought logically when declaring a verdict.

That was a lesson he'd learned at school. He'd gotten so good at avoiding people that he'd gone nearly a year without speaking privately with anyone other than Oliver and Graham.

"If we're going to share ludicrous tales, Father, do include the one where someone asked if he'd dressed a boy up like a lady to make a point," Lady Rebecca scoffed.

"I think it was the trousers that inspired that one," Oliver added.

"If I'd been of that mind, I'd have dressed Miss Fitzroy as a lad, not the other way around," Aaron said dryly.

"None of this matters," Lord Gliddon said, getting himself worked up again. "The Jockey Club can make a rule no one in their right mind ever thought they'd need, and this nonsense will be done with. What I want to know is what she was doing in Hezekiah's stall this morning. If I hadn't found her, she'd have stolen away with my horse!"

Aaron snapped his attention to Miss Fitzroy, who was looking up at him with wide green eyes and shaking her head so hard her low knot came half undone.

She'd been in Hezekiah's stall? Why even be in Lord Gliddon's stable to begin with? He didn't think she'd intended to steal the horse, but that she'd been there at all added another piece to the puzzle. Why weren't the things he knew about her fitting together?

"Was she leading the horse away?" he asked, turning and stepping over to the low wall to better block any chance of Miss Fitzroy being noticed.

"No." Lord Gliddon looked a bit abashed for a moment. "She was sleeping."

"You put her in the stable?" Oliver asked his fiancée.

"Of course not. I gave her a maid's room," Lady Rebecca said.

"In my house!" Lord Gliddon turned his accusatory finger to Oliver. "I haven't written your father before now because, while I too thought Mr. Whitworth was making a point, I assumed it was a different one entirely. He could have made it so she'd lose, you know, thus establishing the way things *should* be. A rather strange way to go about it, but what else can you expect from someone like him?"

Someone like him. Aaron's blood ran cold. The hairs on his arm pricked up and rubbed against his shirt, leaving his skin feeling raw. So much for all the time and care he'd spent building a reputation in this town. He expected such comments in London, knew the scandal had followed him here, but until Miss Fitzroy came into his life, it had all seemed carefully contained.

"You can leave now."

Aaron blinked. He'd never heard Oliver so firm, and he'd been witness to most of Oliver's serious life choices. More often than not, his passionate feelings left him sounding somewhat manic, but in this moment he was as hard and firm as a forged horseshoe.

"What?" Lord Gliddon asked.

"Get. Out. Insults to Mr. Whitworth are not welcome here or on any of my other properties."

"They aren't your properties, boy."

"They are more mine than they are yours."

"I'll be writing to your father about this. And I'll be going to the magistrate. If you won't investigate why that girl was in my stable, I'm sure he will!" Lord Gliddon spun around on his heel. "Come along, Rebecca."

"Oliver can see me home later," she said in a sweet voice. Her ever-present half smile was back in place as she looped her arm calmly through Oliver's.

No one moved until the echoes of Lord Gliddon's boots faded from the stable.

"Well," Oliver said, sounding more like himself, "the stable boys have to be around here somewhere. How long do we think it will take for word of that little tiff to get around town?"

"It will be in the alehouses tonight and the drawing rooms tomorrow," Lady Rebecca said. "But I can head it off. Take me home, Oliver. If Mother and I make the rounds today, I can present a different version."

Oliver looked at Aaron, as if making sure he hadn't taken any of Lord Gliddon's insults to heart. Though they'd stung, they were nothing he hadn't heard before. He gave Oliver a nod, and the couple headed out.

Now to see what Miss Fitzroy had to say about the whole business.

When he turned back to the horse, though, she was gone. When had she slipped away? How had she done it without him—or anyone else—noticing?

He ran from the grooming area and walked speedily through the stable, checking the stalls as he went.

Nothing.

He stepped outside as a flash of color whipped around the side of another stable. While he didn't blame her for running, where was she going to go?

He set off after her. Maybe now he would find the final piece to make the rest of the puzzle make sense.

Twenty

Sophia nearly tripped over her own feet as she hastened away from the training yards, constantly checking over her shoulder to see if anyone noticed her.

Mr. Whitworth had said she was trouble and things would be bad if she rode. She'd thought it was more the type of trouble that made someone uncomfortable or doubled their workload for a day. Instead, she was the sort of trouble that crushed a man's life, if Lord Gliddon's claims had been anything to go by.

She couldn't do that to Mr. Whitworth. He was a good man. Yes, it would be nice if he talked more, but any man who risked such derision just to keep his word and keep her from being out on the streets was a good man. She refused to be responsible for the demise of a good man. She didn't want to be the demise of any man, but particularly not a good one.

So, she would go.

She started to head straight for the cottage but took a turn toward town at the last minute in case someone had seen her leave the stable. The excitement of the morning, the lack of breakfast, and the uncertainty of her future had her trembling by the time she'd entered Newmarket and turned north on Wellington Street.

The scent of the bakery made her stomach growl. The sight of a woman hanging clothes on a drying line made her worry. By the time she was surrounded by farms and fields, even her brain was shaking. She gave a quick glance around and didn't see anyone, so she cut across the land toward Jonas's hiding spot.

Every dense grouping of bushes or stand of trees was an opportunity to stop, remind herself to breathe, quote every Bible verse she could remember—which was approximately three in her current state—and check to see if she was being followed.

By the time the cottage came into view, her heart was pounding harder than Equinox's hooves had done an hour ago. She ran inside, breaking what was left of the upper hinge and sending the door to the ground. It took five seconds to look around the room and see that Jonas wasn't there. Rhiannon had been tucked into her stall, and Sophia's wild entrance had the horse tossing her head and prancing in place.

Sophia rushed through the cottage and wedged herself into the stall beside her horse, pressing her forehead into the animal's warm neck as she both gave and took reassurance. What was she going to do?

Mr. Whitworth could lose his position. Mr. Barley could lose his license. Lord Farnsworth was certainly on the outs with his fiancée's family. The money Jonas had tucked away somewhere in this cottage wasn't even enough to get them to London, where they might find work.

Not even Jonas's creative ideas and clear thinking were going to get her out of this one. This time, she just might have ruined it all. She wrapped her hand in Rhiannon's braided mane and cried.

"THE LAST TIME I saw him he was sleeping in an abandoned cottage that was half fallen in."

Aaron pressed his mouth into a flat line as Miss Fitzroy's destination became apparent. This was what he'd been missing.

169

Her hesitancy to search for another job, the way she didn't linger after training despite knowing no one in town, even his initial confusion when hiring the red-haired horse trainer named Fitzroy.

Now that all those questions were answered, a dozen new ones had taken their place.

Why hide the brother? Aaron's offer hadn't contained any competence requirement. Even if the man he'd thought he was hiring couldn't ride as well as Miss Fitzroy, they had to know their opportunities would be greater if he'd been the one to show up on the Heath that day instead of her.

Something else was amiss.

Unsure what he would find inside, Aaron moved toward the cottage slowly. To say the building was not structurally sound was an understatement. At least part of the roof and half of one corner was missing. If it had any furniture at all, it was half-rotten. That someone had been living here, even if only for a week, sent his stomach into knots.

He still held a shred of hope for a reasonable explanation, but he had a feeling his wishful thinking was connected to that moment when Miss Fitzroy had jumped from the horse's back and landed in his arms.

The fact was she'd deliberately misled him. What else had she lied about without actually telling a lie? Desperate circumstances had pushed more than one otherwise honorable person to make less-than-honorable choices. Perhaps she wasn't so deep into this that he couldn't still help her.

The door of the cottage was on the ground, so he was able to ease inside without much noise. Standing in the doorway caused his shadow to stretch across the sad furniture and a pitiful sleeping pallet, but there was no one there to notice. He frowned. Had she somehow known he was following her and managed to climb out over the broken wall without his noticing?

He stepped farther into the room and looked around. The last thing he'd expected to see was a white Andalusian horse standing in a stall made of loose brick and timber.

He swallowed hard. Perhaps she was a horse thief after all.

As SOPHIA'S TEARS soaked her horse's coat, her mind whirred. If they could just get to London, there would be opportunities. Even if she had to go back to performing or rent Rhiannon out for ladies to ride in Hyde Park. Maybe she could dress as a boy and find work as a tiger.

Hysterical laughter threatened to bubble up through her tears. As if Jonas would allow her to pretend to be a boy. If it weren't for that crazy accusation in the training stable, she'd never have come up with such an idea. She hugged her horse tighter. What was her life becoming?

Warm breath tickled her back as the horse curved her neck around to bump her head against Sophia's body. The reminder that she wasn't alone chased away some of her despair.

She must think before she acted next time. Every possible consequence had to be examined, not just the best possible scenario. Was that what God was trying to teach her? Maybe if she matured enough to consider the consequences beforehand, He would give her more to manage.

It was a nonsensical hope, but she'd learned long ago that hope was worth holding on to even if doing so required a little nonsense. Life was far too difficult to go through without hope.

"I'm certainly glad Lord Gliddon isn't here to see this. He's loud enough without having a valid reason to call you a horse thief."

Sophia lifted her head. Mr. Whitworth stood in the narrow gap at the front of Rhiannon's stall, effectively trapping both her and the horse.

"I'm not a horse thief," she said quietly.

He pointed to Rhiannon. "Is that, or is that not, the horse from the circus?"

"Yes," she said and sighed. "But she belongs to me, not Mr. Notley."

"You own two changes of clothes and you expect me to believe you own a horse that you could sell and cover the rent on a modest cottage for a year?"

"Three."

"I beg your pardon?"

"I have three changes of clothes. Though now I suppose I have only one. I don't think Lord Gliddon would take kindly to my returning to his house to retrieve the others."

Mr. Whitworth's exasperated expression was easy to make out even in the shadows of the cottage. "Three, one, two, it hardly matters, considering they by no means indicate a person with the means to care for a nag, much less a mount of quality."

Sophia frowned. "Does a nag require less money to feed and house? I wouldn't have the funds to purchase Rhiannon now, but . . ." Sophia swallowed. "You have to believe me, I didn't steal her."

"You have to do better than that, Miss Fitzroy."

She licked her lips and wrapped a braid from the horse's mane around one finger. "Can I be honest with you?"

"I don't know," he grumbled. "Can you?"

She couldn't blame him for his frustration. Still, she had to protect Jonas. If Mr. Whitworth didn't believe her, took her to the magistrate, and backed up Lord Gliddon's claims, she had to make sure that Jonas would still be free to start over. "Is it *safe* to be honest with you?"

"I don't think you can afford anything else. The only safety you'll get from me will be in exchange for an honest—and expeditious—explanation."

She swallowed and tried to give a smile, to look unbothered. "It's not as if you've tongue enough for two sets of teeth. Chances of you spreading the tale are slim."

He didn't smile back.

She winced and rushed ahead before he lost what little patience remained. "My father trained in Spain. When he came back to Ireland, he brought horses to start his school. He bred them, training the foals from the beginning to be fancy riding horses. He gave me one of the fillies. We started training her together."

Mr. Whitworth said nothing, but the tension emanating from him abated somewhat. She pushed on, anxious to get through the story without getting tangled in her own emotions. "My father loved my mother and me and Jonas and the horses and his students. He was very good as a father and trainer. He wasn't very good at managing money."

Mr. Whitworth grunted.

"After he died, we discovered how tenuous everything was. Within months we lost the riding school and the house. Soon after that, we lost Mother. I kept my horse, though, even as we sold the rest of them. Horses were all I knew, and I couldn't imagine how I could make my way in the world without her."

"I can't imagine how you thought to make your way with her."

Sophia frowned. "We've done well enough."

He gave a pointed look around the dilapidated cottage.

She bit her lip, having to concede his point.

"How old were you?"

"Seventeen."

"So, you left home at seventeen with the intention of joining the circus?"

"I didn't *leave* my home, I lost it." Wasn't the man listening? "And my *intention* was to train horses with my brother, but no one wanted to hire someone so young on nothing more than the reputation of our father. Perhaps they'd hire a stable boy, but not a girl, and not one bringing her own horse."

"Is this the same brother you last saw sleeping in an abandoned cottage?"

A chill shot through her. She didn't remember telling him that. What else had she told him while babbling nervously across the countryside? If she couldn't remember, she couldn't continue her tale. She might contradict herself, or unwittingly give more away. "Abandoned cottages are lovely finds when you don't have anywhere else to call home."

She quickly added, "I don't know where my brother is now." That was technically true. She didn't know *exactly* where he was.

Mr. Whitworth's eyes traveled over her face, jerking from point to point as if trying to see past her words to the truth beyond.

Wind blew outside the cottage, wailing past the openings and rattling the loose, broken edges. A chunk of roof fell into the cottage and broke into pieces on the floor. Rhiannon jumped sideways, pushing Sophia into the cottage wall. Air rushed from her lungs as Sophia braced herself against the horse.

Then Mr. Whitworth was there, squeezing in beside her and forcing Rhiannon to shift over and press against the other side of the stall.

She was now snugly trapped between the heat of the horse and the warmth of the man. She didn't know what to do with her hands or even her feet. Should she turn toward him? Face the horse and stand shoulder to shoulder with him? Duck down and crawl between Rhiannon's legs so she could escape?

Ultimately, she did some awkward blend of none of those and stepped on the man's foot. She tried to scramble away and made the entire business worse by tripping over her own toes and kicking him in the shin as she grabbed the lapels of his jacket to keep herself from falling.

"Are you quite finished? I've never seen you this clumsy."

Would it kill the man to allow a little emotion into his voice? She couldn't tell if he was still mad or had moved on to somewhat amused.

She placed her feet carefully on the ground and straightened. "I am not clumsy."

"Not normally, no, though it seems you're expending all your dexterity on your tongue at the moment and have none remaining for your feet."

She opened her mouth to answer, but he didn't let her. "You do realize this is someone else's property."

She nodded because she could hardly deny it.

"Miss Fitzroy—I assume that is your real name?"

"Yes."

He gave a short nod. "Miss Fitzroy, you are hardly the first person I have met to whom life has been less than kind. Nor are you the first I have employed, though you do have the distinction of being the first woman—a distinction, I might remind you, I never intended. I am no stranger to aiding the less desirable, and my reputation suffers none for it, but I will not tolerate being lied to, used, or manipulated. You have two minutes to convince me not to haul you out of here and let the local magistrate sort out your claims."

Two minutes? She couldn't produce a convincing argument in two minutes, not with his imposing presence looming over her. She wasn't even sure she could formulate something in two hours.

Her heart squeezed and breath rushed in and out of her lungs until her lips began to tingle. Her mouth opened, though she wasn't entirely sure what she meant to say, and the words spilled out without any consideration.

"Jonas tried getting work as a horse trainer, but the men who hired him either refused to let me come with him or were all too willing for him to bring me along. We moved from place to place. I tried to get work as a maid a few times, but I always got in trouble for being too rough with the cleaning or staring out the window daydreaming, and it was . . . hard . . . being away from Jonas and the horses."

Mr. Whitworth was a horseman. Surely he understood the need to be around the animals in order to feel alive.

"We lived in the woods sometimes, saving what little money we had for food and letting Rhiannon and Prancer graze in a field. I suppose we were stealing the grass, but it wasn't as if it wouldn't grow back or the sheep were going hungry."

Not how she needed to spend her two minutes. Admitting she'd squatted in places before wouldn't help her case. Worry loosened her tongue even more, and words tumbled from her mouth before they could form in her brain.

"We thought things were turning around when a man hired us both—Jonas for the stable and me as a scullery maid. We made enough to pay a farmer to keep the horses in his barn. We saved everything we could, hoping to have enough to start a small crop share of our own.

"Then things went missing from the house. Turns out the man was selling heirlooms to cover his gambling debts, but he didn't want the family to know, so he accused Jonas. The magistrate knew our father, knew us, knew we hadn't done it, but everyone in the village believed the claims. The magistrate told us to run, so we did."

She was terrible at this. Why would she bring up other times they'd been accused of theft?

"We crossed over to England and made an act with the horses. It wasn't showy, and we barely made enough to survive. Mr. Notley saw us working with the horses in a field one day and offered us jobs. It was supposed to be temporary, a way to travel to a better place, but we never seemed to get there. Then there was an accident, and . . . and . . ."

Her mind filled with the images of the road giving way and sending Jonas and the horse tumbling down the ravine, the screams of man and beast. The physical pain on Jonas's face had been nothing compared to the anguish when he realized how badly Prancer had been injured, the dark eyes of the horse seeming to apologize for the trouble. Mr. Notley callously telling them to do what needed to be done or stay there on their own.

"J-Jonas was hurt, and Prance—" she hiccuped—"Prancer—"

A strong masculine hand wrapped around her shoulder. "You don't have to say it."

The last of her control crumbled beneath that comforting hand. "Jonas was in so much pain."

Stop it, Sophia, you can't keep talking until you have more time to think.

"Mr. Notley said he wasn't valuable to the show anymore and therefore wouldn't be paid. He could stay if I too took a lower portion." It had been a foolish agreement, but what else could they do?

"There was hardly enough money to feed ourselves and Rhiannon, much less save to start somewhere new. I was trapped. So trapped."

The hand on her shoulder tightened, and sobs shuddered through Sophia's chest.

Sophia, you're getting hysterical.

"I prayed. I prayed and I prayed that God would bring me a way out, real work and real wages and a chance to create a home. I wanted that so badly that I didn't think about what taking advantage of this opportunity would do to you. I just grabbed it and—"

Where were these words coming from? She'd never realized these truths before, never had the courage to turn them into solid thoughts.

"I couldn't pass up the chance to be respected for my riding again instead of trotted out in a display that often drew scandalous jeers from the crowd—"

Really hadn't meant to share that part.

"I felt bad for tricking you, but I didn't know what else to do. I knew there was a chance you wouldn't honor the contract and I'd be on my own again, but you didn't send me away and—"

And she'd gotten to know him, at least a little bit, and she'd landed in his arms, and she'd thought things about him that she had no business thinking, and she really needed to stop talking.

"Miss Fitzroy—"

"You see? No one calls me Miss Fitzroy since Father died. I've been *Sophia* or *Girl* but never *Miss*. This week has been the best my life has been in a long time. I knew it couldn't last, but I never meant to bring anyone else down with me—"

If she didn't stop talking, her blurted words would soon reveal more than she even wanted to admit to herself. She needed something—anything—to help her shut up, but her eyes were captured by his and couldn't pull themselves away to find something else.

So, with all the emotion and desperation and unacknowledged feelings of the past week driving her, she wrapped her hands in his lapels, rose up on her toes, and smashed her traitorous mouth against his.

Twenty-One

First the woman scrambled his thoughts with her onslaught of words and now she was addling his brain, sending his senses rioting with the press of her lips against his.

His shoulders were hunched over, weighed down by the pull of her fists on his jacket, but he was more than strong enough to lift himself away.

At least he should have been.

Her grip slackened, but still he didn't straighten. He stayed, head lowered, the hand on her shoulder sliding until it braced against her upper back, pulling her forward, closer.

Her mouth shifted against his, no longer smashing tightly against his teeth but leaving their lips connected in a way that made him forget everything else. Forget that she'd lied, forget they were crammed into a corner of a falling-down cottage with a horse that may or may not be stolen, forget that she'd made his already tenuous life more difficult.

Or maybe he hadn't forgotten so much as he no longer cared.

The skim of her hands sliding against his face tossed his thoughts sideways again. She cupped his jaw, the roughness of the stubble on his cheeks keeping her movements from being too fluid, but the pull made it impossible to ignore. When was the last time someone had touched his face? He even did his own shaving.

Her fingers brushed his ear, the sensation strange and new

enough to break through his trance and provide the presence of mind to lift his head. He didn't go far, as his arms had done more traveling than he'd realized and were wrapped solidly around her, keeping them pressed together as their rough breathing joined the shuffling noises of the horse beside them.

Her eyes were wide and round, as if she was as stunned as he was, even though she'd initiated the kiss.

"That isn't how I meant to convince you," she whispered.

"That isn't why I believe you," he answered, knowing it was true. Somewhere in the rant of words tripping over themselves far too quickly to be false, he'd concluded that she was telling the truth.

Despite the fact that what he wanted most at this moment was to dip his head and kiss her again, removing her lips from his had allowed a trickle of sanity to return to his mind. She may be telling the truth about the horse and accepting his job offer, but she was still attempting to hide the presence of the brother.

She shifted, drawing his attention to how she was still wrapped in his arms. She licked her lips, and his senses threatened to slide away once more. He couldn't seem to look away, couldn't help but analyze and measure the rest of her expression to determine what she was thinking.

He could feel her too, could feel that she wasn't trying to pull away any more than he was. One of them needed to end this embrace, and as had been the case his entire life, Aaron could depend on no one aside from himself to do what needed to be done. The effort required to ease away from her was greater than he'd expected.

"I suppose I should be outraged, but I must confess to needing more information so I know to whom to direct my anger."

Aaron didn't turn. He was more interested in Miss Fitzroy's reaction to this moment than in seeing the brother. "The missing Jonas, I presume?"

Sophia winced, ran her teeth over her bottom lip, and nodded as she looked at her brother in the open area of the cottage.

Aaron turned, slowly following her gaze to the man he'd seen in the paddock behind the circus. He was a young man, but he seemed old enough to care for his sister. There was no question of the legitimacy of their claim to be siblings, either—the same shock of red hair, oval-shaped face, slight accent.

Jonas—presumably Mr. Fitzroy—leaned one shoulder against the wall dividing the two rooms. The pose appeared casual, but unless Aaron was of a mind to climb out a window, the other man was effectively blocking the only escape route.

Mr. Fitzroy tilted his head, keeping his gaze levelly connected to Aaron's. "Protocol in this situation is, I believe, to throw a punch or two. As I'm not of a mind to bruise my knuckles and Soph doesn't appear all that traumatized, for now I'll reserve the right to an altercation, if you don't mind."

Aaron could thank his recent exposure to Trent's ridiculousness that he could make any sense of that maze of a sentence. At least, enough to know he could ignore it. "I saw you at the circus."

"Aye, you did."

Assuming these two made logical choices—a dangerous assumption given his experience thus far with Miss Fitzroy—there had to be a reason this man hadn't presented himself as the jockey. "You were injured recently."

"Aye."

"Does it prevent you from riding?"

Mr. Fitzroy's eyebrows slid upward as he glanced at his sister.

"Is there any of that rambling you didn't catch?" Miss Fitzroy mumbled.

"I might have forgotten the last bit, but not the rest of it." He hadn't meant to admit that her kiss had wreaked havoc with his mind, but whatever she'd said right before going up on her toes was long forgotten.

A flush flew across her skin, and though there was no additional room in the stall-like space they were in, she pressed closer to the horse, curling herself in order to fit halfway under the animal's neck.

Now was when she chose to be embarrassed? Not when her

brother revealed himself without any indication of how long he'd been standing there? He'd never been able to understand women, but Miss Fitzroy confounded him far more than the rest of them.

A quiet chuckle came from the brother. "You aren't much of a man about town, are you?"

"Jonas, hush." Miss Fitzroy wrapped an arm around the horse's neck and tried to tilt her chin up in a gesture of confidence. The position looked uncomfortable at best as she twisted her neck to look at his right shoulder. "You have nothing to worry about, Mr. Whitworth. I shall not jog your memory by attacking you again."

Aaron frowned, mentally walking back through the conversation. Goodness, had she assumed he meant he'd forgotten their kiss? He hadn't exactly been an impassive receiver of her attentions. "That isn't what I meant."

"It doesn't matter." She looked at her brother. "What do we do now?"

Mr. Fitzroy blinked. "I don't even know what we've done, but whatever it is, I don't think what happens next is entirely up to us, Soph." He nodded to Aaron. "And yes, until my injury heals, riding isn't an option."

The man seemed to move well enough. If he was lying about an injury, he'd have made it obvious to support his lie. Walking was different from riding, though. "You were working with the circus horses."

Another short nod. "Aye."

The brother was apparently not afflicted with the same loose tongue as his sister.

"I can find you work in a stable. It won't pay much, but the roof won't leak and you'll have an actual bed."

Mr. Fitzroy cleared his throat. "As wonderful as that sounds, perhaps you two could come out of the stall and tell me what's going on?"

Aaron's own face threatened to flush at the reminder that he was still crowding Miss Fitzroy's space. He moved quickly to the center of the room. Miss Fitzroy followed, moving the piece of wood keeping the horse in the stall and allowing the animal to roam the area and nuzzle a pile of hay scraps. "She won. Not everyone is happy about it."

Mr. Fitzroy pushed off the wall. "Well, I am." He wrapped his sister in a hug. "Congratulations, Soph. I knew you could do it."

She smiled and wiped her hands on her skirt as her brother pulled away. "I couldn't sleep last night."

Aaron's mouth fell slightly agape. Of all the things she could have said, all the day's moments she could have shared, and she chose her difficulty sleeping?

"Today was so important and I didn't"—she waved her hands in the air in front of her, as if creating the words by magic—"I was afraid."

Mr. Fitzroy just nodded.

"I thought a walk might help, and as I went by the stable, one of the horses sounded restless. It looked like colic, so I walked him outside. I was sufficiently tired by the time he was ready to settle, but I didn't want to leave him before I was certain he was well again, and I fell asleep in the stall."

She rattled on about her morning, barely taking a breath. Aaron had either been present for or guessed some of it, but other parts—particularly the way Davers's jockey had pressed in on her even more than he'd realized—were new, and he tucked the information away to think on later.

"And then Lord Gliddon came to the stable. I didn't think about how my racing would affect other people, Jonas, but Mr. Barley and Mr. Whitworth might lose their jobs over this. But if I don't work, we won't have enough money to start over, and you won't get better if you don't rest, and—"

Had she forgotten that Aaron was still in the room? He softly cleared his throat. She didn't notice.

"If we go to London, I can perform again. Maybe get a job with Astley's Circus." Her voice wobbled. Aaron's heart seized.

Was she going to cry? "At least Astley's stays in one place and we wouldn't be constantly moving. We could find rooms. Build a life."

"You don't want to live that way," Mr. Fitzroy said, wrapping his arm around her shoulder.

Had they both forgotten he was here?

"We haven't been able to live the way we wanted to for a long time. You said when we lost the riding school that it was more important to live the best we can."

"Hmm, so I did." Mr. Fitzroy glanced in Aaron's direction. "And I think I've let you ramble on long enough to elicit pity, if Mr. Whitworth has any."

Miss Fitzroy blanched and buried her face in her brother's shoulder.

"I've pity enough to want to get you out of this cottage before it falls down around you. We've not had rain in a week, but that won't last. Pack your things and bring the horse. We'll determine what else is to be done later."

There was a part of him that wanted to throw them a bundle of money and tell them to hightail it out of town. They needed more than money, though. No matter how he looked at it, Aaron didn't think he could stay on the fringes this time.

Miss Fitzroy wrapped her arms around her middle. "I've caused you enough issues. I'm not going to invade your life any more than I already have."

Of course she wouldn't make this easy on him. "We had an agreement."

"I'm sorry?" She frowned.

Aaron didn't blame her. He couldn't believe what he was about to say either. "We agreed that you would continue riding for me if you won. Do you mean to leave me without a jockey again?"

"I . . . well . . . but . . ."

While Miss Fitzroy floundered for words, her brother started laughing. He clapped her on the shoulder before turning to gather his meager belongings. "You know, Soph, I think this is the first man you've ever worked for that I like."

Compliments never sat well with Aaron, so he looked around, seeking a change of topic. Carvings covered the room. "Did you do these?"

Mr. Fitzroy nodded as he folded a blanket. "Had to amuse myself somehow."

"They're good."

The other man nodded his thanks and went back to work, leaving Aaron grateful for a normal exchange.

The siblings moved about the cottage, efficiently bundling the few belongings scattered in the room. A tattered Bible and a miniature, along with practical items related to caring for and training horses. At one point, Miss Fitzroy strained to break off part of the table, careful to do it behind her brother's back. He guessed she was saving one of the carvings. He considered offering assistance, but she had been embarrassed enough today, so he kept her brother distracted while she finished.

It didn't take long to load everything on the horse and lead it into the sunshine. Seeing such a majestic animal used as a packhorse hurt Aaron's sensibilities. That the horse's owner had been forced to peddle her skills instead of glory in them seemed a similar plight.

No matter how lofty one's origins, in the end they did what they had to do to survive, even if it meant carrying a bundle of blankets instead of a member of royalty.

Aaron walked ahead of the siblings, giving them a semblance of privacy as they went the long way around town. For now, the fewer people who knew about Mr. Fitzroy and the horse, the better.

Aaron rubbed a hand over his face and glanced back to see Miss Fitzroy talking animatedly to her brother. He didn't see any missing pieces when he looked at her anymore.

Now if he just knew what he was going to do with the picture he saw in front of him.

Twenty-Two

With the relative privacy of a few feet, Sophia held nothing back as she filled her brother in on everything she hadn't already said.

"We prayed for a new start." Jonas nodded ahead to Mr. Whitworth. "Looks like it might be. Just not the one we envisioned." He paused. "God works like that, though. Moves in us in ways we don't understand. He hasn't failed us yet, and I'm going to trust that this is the best start for us, just like He provided a new start the last time we needed one."

Sophia snorted. "You think the circus was the best path for us?"

"Better than scrounging for berries." Jonas shrugged. "Think about it. We're together. We're alive, healthy—well, healthy for the most part. Once this injury heals, I'll be good. Things could be worse."

They could also be a lot better. What was Mr. Whitworth going to do with them? For that matter, where were they going? Every now and then she thought she recognized an area, but given they were walking through the countryside, it could just be that one tree looked similar to another.

Her stomach grumbled, reminding her she still hadn't eaten today. The sun was on its way down as they approached a building she could definitely identify.

Hunger turned to nausea.

"This is Lord Farnsworth's stable," she hissed to Jonas. "Could Lord Gliddon be here? Or the magistrate? What if Mr. Whitworth brought us here to turn us in?"

"You're being nonsensical," Jonas answered. "For one thing, he hasn't had time to plan anything like that. For another, what would he turn you in for? Last time I checked, there were no penalties for not stealing a horse."

She took a deep breath. Jonas was right. He always was.

Still, she didn't breathe easier until Mr. Whitworth passed behind the stable and continued down the lane that extended away from the house. It was little more than a wagon road, with a well-worn path between the ruts.

She wasn't sure what to expect, but the small, well-tended cottage wasn't it. A second building, almost as large as the first, sat behind, the wide door open to reveal two box stalls.

Mr. Whitworth gestured to the back building. "You can put the horse in there."

Jonas took Rhiannon's lead from Sophia. "I'll take care of it."

Sophia wanted to protest, but the events of the day were catching up with her, and she wasn't sure she had the strength to take care of everything.

Unfortunately, not going to the stable meant—what? Entering the cottage?

Apparently. Mr. Whitworth disappeared inside, leaving the door open in silent welcome.

She followed him in, unsure of what she would find. The cottage was a single room divided into sections. To her immediate left was a small cookstove, worktable, and a set of shelves against the wall. A table with four chairs sat in front of it. A large overstuffed sofa and bookshelf were to her right. In the back corner was a bed; the other corner was walled off into what she assumed was a washroom and dressing room.

Mr. Whitworth was at the cookstove, putting a pot of water on the surface and poking at the fire inside before throwing a small log into the growing flame.

He put his hands on his hips and looked around.

The silence was awkward.

The way her grumbling stomach broke the quiet even more so.

Mr. Whitworth quirked a half smile as he sent her a quizzical glance. "The water should boil soon." He set a tin on the table. "Here's tea. I don't have food here, though. I'll go up to the main house to have something brought down for you."

She was in his house. Her invasion of his life was complete. Guilt speared through the hunger. "What are you going to do?"

He rubbed a hand across the back of his neck. "Right now? Nothing." He turned on his heel and strode to the door. He paused halfway out. "Stay here tonight." He gestured toward the bed. "If that doesn't work for you, you know where the stable is."

Then he was gone.

THE KITCHEN SERVANTS looked surprised by his request for a fully laden tray to be left at the door to his cottage as soon as possible, but they didn't question him. Normally he let them in so they could set it on the table, but until he knew what was coming next, he didn't want to advertise the siblings' presence in his home.

Forget his professional reputation. His personal one would be in shambles if it became known that the female jockey was sleeping in his home for the night.

After leaving Trenton Hall, Aaron made his way toward the Heath. Shadow was still at the training yard, and he needed to know the potential repercussions of the race. If Lord Gliddon was right, this was going to be an uncomfortable walk through town.

It started with ugly stares.

Then a yelled insult from a man walking into a tavern.

When he passed the Jockey Club, there was no avoiding it anymore as a group of men called him over. His tainted blood would never be allowed in the building, but they would talk to him in front of the door. He was inclined to ignore them, but the ensuing ruckus wouldn't be worth it. That didn't mean he had to give them any reaction. He would simply let them talk around him.

"Tell me this nonsense is over, Whitworth."

"It's not nonsense. It's a novelty, don't you think?"

"A novelty. Bah. I heard my daughters talking about racing their horses when they go for their ride tomorrow."

"Gliddon said he caught her in his stable. If she steals a horse, being female won't save her."

Aaron gritted his teeth. His usual course of action in these scenarios was to wait them out. Eventually the men would tire of pretending he was part of the conversation and let him go. Since they didn't truly care about his thoughts or opinions, his stating them wouldn't change the conversation in the least.

But now they were questioning the character of a woman who was willing to race. Aaron couldn't remain silent.

"Gentlemen," he said, aiming to keep his voice light and conversational when what he wanted to do was run each of them through with a verbal rapier. Well, maybe not Turner. He seemed to think the whole thing a lark. "What are you more afraid of—having your horse beaten by another with a woman as the rider, or having your women realize they can challenge *you* as well?"

"Are you advocating for more women jockeys, Whitworth?"

No. He couldn't stomach it, but not for the reason some of these men couldn't. He was sure there were plenty of men like him who wouldn't care for the idea for safety reasons and the practicality of how to treat a lady properly in the grimy, sweaty sport. But most of these men simply didn't like the idea that a woman could do anything she wanted.

"I am advocating for Miss Fitzroy," he said. "She has proven her abilities. She shall race in the October Meeting. After that, when tempers have cooled, you can discuss whether you will honor her achievements and what to do about this situation in the future."

Mr. Turner smothered a laugh but couldn't hide his grin. "Well said, Whitworth."

The others were not of the same mind. "I gave you a chance, Whitworth," Mr. Wainbright said. "It took you a while, but we're finally seeing your true breeding."

Aaron's thoughts and feelings had tumbled about enough today, and he did not need these men muddying up his life even more by bringing the insults of London into Newmarket. "Then I shall save you from the tarnish of my presence. Good day."

He departed before they could answer, striding down the street in long steps that ate up the ground but did nothing to calm his mind. He didn't like not knowing his own mind. Didn't like sorting through emotions even more. If he *had* to feel things, he wanted to be able to label them.

He hadn't wanted to like Miss Fitzroy, but she'd made it almost impossible not to. He had to admire her spunk and her dedication to her brother. Her skill on a horse was as good as anyone he'd ever seen. Obviously he found her attractive.

By the time he got to the training yard, where, thankfully, Shadow had been properly seen to, his entire body was vibrating. He needed to decide where he stood on everything without anyone else's input.

He saddled Shadow and swung into the saddle with grim determination. In his experience, there was no better place to think than on the back of a horse.

Sophia eased into wakefulness, feeling far more rested than she had in days, maybe even years.

She tried to roll over and couldn't because she was wedged into the corner of a soft, comfortable sofa. She blinked. A sofa?

Oh yes. Mr. Whitworth's sofa.

It took several wiggles that she was glad no one could witness, but she freed herself from the corner and rose. A light, familiar

190

snore came from the bed. Jonas had tried to get her to take the better sleeping spot last night, but the thought of lying in Mr. Whitworth's bed had felt too strange, especially after that kiss.

She stretched her arms up and lifted onto her toes, enjoying a sense of peace she'd been missing. Despite the worries waiting for her today, she was at least done with the lying and sneaking about.

Leaving Jonas to sleep, she went out to check on Rhiannon. The horse was standing in one of the two boxes, munching happily on hay. Her coat was clean and gleaming, and her mane and tail had been combed through until they lay without a single tangle. Considering Jonas had merely given her a quick brushing along with food and water last night, someone else had been busy.

Perhaps one of the grooms? Who else could it have been? Had Mr. Whitworth sent them, or had they come on their own? Had they known she was occupying Mr. Whitworth's home?

She took a deep breath and pressed a hand to her forehead, trying to shut down her thoughts like she shut up her mouth. It worked. Sort of.

The sky was still pale, with a tinge of the night's greyness at the edge, and a damp chill wrapped around her as she walked along the lane toward Trenton Hall. She passed the main stable and poked her head in long enough to see Shadow resting in one of the stalls, then continued toward the house without a single notion of what she'd do when she got there.

A decorative walled garden sat between the stable and the house. Perhaps she would dally in there while she waited for Mr. Whitworth to make an appearance. She left the gravel drive and stepped across the stretch of manicured lawn. The old stone walls with the creeping green ivy reminded her of the vine-covered home she'd grown up in. Hopefully whoever lived there now had children who could enjoy the romance of the place.

Just as she got to the corner of the garden, the front door of the house slammed, and she instinctively jerked back into hiding. Easing her head around the corner, she saw Mr. Whitworth on the drive, scooping up handfuls of small stones and chucking them one at a time toward a distant post as Lord Farnsworth came down the steps to join him.

The aristocrat looked somewhat ridiculous in riding boots, breeches, and a bright blue dressing gown. He was frowning as he joined his friend. Did he regret standing up to his fiancée's father?

"Blast it, Aaron, it's cold outside. Why can't you come inside? Or better yet, come at a normal hour and join me for breakfast?"

"This is a normal hour," Mr. Whitworth said, his tone lighter than she would have expected based on the agitated way he was throwing rocks. "Still having trouble remembering you're in the country now?"

There was a grumble Sophia couldn't make out, then Lord Farnsworth replied, "Couldn't we at least be inside?"

Mr. Whitworth dropped his remaining rocks and brushed his hands together as he glanced from the house to the drive that led around to the stable. Sophia ducked a little more behind the ivy. "I don't want extra ears."

Heat flared up Sophia's ears.

"What's wrong?" The disgruntlement was gone from Lord Farnsworth's voice, replaced by a clear note of concern. "We discussed everything last night. Or rather, you told me the conclusions you'd come to. I'm in full agreement with them."

"Barley quit this morning."

"What? Why?"

"And the Jockey Club is already at the table. Their discussion is rattling the windows. Given the early hour, I'm inclined to think they've been there all night."

"Not taking your advice to wait until cooler heads can prevail, I take it."

"So it would appear."

Lord Farnsworth fell silent. Sophia bit her lip to keep from demanding Mr. Whitworth get on with it. That couldn't be all he intended to say about it, could it?

Finally, Mr. Whitworth sighed. "I don't blame Mr. Barley, and the Jockey Club can't do much at this point, at least not about the first meeting. That's not what I wanted to talk to you about."

Silence again. Sophia bit her knuckle to keep quiet.

"Whatever I do next is going to affect you and Hudson."

Sophia almost groaned aloud. She'd forgotten about Lord Stildon. How many people's lives had she loused up trying to fix her own? She should go back to the cottage, collect her brother and her horse, and leave.

"I'm not going to fire her," Mr. Whitworth said.

"I should think not. You were rather firm in your proclamation that she would be riding in the meeting."

A sharp inhale filled Sophia's lungs with air and her mouth with leaves. She jerked her head to move her face from the proximity of the vine, but that didn't stop the burn at the back of her eyes. The idea of someone else caring about her fate, of someone other than Jonas supporting her, filled her with a warmth she hadn't known she needed.

She'd make him proud. He wouldn't regret it. She would be the best jockey anyone had ever seen. No one on the Heath would work harder.

Assuming Lord Farnsworth was in support.

"You know I'll support whatever you decide. You have more to lose with this than I do."

Sophia's knees nearly gave way.

Another heavy pause stretched out, and her chest hurt from the breath she was holding. She opened her mouth wide to ease the air from her lungs without gasping. To be discovered now would ruin the goodwill Mr. Whitworth had apparently formed of her.

"I could do the training," Mr. Whitworth said, "but I doubt they'll be inclined to issue me a license, at least not quickly."

"Which means you can't use the training yards or the practice gallops. You could run them from Hawksworth during the public hours."

A snort of laughter preceded Mr. Whitworth's lighter tone. "Kind of you to offer Hudson's resources."

"You can't tell me he wouldn't agree. He had misgivings a week ago, but you brought him around—or rather Miss Fitzroy did. The man is going to marry a fanatical horsewoman. If he didn't support Miss Fitzroy after yesterday's run, his life would be far more difficult than dealing with a questionable connection to you." He chuckled. "Between Miss Snowley and Rebecca, you can believe you have my and Hudson's support."

Sophia sagged against the wall. She'd only briefly met the other two women, but the next time she saw them, she'd be tempted to kiss their feet. The power they held over these men was something she didn't understand, but she was grateful for it.

"My life was so much simpler without any women in it," Mr. Whitworth grumbled, sounding more like himself.

Lord Farnsworth laughed. "Simpler, maybe, but far less interesting."

Twenty-Three

"Explain this to me one more time." The amusement in Oliver's voice was undeniable. He'd finally convinced Aaron to bring the conversation inside, and now he was seated at the head of the breakfast table, chair turned so he could watch while Aaron stared out the window and tried not to pace. "You're saying that while our jockey isn't a horse thief, she does have a horse? And a brother? And they spent the night in your cottage?"

"The horse was in the stable," Aaron grunted, curling his toes in his boots to keep his feet from moving. Pacing was what Oliver resorted to when upset, and more than once Aaron had mocked him for it. He understood the impulse now. Nervous energy could drip from the mind, form a constricting band around the chest, and then swirl down to a man's legs until standing still seemed impossible.

"And now you've sent someone to collect them for breakfast."

"Well, not the horse." Now he was repeating his own jokes.

Aaron turned from the window, the desire to move too compelling to resist, though he refused to pace the room. Instead, he walked the long way around the table to the seat at Oliver's right. The journey wasn't enough to even take the edge off the compulsion.

The Fitzroys would be arriving any moment, and Aaron couldn't let them see his agitation. While he still wanted Miss Fitzroy off

195

his racehorses, he didn't want to scare her into running off to London because she'd caused too many people problems here in Newmarket.

To get his mind off that unsettling thought, he returned to prodding Oliver. Perhaps he could make his friend uncomfortable enough to start pacing and Aaron could join him in a show of support. "I'm glad you find this amusing, since it all connects to your stable."

"Ah-ah." Oliver waved a finger in the air. "My *father's* stable, as you and everyone else has reminded me of late." He shrugged. "In a few weeks, I'm marrying Rebecca. If things get too bad here, we can retreat to the city for the winter."

Maybe Aaron should go to ground in London. He'd always spent part of the year there, though not as much since Graham had married. It would smack of running away, but he could eventually convince himself he was just letting things settle down until he could come back and pretend it had never happened.

Rather like he needed to pretend that kiss had never happened.

Forgetting it was a true impossibility, as every moment of it was etched into his brain like one of her brother's carvings. He shuddered. Best not to think of her brother in relation to kissing Miss Fitzroy.

"Where did you find the brother?" Oliver asked.

"An abandoned cottage."

"Odd."

Aaron shrugged one shoulder and dragged a hand across his face. "Answers were in short supply yesterday, but I intend for them to be the main course this morning."

"And I had Cook prepare a full spread. How foolish."

How long did it take to fetch two people from his cottage? Aaron's fingers itched to drum against the table, so he clasped them together until the knuckles turned white. Drumming fingers was a sitting man's pacing, and he would not give in to it.

Then Oliver clapped his hands, jumped to his feet, and crossed to the door, throwing it open to say something to the footman standing outside the room. After a murmured conversation, he returned to the table and flopped back down in his chair, arms banging against the table.

"Do you know what you need?" Oliver asked.

Aaron gave his friend a wary, side-slanted look. "What?"

"I haven't the slightest idea." The footman returned with paper, ink, and a pen. Oliver continued speaking as he scribbled out a note. "I was hoping you could give me some direction. Since both of us are at a loss, I'm calling in reinforcements."

He folded the note and passed it back to the footman. "Have this delivered to Hawksworth and placed directly into the hand of Lord Stildon immediately."

"We do not need Hudson."

"I've never been the best head in these situations, and since Graham has yet to materialize, Hudson is the next best choice. I haven't known the man long, but you trust him, and since this is your problem, that's good enough for me."

"This isn't *my* problem. It is *our* problem. She's riding your horses."

"All the more reason to invite Hudson. If this is a problem in a professional capacity, he should have a say, don't you think?"

Considering Aaron would have had this meeting without Oliver if there'd been a way to do it, he most certainly did not agree. "I do not need Hudson's assistance."

"Maybe I do," Oliver grumbled. "I've never had to be the solid one on my own before. I do think there's something to the biblical sentiment of having a cord of three strands in your life. I could send for Trent if you'd rather."

"No!" The word rushed out of Aaron's mouth a little too quickly, but the last thing he needed was Trent becoming part of this farce. The man was far too cheerful and entirely too conniving. "If we must invite someone, Hudson will do."

"That's convenient, since I've already sent the missive."

"Miss Fitzroy and Mr. Fitzroy, my lord."

Oliver and Aaron both stood at the butler's announcement. The urge to pace, to move, even to simply fidget with the serviette on the table grew as the reason for his agitation entered the room.

Miss Fitzroy's clothes were the same ones from the day before, and they were wrinkled to the point of possibly being beyond redemption. He'd need to send someone to Meadowland Park to retrieve her belongings. Actually, that would have been the perfect thing to occupy Oliver. If only he'd thought of that five minutes ago.

As the four of them stared at one another, a small line of servants slid through the room, depositing tray after tray on the sideboard. Without a word, they removed themselves, leaving behind the delicious smells of a host of breakfast delights.

Mr. Fitzroy cleared his throat and glanced at the room's occupants. "Given that this is one of life's awkward moments, I do hope you won't mind if I uncouthly help myself to the food." Another glance swept the room before he shrugged and moved toward the sideboard. "My pride has never been as comforting as food, I must say."

A smile tugged at Aaron's mouth. He had wanted to find fault with a man who would hide while his sister trod into danger, but he had to respect someone who stated facts as they were and didn't bother with the consequences.

The clink of serving dishes prodded everyone into movement, likely in the hopes that eating would ease the awkwardness.

Though Mr. Fitzroy had been the first to get his plate, he was the last to approach a chair. After staring grimly at the piece of furniture, he carefully lowered himself into it, wincing as he settled into the seat.

If that was genuine, it was no wonder the man refused to sit on a horse.

"Talk." Aaron poked at his food and took a bite before looking expectantly at the pair on the other side of the table.

"That's a dangerous command to give Sophia."

The brother's dry statement pulled a grin from Aaron before he could stop it. The woman's tongue did like to run away with her. Then he recalled all the unorthodox ways she'd stopped herself from talking, which led to the kiss he was trying not to remember. "Be that as it is, I want to know anything I don't already know."

"I rattled on about most of it last night." Miss Fitzroy's face flamed. Was she too remembering what had stopped the rambling? The embarrassment didn't make her shove food around on her plate in despondency, though. Despite the slump in her shoulders, she ate steadily.

"Perhaps the less jabbery version, then?"

She set her fork down and speared him with her gaze, her cheeks still flushed. "Father died when we were seventeen."

When *they* were seventeen? Not just siblings, but twins?

"Mother passed within the year," she continued in a brisk tone. "No one would hire us to do the horse training Father had done, and we eventually had to sell the house, land, and horses, along with most everything else, to pay his debts. Searching for work took us farther and farther from where we'd grown up."

Mr. Fitzroy set his fork down and placed a hand on his sister's shoulder. "I think I can condense this down to the parts you care about."

"By all means." Aaron stared at Mr. Fitzroy, daring the younger man to be the first to break eye contact.

He didn't. "We left home with the last two horses our father bred and the few mementos that had more value to us than the pawnbroker. Staying together was difficult, but we managed. We left Ireland after being accused of stealing items we'd never even seen before." He gave a wry grin. "Turned out the pawnbroker got those items as well, but he didn't get them from us."

"After that, we joined the circus," Miss Fitzroy chimed in, looking from Oliver to Aaron and back to her plate. "You know the rest."

"That seems rather simple."

"Living it was complicated." Mr. Fitzroy took a bite of ham and chewed it slowly, a contemplative look on his face. "I wonder if that's why people find a lie so much easier to swallow."

"You were injured." Aside from the wince and careful sitting, there seemed nothing wrong with the man.

Mr. Fitzroy nodded. "Broken coccyx, according to the surgeon. Nothing to do but wait it out and try not to sit." He shook his head. "It's rather difficult to work on a horse when you can't sit."

A footman appeared in the doorway. "Lord Farnsworth, Lord Brimsbane has arrived."

Oliver's eyes met Aaron's and widened before he turned to the footman. "Show him in, please." He leaned forward and hissed, "I did *not* send for him."

Aaron ran a hand over his face. This had the potential to get messy.

Brimsbane, otherwise known as Lady Rebecca's brother and Lord Gliddon's heir, strode into the room, taking in all the occupants with a sweeping look. "Rebecca will be relieved to know Miss Fitzroy's whereabouts at least, though it looks like the rest of the story could be far more interesting."

"We're not gossiping about our jockey." Aaron rose to refill his plate. He wasn't hungry anymore, but he needed something to do.

"I would introduce Miss Fitzroy's brother, but I haven't been acquainted myself," Oliver said.

Aaron rolled his eyes as he selected a slice of ham.

Before Brimsbane could respond, Oliver gestured toward the sideboard. "Help yourself to the food, Brimsbane. How is your father this morning?"

"He's not meeting with the magistrate, if that's what you're asking." He sent another quick look toward Miss Fitzroy.

Aaron put down his plate and stepped into Brimsbane's line of vision.

The other man cleared his throat and continued, "That doesn't mean he's happy. Rebecca asked me to offer assistance in finding Miss Fitzroy, since no one has seen her since the race."

"At least you'll be able to brag of your remarkable efficiency when you tell her you found her before breakfast."

Everyone in the room turned their attention to Mr. Fitzroy, who was hunched over his plate, eating without an apparent care in the world and leaving only the disheveled spikes of his red hair visible.

"Sisters don't find efficiency impressive," Miss Fitzroy added quietly, apparently not as bold as her brother but unable to let him have the final word. "He could roll around in the grass and wait until this afternoon to return and it will look like he put in some effort."

The only sound in the room was that of the twins' forks against their plates. No one else moved. Aaron wasn't even sure the aristocrats were breathing, and he needed one of them to say or do something because Aaron couldn't hold his amusement much longer.

"There you have it, Brimsbane," Oliver said as he put his own fork back into action. "I'll support anything you claim when you report back to Rebecca."

Brimsbane sat at the table, his expression giving no indication of whether he saw any humor in the moment. "In exchange, should I refrain from saying I found her in your house?"

The implication quickly dissolved Aaron's laughter. "She *and her brother* are only here for breakfast."

Brimsbane's gaze connected with Aaron's. "She didn't stay the night in my house."

"Nor did she stay in Oliver's."

Most of the time, Aaron tried to remember to use Oliver's title when in mixed company, but in this case, he wanted to knock Brimsbane off balance as much as possible. He really didn't want the other man to guess Miss Fitzroy had been in Aaron's home for the night, even though Aaron had stayed at Oliver's.

The footman came to the doorway again. "Lord Stildon."

Hudson walked in, his brisk steps faltering as he encountered the tension in the room. His attention flew straight to the jockey.

Oliver stood. "Good, good. You're here. You can be part of the solution for our current dilemma."

"I'm at your service." Hudson gave a nod.

"Lord Stildon, may I present Mr. Fitzroy, Miss Fitzroy's brother?" Aaron said with a pointed look in Oliver's direction.

Hudson gave the man a nod, then looked to the jockey. "That was an admirable ride yesterday, Miss Fitzroy. You can count me among your supporters." He looked at Aaron and nodded before taking a seat at the table. "What do you need, Oliver?"

"Mr. Barley quit this morning. Aaron will be training my horses, but he needs a yard to work from. I was hoping he could use Hawksworth."

Hudson tilted his head. "I'm sure we could move some horses around and free up the loose-boxes."

"You're free to move them here if you need to," Oliver offered.

"Hmm. Possibly. The weather's been fine, so we may rotate a few more out to pasture."

Aaron frowned. Hudson had only taken possession of Hawksworth a month ago. He might not know there was another stable. "There's also the old—"

"You won't get the Jockey Club to license you as a trainer in time for the first October Meeting," Brimsbane said.

"I know, but—" Aaron began before being cut off again.

"It will make my father livid," Brimsbane continued, "but my trainer would agree to putting his name down for you if needed. He too was impressed by Miss Fitzroy yesterday."

"Everything is working out nicely, then." Oliver sat back, a wide smile on his face. "This was easier than I thought it would be."

It would seem the night Aaron spent staring up at Oliver's ceiling had been wasted. These titled men could square it all away over breakfast. They didn't even need Aaron.

His chair scraped along the floor as he shoved it back from the table. "As you have everything under control and I am no longer needed, I'll be leaving."

He didn't look around, didn't want to know what they were thinking, didn't want to see the expressions on their faces. He simply headed for the door, intent on retrieving Shadow and getting out of there.

It was obvious that once their lordships got together, his voice would be the last one heard.

"I'll be at Hawksworth," he said as he exited the room. At least if he got there before Hudson, he'd get a word in edgewise.

Twenty-Four

Was there a way for Sophia to become a part of the dining chair? If so, she was ready to do it. She slid lower in her seat, giving serious contemplation to going entirely beneath the table.

Jonas leaned over and whispered, "Chin up, Soph. They think you're amazing enough to defend."

She blinked at him. Was that what that was? Having three men with *Lord* before their name pin hopes upon her was terrifying.

She wanted to go back to being invisible.

Lord Brimsbane stood first. "Send me word if you need my trainer's assistance."

All the noblemen congregated near the door, talking in low voices for a moment before Lord Brimsbane broke away and left.

Lord Stildon glanced over at her and Jonas. "I'll escort you to Hawksworth whenever you're ready."

"Don't worry about your horse yet. She's fine where she is." Lord Farnsworth's smile was likely meant to be reassuring.

Moments later, Sophia and Jonas were leaving Trenton Hall in the company of Lord Stildon. Leaving Rhiannon behind felt strange. Either she or Jonas had been in the mare's vicinity almost her entire life.

The two men talked as the trio walked toward Hawksworth, but all Sophia could do was remember the way Mr. Whitworth had

KRISTI ANN HUNTER

stormed from the breakfast room. He'd tried to interrupt the men multiple times. Had he something to add, or was he trying to tell them she wasn't worth risking their reputations and relationships for? That had certainly been what she'd wanted to say, what she still wanted to say.

Or was he mad at her? It wasn't as if she were at fault for the situation.

Very well, she was completely at fault. If she hadn't come to Newmarket, his well-ordered, meticulous life would be going on just as it always had. Even losing the challenge race wouldn't have caused him this many problems.

A familiar hand landed on her shoulder, and she looked up to find they'd moved from open countryside to fenced pastureland. Lord Stildon walked a few feet ahead, leading his horse.

"You can't change the past," Jonas said softly as he closed a gate behind them.

"Of course not." She tried to brush off her brother's statement, as if the idea that she'd been contemplating, of how things could have been different, was far from what she'd been doing. Her brother knew her too well.

"I'm serious, Soph."

"I know." She tried to leave her response as a simple acknowledgment, but holding back words had never worked for her. "If I hadn't been here . . . If I hadn't come . . . If I hadn't raced . . . What if I'd just taken the money he offered and left?"

"Then he'd have another problem to deal with. He didn't hire you on a lark, Soph." Jonas sighed. "If Father had not taken that last loan. If Mother hadn't gotten sick. If we'd sold the horses and taken service jobs in Ireland." He shrugged. "Our paths could have gone in other directions at a hundred different times, but we have no idea where they eventually would have led. You can't change what path you're on. You can only change what you do next."

As usual, Jonas had managed to go straight to the heart of the matter. No more looking back. She would focus on what was ahead, on working with Mr. Whitworth to do better in next week's races, on riding the best she could. She would make mistakes. Some people wouldn't like her. But all she could do was put one foot in front of the other and make each next step as right as possible.

But what if her best step was not in the direction of Hawksworth?

"Stop," Jonas groaned. "I can hear your head spinning."

She nudged his shoulder. "No you can't."

"Mm-hmm," he said with a nod. "It sounds like a wagon with a broken wheel."

She was laughing as they approached the stable. The last time she was here, she'd stayed outside. The inside was like nothing she'd seen before. Stone walls separated the stalls. A wide, clean aisle led the way to loose-boxes at the end. Large open doors let in air and sunlight. She could only imagine the amount of work it took to maintain a place like this.

Mr. Whitworth stood in the center of a great bustle, in complete command of his domain. He had grooms cleaning out box stalls to make room for the racehorses, grooms heading to the training yard to collect those horses, and grooms saddling mounts. It was a fascinating controlled chaos.

He might not have been able to get out a word in the breakfast room, but no one was interrupting him here.

He gave Sophia no more than a glance before turning back to the thin man next to him. His weathered face was creased and tan, proving he spent more than a little time in the sun, squinting at the horizon.

"Fitzroy!"

Both Sophia and Jonas jumped forward, looking at each other with wide eyes.

Mr. Whitworth groaned and rubbed a hand across his face. "You can't both be Fitzroy." He pointed to Jonas. "Since you'll be working in the stable here, you'll be Fitzroy for now."

206

Jonas frowned in mock surprise. "Does that mean I get to be someone else later?"

Sophia nudged him with her elbow. Now was not the time to be witty. Then again, Jonas always seemed to know how to get the best possible reaction out of people. It had worked for a moment in the breakfast room. Maybe it would work here.

Trying to follow her brother's lead, she chirped, "I suppose that makes me Sophia." Unlike Jonas, she never knew when to leave a quip as the final word, so she also said, "Does that make you Whitworth or Aaron?"

Two dark eyebrows shot up toward the curls that drifted down across his forehead. He didn't dignify her question with an answer, but when he resumed giving orders, he seemed somewhat less perturbed.

"Mr. Knight," he said, turning to the thin man standing beside him, "put Fitzroy to work. He'll be an extra groom while I'm using part of the stable. He can't ride." Mr. Whitworth frowned. "I say, Fitzroy, what can you do?"

"Most of the care work. Anything I don't have to sit for, really." Jonas grinned. "Just pay me no nevermind if I take my break lying down in the hay. It doesn't mean I'm sleeping on the job."

Lord Stildon cleared his throat and stepped away from the door-frame he'd been leaning on. "Speaking of lying down, have you given any thought to where they're sleeping?"

Sophia took a step closer to Jonas. "I don't know if this is the right path," she whispered to her brother.

"We can't exactly change it at the moment."

"We could leave."

"Or . . ." He dragged the word out for several seconds. "We could try staying." He nodded toward Mr. Whitworth, then said in a slightly louder whisper, "I don't think our employer is taking kindly to our whispering."

"No, he isn't," Mr. Whitworth said flatly. "I'll have your word now, Sophia. You won't be running away from this."

She hadn't thought the man could appear any colder, but his entire being conveyed no emotion whatsoever. Even the frustration of moments before was gone.

"I won't leave," she promised softly.

Lord Stildon stepped forward. "I can arrange—"

"Don't you have somewhere you are supposed to be this morning?" Mr. Whitworth interrupted.

"Urgent matters have arisen here."

Mr. Whitworth shook his head. "I don't need you cleaning up my messes."

Sophia's throat tightened. Jonas's heavy squeeze of her shoulder kept the burning in her eyes from becoming hot tears.

Lord Stildon crossed his arms over his chest.

"You are supposed to be meeting with Bianca this morning, are you not?" Mr. Whitworth asked. "The woman you intend to marry?"

"I am."

"Then off you go. I've been solving life's unfair problems since I was born. This one shall be no different."

He'd called her a problem that first day. Somewhere along the line she'd thought—hoped—that she'd risen above that distinction.

Apparently not.

Equinox and Sweet Fleet arrived then, along with a draft horse pulling a cart of equipment. Another flurry of instructions flew from Mr. Whitworth's mouth, and everyone, including Jonas, went to work.

In short order, three horses stood ready to be mounted. Equinox with his sidesaddle, the grey she'd ridden that first day, and Shadow. Jonas gave Sophia a small salute as he passed by, pitchfork in hand.

He was doing his job. Now she would do hers.

She remembered where the mounting block was this time and took Equinox over to it so she could get into the saddle on her own. Mr. Whitworth and a groom with heavy-lidded eyes and a permanent scowl mounted up as well.

Without a word, they rode out to the Heath.

"Since I'm not an official trainer, we can only be on the Heath during the same hours as everyone else," Mr. Whitworth said. "It will be difficult but doable."

"Difficult but doable seems to be our way of life recently." Sophia forced herself to grin at her own joke, hoping to put them back on semi-friendly footing.

Mr. Whitworth's reply was a set of instructions. She was to take Equinox through a shortened version of the brush runs from last week, then a long, straight ride before returning to the stable. "Roger will go with you."

"Oh." His plan was to go back to avoiding her. It was probably for the best, but it still hurt.

His lips pressed into a thin line. "You can tell me how it goes when I return."

Was he coming back this morning? This afternoon? Tomorrow? The lack of emotion and information had her pushing back. "If I'm not at Hawksworth, I'll be at Trenton Hall with Rhiannon."

He didn't respond, so she pushed harder. "Where will you be?"

"Finding you a place to stay." He nodded toward the Heath. "Get going. And keep your back straight on the runs."

Then he rode away, quickly blending in with the other horses and riders scattered across the rolling expanse of grass. She didn't move, staring in the direction he'd disappeared until Roger cleared his throat.

Right. She had training to do. As she readied herself and the horse to go through the paces, her mind was only half on the task at hand. The rest was pondering what she could do to bring back the if not almost-friendly man, at least the one who seemed to care.

WHEN GOD MADE man, He'd said it wasn't good for man to be alone.

Aaron was ready to debate Him on that topic.

In his experience, inviting people into your life only made it complicated. If a person didn't ask anyone for anything, they never had to suffer the pain of being denied. As far as safe strategies went, it was a good one. It also prevented him from having to deal with someone doing things in a way he didn't like or feeling like an obligation to anyone, especially those he considered friends.

He'd grown up knowing that the man who'd provided everything from his shoes to his blanket to his morning toast saw him as nothing but an obligation. It would do him just fine to never thrust himself upon someone like that again.

But Aaron finally had to admit he couldn't solve this on his own, and he had to go to someone other than Graham or Oliver to get assistance. Well, he could have gone to Graham, had he been in the area, but his friend's nomadic existence did not help with the question of where to put Sophia.

There were a lot of angry men in Newmarket at the moment, and while he didn't think any of them intended to do her bodily harm—yet—she needed a place that was safe, secure, and above reproach. Going through his options had been just one of the things keeping him up all night.

Sophia couldn't continue staying in his house. Not even if he publicly moved himself into a hotel in the center of town could he protect her reputation if those lodgings came to light.

Lodging her at Trenton Hall would be even worse. Hudson's house was likewise not an option. Bianca would probably welcome the visitor, but Aaron would have moved her out of the same house as her vile stepmother long ago, had he had the ability. He certainly wasn't putting another woman there.

No matter how many times he ran through his available options, he could only come up with one solution.

He didn't want to do it, but for Sophia, he was going to swallow his pride and discomfort. He had to. He wasn't asking for a large favor, but that didn't make it any easier to ride south to see a man he didn't know well enough to trust fully.

"Ahoy there," called a blond man with a wide smile. He stood outside a large greenhouse, eyes shielded from the sun, as Aaron and Shadow crossed the remaining expanse of lawn between them. "Quite a bit of excitement yesterday."

Aaron dismounted with a nod, gave Shadow a comforting pat on the neck, and then turned. His throat was tight, and he had to swallow twice before he felt like he could talk in a normal voice. "Lord Trent, I'm afraid I need a favor."

Twenty-Five

Aaron braced himself for the smugness of a man who had something someone else needed or the wince of someone who didn't want to be bothered.

He got neither.

Trent clapped a hand on Aaron's shoulder and started walking toward the stable. "What do you need?"

"Uh." Aaron paused to clear his throat. "A room."

"For you?"

"For my jockey."

"Ah." Trent nodded. "Come along. Adelaide usually has a tea set up about now. We'll make arrangements over biscuits."

Even though Aaron had been inside the house several times in the past few weeks, he still hesitated before walking in the door. Trent had been something of a business associate for a couple of years, but in the last month he'd decided Aaron was part of his chosen social circle. Or perhaps Trent had decided Hudson was going to be a close friend and Aaron had simply got caught in the net. The association had then extended to Oliver.

It had all happened at a speed that made Aaron's head spin and his wariness rise. Until Trent did something to negate the fledgling connection, though, Aaron had to accept it for what it appeared to be. That didn't make it easier to follow the man into the casual family sitting room.

"Adelaide, my love," Trent said as he greeted his wife with a squeeze of her shoulder before moving to a wingback chair and waving Aaron forward. "How do you feel about making up the guest room for the young lady who is turning Newmarket on its collective ear?"

"It doesn't need to be a guest room," Aaron said as he sat. "She can sleep with the maids."

"I can't put a guest in with the maids," Lady Adelaide said with a small frown. "When will she be arriving? Aaron, how do you take your tea?"

Numbly, Aaron gave his preferences and accepted the offered cup. Was it really going to be that easy? "I can pay rent for her boarding."

"Nonsense," Trent said. "If she's paying rent, then she's not a guest, and since we've already established her as a guest, rent would make us start over."

"You won't win this argument." Lady Adelaide gave her husband an indulgent grin. "If you push, he'll only make it worse."

"What would be worse?" Aaron asked before he could stop himself.

"I've an unmarried cousin," Trent mused. "Should I invite Robert down for a few weeks?"

Lady Adelaide gave Aaron a pointed look and sipped her tea.

"That's not necessary," Aaron said hastily. A romantic entanglement was the last ingredient this situation needed. Not to mention the idea of her kissing another unsuspecting man made him irrationally angry.

He pushed the thought aside and moved ahead. "There's also a horse. I'm moving Oliver's racers to Hawksworth, so there isn't room to stable the mare there." There was room at Trenton Hall, but he had a feeling Sophia would rather the horse be closer.

"That's not a problem. I don't have any loose-boxes, but we do have empty stalls. I'm assuming the horse is hers and not Gliddon's?" Trent bit into a biscuit.

Aaron almost choked on his tea. "How is it possible that you barely participate in society yet always seem to know everything?"

He shrugged one shoulder and grinned. "People tell me things. I must have one of those faces."

Aaron resisted the urge to roll his eyes, though he made a note to keep Sophia's brother as far away from Trent as possible. Both men thought themselves a little too funny. "The horse is hers."

"Of course it is," Lady Adelaide said. "Where are her things? I'll send a footman to collect them."

"Her brother left a few items in my cottage." Aaron shifted in his chair, realizing he was taking a page from Sophia's book by stating the truth but implying something different. "Her clothes are still at Meadowland Park."

"Oh dear," she murmured. "No matter. I'll pay Lady Rebecca a call and have my maid retrieve them while we're there."

"See? All handled. We've space for the brother as well." Trent turned to his wife with a sudden frown. "I didn't know about the brother."

"Er, I don't think anyone knows about the brother." Though Trent seemed to eat up local gossip with his morning tea, Aaron had never known the man to spread it. "He's going to be working with the racehorses at Hawksworth."

"We'll have a room made up for him anyway, in case he wants to stay over with his sister. I can have my man wake him at whatever horrible hour he has to rise to get to the stable." Trent saluted Aaron with his teacup.

Somewhere Aaron had lost control of this conversation, assuming he'd ever actually had it.

Aaron's head was still spinning when he returned to Hawksworth, only to find Bianca standing in the stable doorway, waiting on him. Aaron did not have it in him to do anything with anyone else today. He shook his head as he handed Shadow's reins to a groom. "I'm not discussing it with you."

Bianca fell into step beside him as he walked into the stable. "I only wanted to ask you which thoroughbred you wanted me to exercise tomorrow. Mr. Knight flatly refuses to allow me to do it without a direct order, and Hudson seems to think it important he not go against your wishes on the matter." She crossed her arms over her chest. "I need you to tell them you've decided I am perfectly capable of riding the retired racehorses."

Aaron kept walking. People were annoying. "No."

"Why not? You let Miss Fitzroy ride in a race."

Aaron rounded on her. "Perhaps I care more about your well-being than Miss Fitzroy's."

As soon as the words came out of his mouth, he knew it was the wrong thing to say. This was why Aaron didn't speak without thinking, why he didn't enter situations without examining all the possible angles. Acting without thought led to error.

Bianca's gasp wasn't quite loud enough to drown out the squeak from his right.

Knowing whom he'd find, he turned his head.

Sophia had looked like a laundry heap before she'd taken Equinox out. Now she resembled a discarded pile of rags. He wasn't at fault for that part, but the stark paleness of her face and the wide pain-filled eyes could be laid at his feet.

Guilt and shame kicked him with the force of an angry plow horse. He ran both hands across his face, pressing hard around his eyes, as if that would somehow release the pressure building inside him. "I didn't mean that."

"I should hope not," Bianca scoffed.

"You"—Aaron pointed a finger at Bianca—"stay out of this. Until you marry the owner of this stable or he absolves me of my responsibilities, which horses you ride is up to me, and I say no." He turned his back on the woman who'd become the annoying younger sister he'd never wanted and faced the woman currently wreaking havoc on his life.

Was there any apology to fix what he just said? Perhaps if he showed her he did indeed care for her well-being. "I have a safe place for both you and Rhiannon to stay. Fitzroy as well, if he's so inclined." He looked about the stable. "I'll take you there when you're ready to leave."

Sophia didn't say anything.

That was all the evidence he needed to prove she hadn't accepted his apology. Though a little distance between them after the events of yesterday was a good thing, this wasn't how he'd wanted to achieve it.

He liked Sophia, and that was dangerous. When he let himself stop thinking about everything that could go wrong, he enjoyed their conversations. He told her things he didn't even tell Graham and Oliver. If he didn't keep a rein on that, it would run away from him and leave him somewhere he'd never wanted to be.

He'd made promises he needed to keep. Just because he'd made them to himself didn't make them any less binding, and he couldn't let the confusion one woman inspired overshadow decisions made over years of sober thinking.

"I've finished the tasks you gave me, and Jonas is brushing Equinox down. Unless you've something else?" She tipped her chin up, and if he wasn't mistaken, it quivered slightly.

He couldn't take her to Trent's house now. She'd spend the afternoon crying into her pillow. If they did more training, maybe she'd realize he believed in her, or at least in her abilities.

"Let's get you another horse saddled. We need to make sure you don't fall off in your next race."

She crossed her arms over her chest. "I didn't fall off in the first one."

"Nor were you secure in the saddle."

Her lips pressed tightly together, but she didn't correct him.

He took her and the horse to one of the fenced-off areas of pasture beyond the stable. This training could quite possibly be an utter disaster, and they didn't need an audience. She knew how to ride but didn't know racing. He knew racing but not the first thing about riding aside.

For the next hour, she did whatever he asked but said nothing in return. There were times in the past week he'd have welcomed the silence, but now he found himself prodding her, trying to break through the wall she'd put in place.

She didn't break. She focused on staying upright in the saddle as the horse ran through a curve. Sometimes she managed well, other times she ended up half bent over the horse's neck. Pieces of his advice were useless since the sidesaddle situated her farther back on the horse's back than he would have been.

After one attempt Sophia winced and she pressed a hand to her side. It was only for a moment, but it was enough to swell Aaron's guilt. If she was in pain, she wouldn't believe he wanted her to remain unhurt. "That's enough for today."

She gave a nod and pulled the horse to a stop. Then she kicked her foot free of the stirrup and jumped down before he could reach her side.

"I was coming to help you," Aaron said with a frown.

"Afraid for my well-being?" Sophia bit out.

"As a matter of fact, yes, I am." He sighed and placed a hand on the horse's neck, moving to the opposite side of the horse so he could see her clearly without invading her space. "I didn't mean what I said, Sophia."

"You always mean what you say." She gave him a sad smile. "That's why you say so little."

"I don't wish you ill."

"That's rather different from not caring if it befalls me."

She had a point, and he hated that he couldn't entirely refute it. He didn't wish any harm to come to Sophia, but part of the reason he'd initially agreed to her racing was because of how little any injury she obtained would affect his life. That first day, he'd have said that was what she'd insisted on risking.

It was different now. A week of getting to know her had changed his mind. Davers's jockey actively trying to unseat her had changed the situation. He'd already promised she would race again, but what if the five or six jockeys she rode against were all bent on making her feel their resentment?

The sun caught her disheveled hair, turning it into a glowing halo about her face. Streaks of red slashed across her cheekbones, likely a sign of her anger and not her recent exertion. Her arms were crossed tightly over her chest. She was the picture of hurt obstinacy, and he didn't like seeing her that way. Especially when the truth was that if she got hurt now, he'd be devastated.

"Do you want to race?"

His quiet question brought her attention swinging toward him. Some of his intentions must have come through, because it wasn't an angry, narrowed gaze that connected with his across the saddle, but a wide-eyed one. Somehow, her brilliant eyes were reflecting the sky, shooting streaks of blue through the green depths.

Thank goodness the horse was between them, because she looked far too similar to the way she'd been right before she'd kissed him. The urge to repeat the experience hit him full force, and he wrapped his hand around the back of the saddle to keep from circling the animal.

Her arms shifted down until she was hugging herself instead of creating an angry shield. When she spoke, her voice was soft, and he had to strain to hear her over the birds and the whistle of the breeze through the grass. "Mr. Notley only kept me on because of Rhiannon. She's been my ticket into a lot of places, but horses get old. They get injured or sick. I can't depend upon her forever." She hugged herself tighter and looked down. "I don't know anything but horses. I need a name to make a living."

If asked, Aaron would have said the same thing about himself. He'd made passable marks in school and could have made a simpler living somewhere else, but working with horses was the only thing that made his life feel fulfilled.

"I don't think Rhiannon was the only reason he kept you." Aaron remembered the act with clarity, and it hadn't been the horse's striking beauty that captured him. "The horses were only amazing because of what you taught them, and you were the one the crowd was enamored with. Did you not like performing?"

She shook her head. "Hated it. All those eyes on you . . ."

Aaron choked out a laugh. "Because no one is looking at you now."

A half grin flashed his way as she lifted her head. "It's different."

"How?" She was still performing impossible-looking feats on the back of a horse while dozens of eyes analyzed her every move for flaws and others lifted her up as some sort of ethereal entertainment.

She ran a hand down the horse's neck. "There's a goal. It's one thing to strive for undeniable success and another for your every action to be an effort to hold their attention."

Her statement sparked a sensation in him that he didn't comprehend. He wasn't sure if he wanted to stop the world so he could slow down and understand what was happening or speed everything up so it would all go away.

Sophia made the choice for him by taking the reins and stepping toward the gate. "You said we're done for the day?"

Since Aaron still held the bridle, the move put them in close proximity. It would take barely any movement at all to lean down and kiss her again.

Acting on that impulse was out of the question. He had decided long ago not to subject any woman to the middling existence he waded through, and he wasn't about to make a habit of kissing a woman he had no intention of marrying.

Dallying with a woman was not an option. Ever. In any way.

He allowed his gaze to connect with hers, and the impact rolled all the way to his toes.

She apparently felt it all the way to her vocal cords, because a sudden outpouring of words tried to make up for two hours of silence in the span of two minutes.

He'd heard it before, her ramblings on the belief that people would take her seriously once she succeeded, that if she did well, they would respect her. What he didn't expect was that this time he was a part of her thought process.

"If I lose, it will reflect directly on you, which is all the more reason I need to do well. Everyone will know you've taken over the training. Though I've heard you talk to Mr. Barley. You make most of the training decisions anyway. I don't know if that's common knowledge. Now anything that happens will be attributed straight to you. People will know they're your ideas."

Panic crawled up his throat. He did not need her thinking about him in connection to her life or how her actions affected him. Could he make the outcome turn out the way she hoped? After the race, could he convince a few people to give her a chance? Maybe.

"Monday we'll run a lap before the official training hours. Remind people you are a serious threat. They'll be watching you differently now."

She nodded. "I won't let you down."

"I'm not worried about that."

"Well, I am. If I cross the finish line clinging to Equinox's neck again, it will look like you couldn't teach me. They won't consider that it might have been because you've never ridden sidesaddle." She tossed him a grin. "Or have you?"

Aaron coughed. He should let go of the horse and step back. He should.

But he didn't. "No, I've never ridden aside. I've balanced a horse through plenty of turns, though."

"One would think I'd excel at anything involving balance, but riding in a race is different from anything my father taught me."

She did what Aaron couldn't, dropping the reins and leading the way back to the gate. As they walked, she chattered about the differences between riding in the circus and running in a race. Interspersed were small bits of information about what her life had been like before.

He found those more fascinating than the equine discussion.

Instead of opening the next gate, she hopped up on the fence.

"See? My balance is spectacular." She put one foot in front of the other and walked along the rail. "When we first joined the show, there was a balance walker. She taught me a few tricks that made standing on Rhiannon's back easier."

Her ramblings had turned to telling happy stories about the circus, and while he was glad to know her time there wasn't all bad, he didn't like how his fascination with listening to her was distracting him from ensuring she stayed safe. If she fell now, the height would be like toppling from the back of a horse. She could hit her head, break a leg, hurt her back.

She hopped from the support down to the crossbeam, and it wobbled beneath her foot. She bent over, arms spinning through the air as she adjusted her balance. That was enough for Aaron. He grabbed her about the waist and lowered her back to the ground.

That was a mistake. His gaze held hers as the sentences tumbling from her mouth stuttered to a halt. Was she thinking about the kiss too? Had she thought about it since then, like he had?

No. He did not need the idea of them both lying awake, staring at the ceiling, pondering what might have been if things had been different. He did not need any part of him wanting to make things different.

She still had one foot hooked on the fence rail, so he held his breath as he pulled her the rest of the way down. Her breath rushed past his ear as he lowered her to find her footing.

Though he knew it was a bad idea, he allowed his eyes to remain fixed on hers, watching the emotions swirl openly across her features. The greedy side of himself enjoyed that he wasn't the only one struggling.

Her lips parted, and she licked them.

His heart pounded and the roar in his ears signaled the threat, as if a charging horse were bearing down on him. In a way, it was. If he didn't find her a better life, she would destroy him. Trample him and every protection he'd built.

He stepped away, fingers trailing lightly from her body. The separation made his heart seize and caused that strange sensation to pierce him once more.

He cleared his throat before he turned, grasped the horse's reins, and flung open the gate to the corral. Without a word, he led the animal through, leaving her to shut the gate behind them. As he headed toward the stable, he assured himself that the last emotion on her face had been relief instead of disappointment.

Twenty-Six

Mr. Whitworth moved quickly toward the stable. Sophia didn't know what to think—didn't know what she *wanted* to think. Normally she talked out her feelings and uncertainties until she understood herself and the world better, but whom would she talk to about this?

It had been a long time since she'd felt the absence of her mother so keenly. It would have been nice to have a more experienced woman explain the way Mr. Whitworth seemed to shift from caring to ambivalent and back again so quickly.

Sophia sighed. Trying to decipher that man was a waste of time. It wasn't as if he was going to become her friend or . . . or . . . well, any sort of permanent part of her life. Right now, she and Jonas needed a future. That was all.

She'd dawdled too much, because Shadow and another horse were already waiting outside the stable when she came around the front. The second horse was beautiful but not a thoroughbred. Somewhat shorter than Shadow and with a sleek red-brown coat, it was a mount any woman would be proud to ride, but given what she'd been on the past few days, it looked, well, it simply looked *less*.

Jonas was standing next to the horse, waiting to help her mount. "This is Midas. I've still got some chores to do here, but Mr. Whitworth said someone would show me where you're staying later."

223

Sophia nodded. "I'll be fine." Her brother looked so happy to have something to do that didn't leave him in pain. Even if she'd been comfortable talking to him about her confused feelings, she wouldn't do it now, not when he was smiling without a trace of tension around his eyes.

He helped her mount, and she gave him a wave before joining Mr. Whitworth. They headed down the drive at an easy walk. Carefully, so as not to cue the horse to turn, she tried to stretch her right leg. Though she was accustomed to riding for hours every day, she'd never spent a week in the aside position.

"You'll be staying at a house south of town," her companion said as they rode across the countryside. "It's far enough from here that you'll be out of sight of those who are less than happy with your presence. It's respectable, so there won't be any rumors." He paused. "It might even dispel a few of the existing ones."

What sort of house could do that? She'd already stayed with an earl. In a way. Of course, his agreeing to her being there might have helped. "They know I'm coming, don't they?"

"You'll be going in through the front door."

"That's not necessary." It sounded rather daunting. "I can come in the side. Or even a parlor window."

And that sentence made no sense whatsoever.

She dropped her head and waited for him to say something. A teasing comment or even a chastisement would be welcome. For a moment in the pasture, it had seemed they were going to return to his finding her equal parts amusing and irritating.

Instead he was once more a blank wall of grumpy apathy. If she started to ramble, how far would she get before he told her to just be quiet? As if deliberate aggravation was a great way to encourage friendship.

Since he seemed to like silence, she did her best to give it to him.

They rode away from the town, past farms and fields. There were a few larger houses out here, but the landscape was dotted with far more modest homes.

Maybe she was staying with a nice farmer. Tension eased from her spine, and she rocked a little easier with the horse's gait. A farmer would be perfect. She could help with the chores, perhaps play with the children.

She was so busy with her imaginary farm family that she almost missed the turn they made onto a drive.

Farmers did not have manicured trees lining the entrance to their homes.

All the ease left Sophia's body, and when the house came into view, she thought she might be ill.

"Don't you know any normal people?" she grumbled.

Mr. Whitworth turned to her, surprise on his face, but before he could say anything, the front door opened and a couple emerged.

Their clothing and confidence left no question as to whether they were the inhabitants of the fine house. "You made it," the man said with a wide smile.

"I have been here before." Mr. Whitworth dismounted, looped his reins over his arm, and approached to help Sophia down.

She did not want a scene like earlier, where she lost every thought in her head as soon as he took her in his arms. On the other hand, she also wanted to make a good impression on her new hosts.

Self-preservation won out. The likelihood of her maintaining the respect of these people was slim, and she had to live with herself far longer than she would live with them. She freed her foot and dropped to the ground.

Mr. Whitworth frowned.

The gentleman at the bottom of the stairs laughed.

The woman shook her head at the man, then sent Sophia a serene smile.

Lady Rebecca had smiled like that. Was there a school where wealthy women went to learn that skill, or was it something they inherited?

Mr. Whitworth sighed and swept his arm out toward the couple.

"Sophia, I would like you to meet Lord Trent Hawthorne and Lady Adelaide." He turned to the couple. "This is Miss Fitzroy."

"How do you do?" Lady Adelaide inclined her head politely.

"Everything is taken care of." Lord Trent rocked forward on his toes, grin still in place, hands clasped lightly behind his back.

Mr. Whitworth's jaw tightened, and the tendons of his neck stood out for a moment before he nodded. "Thank you."

Lady Adelaide frowned. "I'm not sure my maid was able to find everything."

"If she found anything, she found it all." Mr. Whitworth cleared his throat. "We'll put the horses away, then come up to the house."

"Pleasure to have you here," Lord Trent called out as Sophia followed the retreating Mr. Whitworth and his horse. She glanced back to see the man waving as they left, his grin so wide it couldn't possibly be real.

Was she staying with a madman?

Perhaps. But they seemed kind, if a little light in the attic. It was nice of them to at least pretend to be happy she was here. She took a deep breath. Everything would be fine.

She stepped into the stable and every worry dropped away as a familiar white tail, long and silky and perfectly combed, swished at her from one of the stalls. The moment a stable lad took Sophia's reins from her, she rushed to Rhiannon's side, squeezing into the stall beside her beloved horse.

She ran her hands over her smooth coat and hugged her tight. "I'll be able to ride you here," she whispered. "You and me on those open fields. It will be glorious."

Once again she was confused by the man she worked for. Mr. Whitworth had arranged this, for her to be able to see to her horse and her obligations. She'd thought his dark mood was because he was angry with her, and maybe he was, but he'd still cared enough to include her horse in his arrangements. She needed to thank him. And perhaps offer a less frantic apology for the turmoil she'd created in his life over the past week.

226

He joined her in the stall, stepping in just enough to avoid being accidentally kicked by the horse.

"Thank you." Her voice was quiet, though she didn't know if it was an attempt not to disturb the peace of the moment, the reverence of her sincerity, or fear that her gratitude would be rejected.

Mr. Whitworth glanced at her before redirecting his attention back to Rhiannon.

Was that in acknowledgment or rejection? Her gaze dropped to the floor, where a scattering of hay seemed to shine against the dark wood floor. "Also," she said, then swallowed hard and peeked her eyes up in his direction, "I'm sorry."

His face swung toward her once more, and this time his eyes stayed fixed on her. "What for?"

She opened her mouth to verbalize her apology in greater detail, but then she wasn't entirely sure herself. She was simply sorry she'd put him through everything.

He leaned a shoulder on the stall wall and tilted his head. "There are several options, don't you think?"

The breath she'd taken in to voice a more detailed apology rushed out of her mouth in a huff. "Pardon?"

"For you to apologize for. You have a lot of options."

She crossed her arms and lifted her chin to look him in the eye. Just because she'd had the same thought didn't mean he needed to voice it out loud. "There's hardly a pile of transgressions."

"Shall we list them? Just so we're in the same place for this apology."

Her eyes narrowed as she examined his face. Was he . . . teasing her?

"There's tricking me into hiring you in the first place."

Well. Yes. That had started the whole thing. Claiming she had merely taken advantage of an opportunity wouldn't negate the offense.

"One could even surmise you feel the need to apologize for not taking the money I offered you to walk away."

The man definitely appeared to be enjoying this. She fought a smile. Before she could defend herself against that non-iniquity, he held up a hand. "There's nothing wrong with that. I understand why you didn't, but there's still room for regret, all things considered."

He did have a point. But she wouldn't trade the past week's experiences even if she could. "I'm not apologizing for that."

"No?" The teasing glint fell from his eyes. "Perhaps for hiding your brother?"

Guilt weighed down her middle. Being generally apologetic was far preferable to dealing with the specifics. "I was thinking more of apologizing for how difficult I've made your life."

He frowned. "You mean the accusations? The conversations I've had to endure with people who think they get a say in my life? Or the establishment owners who threaten to ban me from the premises?"

Her knees trembled. He'd gone through all that? Because of her? "I—" She had to stop and swallow before she could continue in anything louder than a croak. "I didn't know about all that."

"Good." He lifted one hand and smoothed a stray hair back behind her ear, his dark eyes flicking over to watch the strand before falling back to connect with her own gaze. "Because those are the fault of the people who can't see past the dirt on their own noses. You've plenty of other issues at your feet without picking up theirs."

"Oh." What was she doing again? Oh yes. Apologizing. But not for other people. "I guess I won't apologize for that either, then."

"No, you shouldn't."

They stared at each other, the air thickening around them. He cleared his throat and eased back, leaning his shoulder against the wall again. "There's making my trainer quit."

"He doesn't count among the people making their own decisions?"

He gave her a nod. "Fair point." He looked at the horse, the floor, and then her, eyes serious. "There's also yesterday's kiss to consider."

Of all the things he'd listed, that was probably the one she should apologize for the most. And the one she regretted the least. "There is that."

"But one shouldn't apologize unless they truly regret their actions."

One more thing she *shouldn't* apologize for, then. "Do you regret it?"

That half smile quirked up again. "Do I regret your using my lips to shut your own?" He took a deep breath and blew it out between tight lips. "I should. But I'm finding I don't. I told myself I wasn't going to have anything to do with you aside from the racing."

"But you changed your mind?" she whispered.

"About a minute ago."

"Why?"

"You hugged your horse."

She ran a hand down Rhiannon's neck. "I don't understand."

"I'm not sure I do either. Would it be enough to say I wanted you to be that happy to see me? That I wanted that bright joy directed at me?"

He'd been jealous of her horse? She bit her lip to keep from grinning. She did not want him to think she was laughing at him. Nor did she want him to think kissing strange men was how she normally got out of scrapes. "I've never done that before."

"Hugged your horse?" He chuckled. "Somehow I doubt that."

"No, the . . . the tricking and the . . ." She waved a hand toward his face. "The kissing." She sighed. "I'm not sure why I did it yesterday. I couldn't stop myself—not from talking, not from wanting to tell you more than I should have, not from kissing you. None of it was planned."

"Sophia."

"I'm glad you aren't angry at me. That is, you don't seem angry. At least not at me." She didn't mind if he was angry at other people, particularly those who were deliberately making his life difficult.

"I'll try not to do anything to upset you again. I mean, if you were upset. I don't really know. I can't read you very well."

"Sophia?"

"Yes?"

"You're doing it again."

"I am, aren't I?"

He nodded, relaxing further against the wall, with a small, real smile on his lips.

"I'm very good at rambling. I'm not very good at stopping."

He watched her intently but didn't move. "I've noticed."

Sophia started shaking again, but this time for an entirely different reason. Gone were the fears over apologizing, over disappointing him. Instead, she was terrified she would misunderstand him. Was he inviting her to kiss him again?

Hesitantly, she reached up to cup his cheek. He slid his hand up her free arm until he was copying her position, bracing her cheek with his palm.

She went up on her toes, his face low enough from his leaning against the wall that she didn't have to pull him down. This time the kiss was slow and sweet, lighter than the first one they'd shared.

And most definitely shorter as he broke the contact and stepped away, his face once more unreadable.

Had it been bad? Had he changed his mind?

"They'll have dinner ready at the house." He stepped backward until he was out of the stall. "Are you hungry?"

Dazed, she nodded. He gestured for her to precede him, and she walked outside and toward the house. Lord Trent and Lady Adelaide were seated on the veranda.

"Sophia?" he asked as they crossed the manicured lawn.

"Yes?"

"It's Aaron. But maybe only in private, hmm?"

She was so busy grinning as they climbed the veranda steps that she forgot to be afraid.

230

Twenty-Seven

Aaron hadn't meant to stay for dinner, but even he knew he couldn't dump Sophia on the veranda and leave after sharing that kiss with her in the stable. Especially after giving her permission to use his name.

He had to stay away from her and that horse in confined spaces. Something about the way she cared for Rhiannon like she was family ripped through every defense he had. She'd gotten so much pleasure out of the idea that she'd get to ride Rhiannon again. When was the last time he'd taken that much pleasure in something so small?

He hadn't been lying when he'd said he wanted that joy aimed at himself. Somewhere along the way, everything in his life had become carefully guarded. Even his blunt acknowledgment of his illegitimacy was designed to keep distance between him and other people. Never had he felt delight as strongly as she experienced her happiness, and he'd wanted a glimmer of that splendor for himself.

"Adelaide, I think this is the year we venture out to the courses," Trent said as they passed potatoes around the table.

"You don't normally attend?" Sophia asked.

"Not to watch the races." Trent leaned back in his chair. "I often ride over on race day to get a sweet bun from the baker walking through the crowd. You must try one. Best sweet buns in the world."

Sophia grinned. "I'll have to remember that."

Aaron shouldn't have worried about Sophia feeling comfortable enough to relax and talk to her hosts. Getting people to talk was Trent's specialty. Even Aaron said unintended things around the man.

Trent had taken one look at Sophia and asked if she'd be more comfortable if he and Adelaide rolled about in the hearth before dinner. It was a ludicrous statement that no one should have been able to say without being utterly insulting, but Trent had managed.

It had unleashed the woman he'd encountered on their rides—charming, engaging, personable. That she'd felt obliged to repress that light around him made him feel like a boor. No longer. Even if he was uncomfortable, he'd make sure she felt free to be herself.

Was this giddy tingle and irrational absurdity what Graham and Oliver had endured when they'd met the women who would be their wives? Hudson had been a blind fool when he'd first met Bianca, but perhaps he'd experienced this and not identified it until later?

What should he do about it? If this was the beginning of falling in love, shouldn't Aaron find a way to halt the process? He'd known her a week. While he couldn't deny he enjoyed kissing her, nothing that grew in such a short timespan should be allowed to overthrow thirty-two years of other plans.

Sophia's animated face flew from emotion to emotion as she told a story about a baker trading fresh bread in exchange for getting his child a ride on Rhiannon's back. The silly story about the child's antics should have inspired little more than a roll of Aaron's eyes, but the way she told it inspired a smile. She talked so much that the conversation flowed easily around him without excluding him, despite his lack of participation.

This comfortable familiarity would get in the way of sound thinking if he experienced too much of it. He needed to limit his exposure until he knew what to do.

He didn't want to. When was the last time he'd felt no need to prevaricate? Whenever it was, the moment had certainly included Oliver and Graham, neither of whom was at this table.

It was even possible that this strange feeling swirling in his gut was him being . . . happy.

DINNER HAD BEEN cleared by the time Jonas arrived, so he retreated to the kitchen to eat. Whether by luck or design, he didn't reappear before Aaron took his leave. Sophia alone escorted him out to the veranda.

He'd invited a second kiss, given her permission to use his name. The wonder of it all made her forget how to use her voice.

"You'd no end of stories at the dinner table and now you go mum?"

She blinked up at him, mesmerized by the easy smile. It barely tilted up at the corners, but the way his eyes crinkled made it much more real. He'd done nothing at dinner but eat. What had caused such a change in him?

"I'm afraid I don't know what to say."

He took a deep breath and let it out slowly as he looked out toward the stable. "That's the beauty of it, Sophia. When everything is good with me, you don't have to say anything at all." He brought his dark gaze back to her, stealing her breath with its intensity. "But if there's something you want to say, know that I want to hear it, even if I'm not talking back."

"Why?"

"Because . . ." He ran a hand behind his neck, looking more nervous than upset or uncomfortable. "I've never met anyone like you."

"Is that good?"

"I think it's the only way it could be, because I don't think there *is* anyone else like you."

So many thoughts swirled through her brain—emotions, sensations, impulses that part of her wanted to share—but the words were clouded behind the uncertainty.

"Don't make more of this than it is," Aaron said with a sigh.

Ah, there was the discouragement she'd come to expect from him. The statement should have been negative, but instead it settled Sophia's uncertainty and freed her tongue.

"Are you afraid I'll never leave now that you've shown me a bit of kindness, Aaron?" She grinned up at him.

"Why don't we just see what happens tomorrow, hmm?"

"I can do that."

He nodded, then headed for the stable. He paused on the second step down from the veranda and turned to look at her over his shoulder.

"What?" she asked after he'd stared long enough to make her toes wiggle in her boots.

"I like hearing you say my name."

Of all the things he could have said, that was one she'd least expected. By the time she'd gathered her wits, he was halfway across the lawn.

A rustle of skirts indicated she was no longer alone on the veranda. Lady Adelaide waited until Aaron had disappeared into the stable before saying, "Are you ready to see your room? I know it's late, but I've had them prepare a bath for you. I hate sleeping in travel dust."

Travel dust was a kind way of describing the filth that currently coated Sophia's person. The last two days had been approximately one month long, and she felt like all of it had accumulated on her skin. She'd cleaned half of Suffolk from beneath her fingernails before dinner.

"That would be lovely, thank you." Sophia bit her lip and folded her skirt through her fingers. "If it isn't too much trouble, may I see if one of the maids has a spare night rail?"

"I've already had one laid out on the bed in your room." Lady Adelaide blinked at her, blue eyes looking enormous behind black-rimmed spectacles. "I hope you don't mind my taking the liberty."

She should be embarrassed, but she was suddenly too exhausted to care. "I don't mind."

"Good." Lady Adelaide led the way to the first floor and pointed to a door on her right. "We put your brother in that room. He intended to come back down after cleaning up, but the footman said he found him snoring in the bed when he went to clear the water."

"Understandable." Sophia could imagine how nice a bath had felt after a week in that cottage.

"This is where you'll be staying." Lady Adelaide swung open the door to a room Sophia couldn't have even dreamed about.

Tasteful elegance covered every surface, from the rose-and-cream-colored carpet, to the gold bed with its green canopy, to the brilliant white trim around the two large windows. Two windows!

"I can't stay here," she breathed.

Lady Adelaide frowned. "It's the windows, isn't it? This is my favorite of the guest chambers, but it's the only one that faces east. I assumed you were an early riser because of the riding."

"It's not the windows." Sophia took two steps into the room, reality catching up with her wonder. She twirled about in the middle of the grand room and laughed. "This is the most beautiful room I have ever seen."

Lady Adelaide cleared her throat. "Good. Hopefully that will make up for everything else I did."

Sophia stopped twirling, a smile still spread across her face. She couldn't imagine this woman doing anything awful. She was sweet and demure and everything gentle.

But the grin on the lady's face showed a heretofore unseen impish side. "All that can wait until tomorrow. You must be tired, and your bath is getting cold." She gave a smirk and then froze, her eyes widening. "Goodness, I think my husband might be corrupting me after all. He'll be so proud." She strode toward the door. "I'll send in a maid to assist with your bath and take your clothing to be laundered."

An hour later, Sophia was still confused but clean and wallowing in a cloud that someone had managed to tie to a bed frame. Whatever her hostess had planned no longer mattered. Even before the maids finished tidying up, she was asleep.

IN SOPHIA'S EXPERIENCE, wonderful moments were often followed by terrible days, so she rose the next morning half expecting life to go horribly wrong.

The day decided to pleasantly surprise her.

Her old clothing, cleaned and neatly pressed, sat in hilariously prominent display in the dressing room off the bedchamber. Jonas greeted her at the bottom of the stairs with a tight hug and a grin. Neither of them sported circles beneath their eyes, and no stomachs grumbled in empty protest.

He had to leave before her, but she didn't mind eating by herself before going to the stable. She promised Rhiannon they would go for a ride that afternoon, then mounted Midas for the journey back to Hawksworth.

Aaron took her out to the Heath himself this time, showing off her abilities just as he'd promised. In between practice runs, they rode in comfortable silence, or he would ask for more circus or childhood stories. When she shared something embarrassing, he would tease her good-naturedly.

He never reciprocated with stories of his own, though. Given that a full sentence was a significant occurrence, she wasn't all that surprised. She didn't let it bother her. Much.

Back at the stable, she'd been prepared for the grooms to discourage her from caring for the horse, but they didn't. One of them even told her where he hid the good currycombs. This was the type of unconventional life Sophia could learn to be a part of.

She needed to be careful about getting too attached to any of it.

Aaron had asked her to just see what today brought. So far it had been wonderful, but the day wasn't over yet. One day and then the next. It wouldn't do for her to build castles in the sky over a man she didn't really know.

Perhaps daydreaming up a cottage or two wouldn't hurt, though.

She rode Midas to her new home again, this time without any resentment. Rhiannon was waiting for her, so her mount could have been a pony and she wouldn't have cared.

The veranda was occupied by at least four people. She eyed the figures as she approached the stable. Was she expected to join the guests or avoid them? If she guided her horse a little closer to the terrace, she could see if they acknowledged her or made a point of ignoring her.

A woman with black hair coiled up in a mass of braids and decorated with green and white feathers leaned over the railing. "I say," she called, "are you Miss Fitzroy?"

"Of course that's Miss Fitzroy." Miss Snowley, whom Sophia hadn't truly met but still recognized, came to the railing. "Did you expect another young lady to be strolling about Newmarket in a skirt and trousers? I promise you, I was the first to order a set. The modiste hasn't finished them yet."

"Do let me know if they're comfortable," the first woman said. "I don't see myself wearing anything of the sort, but I am curious."

Lady Adelaide joined the duo at the railing. "Miss Fitzroy, come join us. I'll have a man take your horse to the stable."

Almost before she'd finished speaking, a footman was coming down the steps to meet Sophia. It felt strange, letting someone else take care of her horse while she . . . socialized? She felt off balance as she slowly climbed the stairs.

Lady Adelaide introduced the black-haired woman as Miss Hancock.

"I've heard about you," Miss Hancock said with a sly smile.

Sophia gulped. "I'm sure you have."

"You can do amazing things on the back of a horse. Would it be too much of an imposition to ask for a display before dinner?"

Ah. She was the entertain-everyone-but-still-get-invited-to-dinner sort of guest. She could handle that. "It would be my honor."

"Wonderful." Miss Hancock moved back to the railing. "Will that area do?"

The expanse of lawn beyond the veranda was large and so pristine a gardener must spend a great deal of time on it. "If Lady Adelaide and Lord Trent don't mind, it will do nicely."

Miss Hancock waved a hand through the air. "She won't mind."

Miss Snowley shook her head. "You'll soon find that Harriet doesn't know the meaning of the term *guest*. Or *discretion*."

"All the world's a stage, my dear, and it's amazing how many people will believe you're the lead if you simply act like it."

Sophia laughed, but she wouldn't be pulling Rhiannon out without the permission of the actual owners.

Lord Trent squinted at the area in question. "It's grass. You can't eat it. Might as well have fun on it."

Sophia all but skipped to the stable. Yes, she was going to perform again, but unlike the circus act, this would be a sophisticated display. The kind of demonstration her father had put on.

Rhiannon danced about as Sophia led her out of her stall, as if she were as excited for the opportunity as Sophia was. Horse and rider both sighed as she settled into the saddle. A few muscles protested being astride once more after putting in so many hours in the sidesaddle, but the pain was gone by the time they reached the house.

Her audience had grown while she'd been tacking up her horse. Lord Stildon now stood at Miss Snowley's side. Lord Farnsworth and Lady Rebecca were occupying seats near the top of the stairs. Sophia's heart jumped at seeing them.

A movement behind them revealed Jonas standing near the wall, far back from the crowd, grinning at her. Finally, she shifted her attention to the group standing at the balustrade to see that Aaron had joined them, watching her intently as he swirled the liquid in his glass.

"Show them what you can do," he said quietly, giving a nod toward the lawn.

Because she was nervous and hadn't been on Rhiannon in over a week, she began with a portion of the circus show. As the horse trotted tightly in place, then pranced through a series of tight circles, there was a smattering of polite applause and a few murmurs from the terrace.

She took a deep breath and sent the horse dancing sideways across the lawn. The lateral movements and quick lead changes made Rhiannon appear to be flying. Gasps of pleasure joined the applause.

Then she reached the portion of the routine where she would normally stand on Rhiannon's back. Standing on the horse was purely a trick for the circus, but making the horse stand on her hind legs was a show of skill and elegance.

An enthusiastic response rose as Rhiannon's front hooves lowered back to the ground. Sophia sent the horse into a *passage*, trotting in a circle in such a way that the animal seemed to be moving slower than the rest of the world, suspended in the air without answering to time. Finally, she had the horse bow before the crowd, but this time she bowed as well, without dismounting or handing anyone a rose.

Applause and cheers washed over her. Rhiannon shook her head, making her mane billow about in a soft white cloud. The horse enjoyed the praise as much as Sophia did.

Though it still felt strange to let someone else care for her mount, she allowed one of the stable boys to take the reins before she climbed the stairs to join everyone else.

"You didn't stand," Aaron said in a low voice near her ear.

Hoping he would understand, she answered, "My father didn't teach me that."

Chaos swirled around them as she received so many compliments that she didn't know whom to thank for what. Still, she felt Aaron's silent scrutiny. Then he nodded, took a sip of his drink, and turned to say something to Lord Farnsworth.

Jonas came up and wrapped one arm around her shoulders in a light hug. "This is a fancy dinner we're about to eat. You may want to go change first."

He had washed and donned his Sunday suit. A glance down at her riding ensemble had her wincing. Was she going to have to change every night? They were going to get awfully tired of seeing her one good dress. It was the best she had, though, even if it couldn't begin to measure up to the other ladies' gowns.

As she went up to her room, she fought to hold on to the joy she'd felt being on Rhiannon again. These women were the type she hoped to teach one day. It shouldn't bother her that she would never be one of them.

Twenty-Eight

The following days went much the same. There were always guests at dinner, though the number varied from night to night. The other two jockeys made it back to Newmarket, and though they didn't seem delighted in the new developments, they never protested her presence at morning training. Having someone nearer her stature to watch was helpful, even if they never deigned to speak with her.

She rode Rhiannon every afternoon, though she didn't give more demonstrations. The first October Meeting was closing in, and if the increase of riders on the Heath was anything to go by, the surrounding area was filling up.

Sunday morning was the first break in her happy little haze. Walking with Jonas to church, she couldn't help jumping at every bird call, every snapped twig. It was the first time she'd gone out in public since the challenge race.

St. Mary's was full as she and Jonas slipped in at the last minute. Relief that they might have to leave because of the lack of space was cut short when Aaron called their names. He'd saved them seats in the back corner.

They didn't talk during or even after the service, but she found herself mooning over the encounter all the same. Though Aaron had been at dinner every night, they hadn't been alone since that first evening in her new home.

She probably shouldn't think of it as home. Her temporary quarters?

After church, she and Jonas went to Hawksworth to help with the animals. "At least church is on this side of town and we didn't have to venture too far into Newmarket," Sophia mused as she brushed down one side of a horse while Jonas worked on the other side.

He shot her an unreadable glance. "Enjoying the isolation, are you?"

"I suppose." The hairs aligning with the brush mesmerized her for several strokes. "We've had a lot of people in our lives the past few years who always wanted something from us."

"And you don't feel that way now?"

"Well, no."

Jonas propped his arm on the back of the horse and pinned her with a serious look. "You do realize we work for them, right? We haven't even been here two full weeks yet."

"I know." But it felt so much longer. It felt right. "It's just . . . nice." She moved the brush more vigorously over the horse. "My enjoying the moment isn't harming anything."

He sighed.

She stopped working and forced herself to look Jonas in the eye. "What?"

"I love your dreams and your optimism and, quite frankly, I can't imagine life without them. No matter what life has thrown at us, the fact that you've always seen a brighter place on the horizon has given me more hope than I've ever admitted."

A warm glow spread through Sophia at the compliment, but a spear of dread cut through the middle, because Jonas's statement sounded too much like it was leading to something bigger. Something painful.

"Just this once, though, I need you to recognize the distance between you and that light." He watched her silently, holding her gaze until she was near to trembling. "Promise you'll stay with me in reality this time, Soph. I don't want you to get hurt."

Pain was usually inevitable, but she didn't want him worrying. She wanted him to be as happy and relaxed as she felt, and if that could only happen when he thought she wasn't headed for trouble, she would find a way to lie.

Rolling her eyes and grinning, she resumed working the comb along the horse. "I'm not going to get hurt, Jonas. I'm simply happy. Life is finally making a turn for us. You watch. This time next year, we'll have our own little school. When we go to the market, people will wave instead of glare, and we'll be well on the way to reclaiming our lives."

Jonas didn't answer, but Sophia hadn't expected him to. They both knew dreams were thin and examining them only poked holes. It was much better to just let them be. Some dreams were thinner than others. They would unravel under the act of simply speaking them aloud.

That was why she didn't tell him that at night, when she was snugged down in that heavenly bed and surrounded by tasteful elegance, she would picture their little riding school with its breeding stable and training rings. Only Jonas wasn't alone at the fence. Aaron was there too.

It was all too easy to envision. They could work all day, then return to his cozy little cottage at night, where he would banter and tease with her the way he did with Lord Farnsworth. That dream could hardly be shared with Jonas. She barely acknowledged it herself. There was no substance to support her fantasies, and even a hint that they might come true would have scared her to pieces. She just liked to imagine a better world. It had gotten her through the last six years without any great pain when life went a different way.

As Jonas said, there was always another bright light to look forward to.

This was no different, but Jonas wouldn't understand that. She couldn't blame him. It was taking all she had to believe it herself.

VOICES DRIFTED FROM her room as she approached it that evening. Cautiously, she pushed the door open and poked her head inside.

Lady Adelaide's presence wasn't much of a surprise. She lived there, after all. Her lady's maid, Abigail, was also to be expected, as the woman had, on more than one occasion, offered to do Sophia's hair. Last night she'd nearly begged. Something about playing with curls of fire?

The other two occupants were a little disconcerting. Miss Snowley and Miss Hancock flanked Lady Adelaide, and all of them were grinning at Sophia.

"Is something wrong?" She edged into the room.

"No." Miss Snowley grinned wider. "The first races are two days away. Tomorrow everyone will be nervous and busy, but tonight, we celebrate."

"Come, come." Lady Adelaide waved her toward the dressing room. "Your wash water is ready. Abigail will brush out your hair for you."

When Sophia didn't cross the room fast enough to suit her, Miss Hancock placed a hand on Sophia's back and encouraged speed with a significant push. "Don't dawdle now. We have a surprise, and I get impatient easily."

Curiosity tinged with fear had her washing swiftly. With a borrowed dressing gown wrapped over her good chemise, she returned to the bedroom, where the ladies still waited.

"Before you say anything," Lady Adelaide said as soon as Sophia appeared, "let me tell you that I don't want to hear it."

How did one answer that?

"Voilà!" Miss Hancock sang as she stepped aside and swept an arm toward the bed.

Atop the covers lay an evening gown. A real one. She didn't know enough about fine fabrics to identify what it was made of, but she could appreciate the beauty and uniqueness of the gown.

Long vertical stripes of pink and gold blended around the skirt, while the bodice, which boasted a simple neckline and the same high waistline of the other ladies' gowns, was decorated with three angled rows of shirred fabric.

She twisted her hands into the dressing gown to keep from reaching for the dress. "You can't give me a gown."

"Whyever not?" Miss Hancock *tsk*ed. "It isn't as if the three of us don't have plenty of them."

The frank statement likely wasn't meant as an insult, but that didn't stop Sophia from pulling the wrap more tightly closed to hide the threadbare chemise beneath.

She tilted her chin up, in part to give her fists room to secure the robe's edges together, but also to show these women they couldn't order her about, even if they meant well. "That gown is not cast-off. I'm not the same size as any of you."

"A few inches off the hem and you could wear most anything in my closet." Miss Snowley tilted her head, looked Sophia over, and frowned. "You might have to take the waist in a little as well. My goodness you are tiny."

"Like a faerie?" Sophia asked dryly.

"Yes." Miss Snowley beamed back, unrepentant. "It's a moot discussion anyway. You have to take the dress."

"Why?"

"Because it would be rude not to," Lady Adelaide said.

"Here." Miss Hancock whipped the dress from the bed and held it up in front of Sophia. "The maid took it in this afternoon, using your other gown as a guide. Don't worry, we saved the measurements so we won't have to dig through your clothes next time."

"There won't be a next time." Sophia took a step back to keep from reaching for the dress. All resistance would crumble the moment her hand touched the fabric. "There shouldn't be a this time."

"Too late!" Miss Hancock grinned. "Be glad these other two have more restraint than I do. I wanted to provide the entire outfit right down to the stays. Adelaide said that might be too overwhelming."

Even the idea was too overwhelming. Sophia licked her lips as her fingers released their hold on the wrap. She wanted so badly just to try the dress on. She could see herself in it, the women would be appeased, then she could slip back into her old dress before going down to dinner. That would be enough.

If she pretended this was real, even for an evening, her dreams would gain too much power.

"Very well. I'll put it on."

The women clapped, and in no time at all, Sophia was in the gown and seated at the dressing table with Abigail brushing her hair. She couldn't believe how well it fit.

"This hair is lovely." Abigail twisted a strand and held it up. "See how it catches the light?"

Sophia glanced in the mirror at the three women hovering nearby, offering opinions on hair and accessories. As sweet as it was, it was also disturbing.

Lady Adelaide broke away first. "I leave you in good hands, Miss Fitzroy. I want to save my first look of the total package for when you enter the drawing room."

Instead of following Miss Snowley and Lady Adelaide to the door, Miss Hancock went into the dressing room. She emerged with a tidy bundle of clothing. Sophia's clothing. "I'll take these with me, shall I? Wouldn't want you to get ideas. Not to worry, I'll have them put back as soon as you come downstairs."

Sophia fought to tamp down the panic as the door closed behind the women. Just when she was about to jump up and run after them to retrieve her dress, the door opened and Miss Snowley stepped back inside. "I almost forgot."

She skipped over to the bed and picked up a pair of trousers in the same material as the gown. They weren't as wide legged as Sophia's riding trousers, but there was no denying what they were. "You don't have to wear these, but we didn't know if you'd be more comfortable in them."

"I only wear them when I'm riding," she choked out. Only the hot iron Abigail had wound into her hair kept her from melting to the floor.

"No matter. I'll just leave them here if you want them."

Then she was gone again, and Sophia was alone with the maid, her new dress, and a thick, twisted emotion in her gut. Fear? Excitement? It didn't matter. Whatever it was, she knew the only way to get through this evening was to do exactly what Jonas had asked of her.

Stay here. Stay in the moment. See the distance between reality and the horizon.

For tonight, the dreams had to be left on the pillow where they belonged.

AARON TUGGED AT the sleeve of his jacket. Oliver's jacket, actually, since all Aaron's formal clothes were in London. More evidence that his life wasn't staying in the boxes he'd organized it into. He didn't attend social gatherings in Newmarket, at least none that required full evening kit, but he hadn't been able to tell Trent no when he'd said tonight's dinner would be a celebration of the upcoming races.

Why tonight had to be different from the other dinner gatherings the man had been hosting, Aaron didn't know.

Then Sophia walked into the drawing room.

Every inch of her looked exquisite. Just yesterday she'd been racing him across the Heath, a streak of mud on her cheek, a joyous laugh erupting as the wind pulled locks of hair from her bun. She'd been comforting. Approachable.

Now she looked . . . well, she looked like she belonged in this drawing room far more than he did. Unlike his ill-fitting sleeves, the dress fit every curve to perfection, as if it had been made for her. Guessing whom the dress must have come from, it probably had been.

It made her look perfect. Untouchable.

And yet, she was here only by the grace and invitation of the hosts, just like he was.

The swirl of conflicting ideas and logic made him dizzy. This was why life needed to stay in the little niches he'd carved out. Everything was simpler when he knew where he was, who he needed to be, and what was expected of him.

Nothing had been simple since he'd set his eyes on Sophia Fitzroy.

He crossed the room to offer her a glass of sherry. "You're lovely."

"Thank you." She accepted the glass but shifted it slowly from one hand to the other instead of drinking. "It's strange."

"What is?"

"Being in this room."

"You've been in here every night."

She ran a hand down her skirt. "Not like this."

"Did you not socialize before?"

She shook her head. "My parents attended local assemblies, but I was too young. Then Father died. I've attended a few servant parties since then, and people often celebrate at fairs, but those aren't elaborate gatherings. People don't change clothing before attending."

Aaron took a sip to hide his reaction. These dinners and this party were her first polite entertainments. "I'm beginning to realize my life hasn't been as difficult as I thought."

He hadn't meant to say the musing aloud, but he was glad he had when her fingers stopped dancing along the stem of the glass and the clever smile he'd seen so often the past few days returned. "Do tell. And I mean that. I have to hear all your stories from Lord Trent and Lord Farnsworth."

"They tell them better than I could. I haven't the flair."

For every story his friends shared, Aaron had a matching, far less pleasant tale. Much better for her to hear from someone who hadn't endured the pointed glares, who hadn't pretended not to hear the whispered slanders, who hadn't learned to sew so he could buy his school robes too large because his father refused to replace them if he grew in the middle of the year.

"Where did you grow up?"

He shook his head. "Not here."

"Obviously not here. You aren't even related to Lord Trent."

"I think this estate came with Lady Adelaide."

"Not my point."

"Not mine either." He looked around the room at the elegance and the beauty, the richness of both the people and the surroundings. "I meant I'd rather not tell you here."

She stood a little straighter, her eyes brightening. "But you will tell me?"

His eyes roved her face, and despite the dismal feeling the promise inspired, he couldn't help but absorb some of her excitement. "I'll tell you."

"Good." She lifted the glass to her lips, eyes widening as the drink slid over her tongue.

"First time having sherry?"

She nodded. "First time for a lot of things."

"So I gather."

She fanned her skirt out with one hand. "I don't know what this fabric is, but it's the first time I've felt it. Nor have I ever worn a dress like this."

Aaron glanced down at the gown but didn't give it too much attention. He was already having a difficult time ignoring his easily created excuses to end up in a horse stall with her again. There would be no more kissing unless he changed his mind and embraced the foolish ideas she inspired.

Still, he'd been in enough social situations to know a man could not allow a woman to mention her dress and not receive a compliment. "The dress is pretty." His clumsy attempt made him wince.

"It seems so delicate. I don't want to ruin it."

"How would you ruin it?" He gave the dress another look, taking in the tiny waistline and flowing drape of the gown. "It's not as if you'd wear it down to the stable."

"I think they want me to. There are matching trousers."

Aaron's gaze drifted back toward her legs, even though it shouldn't.

"I'm not wearing them right now," she said, nudging him in the shoulder. "But they made sure I knew they were available. I think I'm tonight's entertainment."

Aaron's brows drew together as he studied her face. The wistful sadness he saw stabbed him in the chest. "That's not how these evenings work."

She gave him a small smile. "I thought you were a hermit. How do you know how dinner parties work?"

Because he had another life in London. "Because this group loves dinner parties."

"So, they don't want me to ride?"

He shrugged. "Ladies tend to exhibit at dinner parties, so you're welcome to if you'd like." He resisted the urge to reach up and loosen his cravat. This conversation was veering into strange territory. "I'm sure Lady Adelaide will play the pianoforte after dinner."

"That seems rather different from a riding exercise."

"Only if you make it different." He swallowed the last bit of his sherry and set the glass aside. "Whenever you ride for them again, do you intend to stand up?"

She frowned. "Why do you want me to?"

"It's impressive."

"It isn't classical."

"Just because your father didn't teach it to you doesn't mean it has no merit. It's part of who you are. You shouldn't have to hide it."

She laughed and shook her head. "That is quite the statement coming from you."

Aaron blinked. "What?"

One slim-fingered hand came up to rest on his arm. "You can't tell me you aren't hiding some of who you are. I should know. I've been looking."

As the twin slashes of red immediately crossed her cheeks, Aaron hid a smile.

"That is to say, I haven't met many people, and you're one of them."

He would not laugh. "Profound."

She sighed. "I'm trying to get to know you."

Aaron couldn't hold the soft laugh in anymore. "Just because I'm quiet doesn't mean I'm hiding. There simply isn't much to learn."

"If you believe that, you're as good at lying to yourself as I am."

Twenty-Nine

The population of Newmarket swelled every year around the October and April Meetings, but this year it seemed to grow more than ever. Since Sophia's first race, people had been pouring into the area. Many were of the higher classes, following the horses because they had a stake in the racing, enjoyed the accompanying social life, or couldn't stay away from the betting.

It made Newmarket feel far too much like London for Aaron's peace of mind. The first of three October Meetings started tomorrow. Twenty-three matches were scheduled to run over the next two days. Aaron had horses in eight of them, but there was only one he was truly concerned about. Tomorrow, Sophia and Equinox were slated for the fourth race.

Standing alone near one of the training gallops, one foot propped on a fence as he watched the competition practice, he could admit, if only to himself, that he was terrified. So many things could go wrong. What if their preparations weren't enough? He'd promised her this race, but he prayed it would be her last. If her jockey career didn't end soon, his heart would give out. He ran a hand over his face. Just twenty-four hours to go.

These days, the training stables felt more like his London club, a place that had only let him in because Oliver and Graham made it a requirement for their own memberships. Before Sophia, he'd been either cautiously accepted or politely ignored at the yards, but now he'd finally rocked the boat enough to overwhelm his skill, record, and reputation.

Glares came his way. Whispered comments made a clearer trail than his footprints, some uttered so loudly they were meant to be overheard.

Fortunately, Aaron had years of experience ignoring such comments. He wasn't about to give them the satisfaction of a reaction.

"Why is he showing his face here?"

"He built up his reputation just to take a swing at his betters."

"One can't really expect true honor from someone with his birth."

Lord Davers, who'd never liked Aaron in the first place, at least had the nerve to speak to him face-to-face. "I'm surprised to see you here, Whitworth."

"There's a race tomorrow. Where else would I be?"

"At Hawksworth, making a mockery of the sport."

"I hold this sport in the highest regard, Lord Davers. To suggest otherwise reveals ignorance of the evidence."

Davers laughed loudly enough to draw the notice of other men in the vicinity. A small crowd gathered. Aaron nearly rolled his eyes. Did they think the two men were going to engage in fisticuffs behind the nearest stable?

"Having a woman in the challenge race was bad enough," Davers sneered.

"You mean the race you lost?" Aaron folded his arms across his chest and allowed a touch of smugness to enter his expression.

"My jockey was flustered at the idea of riding against a woman. He was too much of a gentleman to ride as he should have." He leaned in and said in a low whisper, "I have corrected his assumption."

He shouldn't ask. "What assumption?"

"That every female is worthy of being treated as a lady. It helped to remind him that every man who presents himself as one of good breeding isn't a true gentleman." He raked Aaron over with a judgmental glare. "Sometimes they are just fooling themselves."

Dozens of retorts came into Aaron's head, but none of them would smother the man's inflammatory statements better than silence. Better to be quiet than give his opponent words that could be twisted into another attack.

One of the men in the circle stepped forward. "Stop acting like you were bobbed, Davers. Whitworth may be touched in the head, but he's not a jack-in-the-box. That girl rides better than you or I ever will." He cast a nervous glance Aaron's way. "Not saying I approve of her exactly, but you can't stand there and say she didn't ride to win."

The smug smile on Lord Davers's face slid into a sneer. "It will be a miracle if Newmarket recovers from this blow to its reputation. I wouldn't be surprised if the Jockey Club decides they'll be better off in York."

It was an empty threat, given the amount of land the Jockey Club members had in the area, and the scattering of coughs and tight laughter that filtered through the crowd proved everyone knew it.

Even though Davers no longer had the group on his side, he stepped closer until Aaron could smell the stench of his breath. "There's still time to pull her. I suggest you do. If not, an example will be made."

He stormed off, leaving Aaron's insides more twisted up than ever. Were there plans to harm Sophia? Davers didn't have a horse in the race Sophia was going to run.

That didn't mean the man hadn't gotten to the other jockeys.

Aaron left the stable area and found a spot away from the crowd where he could still watch over the mass of horses and people. Should he pull Sophia from the race? Letting her run had dire possibilities. Pulling her had definite consequences.

But she would be safe.

KRISTI ANN HUNTER

A man approached and joined Aaron at the fence. Aaron ignored him, not even turning his head to see who it was.

"My jockey informed me of a rumored plan to keep your girl from winning."

Aaron glanced sideways at Rigsby. He'd propped one foot on the fence, looking on the horses beyond.

"They may not even let her finish," he continued.

Visions of her being physically pulled from the saddle and trampled by the horses sank claws into his chest. That wouldn't happen. A violation such as that would be too obvious. Too many people would see it, and some would be willing to testify. Aaron forced a deep breath through clenched teeth, allowing the logic to soothe some of the tumultuous emotions.

"Some say you planned this as revenge against those of better birth."

"So I've heard," Aaron said dryly. "It's strange. Usually I'm the only one willing to mention my origins."

Rigsby gave a light laugh and shook his head. "People talk about it plenty when you aren't in the conversation. It's only your face that makes them uncomfortable."

Aaron couldn't help the laugh that sputtered out. It was the sort of thing Graham or Oliver would have said.

Or a brother.

He didn't have the time or energy to examine that thought.

"What are they saying about Miss Fitzroy?" he asked.

"Some say she's made her point and should be done. Others are glad she's riding again since they didn't see her the first time."

Aaron waited. There was more. Her adversaries had been very loud, and it wouldn't take many of them to cause a problem.

Rigsby withstood his silent stare for an admirable amount of time, but then he sighed and said, "Most aren't being that kind."

Aaron felt Sophia's dreams wither. Her hope to win over these people had been fragile to begin with. Even if she did impress

255

them enough to hire her, they would insist upon a fee that was far lower than fair.

"If she weren't riding for me . . ." He couldn't complete the statement, but Rigsby knew what he was saying.

"Maybe." He sighed and ran a hand over his face in a gesture that was familiar enough to make Aaron uncomfortable.

"Look." Rigsby paused. "I'm always going to hear the worst about you. Everyone assumes I hate you, and I've never seen the point of correcting them."

Aaron had to give the man marks for honesty.

"Most of what I get told is what people think I want to hear. My trainer and my jockey are hearing similar things, though. Some think she's trying to catch the eye of an aristocrat with racehorses; others think she's been bribed to throw the race." He shook his head. "There are even a few rumors so unsavory I won't insult her by repeating them, even to you."

"Thank you."

"One man asked me if she was our half sister. I nearly punched him for that one. She's what—twenty-two?"

"Twenty-three," Aaron said. Nearly ten years younger than he was.

"At least Father was unmarried when you were born."

Aaron hadn't thought anything could make him smile right then, but there was something humorous about Rigsby finding that particular charge insulting. "I very much hope she's not related to me in any way," he murmured. "That would be awkward."

Rigsby gave a small smile of his own. "That answers my question about the validity of one rumor."

"Do I need to pull her?"

"It'd be safest." Rigsby shrugged. "Don't know that it's wisest. Some of those jockeys are discussing rather underhanded tactics, but I think they feel safe saying it because they aren't racing against her. She's in the two hundred guinea?"

Aaron nodded.

"I've got a horse in that one as well and a jockey I trust. I can't ask him to throw the race, but he'll keep an eye out for her, try to position his horse between her and some of the others."

"Why are you doing this?"

"Because it's the gentlemanly thing to do. No lady deserves to be treated ill."

"Davers said she wasn't a lady." Of all the insults he'd heard, that one cut him the deepest. Sophia only wanted a chance to do what she loved. No one should be disparaged for that.

Rigsby snorted. "Then perhaps it is Davers's breeding that should be called into question. Sadly, the sport of kings has not enough gentlemen and more than its share of addlepates."

Stepping away from the fence, Rigsby turned to Aaron. "I received your notes on the three properties. Thank you. I'd rather not have it get around that I'm looking for land."

"That would increase the price."

"And get back to Father." He sighed. "When he gets angry, he tightens the purse strings. At the moment, he isn't looking into my spending too carefully. He knows I want land, but he hasn't asked where. I'd like to keep it that way." With a quick nod, Rigsby strode back toward the stables.

Somewhere along the way, his younger half brother had developed an impressive, refined dignity. There was no question he was a gentleman both born and bred.

Things would be different if Sophia were riding for him.

They would be different if Sophia were kissing him.

Aaron frowned and shook his head free of that thought. Things would be different if Sophia were kissing someone *like* him. Someone who had the respectability to go with the manners.

The hope for a future that Aaron had allowed to sprout in Sophia's presence was as substantial as his childhood wish that his father would come back and claim him in truth. Reality had shattered both that dream and him. Hoping for something real with Sophia made him as foolish as the rest of the addlepates in the yard.

No more. He may not be a gentleman, but he still had his wits about him. He'd gone too long thinking he had nothing, but that wasn't true. What little he had could be pooled together to see that Sophia got everything she wanted. A home. A school. Security. And he would make sure all of it was safely away from him.

Thirty

At first Sophia had been upset that she was only running one race, but as morning dawned with a dismal grey that could just as easily turn into rain as brighten into watery sunlight, she was glad. Her legs were going to turn to jelly the moment she no longer had anticipation holding them up.

Never would she have dreamed that turning up that day, defiantly holding aloft Aaron's job offer in desperate hope, would turn into this. There were reports of people sleeping outside last night to ensure a good position from which to watch today's race.

She didn't want to know if that meant they wished her well or ill. Of much greater concern was whether there were any among them who wanted to hire a female riding instructor and horse trainer.

Lord Trent parked his carriage atop the dike near the course she would soon be barreling down. She watched two races from the confines of his vehicle.

All too soon she was slipping out of the carriage, the calls of "Good luck!" from Lord Trent and Lady Adelaide echoing in her ears as she made her way toward Aaron and the horses. Thankfully, she was wrapped in one of Lady Adelaide's coats and a bonnet that was large enough to shield her from any onlookers.

Aaron was waiting with the horses, his attention fixed on her from the moment she came into view until she stood next to him, shucking the coat and bonnet. Without a word, he cupped his hands to give her a leg up. Situating her leg and skirt was as familiar as the horse's height and movement now.

The way Aaron avoided her eyes was new, though. Was he worried?

Should she be worried?

All morning she'd been nervous, excited, maybe even a little frightened, but not concerned. "Aaron," she leaned over to whisper, "is everything all right?"

He kept his head down, rechecking the girth and the squareness of the saddle. "Just be careful. You've never ridden in a field of six before."

The worry she'd been avoiding flooded through her until she was very glad she hadn't accepted Lord Trent's offer of a sweet bun earlier. Now was not the time to be ill. She took deep breaths in through her nose, letting the scents of horse and leather, grass and dirt ground her to the moment.

She lined up Equinox at the starting pole. Though she did her best to position herself on the end because of the sidesaddle, her competitors were not interested in allowing her to do so. At least two of them were giving her unkind looks. One of them sneered as he guided his horse into place on her right.

Moments later, another horse wedged its way between her and the sneering jockey. That rider gave her a nod before facing forward and preparing to race.

At least she wasn't entirely alone out here.

In the stillness before the gun, a moment of clarity cleared the trepidation from her middle.

She did not want to do this.

Equinox and Aaron both deserved for this run to happen, not to mention Lord Farnsworth, but she did not want to do this. As much as she loved the animals, the riding, and showing people the joy to be found on the back of a horse, she did not love racing.

At least not from this position.

It wasn't the same, and she'd been fooling herself that it was. No one was going to see this race and know she could teach them how to high-step a mount through the park and impress their friends.

This race wasn't for her anymore. It was for Aaron. She would not let his reputation be damaged by her inability to think things through.

Resolve in place, she firmed her grip on the reins and adjusted her hold on the whip. Her position in the middle of the field would make it difficult to use, but she didn't want to drop it.

One race. She could do it.

The race started, and Sophia's heart pounded in rhythm with the hooves far beneath her. The energy of the larger group of horses and the enormous crowd rippled over her skin. Sweat beaded on her face and dripped into her eyes before they'd covered the first mile.

She blinked hard and used the back of her wrist to clear the sweat from her forehead as she yelled for Equinox to run.

A jockey in green pressed in on her left. Only years of experience kept her in the saddle as a sharp sting crossed her back.

The man who'd wedged his way in and given her an encouraging nod pulled ahead, and another horse pressed in on her in his place.

Another burn slashed across her leg.

Great heavens, she was getting hit with the other riders' whips.

She tried to maneuver Equinox, find somewhere to go, but short of pulling him up and quitting, there were no options. Her eyes searched the turmoil in front of her, looking for a hole that would allow her to press the horse forward.

Three more stings drove home that this was not an accident caused by the proximity of rushing horses.

She dropped her whip, refusing to allow herself even the temptation of lowering to their level. She regripped the reins and settled deeper into the saddle.

Time to make a way even if there wasn't one.

Praying the horses wouldn't tangle and fall, she steered Equinox to the right, forcing the jockey in blue to either give way or collide with her.

The jockey on her left stayed with her.

Tears were stinging her eyes as they approached the final curve. The way her legs and back were burning, she may never be able to use a whip on a horse again.

Sweat coated her palms until she feared her riding gloves might slip off. Her fingers cramped and spasmed as she gripped the reins tighter and used every method she knew to compel Equinox forward. More speed was her only hope. Even half a length would put her out of the range of those infernal whips.

They rounded the curve, rushing toward the end post. The crowd gave Equinox a burst of motivation, and he surged forward. Sophia nearly cried in relief as she urged him to go even faster.

This was no longer about racing or people's opinions. This was survival.

When the horse crossed the finish line, she wasn't going to pull up. They'd ride straight to the weigh house, and she wasn't getting down until she was back at Hawksworth. Her torturers were behind her as she passed the finish post, so at least she hadn't been last. She rather doubted she'd been first, though it didn't matter. The race was done.

The horses from the previous race were still milling about the weigh house, but no one stopped her from moving to the front of the line. As soon as the horse's weight was recorded, she fled the area. They weren't running at a race pace anymore, but they were certainly going fast enough to make everyone get out of their way.

As the noise of the crowd fell away, she allowed Equinox to slow and her tears to fall. Perhaps she could get the worst of the crying out while she was alone. With any luck, the stable would be empty, with everyone still on the Heath to watch the races.

Instead of jumping from the saddle, she rolled onto her stomach and slid down the horse's side. Her legs gave out, and she crumpled to the gravel drive. A dark sweaty muzzle bumped her face, inspiring a laugh to cut through her falling tears.

"You ran well, Equinox. You deserve a good brushing and an entire trough of oats."

Using the horse for leverage, she managed to get to her feet and limp her way into the stable and down to the farthest box stall.

Without the excitement of the race, the pain of every single blow pulsed all the way to the bone. Her leg was certainly the worst, though she might be sleeping on her stomach for a few days.

She was struggling with the saddle buckles when Jonas arrived, riding Midas right into the stable and up to her stall before dismounting with a wince. He dropped his horse's reins and wrapped his arms around her.

The last of her control broke. She sobbed into his chest and clung hard to his shoulders. Once the surge of emotion subsided, an eerie calm followed. She pulled away from him with a shuddering breath. Callused thumbs wiped her tears away, and she finally looked up into eyes the same green as her own.

"You didn't win."

She couldn't stop the laughter. "I guessed as much. Seeing the tail of another horse for most of the race is a good indicator."

"It looked rough."

"It was nothing like that challenge race. Nothing like running the Heath with the others." She sighed. "They hated me."

"What do you mean?"

She took a step back and looked around the stable. "You can't tell anyone, Jonas. It's done, and chances are no one would believe it was intentional."

"Sophia, what happened?"

"Looking back, I can think of several things I could have done differently, solutions I could have tried. It was a race, though, and all I could think was go forward, go faster. At least two of the other jockeys didn't like me. I think a third was in on it too, but I can't be sure."

"Soph."

She leaned over and pulled up her riding skirt and the trouser leg beneath. "Part of me couldn't believe it was happening. I didn't want to believe anyone could do this." She tugged the fabric higher. "Having trousers beneath the skirt helped, though. Fewer layers would have made it worse."

She finished pulling the skirt and trouser up her leg, exposing her thigh and the scattering of red welts forming on it. "There are some on my lower right leg as well, but these were—"

"What happened?"

The animalistic growl had Sophia snapping her head up and dropping her skirt. Jonas stepped immediately in front of her. Even Equinox skittered sideways.

Aaron stood in the opening of the box stall, staring at her now-covered leg.

"Aaron, I—" Sophia glanced to her brother, realizing she'd just slipped up and called Aaron by name in front of another person, but Jonas wasn't paying her any attention. He was watching Aaron.

"I don't think I want to ride racehorses anymore." Sophia was quite proud of the calmness in her voice. Considering the tension of the moment, calm and steady was a necessity.

Aaron said nothing. Sophia pushed on.

"I might stay in the area, though? Some people must be sympathetic. Maybe they need a maid. Dusting can't be that different from brushing down a horse." The energy building in her needed somewhere to go, so she busied her hands by pulling off her riding gloves and balling them into her fists. "It's realistic, don't you think? Not everyone is meant for grandeur, right? What would the world be—"

The twisted pain Aaron wasn't bothering to hide from his features had Sophia stuffing one of her gloves into her mouth to stop the talking. She was hurting him with every word, exactly the opposite of what she'd intended.

Once she was back in control, she spit the glove to the ground and took a step toward Aaron, hand outstretched.

He spun and stomped from the stable.

Sophia stared at the empty doorway for a long time. A stool appeared at her side and firm hands urged her onto it. Hay rustled and buckles clinked as Jonas saw to Equinox. Still Sophia stared.

Wheels and hooves rattled on the drive outside, and soon people spilled into the stable. Miss Snowley and Lord Stildon were first, with Miss Hancock, Lord Farnsworth, and Lady Rebecca immediately behind them. A man and a woman Sophia didn't recognize entered last, but the man circled the group to join Lord Farnsworth at the front, looked about the stable, and then moved to the stall where Sophia still sat.

"Where is he?" the unknown man asked. His tone wasn't unkind, but Sophia was still reeling from the expression on Aaron's face as he'd departed.

"I . . . I don't know." Sophia's voice barely managed to scrape past the shock clogging her throat.

He'd left her. Was it for good? Was he waiting for her to leave before he came back? She would. She would leave the stable, leave Newmarket, leave the entire county if she had to. He had a life here. Friends, a home, a job he loved.

Jonas's quiet voice slowly broke through her mental ramblings. He was telling the others that Aaron had been here but departed several minutes ago.

The new man pressed his lips into a thin line and turned to Lord Farnsworth. "If he's not here, where would he go?"

Lord Farnsworth frowned. "There's more races. He'll likely be on the Heath."

A throat clearing pulled everyone's attention to the stable door, where Mr. Knight, the wiry head groom of Hawksworth, stood. "Considering he just asked me to see to the start of the rest of his races, I wouldn't count on that."

Thirty-One

Aaron would never get the image of Sophia's leg out of his head no matter how long he lived.

Even though he'd never seen a woman's leg before, he couldn't imagine all of them were that shapely. If it weren't for the welts, he'd have stood there, mesmerized, for ages.

But there had been welts.

A lot of them.

And then her words had slashed him just as effectively.

They'd broken her. He'd broken her.

Nothing was more important than making that right, and he couldn't let anyone convince him otherwise. They would tell him it wasn't his fault, that he shouldn't blame himself.

But he'd known something like that was a possibility, and he'd let her race anyway because she'd have been hurt if he hadn't. And those words? The ones she'd said as she tossed her dreams aside? They'd been his words. He'd put them in her head.

A plan he didn't realize he'd been forming fell into place as he strode away from Hawksworth. He'd ignored it because it meant sending her away and it meant asking for favors. Lots of favors.

She was worth it.

He'd failed her today. And if he stayed in her life, he'd fail her over and over again. Because while he'd never allow anyone to horsewhip her again and would do everything in his power to make sure the men who had done it this time paid for it, there would be nothing he could do about the verbal attacks. The social attacks.

How would she feel when Lady Adelaide had to leave her off the guest list for her larger parties because she was associated with a man like him? When she had her own household and had to carefully time her trips into town so she could shop without derision?

He could give her more money than any of those shopkeepers made in a year, but they would still consider her beneath them because *he* was beneath them. And yet he wasn't. It was a delicate social balance he'd learned to navigate, but how could he ever entertain bringing a wife into it? And what was the point of staying connected to her if he would never let it get to marriage?

He had to move forward alone.

They'd be looking for him soon. When Mr. Knight told them what he'd done, they'd form a search party.

The head groom would do fine for the rest of the meeting. Aaron had given him his notebook with race times, jockeys, horses, and preparation details. The truth was, if the horses and jockeys weren't ready at this point, there was little Aaron could do for them. He'd tried to tell the man it was no different from readying a horse for Lord Stildon.

The groom had coughed. "I'd say it's remarkably different."

"Only if you let it be. I need your help, Mr. Knight."

The words had been difficult to say and, apparently, difficult to hear, because Mr. Knight's eyes had widened and he'd responded with a silent nod.

Aaron hadn't waited around for more questions. He didn't have any answers anyway.

He checked his pocket watch. The mail coach would leave for London in four hours. That was enough time. Possibly too much time, but he could avoid his friends.

None of them would expect him to run off to London, but he would.

None of them would expect him to call in every favor he could, but he was going to do that too. He would give Sophia something as close to her dream as he could, and he wouldn't allow himself to see her again until it was complete.

If he did, he might convince himself that a life with him wouldn't be so bad.

He scoffed. Look what had happened with that logic this morning. He had no doubt she'd have hidden her leg from him if she could. He didn't want to have to wonder if she was hiding wounds on her soul.

Best to step out of her life now.

He bought a ticket for the mail coach, then a stack of paper from the innkeeper. He methodically worked through all the necessary steps as he wrote note after note, marking each one with a time and date to be delivered.

Coins in the innkeeper's palm ensured they would be delivered as requested. Timing was important if everything was going to go right. If anyone got their note too early, it would give them time to ruin everything by trying to convince him to change his mind.

Even worse, they might succeed.

THE DISCUSSION OF where Aaron had gone and what he might be doing swirled around her, and Sophia wanted to be anywhere other than that stall. She'd even rather be doing another circus show.

Miss Hancock had finally stepped in and wrapped an arm around Sophia's shoulder, guiding her out of the stall and past the hovering group of concerned aristocrats. "Since you are already home, Stildon, I'm borrowing your curricle."

If Lord Stildon answered, Sophia didn't hear him. She was too thankful to be out of there.

Miss Hancock drove the curricle with an ease Sophia envied. She'd never been able to drive. Normally Sophia fought feelings of jealousy, but right now she embraced them. Anything to ward off the numbness lurking at the edge of her mind.

They returned to Lady Adelaide's, and Miss Hancock had a hot bath prepared. Sophia stayed in it until the water turned frigid. While she was soaking, Lady Adelaide returned and insisted on calling for a doctor, though in the interest of privacy, she sent the footman to fetch one from Cheveley instead of Newmarket.

There wasn't much the doctor could do aside from bandage the strikes that were bleeding and suggest she rest. Because the perfect thing for her to do right now was lie around and think over every minute of the day and wonder what on earth had happened.

Maybe Lady Adelaide could recommend a good book.

After the doctor left, Sophia was tucked into that enormous cloud of a bed and a tray of food was brought in. Miss Hancock accompanied the meal and proceeded to distract her with story after story. Half of them couldn't possibly be true, but Sophia didn't care.

Miss Hancock was the only daughter of the only son of a wealthy businessman. The sum she'd inherited from her grandfather meant she could travel the world and never marry if that was her wish. According to her tales, plenty of men sought to change her mind, but a grand heiress with complete independence was a hard woman to tie down.

Sophia was just thankful the woman didn't mind carrying the conversation by herself. As fascinating as her stories were, responding to them was outside Sophia's capabilities. The way she saw it, her only task was to maintain her composure while deciding what to do next.

She fell asleep listening to Miss Hancock speak of ice skating in Russia.

AFTER AN INTERMINABLE wait, Aaron climbed aboard the mail coach. As much as he would prefer to ride Shadow to London, it would take too long. The coach would drive through the night, changing horses and passing tolls.

It wasn't as if he intended to stay in London more than a few days. He'd be too busy to ride in Hyde Park anyway.

Sleep came in fits and bursts, and exhaustion rode him hard by the time he exited the coach at a London inn. Rest could come later. First, he had to see to the most important part of his plan.

He took a hack to a perfume store on Bond Street and climbed the stairs to the set of rooms he rented above the shop. He paid his landlord's daughter to keep it clean and ready for whenever he came to town. It appeared she'd been doing an excellent job. The only dust and dirt in the place was what came off him as he shed his travel clothes and cleaned himself up.

Though the room felt fresh, the clothes he took from the armoire were rough and stiff, the boot leather creaking from lack of proper care. It all felt ill-fitting and out of place.

Rather like him.

Dressed and clean, he set out across Mayfair to a house he'd been to countless times.

Never without Graham, though.

Standing on the street, he looked up at the building, hoping he could trust the assurance he'd been given that this was the one place in London that would always grant him entrance. Would they still mean it when Graham wasn't in residence? Even more important, once he was inside, would they want to help him?

Graham's parents had always treated Aaron well, but Lord Grableton was still an earl. The idea of walking up those stairs and asking to see him rather than his son was daunting.

The door opened, and the butler appeared. He cleared his throat. "Lord Grableton wanted me to see if you intended to stand on the street all day." The man held out a coin. "If you do, please purchase a copy of *Sporting Magazine* when the lad comes by."

Aaron shook his head and climbed the stairs. "I don't mind getting a paper, but perhaps I could find the lad after I've completed my business."

"That shouldn't be a problem, sir," the butler said, face devoid of any judgment. "He doesn't come by until tomorrow morning. This way, please."

To Aaron's amazement, he was chuckling as he followed the servant. Everything seemed possible in this house. If a miracle could happen for him, it would happen here.

Lord Grableton stood and shook Aaron's hand as he entered the drawing room. "Nice of you to join us."

"Grableton, be nice." Lady Grableton smiled at Aaron. "Do sit down. I've rung for tea, so it should be here momentarily. Is this a simple visit, or have you business with Lord Grableton?"

Aaron lowered himself to the settee. "Actually, my lady, I needed to speak with you." He took a deep breath and pushed on. These words were for Sophia. He could get them out. "I need a favor."

When Sophia woke, the sun was streaming in the window, and the chair Miss Hancock had occupied had been replaced by a chaise in which Jonas lounged. Sophia shoved her hair out of her face and sat up with a small wince as every muscle in her body announced its displeasure. "What time is it?"

"You might want to start by asking what day it is."

Sophia blinked at her brother. "I slept more than a day?"

"No, but it isn't the day you fell asleep anymore." He frowned. "I suppose that's normally the case when one goes to sleep, though." He shrugged. "We just don't usually start at five in the afternoon."

Sophia blinked again, not yet awake enough to follow his thoughts.

He sighed. "Last I looked it was almost eleven." He stood and crossed to the bellpull Sophia hadn't had the nerve to use yet. "They told me to pull it when you woke and someone would bring you a breakfast tray."

Considering Jonas's face when he performed the task, he was as comfortable with the idea of summoning a servant as she was.

He pulled his hand away after yanking the cord and wiped it on his trousers, drawing a giggle from Sophia.

"I suppose they need those in a house such as this one. Otherwise, you'd spend your whole day running about finding people." She enjoyed the feeling of a smile on her face. It seemed like ages since she'd worn one. Was it just two days ago that she'd been thinking how nice it was that she and Jonas might not be on their own anymore, that perhaps they could stop living out of a knapsack?

"How do you feel?" Jonas asked.

"Sore. Surprisingly tired. I shouldn't want to go back to sleep, but the idea of eating and curling back under these blankets is appealing."

"You might as well." He frowned at the windows. "I could get my hands on a ladder if you fancy an escape. Otherwise, they won't allow you two steps past the door until you're sufficiently healed."

Sophia looked about the room, searching for something to keep her awake until the food arrived. A sketchpad and pencil sat on the table beside the bed. "Yours?"

He nodded, looking at the sketchbook as if he wasn't sure where it had come from. "I got paid. It seemed like we were going to be here awhile."

Now Sophia wanted to burrow under the covers for a different reason. He'd turned down her offer to buy him a sketchpad before because they would need the money later. He had cautioned Sophia not to dream too big, but it would seem he too had felt the security of the past week.

"Can I see?"

He grabbed the sketchbook and climbed onto bed with her. The breakfast tray arrived, and they chatted as she ate and admired his drawings.

Her energy bolstered by the food, she climbed out of bed and walked around the room. They even ventured to the library to select a book. The house was quiet around them, and the house-keeper said everyone was out.

"Probably still trying to locate Mr. Whitworth," Jonas said.

A day later and they still didn't know where he was? Worry for him made Sophia forget, at least temporarily, that she was concerned for her own future. "How are today's races going?"

"One win for Lord Stildon yesterday and another for Lord Farnsworth this morning."

And because of her, Aaron wasn't here to celebrate.

ANOTHER TRAY WAS delivered that evening, and if the other occupants had returned, no one saw fit to tell her.

Jonas settled onto the bed with her again to show her the rest of the pictures he'd been working on. He turned the page to a sketch of her riding a galloping Equinox. Her hair was a mess and her face determined.

The image sent a variety of feelings spiraling through her. Pride. Despair. Regret. Anger.

She traced the sketch lightly with her fingers. The horse seemed ready to fly off the end of the page. "Is that really what I looked like?"

He shrugged one shoulder. "I couldn't see the details, but this was the heart of it." He closed the notebook and kissed her on top of her head. "We're going to make it through this, Soph. We don't have to run this time. We have time to plan. Lord Stildon says I have the job as groom for as long as I want it, and I think if you try to leave before the week is out, Miss Hancock will personally tie you to the bed."

Sophia grinned. "She is rather opinionated."

"That's one word for it."

"I don't think I could stay in bed for a week."

"Maybe not, but if you want to go back to sleep now, I say do it."

Though she was sore and tired, she wasn't certain she could fall asleep with the thoughts currently churning through her mind. "Will you draw? I like to watch you."

"I suppose that would be boring enough to put someone out." She laughed and snuggled into the pillows.

Jonas flipped the book open, and the pencil slid over the page, the lines of the Heath becoming apparent. "Rest now, Soph, and cast your worries upon God. He can hold them while you sleep, and when you wake, we'll ask Him what we should do."

"Sounds simple."

"Sometimes the answers are simple. It's doing them that gets complicated." More quick lines became a crowd of people.

As Sophia's eyes closed, she prayed God would take care of her and her brother one more time and that somehow the answer would be waiting when she woke.

She didn't expect that answer to take the shape of three intent-looking women.

Thirty-Two

"Oh good," Lady Adelaide said with a sigh. "You're awake."

"They weren't going to wait much longer," Miss Snowley added.

Miss Hancock crossed her arms. "They will wait as long as they have to. You two might have reason not to fluster their feathers, but I am perfectly happy to tell them to rest their tails."

Sophia shook her head. "What is going on?"

The curtains had been pulled across the windows, giving her no indication of the time of day. The only light came from two lanterns on a table across the room.

It made the women look like specters of doom.

"The men are downstairs," Lady Adelaide said. "They would like to see you."

Men. Did that include Aaron? She swallowed and looked from one woman to the next. They'd have told her if he'd come back, wouldn't they?

Feeling fully rested and more than ready to be somewhere other than bed, not to mention anxious to find out what the women weren't telling her, Sophia flung aside the covers and rose. She crossed to the window and pulled back the curtain to reveal the early edges of dawn. A common time to rise when she'd been meeting Aaron on the Heath, but people didn't come calling at this hour unless it was an emergency.

275

She turned to see Miss Snowley holding up a garment. "This is for you."

It was a riding habit. A normal one. With a green jacket and a long red skirt. "What . . . why?"

Miss Hancock took the dress and pressed it into Sophia's hands. "Because there's a drawing room full of men down there, and if you go in feeling polished and put together, it will be harder to pick you apart."

"I hardly think they mean her harm, Harriet," Lady Adelaide said gently.

"They don't need to do a thing when she's capable of shredding herself on her own." Miss Hancock frowned. "This is for her, not them."

As much as Sophia wanted to deny it, Miss Hancock's claim had a nugget of truth to it. Her normal clothing reminded her often that she was different and at somewhat of a disadvantage in life. Perhaps a nicer dress would allow her to better fake composure.

She took the edge of the soft wool skirt and fanned it out. This dress inspired more excitement than the evening gown. "It's lovely."

"And you will look lovely in it." In short order Abigail was summoned and the ladies took their leave, telling her to come down whenever she was ready. Twenty minutes later, even the elegant riding habit with its pinned-up skirt and wide shoulders wasn't enough to bolster Sophia's confidence. She stood at the drawing room door, staring at the portal until a maid cleared her throat.

"Beg pardon, miss, but are you going in? I need to deliver this tea tray."

"Right." Sophia swallowed. "Yes." She preceded the woman into the room, cheeks flaming.

As the women had said, the drawing room was full of people. Lord Farnsworth stepped away from a group of men clustered by the window. "You look well, Miss Fitzroy."

"I am much improved, thank you."

"Good." He gestured to a sofa. "Have a seat, if you will. We were hoping you might remember more. Perhaps Aaron said something in the past two weeks to indicate where he went?"

"He didn't do much talking," Sophia admitted. "Just a lot of staring and frowning."

"He does tend to do that," said the stranger who'd spoken at the stable.

Introductions were made, identifying the man as Lord Wharton, whom Aaron had mentioned as Graham in the rare times he'd discussed his travel or school days.

His wife sat on a settee beside Lady Rebecca.

Knowing who everyone was didn't make the scene less intimidating. She fleetingly wished Jonas was there to support her but then was glad he was absent. This conversation could go many ways, and though Jonas was mild mannered compared to other men, he wouldn't hesitate to throw aside his new job and defend her.

Not that she thought anyone here meant her harm, but their loyalty was—and should be—with Aaron. She licked her lips. "I'm sorry. I've nothing to add. The only place I know of is his cottage, and I'm assuming you've checked there."

The potential implications of her knowing where his home was entered her mind too late to stop the sentence. Embarrassment heated her cheeks, but no one else seemed to care. They'd all moved on to other possibilities.

Lord Farnsworth started pacing. "He wouldn't have gone to his rooms in London, would he?"

Lord Wharton leaned on the back of a chair, his head turning to follow his friend. "I've never known him to go without at least one of us being in Town."

Aaron had rooms in London? As in a residence he paid for all the time but only used occasionally? Wasn't that expensive? While his cottage was cozy and comfortable, it was hardly the abode of a man who could afford to keep rooms in another city, much less London.

Did she know him at all?

Lady Adelaide stepped forward. "Breakfast has been laid out in the dining room. Perhaps we could move this conversation there?"

Lady Wharton pushed off the settee and wrapped an arm around her rounded middle. "We would certainly not mind eating."

Her husband coughed out a laugh. "You never mind eating."

"It's your child's fault, you know."

"I do." Lord Wharton hugged his wife to his side and kissed her on the head. "I also know everything is going to be that poor child's fault for at least the next ten years."

Lady Wharton sniffed but didn't deny the claim.

Tension flowed beneath the civility of food and conversation. Once in a while the talk would turn to speculation of Aaron's whereabouts. Inevitably, someone would comment that the man had been taking care of himself for years and everyone's concern was needless. That it was someone different pointing it out each time amused Sophia even as it worried her.

Breakfast was interrupted by the butler stepping in to address Lord Trent. "My lord, there is a lad here who says he has an urgent message that must be delivered straight into the recipient's hand."

Lord Trent frowned and started to rise.

The butler cleared his throat. "The letter is not for you, sir. It's for Miss Fitzroy."

Every eye in the room swung toward Sophia.

"Is it the boy from the inn?" Miss Snowley asked.

"Yes, miss."

"Finally," she said on a sigh, exchanging glances with Miss Hancock. "You might as well send him in. I'm guessing he has more than one letter to deliver."

"Why would you think that?" Lord Wharton asked.

"Because Aaron sent me a letter before he left town and said it would make more sense in a day or two. I would surmise it's time for the rest of the puzzle pieces to be placed."

A beat of silence preceded the ruckus of voices.

Miss Snowley crossed her arms and lifted her chin in the air, looking entirely unrepentant about remaining silent. Miss Hancock beamed, glancing about as if they were putting on the best show ever.

Lord Trent wore an expression of similar amusement. After a few moments of chaos, he lifted his hand, and the room stumbled into a tense restraint. He nodded to the butler. "Send the boy in but give us a minute first."

The servant departed with a nod.

Lord Wharton was the first to speak. "Why didn't you tell anyone?"

"Because Aaron asked me not to," Miss Snowley said. "Pleasant as you all seem to be, I've known him a sight longer than I've known any of you."

Sophia had to applaud that reason, but why would Aaron contact no one other than Miss Snowley?

Sophia glanced at Lord Stildon to see if he was battling the same frisson of jealousy she was.

"Besides," Miss Snowley continued, "I did tell someone. I told Harriet."

Miss Hancock smiled. "Of course you contacted me. This lot wouldn't have been the least bit of help."

"What did he ask you to do?" Lord Stildon asked.

"Pack a trunk."

He laid his fork down slowly. "Are you traveling?"

"I didn't pack it for me."

The butler showed the boy in. His wide eyes looked around the table before he pulled out a handful of folded letters. "Blimey, are you all here?"

"Perhaps you should start with Miss Fitzroy's letter and then go through the stack?" Miss Snowley suggested.

The boy nodded. "I'm supposed to put it directly in her hand." He swallowed and eased farther into the room. "This one's for you, Miss Fitzroy."

"Thank you." Sophia bit her lip as she reached out to accept it. "I'm afraid I haven't any coin—"

"I'm not supposed to take one even if you do," the boy said in a rush. "Mr. Whitworth took care of everything."

"So it would seem." Sophia opened the note with more than a little trepidation. She mumbled to herself, "Aaron, what did you do?"

The letter was short, but the ache it brought was enormous.

Dear Miss Fitzroy,

The formality of the greeting alone brought tears to her eyes.

Despite your performance, I'm afraid tying your introduction to me has made it impossible for you to gain the respect your abilities deserve. I cannot let you throw away your passion when you deserve so much more.

Mrs. Carlton's School for Girls is in need of a riding instructor. You'll start as soon as you can get to London. They have one of the finest reputations in England, and you will only add to the quality of lady they turn out.

Don't worry about logistics. The boy from the inn has other letters to deliver once he's given you this express. Those letters should arrange everything you need. It may take a day or two for it all to come together, but I trust everything will happen.

Once your brother is healed, I'll help him find a job near you. Perhaps he can even work in the school's stable.

You deserve your dreams, Sophia.

He hadn't signed it, but it was clearly from Aaron. She looked up to find everyone staring at her. Some held open letters of their own.

Miss Snowley cleared her throat. "There's a trunk waiting for you. It isn't much. A few of my old riding habits and a couple of dresses, including the one you're wearing. Six in total, I believe. And boots."

That was twice her current wardrobe. Sophia swallowed.

"Harriet and I spent yesterday altering them according to the measurements she took last time."

Sophia's grip tightened, causing the paper in her hand to crinkle. How was she to respond to such generosity?

Lord Farnsworth held up a note. "I'm to pay your way to London on the mail coach, but he doesn't say why." He looked to Lady Rebecca. "What does yours say?"

"That he'll be back in Newmarket in time for the wedding but understands if I would rather he not attend." She looked up at her fiancé and frowned. "Apparently he'll come up with an excuse so that you don't have to know I was uncomfortable with his presence." She scoffed. "As if we would even be getting married if not for him."

"You know," Miss Hancock mused, "I think that's the first time I've seen you do anything other than smile."

Lady Rebecca's face went blank, and then she looked at Lord Farnsworth. "My goodness. What have you done to me?"

"Loved you just as you are, my dear."

She answered with a soft, gentle smile and folded her hands in her lap.

Lord Trent waved his paper in the air. "My request is easy. I get to stable that beautiful horse until Miss Fitzroy makes other arrangements."

"Well." Miss Hancock threw her letter onto the table. "He asked me to stay out of everything and not interfere."

A round of suppressed laughter was the only response.

Lord Wharton frowned. "I'm rather miffed I didn't get a letter." He gave a pointed frown to Miss Snowley. "He's known me far longer than the rest of you."

"He didn't know we'd be here," his wife said. "It's possible your letter is arriving at the solicitor's now."

"I hope so." He nodded toward Sophia. "What does your letter say?"

"I'd imagine it's far more personal than ours," Miss Snowley warned.

Sophia looked back down at the strong, slanted writing that was to be her last tie to Aaron Whitworth. "He arranged me a job. I'm to be the riding instructor for Mrs. Carlton's School for Girls."

"That's Mother's school," Lord Wharton said, his voice soft with awe. He cleared his throat. "Well, not exactly Mother's, but she is one of the patronesses and volunteers there often." He exchanged a wide-eyed look with Lord Farnsworth. "He did go to London."

"And voluntarily met with your parents."

Both men appeared utterly shocked.

Sophia didn't blame them. Aaron had asked everyone he knew for assistance. Every person he could possibly ask a favor of had been contacted.

For her.

It was a beautiful, difficult, selfless gift that provided a way for her to leave his life with more than she'd arrived with. As much as she wanted to appreciate it, she couldn't help wishing he'd chosen to put the same effort into keeping her around.

Thirty-Three

Aaron shouldn't feel like he'd run clear across the Heath. What had he really done yesterday?

Had a conversation with Graham's mother, who had immediately been intrigued by the idea of a riding instructor with Sophia's abilities.

Assured Lord Grableton he was fine on his own and the other man was free to go to his club.

Cleared the billiard table three times while he waited for Lady Grableton to return from Mrs. Carlton's School for Girls.

Sent an express to the inn in Newmarket that would set everything in motion.

Finished removing Sophia from his life.

Perhaps that was why he'd felt like a horse who'd been sweated and then left standing about in his blankets.

He should have waited until he'd gotten back to his rooms to write the note, but he'd wanted to get it sent before he could call off the entire thing. So, he'd done it in Lady Grableton's drawing room while the footman summoned a messenger.

Once the missive was on its way, he'd sat on the settee.

He didn't know how long he'd been there, but eventually voices in the front hall had broken into his stupor.

"Is he still here?"

"He's been staring at the wall for hours. Peter, I'm worried."

Aaron's first thought had been that he'd never known Graham's father's name was Peter. His second was that if they grew worried, they'd send for Graham. That would make a host of other problems for Aaron.

He'd pushed to his feet and left the drawing room. "Thank you for your assistance, Lady Grableton. It means a great deal. I'll be going now."

"Given the hour, won't you join us for dinner? There's a small group of friends coming, but it will be simple to add one more."

"Your father isn't one of them, by the by," Lord Grableton added. "In case his being in town is giving you hesitation. We wouldn't do that to you."

Panic had gripped exhaustion by the arms and done a jig in his belly. He'd stepped closer to the door. "Thank you, my lady, but I have other plans." Mostly to be anywhere other than there.

He'd taken a hack back to his rooms, shucked his coat, and fallen into bed.

Now it was morning, and he still felt like he'd been kicked in the head.

Then again, it had been one emotional blow after the other for the past two days. It was a lot for a man to deal with when he avoided emotion like it was a venomous snake.

Everything was done. He could return to Newmarket.

He probably shouldn't, though. It might take some time for his friends to put everything together and get Sophia to London. He didn't want to be there when she left Newmarket. The last thing he needed was to be forced to tell her good-bye and watch her walk away, smiling as if he was happy about it all.

He was happy *for* her—happy that he could give her what she wanted, or at least had the connections to make it happen. *God, please don't ever make me have to do anything like that again.*

If this was how people made changes in their lives, he would gladly remain a stable manager forever. How did others do it? How did they decide who wouldn't mind being asked and how big a favor was appropriate? He still wasn't sure he'd gotten it right. He'd have to follow up with everyone when he returned to Newmarket and ensure they didn't resent his appeals.

Three days should be enough. If they were going to grant his requests, they'd accomplish it within three days.

Until then, he'd stare at the walls of his room.

It took him five minutes to determine he was terrible company.

He went to a coffeehouse but found strangers made even worse companions, so back to his rooms he went. He shucked his fashionable coat and rolled his shoulders. The looser cut of the coats he wore in Newmarket was far more comfortable, but he wasn't about to give anyone in London more reason to look down on him.

What was wrong with him? He was a man who'd found comfort in his own company his entire life. Now it was agitating, and he was the one person in the world he couldn't walk away from.

Two large, neat piles of correspondence sat on his desk, everything that had been sent to him since his last visit. Correspondence wasn't really the correct word for it, since not a single letter was personal. The only mail delivered to his London address was invitations sent by people who wanted to stay in his father's favor.

Graham and Oliver thought Aaron chucked them in the trash, but he didn't. He opened every single one. Then he tortured himself imagining how Rigsby would be welcomed while the hostesses lived in terror that Aaron would accept.

The first time he'd heard his father insisting that the *ton* acknowledge his illegitimate son, Aaron assumed it was his father's way of trying to make up for the stigma he'd saddled on Aaron. It wasn't until he attended an event that he realized it had nothing to do with him. His father had a need to play the penitent martyr in public, paying for his mistake and providing an example for others to do better.

That was Aaron's role in life. His father's punishment. A symbol of society's underbelly. A walking embodiment of the reason social classes existed.

It wasn't *who* he was. Aaron knew that. At least, he knew it now, but that was the role he had been given. Every now and then, when he was tempted to reach for more, he carefully chose one of those invitations and used it as a reminder.

A reminder of where he'd come from, of what could have been if he'd been born someone else. A reminder that trying to have a peaceful life meant walking away from his aristocratic friends and admitting he'd never belonged in their world.

Perhaps a reminder was what he needed now. The fact that the Marquis of Lindbury was in town and not relaxing at his country estate made it the perfect opportunity. Aaron never saw the man by accident. Every one of their encounters over the past six years had been carefully planned.

And they always went the same way.

They would see each other, make everyone uncomfortable, and spend five minutes in rudely polite conversation.

Then Aaron would leave, throw up in the bushes on his way home, and spend the next day and a half staring at the ceiling as penance for thinking he could change his lot in life.

He couldn't think of a better way to spend an evening.

AARON HAD TO shuffle through most of the stack to find the perfect opportunity, but one was happening in an older home halfway across town the next evening.

Aaron had performed this penance enough that he knew the necessary ingredients. A large gathering, so that his presence reached his father via gossip first and everyone in attendance couldn't witness the confrontation for themselves. A well-established hostess, so that he didn't inadvertently bring anyone down with him. Normally the hostess needed an unmarried daughter in attendance to keep Rigsby from setting foot in the place, but Aaron's brother was safely in Newmarket.

Fashionable, perfectly tailored clothing was also required. His evening kit had been made by the best tailor who had been willing to have him as a client, and it was so exquisitely fitted that it was almost as comfortable as his Newmarket ensembles.

As he presented the invitation to the footman, the settled feeling he normally got remained evasive. The internal discomfort, wariness, and heaviness were familiar, but the resigned satisfaction that usually accompanied those other feelings was nowhere to be found.

When was the last time he'd done this? February? That stretch was longer than he'd gone in years. Perhaps that was how Sophia had gotten past his defenses so easily.

The footman granted him entrance without a blink, but the first guest he saw stared at him agape and then rushed across the hall to whisper to someone else.

And so it began.

Tonight's ball was in one of the old manors that hadn't yet been torn down to make way for terraced houses. He could see a large open expanse at the top of the stairs and knew the ballroom lay beyond.

Most people gave him a wide berth but followed him with their eyes as he climbed the stairs. Aaron and the marquis had never had a shouting match, a physical altercation, or even an exchange of spiteful insults. Their meetings only made the gossip papers on very boring days, and even then it wasn't more than two lines.

Still, everyone watched, wondering if this would be the first time.

Aaron was so focused on maintaining his composure as he entered the ballroom that he nearly collided with the man who stepped into his path.

"What are you doing here?" Graham stood in front of Aaron, refusing to let him go any farther unless he wanted to engage in a public tussle.

That would most certainly make the gossip sheets.

Aaron crossed his arms and stood as tall as he could, which

put him approximately half an inch taller than his friend. "I was invited."

"You're always invited."

"Then why were you asking?"

"Because you never attend."

"Obviously I do." Aaron frowned. "What are you doing here?"

Instead of answering, Graham narrowed his gaze and leaned in. "He's here."

Since that was the entire point of attending, Aaron had hoped as much. Graham's being in attendance was mucking up the plan. "The hostess has nothing to worry about. We've always been civil."

"I've never known you to attend gatherings without me or Oliver in attendance."

Aaron should have known his two best friends would never stay in Newmarket after learning he'd gone to London. "Is Oliver here?"

"You hate balls," Graham said, resisting Aaron's attempt at distraction.

"I can't say that I've been to enough balls to have any solidified opinion about them."

Graham snorted. "And you'd like to rectify that?"

"Perhaps."

"I'll have Mother arrange one for next Wednesday, then."

Aaron's father never attended Lady Grableton's functions. "That wouldn't provide a fair assessment. Your family is rather biased in my favor."

"You annoy my mother."

"You've always said she adores me." She might currently be annoyed that he wouldn't allow her to meddle in his life more. "Besides, I entertain your father."

"He doesn't make the social arrangements."

This was a pointless argument that served no purpose. "We are blocking the pathway."

Instead of stepping aside and letting Aaron continue into the ballroom, Graham took Aaron's arm and none too gently guided him over to the side of the antechamber. "Why are you here?"

Aaron made a show of looking about their new position. "Do you expect the change of scenery to prompt a different answer? Where is Oliver?"

"You think he came to London a week before his wedding?"

A pang of guilt shot through him. Still, he knew these two men. "Yes."

"You're right. He's on his way to your rooms. I was going to join you both there later, but Mother asked me to make an appearance here because she and Father didn't feel like going out. Now I have to wonder if she suspected you would be here."

Possibly. Lady Grableton was a rather meddlesome, if lovable, woman, and if anyone had noticed the pattern of Aaron's appearances, it would have been she. "As we have already established, this is not a normal evening activity for me. Where is your wife?"

Maybe mentioning Kit would distract the man.

"Newmarket. She could not endure such hasty travel in her condition."

Her condition? Aaron swallowed. More chances to be an uncle. "Congratulations."

"Thank you."

They fell into a silent staring match. Graham's frustration was nearly palpable. The other man had Aaron's best interests at heart, but Aaron couldn't begin to explain to someone else what he himself barely understood. It was a compulsion to know what he was missing out on, to remind himself where he belonged, to remember whose blood ran in his veins.

"And here I'd hoped you decided to give this up."

Aaron and Graham turned to find Rigsby standing next to them.

Because that was what this evening needed. Aaron and the marquis in a room together was a boring event the gossipmongers barely noticed. Rigsby and Aaron in the same vicinity would make the rounds in seconds.

That they were having a private conversation would be in every paper by morning.

Graham stepped in front of Aaron. "Rigsby," he said in a firm but congenial tone. "What brings you to Town?"

Aaron placed a hand on Graham's shoulder. "It's okay."

He glanced back. "It is?"

"It is," Rigsby said as Aaron nodded.

Graham resumed his earlier position, adding a set of crossed arms to the glare he aimed in Aaron's direction. "Explain."

"After the number of times you've reminded me Rigsby had as little choice in his situation as I did, you're going to quiz me for finally listening?"

Rigsby laughed.

Graham lifted a single brow in the other man's direction. "Didn't know you had a defender, did you?"

"Didn't know I needed one."

"You were never in danger," Aaron grumbled. "I know how to avoid you."

"It helped that I was staying away from you."

Aaron shrugged in agreement.

Graham looked from one man to the other. "What is happening here?"

"Here?" Aaron asked. "You're stopping me from entering the ballroom. As I've never been in this house before and have only managed to make it up the stairs, I can't speak to anything else."

Maybe if Aaron was sufficiently annoying, Graham would stomp off and Aaron could sip punch while staring down his father. They'd eventually say hello. Then Aaron would leave. It was a plan that had worked numerous times.

Rigsby was determined to muck it up, though, by keeping the conversation flowing. "Are you referring to our cordiality or Aaron's petty need to remind our father of his fallibility?"

"It isn't petty," Aaron grumbled. As long as he never admitted it out loud, he could convince himself it wasn't. What Rigsby didn't realize was that it was as much for Aaron as it was for their father.

Graham frowned at Aaron. "You avoid your father. When we stumble into him, neither of you does more than exchange perfunctory greetings."

Rigsby laughed and shook his head. "Do you even know what it does to him?"

Aaron had never considered what the man did after he left. His normal uneasy tension curled tighter in his gut.

"He's broken several brandy glasses by throwing them into the fireplace after one of your appearances. Yells about how you refuse to understand how life works and how he did right by you by forcing everyone to acknowledge your existence. You were supposed to repay the favor by disappearing."

Graham flicked a finger back and forth between them. "When did this happen?"

Rigsby shrugged. "When he needed my horse as a stud."

"Ah." Graham nodded. "Anything for the horses."

Sending Sophia away hadn't been for the horses. And it hadn't been for Aaron. It had been for her, and no matter how much he told himself to be happy for her, it wasn't enough to cover the pain he felt that he couldn't be like Graham and Oliver and Hudson and fall in love and offer the girl the world.

And the man at fault was right through those doors. If Aaron could just get past these two brutes, he could spread a little of this pain around and then maybe it wouldn't hurt so much.

Rigsby tilted his head. "It will be worse tonight. He's not prepared. You never come to London in October. He thinks he's safe."

"He considers when I might show up?" Aaron asked.

"That would make sense, given how little he likes to see you," Graham muttered. "Unfortunately, you attend so few social events that your appearance is unpredictable."

"Hmm, yes." Rigsby examined his fingernails. "If, say, Aaron were to always appear at a musicale approximately two weeks before the first ball of the Season, our father could make other plans." He looked up to meet Aaron's eyes. "Or perhaps you would choose to attend one of the last soirees before Parliament recessed. If you did that on a regular basis, missing the encounter could be easily arranged."

A deep wrinkle formed between Graham's brows. "Wait. That's exactly what you do."

Aaron glared at his brother. His father could have avoided him. Easily it would seem.

Penitent martyr. Like father, like son.

Aaron looked away from both men. A handful of guests nearly tripped over their feet as they tried to enter the ballroom and watch the conversation at the same time.

Aaron turned back to Rigsby. "By now he's heard that I'm out here talking to his heir."

Rigsby winced. "What a lovely role to have—the man waiting for his father to pop off. I would like to think I'm somewhat more than that, even if he doesn't see it that way."

They all looked at the ballroom doors as if they expected to see something more momentous than elegantly clad men and women.

Rigsby cleared his throat and continued. "As it so happens, I've already made my appearance and informed him of my participation in the October Meeting. He isn't happy I'm in Newmarket. Learning you're here may send him over the edge." He pointed at Aaron and then the ballroom. "This need you have to stab each other's wounds doesn't interest me. It's why I stay out of your way."

A brief swell of chatter drifted from the ballroom before the marquis burst out the door. Aaron looked at the man—really looked at him. Deep lines bracketed his hard mouth, and bitter shards of ice dripped from his narrowed gaze. His walk was stiff and halting.

There was enough physical resemblance between the two of them for Aaron to easily imagine himself in the other man's shoes. Would that be him in thirty years? A tortured man, wracked by regret and indignation, unwilling to let the past go because he wasn't sure what sort of life he'd find if he did?

Dear God, what am I doing to myself?

"I'm leaving," Aaron announced, taking a step back, eyes fixed on his father as the man stopped, confused by Aaron's retreat. "Give my regards to our father."

Without looking at Rigsby or Graham, Aaron spun on his heel and walked away. He'd expected each step to bring a sense of freedom since he was walking away instead of doing their sick little dance.

But the truth was he'd gotten what he came for. Guilt. Anger. Pain.

He didn't need his father when he could easily torture himself.

Three streets away, he cast up his accounts in the bushes.

Thirty-Four

Aaron let himself into his empty rooms, though he doubted he'd be alone in them for long.

He'd managed to remove his jacket and waistcoat when a solid knock pounded on his door. Without even asking who it was, he pulled open the door and returned to the bedroom to finish changing.

When he emerged again, Oliver and Graham had made themselves comfortable on the sofa. Aaron took the chair.

No one said a word.

The clock struck the hour.

"It's been a fine visit, gentlemen, but I think I'll turn in. Do see yourselves out." Aaron stood and turned, ready to leave his friends to stare at an empty chair. They'd likely escorted Sophia to Town, so it was safe to return to Newmarket. He'd buy a ticket in the morning.

"It didn't work," Oliver said.

Graham sighed. "I'm aware."

Aaron shouldn't ask. He *knew* he shouldn't. He turned around. "What didn't work?"

"Waiting you out." Graham shifted to lean more comfortably into the corner of the sofa. "You're far too experienced at being quiet."

Aaron laughed dryly. "What did you expect? That I'd spill my innermost thoughts to fill the silence?" He shook his head. "That might work on Sophia but not on me."

Oliver stared with wide eyes, slowly blinking for several moments.

Graham grinned. "How long has he known her?"

Oliver's mouth curved as well. "Two weeks."

"Huh." Graham tilted his head to the side to assess Aaron.

Aaron wanted to kick himself for even mentioning Sophia's name, much less in a capacity that indicated he knew her well. He pulled both hands across his face. "Stop looking at me like that. It doesn't mean anything."

"Obviously it does or you wouldn't think I thought it did." Graham grinned.

Aaron dropped back into the chair and leaned forward to brace his elbows on his knees. "She made my life interesting, I'll admit. Made me consider things I hadn't before. That's all it is."

"Of course." Aaron hated when Graham agreed with him in that tone of voice. It all but called him out as a liar.

Oliver frowned. "When we escorted her to the school this morning, you said Aaron was going to wish she was coming back with us."

Graham sent an exasperated look at Oliver, who winced. "Right. Strategy." He waved a hand between Graham and Aaron. "As you were. I'm just going to sit here."

With a sigh, Graham turned back to Aaron. "Would you like to discuss your departure, Sophia, or tonight's fascinating revelation first?"

He didn't want to discuss any of them, but he absolutely refused to talk about Sophia. "Seeing my father on occasion helps me maintain perspective."

"I can't imagine how."

"Because you are surrounded by people and places that remind you who you are and where you belong."

There was a moment of silence before Graham quietly asked, "And you aren't?"

"Not without careful planning, no." Aaron left the topic there, allowing his friends to build their own conclusions. They'd known him more than twenty years. They wouldn't be far off the mark.

After several long moments of silence, Graham's face softened. Had he shifted into pity, Aaron would have left the room. While there may have been sympathy behind the determined set of his chin, his expression indicated nothing more than a desire to stand shoulder to shoulder with Aaron while he faced his demons, whether they came from the world or from himself.

Oliver was the one to finally speak again. "You left Newmarket. In the middle of the first October Meeting."

"I know." Aaron slid his eyes closed, and the vision of those red welts floated in front of his eyes. "I needed to take a moment, assess my life."

"Did you come to any conclusions?"

He had. But he didn't like a single one of them.

ANOTHER WEEK. ANOTHER bedroom.

This one was somewhere between the maid's room at Meadowland Park and Lady Adelaide's guest chamber. The bed was metal, with silver vines scrolling across the headboard. A dresser and a washstand sat to one side, a desk was beneath the window, and a comfortable-looking chair sat in the corner beside a small table. Perfect for drinking a cup of tea while reading a book.

Her trunk sat at the foot of the bed. It was silly, but there'd been something exciting about not being able to carry her luggage up to the staff quarters on her own.

Mrs. Carlton hadn't been rude, but she also hadn't seemed all that thrilled to have Sophia join the teaching staff. She'd shown her around, introduced her to the students, and then pointed out their small stable. There were only six stalls, and half of them were empty.

"When did your last riding instructor leave?" Sophia asked.

"You're the first permanent one we've had." Mrs. Carlton gave her a tight smile. "One of our patronesses suggested the girls' riding skills be more than rudimentary. I don't see the need. As long as you sit tall in the saddle and don't fall, what does it matter?"

What indeed. Sophia could have told the woman that sitting properly made the ride more comfortable for the person and the horse, but Mrs. Carlton probably wouldn't care. Instead Sophia said, "Often our first sight of a person is when they approach on horseback. The better a lady's seat, the better her first impression."

"Hmm. I suppose." Mrs. Carlton at least looked thoughtful, which Sophia considered a win.

She dined with the rest of the staff before returning to her room, where she started a letter to Jonas. They'd agreed to write one letter a week. It would be strange, not seeing him every day, but perhaps it would be good for them. Independence would only make them stronger once they were back together.

Her window overlooked the small stable and riding ring. Mrs. Carlton's school turned out fine, respected ladies. If she did well here, others would want to hire her. This was the beginning.

She was glad for it. She was.

If only it hadn't come at such a high price.

OCTOBER IN NEWMARKET was always a bustling frenzy. Add the wedding of the daughter of one of horse racing's most successful stable owners and the area exploded with wealthy and titled horse lovers.

Aaron was surprised at how quickly life calmed down after Sophia disappeared from Newmarket. It was proof that he had done the right thing. They were both safe, both getting what they'd always wanted, both moving on.

It would help if Fitzroy didn't glare daggers into his back every time Aaron stepped foot into Hawksworth, which was multiple times a day since he was still training horses out of the stable.

Mr. Barley had asked for his job back, but Aaron declined. He couldn't trust the man not to use circumstances as a weapon. He couldn't trust anyone other than himself.

Besides, he enjoyed the training, enjoyed working with the horses and the jockeys. He'd even hired a new jockey. That he'd once worked for Davers gave Aaron pause, until he learned the man had quit because of the way the other jockeys had treated Sophia.

So far, the fellow was working out well.

Aaron had asked about getting the actions of the jockeys who'd whipped Sophia on official record, but his inquiries hadn't gotten far. The fact that all three men in question were no longer working in Newmarket was telling. As was the fact that Davers and another owner had pulled their horses from the other two October Meetings. The record might not be official, but someone had put the pressure on behind the scenes.

It wasn't enough for Aaron, but it was something. Especially when the Jockey Club had agreed to list Sophia in the books as an official jockey, including her challenge win, if Aaron would let the matter be handled quietly.

The entire exchange made him more determined than ever to do things differently. Every training decision, breeding suggestion, or race subscription would be chosen because it made sense, not because everyone else was doing it.

Sophia's encounter notwithstanding, it was shaping up to be a good October for both the stables he managed. If he could keep his jockeys and his horses healthy and avoid angering the Jockey Club, the next two meetings would be profitable.

Yet every night he paced his cottage. One wall to the other and back again. He couldn't understand why Oliver gave in to the action so often. It wasn't at all beneficial.

With the quiet of the night pressing in on him, he recalled that last image of his father. Angry. Bitter. Ready to confront his sons for simply existing in the same room.

Aaron didn't want to be like that.

He plopped down in a kitchen chair and laid his Bible on the table in front of him. If his normal method of barreling through and making do wasn't going to fix this, he'd try something else.

He would try . . . talking.

"Hello, God."

Aaron growled and pushed himself up from the table. "This is ridiculous."

What was God really going to change for him? He had a steady income, loyal friends, and work he enjoyed. It was more than a lot of other people had and probably more than he deserved. What did he have the right to ask God for?

The bottom dropped out of his anger, and he collapsed back into the chair.

If he had nothing to ask for, was his life really lacking? He'd always seen himself as having less because he couldn't claim life the way his friends did. Yet he had everything he'd ever wanted, everything he'd ever been willing to allow in.

Perhaps what he needed to ask God for was a little perspective.

He looked down at the Bible.

Or maybe it wasn't about asking God for anything. Maybe Aaron just needed to talk to Him.

He adjusted himself in the chair, gaze fixed on the Bible, half expecting to hear a booming voice uttering divine prophesies. When that didn't happen, he flipped it open. It landed in Psalms. He'd always found David interesting. A younger son of a shepherd usurping the king, running and hiding because Saul wanted him dead.

"I don't think my father is a happy man."

Aaron blinked. That had not been what he thought he'd say. Sure, he'd been thinking a lot about what the marquis's storming out of the ballroom meant, but it all boiled down to the fact that Lord Lindbury was not a happy man. He was a tortured one.

"What would make him like that?" Aaron ran a hand over his face. "He was the one who put us in this position. *He* sent me to school. *He* acknowledged me in public. *He* forced his peers to accept me."

But weren't those the best things he could have done for Aaron, aside from marrying his mother? The marquis may have placed Aaron in a hole, but he'd also given him a ladder. Wallowing in the mud had been Aaron's choice.

Aaron sat back in the chair and drummed his fingers on the tabletop.

Was that why the other man was angry every time he saw Aaron? The idea seemed to give the man far more credit than he deserved, but why did Aaron need to know anyway? He was sabotaging his own life to punish a man who may not even care.

His eyes drifted to the Bible. "That's quite the revelation, Lord. Got anything else for me?"

AARON SAT IN the shadows at the back of the church while Oliver married Lady Rebecca. Several other attendees sat closer to the front, including Oliver's father. If the earl knew about Sophia, he was obviously satisfied that all had been handled, since he'd given Aaron no more than his customary nod of greeting.

Soon a large group would gather at Meadowland Park to celebrate the wedding breakfast. Lord and Lady Gliddon were not going to miss this opportunity to impress everyone in the horse-racing world.

He was the first to leave the church and the last to arrive at the house, but as soon as he walked in, Oliver caught his eye and they exchanged smiles and nods.

Then Aaron found himself another corner.

Aside from the fact that there were plenty of people in this room who would rather not socialize with him away from the track, he just didn't feel the need or desire to mingle. Being on the fringe was comfortable.

Besides, Oliver knew he was here, and that was all that mattered. Graham and Kit circled by his corner on occasion, but they both enjoyed people too much to stay. Aaron was content holding up a wall and watching the goings-on while everyone ignored him.

Everyone except Miss Hancock.

If women were mysteries, the one walking toward him was a full-blown enigma. She dipped in and out of society at will and considered the social rules to be mere suggestions.

And everyone let her get away with it.

"Do you always celebrate in the corner?" she asked.

"It suits me." He'd spent more than one night this past week sitting at his kitchen table with an open Bible in front of him, and he'd come to the conclusion that there was comfort in knowing one's place. His was with the horses and with his friends, so he ignored everyone else.

As far as mottos went, it was a work in progress.

"With the wars over, it's safe to travel again. Do you know if they've arranged a wedding trip?"

Even if he did, he wouldn't tell her. He wouldn't tell anybody. It wasn't his information to share.

"I'm considering traveling again."

Lack of response was not an effective deterrent for some people.

"It's not fun to travel alone."

If she even hinted that Aaron might want to be her companion, he was leaving this party and refusing to set foot in any home she was in ever again.

"I thought it might be nice to see the French countryside on horseback. Better views than from inside a coach."

That was why Aaron, Graham, and Oliver had done their tours in a saddle. He'd made it this long without responding to her, and he wouldn't give in now.

"My riding is mediocre at best, though." She frowned. "I wonder if Mrs. Carlton's School would allow me to train there if I made a donation. I must say, Miss Fitzroy was the best female rider I've ever seen, and I do like to have the best in my life."

"Why are you telling me this?" Aaron bit out, the mention of Sophia breaking through the last of his patience.

"Because, in my opinion, which I value rather highly, people in love are stupid."

"I'm not in love."

"No," she sighed. "But you could have been. And there is something to be pitied about a man who avoids even the chance. Oh look, they're bringing out more bacon."

As she strode back toward the food, Aaron moved to the exit. His duty had been fulfilled. There were horses to be seen to, an open Heath to be galloped across. Maybe if he went fast enough, he could outrun Miss Hancock's words.

Thirty-Five

What did it mean when you got everything you wanted but you still weren't happy?

Sophia smiled on, even though her cheeks hurt and her heart wasn't in it. It wasn't her student's fault that her mind and her life were muddled.

When the girl went a full round with her back straight, her skirts properly draped, and the horse in complete control, Sophia congratulated her and ended the lesson. After three weeks, Sophia was coming to understand why Mrs. Carlton had been unsure of her presence.

There wasn't a need for her here. Nor was there any challenge to distract her from the realization that this was one more road that wouldn't lead to the recognition she needed to start a school.

However, it was steady work with horses and riders and no audience.

Every night, she ate dinner at a table. She had a desk, paper, and time to write letters to Jonas. The bed was comfortable. Her clothes filled the drawers and pegs enough that they didn't look empty. The other teachers were kind.

There were times she missed the exhilaration and excitement of the Heath, and she certainly missed the wide-open spaces, but here the sun would rise through the same window every morning and no one threatened to take it away.

Security was better than excitement, even if that meant this was now her home instead of a stopover on the way to something else. Bringing Rhiannon here would help.

She wrote to Jonas every day, making her weekly missive multiple pages long. Jonas's letters, on the other hand, were far shorter and appeared to be written in a single sitting. He must be busier than she was.

She missed her brother and her horse, but both were due to arrive today. With Rhiannon she could show the girls what was *really* possible on the back of a horse, and then they'd all take more interest in their lessons.

Hopefully.

If not, at least Sophia could keep herself busy working with her horse.

She would suppress the niggling urge to show them she could stand on a running horse no matter how much she wanted them to drop their jaws and their attitudes.

Her student returned to the dormitory, and Sophia took the horse back to the small stable. The lack of horses meant that even though she gave several lessons a day, no girl rode more than once a week. That wasn't enough to inspire a passion for the activity.

The horse's hooves clomped on the dirt floor as she entered the stable, but neither of the two grooms made an appearance. "Patrick?" she called. "Robert?"

A man scurried out of the last stall to take the reins. "Apologies, Miss Fitzroy. We were admiring your horse."

Sophia's face broke into a smile as she hurried to the last stall, where her brother was settling Rhiannon into her new home. "Jonas!"

Glad the reunion was happening away from the serious regard of the schoolmistress and the students, Sophia threw herself into Jonas's arms. "I'm so happy to see you."

He hugged her tight, lifting her off the ground and tucking his face into her shoulder. "Me too, Soph."

After lowering her to her feet, he stepped back and looked her over. "You look nice. Polished."

She swatted his shoulder. "You say that as if it's a bad thing."

"Not bad. Different. Are you finished for the day?"

"Yes. Let me change out of this habit, then we'll walk to the coffeehouse. The staff dining room isn't very private." She grimaced. "I'm sorry I can't offer you a place to stay. The hotel above the—"

"I'm taken care of." Jonas gave her a smile as he cut her off but avoided meeting her eyes.

"Oh." An awkward silence passed between them for the first time she could remember. "I'll just . . . meet you out front?"

He nodded. "I'll be there."

She changed quickly and hurried to the front of the school. They walked and talked as if the awkward moment had never occurred, as if it hadn't been weeks since they'd seen each other, as if nothing had ever changed.

Jonas held her chair for her before easing into the seat across the table.

Sophia gasped. "You're sitting!"

He nodded, a huge grin on his face. "All that rest did exactly what the doctor said it would. I won't say riding a horse from Newmarket was comfortable, but it wasn't as bad as I feared. I'll take another long rest before I ride again, but sitting is doable."

They ordered, and the silence fell between them again as they exchanged assessing stares.

Jonas spoke first. "Are you happy, Soph?"

"Yes," she answered, without allowing herself to give it much thought. "I always wanted to teach. Your being here would make it better, but maybe someday . . ."

He glanced down at his hands and then back up. "You still think we should open a school together?"

"Isn't that what you want?"

"I want it if you do. I can be happy anywhere, Sophia, unless you're unhappy. Your letters . . . they haven't sounded like you."

She'd tried so hard not to let her melancholy moments fall onto the page.

"I don't want to go back to wandering, Jonas. If settling means steady work and a home, then I'll settle. I don't know if I'm happy, but at least I'm not worried." Maybe that would have to be enough. As she'd told Aaron the last time she'd seen him, not everyone was meant for grandeur. Jonas looked into his coffee cup for several moments. "If you had another option, would you take it?"

Sophia narrowed her eyes at her brother. "What aren't you telling me?"

"I don't know exactly. But I . . . sometimes I hear rumors, and there's been talk of an opportunity that might be coming your way." He took a swallow of coffee. "You know I moved into the rooms above the stable, but sometimes Lord Trent still invites me to dinner. It's strange, but I go because it's nice too. It reminds me of the parties Mother and Father would hold so the students could show off to each other."

Sophia grinned. "Could you imagine if Father had seen us in the circus? Standing on a horse is not in the least refined."

"But it is amazing." Jonas reached across the table and took her hand. "I want you to be amazing, Soph."

Part of her wanted that too. Would she ever be willing to risk reaching for it again? "This opportunity . . . it would be long-term?"

"From the sound of it, as long as you want it to be."

A kernel of light broke through the shroud that had seemed to cover her life these past weeks. Jonas hadn't mentioned Aaron, but was it possible he had something to do with this? She still thought about him all the time. She missed talking to him. She thought about Newmarket too. Not that she wanted to race again, but she did miss the energy of the place.

306

"I shouldn't have mentioned it," Jonas said, pulling her out of her reverie, "especially since it might not even happen."

"No, I need to be prepared," Sophia said, her heart pounding in her ears. "When do you return to Hawksworth?"

"On tomorrow's mail coach. I'm needed to help with the horses during the third October Meeting."

"Oh." She'd secretly hoped he could stay longer, though it wasn't practical. What would he do all day while she was working? Not to mention neither of them could afford an extended stay in a London hotel. "Where are you staying?"

"Mr. Whitworth gave me the key to his rooms."

And just that quickly, Sophia was befuddled once again.

FOR THE FIRST time he could remember, Aaron was glad to see the end of the final race of the last October Meeting.

None of his horses raced again until spring. He had plenty of time to think about what his next steps should be.

Normally he visited London for the winter or wherever Oliver or Graham were, but Oliver was on his wedding trip and Graham and Kit were staying at Trenton Hall until he returned. Aaron had a feeling it was as much to keep an eye on him as it was that Kit didn't feel up to traveling.

Most nights he dined with them at the house before walking down to his cottage, but tonight he didn't want to do it. He was tired, and being around people, even his closest friend, sounded exhausting.

If he cried off, though, they'd want to know why, and since he couldn't even explain it to himself or the open Bible he'd taken to talking to before bed, he climbed the steps to go to dinner. At least they kept it simple when it was just the three of them. He'd be in his home within the hour.

"Have you decided where you want to live?" he asked as they ate. "I'm assuming you won't be able to travel as much for a while with the baby."

Kit frowned. "No, we won't. We must find a place soon or we'll end up with his parents or Daphne and William. I know I lived with Daphne for years, but that was before we were married. I doubt it would work as well now."

Graham shook his head. "Especially since they're expecting their own bundle of joy. Two new families under one roof would strain even the best of friendships. We need to find a place of our own soon. It will either be here or in Wiltshire."

"There's an estate a few miles south of here. It would be too small for large house parties, but it's perfect for a family. There's not a lot of land by Newmarket standards, but I don't see you breeding horses."

Graham slowly put his fork down. "How do you know about this estate?"

This was why he should never have started talking freely out loud, even to himself.

Aaron stuffed a bite of potatoes into his mouth and nearly choked as he remembered that was Sophia's tactic to get herself to stop talking. He hadn't seen her in weeks, and yet she was never far from his thoughts. He shook his head and swallowed. "I . . . try to keep up with changes in the area."

In truth, it had been one of the properties he'd investigated for Rigsby. Not that Aaron was going to tell Graham that. He'd expected his friend to push for more information about Rigsby after they'd returned from London, but he hadn't. If Graham had forgotten about that exchange, Aaron wasn't about to remind him.

"I'll take a look. Are the neighbors nice?"

Aaron winced. One of the neighbors might soon be Rigsby. The estate Aaron had recommended—and his brother was moving forward on—bordered the property to the south. "Have you ever had difficulty getting along with anyone?"

"Your father isn't one of my favorite people."

He'd likely be too angry to visit often. "Have you had difficulty with anyone you didn't want to have difficulty with?"

Kit laughed. "He has a point."

Though it was rude and uncouth, Aaron indulged himself in a large yawn. "The races left me drained. I believe I'll leave early tonight."

Graham waved him away. "Go, go, get your rest, Little Briar Rose."

Aaron paused halfway out of his chair. "Little who?"

"Briar Rose." Kit sighed and rolled her eyes. "He's been reading fairy tales to me. I try to tell him there's no way for the baby to hear him yet."

"Practice never hurt anyone." Graham grinned as he ate the last bite of food from his plate. "I will be the most impressive father in England."

"I'm sure you will be," Kit said in a tone that indicated this was not the first time they'd had this conversation.

Aaron shook his head as he left the house and strode toward his cottage. His friends had all found women who loved them and made them happy. All of them made him feel welcome in their families. Still, the unsettledness that had plagued him since London made him uneasy in their presence.

The Bible, which had taken up permanent residence on his table, drew his eye as he entered the cottage. After all the reading and talking, wasn't he supposed to be more at ease instead of less?

A sudden knock at the door made him frown, but not as much as who was on the other side. "Rigsby?"

His brother took two steps inside and looked around the cottage with raised eyebrows. "Well. I suppose that answers that."

Aaron shut the door and crossed his arms over his chest. "Did you expect a manor house? I don't have an inheritance."

Rigsby coughed. "It would seem you do, though it's a rather terrible one. You had this built?"

"Yes."

"Designed it yourself?"

"Yes. It's just me, so I wanted the space to be efficient."

"Are you lying to me or yourself?"

"I think you can find the door."

Rigsby sighed. "I didn't come here to argue with you, truly. It's just . . . you didn't do this intentionally?"

Aaron looked around the room. It was quaint, but he couldn't see anything wrong with it. "What are you talking about?"

"It looks exactly like your childhood home. More structurally sound and with a far nicer bed, I'm sure, but the layout is the same."

"No, it—" Aaron stopped and looked around. How had he not noticed? How could he have deliberately rebuilt his mother's rundown cottage and not seen it for what it was? "You were there once. How . . . ?"

"I remember everything about that day."

"You were six."

"Do you think it matters how old a boy is when his father shows him another little boy and says this is what happens when you don't act responsibly? That we have to fulfill our duties, no matter how unpleasant they may be? I couldn't see the difference between you and me, but I saw how you lived and I knew what I was going home to."

"I'm guessing it had more than one room?" Aaron moved toward his small cookstove and threw a log in the glowing embers to build the fire back up. Not that he wanted Rigsby staying long enough for tea, but he needed something to do.

"I learned a lesson that day, and not the one Father intended." Rigsby sighed and pulled at his neck with one hand. "This isn't why I came here tonight."

"I'm sure it isn't, but since it's come up, why don't you finish your story?"

Rigsby's eyebrows rose. "You want to know what I learned?"

"Tell me what I missed."

He shook his head. "That would take all night. No, from that day on I questioned everything Father said."

Aaron stilled. "Everything?"

Rigsby nodded. "I've never been the son he wanted, but he couldn't complain about it because I've also been the son he couldn't criticize. I made sure my grades were good and I didn't get into trouble. I took care to make the right friends, but not be so popular as to anger the wrong people."

"Sounds exemplary."

"Sounds not like you. He complains about you. A lot. I think he needs to feel that the world is trying to punish him. He's hoping one day you'll punch him."

"What?" Aaron dropped the pot he'd filled with water for tea. His leg got soaked from the splash, but he didn't care.

"He only admitted that to me once, after you'd finished school and he lowered your quarterly allowance. He thought that would be enough to prompt you to do something, but you just took it." Rigsby shrugged. "After that, I tried rebelling against everything, hoping that could be my way to finally make him happy. Mother hated it. It didn't work, so I stopped."

"Stopped rebelling?"

"Stopped caring. At the end of my life, I won't answer to Lord Lindbury and neither will you."

Aaron filled the pot again and placed it on top of the cookstove. "You've got it figured out then, have you?"

Shaking his head, Rigsby laughed. "Hardly. That's why I was in London a few weeks ago. No matter how many times I tell myself it is more important to be a man God would be proud of, I keep going back. And I keep getting disappointed."

"What are you wanting?"

"I don't know. Maybe that's why I sought you out. I'm hoping I'll see what I've been missing."

"Is it working?"

"No."

A slow ripple crossed the surface of the water as it began to heat. "I don't know what it was like growing up in that house

311

with Lord Lindbury, and I don't think I want to know." Aaron glanced around the room. He would never see this place the same way again. "You don't want to know what it was really like in that cottage either."

Aaron's gaze fell once more on the open Bible. "Neither of us is going to be the man we want to be if we hold on to the past."

Maybe there was something to this idea of talking things through, because all of a sudden it made sense. God did not define people by their birth but by their hearts. When a man entered into a relationship with Jesus, there wasn't anyone else involved. Not a father or a mother or a friend. It was just him and God. What if, instead of trying to imitate what he'd been taught a gentleman should be, Aaron started living by God's standards for one?

He pulled two mugs from a shelf. "Sit down, Rigsby. I make a terrible cup of tea, but I can't think of a better way for us to start over. And you can tell me why you came here in the first place."

Rigsby was silent for several moments until he answered with the scrape of a chair. "I have a proposition for you."

Thirty-Six

Aaron was waiting in the breakfast room when Graham came down the next morning. "I'm giving up my London rooms."

Graham squinted, blinked, and rubbed his eyes. "I . . . what? Why?"

"Because I don't need them. If I go to London, I could stay in a hotel or—" Aaron took a deep breath—"with your parents."

Graham froze in the act of pulling out a dining chair. "Did you just say you would stay with my parents?"

"They're always offering." The lightness Aaron had been feeling since talking to Rigsby the night before started to dim. "They meant it, didn't they?"

"Of course. Mother was overjoyed that you felt you could come to them for help, even if it was a favor for someone else. There are six bedrooms in that house. You can even claim one and keep clothes there if you want."

Aaron nodded. "Good. Then I don't need rooms."

Graham sat and stared at Aaron until that wretched desire to pace began to rise.

"Could I borrow your carriage to collect my belongings?"

"It's like a dam broke and now you can't stop asking for favors."

Aaron's defenses snapped into place, but he forced himself to stop and think. In a way, Graham was right. Somewhere in the past

313

few months, the fear that he would be alone as soon as he reached out to anyone had receded.

There was a new fear in its place—the fear that he wouldn't take advantage of this fresh moment in life. The fear that he wouldn't know who he was anymore if he stopped expecting the world to kick him in the teeth.

It had taken him thirty-two years to face the first fear. He hoped to handle this new one a little faster.

"Are you going to help me or not?" Aaron asked.

"We'll leave after breakfast."

It DIDN'T TAKE long to gather Aaron's clothes and the scattering of personal effects and let the shop owner know he was vacating the rooms. As they packed, Aaron explored the idea of telling Graham about Rigsby and Sophia.

There were times he couldn't get the words out and times he chose not to be completely truthful, but it was more than he'd ever shared in a single moment and far more than he'd ever given voluntarily.

Graham grinned as they closed the last of the trunks. "Oliver is going to hate that he missed this."

"I'm sure you'll tell him everything."

"With embellishments." Graham moved to one end of the trunk. "Let's strap this onto the carriage. We'll stay the night with my parents and start for Newmarket in the morning."

Considering how long Aaron had partially resided in those rooms, it was surprising how little of him had been in there. Clothing, boots, a few books and office items. Now it was just a room, waiting on another gentleman who didn't quite have the means but wanted to maintain appearances.

Aaron was finished pretending. He was a horse trainer from Newmarket and that was enough. If he fully embraced this role, his friends wouldn't leave him, his schedule wouldn't shift. He would still be a gentleman in manner, even if he couldn't claim the title.

Dinner with Lord and Lady Grableton was relaxed, and as Graham had predicted, his mother offered to let him leave a few items behind. He politely declined. While it would be annoying to pack every time he came to London, he needed a clean break.

THE NEXT MORNING, Aaron and Graham climbed back in the carriage.

"Can we make a stop before we leave London?" Aaron's heart lodged itself in his throat like a rock.

"Where?"

"Mrs. Carlton's School for Girls. Not the actual school, though. Just . . . somewhere nearby."

For once Graham didn't tease or make a joke. He simply gave the coachman instructions and sat quietly in his seat.

When the carriage rolled to a stop, Aaron climbed down. Graham exited behind him, but Aaron didn't wait before strolling down the street to get closer to the school. Through a line of trees he could see the enclosure where Sophia was working with two girls on horseback. She perched atop Rhiannon, giving instructions and demonstrating before the girls made their own attempts.

She wore a blue riding habit that Bianca had worn last year. The skirt draped elegantly over the side of the horse, covering Sophia's legs. It was entirely proper and looked entirely out of place. Could she do the riding she loved in that skirt? Even though she'd raced sitting aside, she'd been astride when she had given demonstrations at Trent's house.

Her laugh drifted to him through the air, and his gut clenched. "Does she look happy?"

Graham looked at Aaron and then Sophia. There wasn't any way to see her face or any real detail. Still, he said, "Yes, she does."

"Good." Aaron could move on as long as Sophia was happy. He didn't want to have made a mistake with her while he was finding his own way.

They stood there too long. When Sophia circled her students, she looked up and saw them, then rode Rhiannon over to the closest corner, the only spot clear of trees.

Her shock was apparent. He gave her a smile and wave, hoping it would be enough.

Her lips moved, and it looked like she might be saying his name.

He couldn't hear it. And he needed to leave before he did. Giving her one final nod, he turned and walked back to the carriage.

It was time to go home.

IF JONAS'S VISIT had left Sophia at sixes and sevens, seeing Aaron on the road beside a carriage loaded down with trunks made her utterly befuddled.

She ate her breakfast and stared into her tea. It was time to admit this was not what she'd thought it would be, yet it was all she was ever likely to have.

She'd envisioned having a handful of students who, even if they couldn't commit to the level of training her father had taught, would be interesting in learning the basics.

Instead, all she had to show for a month of work was many young ladies with a proper seat. Mrs. Carlton still didn't care if they were good at riding. She just wanted them to appear as if they were.

That lack of interest from the school and her students led her to spend more time alone than she ever had before. She amused herself by working with Rhiannon, attempting to perform some of her disciplines while sitting aside. Once she and the horse learned how to use a whip as the right-side leg aid, they started making progress.

Unfortunately, she had no one to share it with. Pouring out her accomplishments in a letter to Jonas wasn't the same as talking to him.

Sophia missed talking.

"Good morning."

Sophia smiled at the other teacher's greeting. The staff were nice, but since Sophia spent her days out of doors or in the stable, they hadn't been able to get to know one another beyond the pleasantries.

The post arrived and with it a letter from Jonas. Sophia tucked it into the pocket of her riding habit to read alone later. It had taken her a couple of weeks to become accustomed to managing the longer skirt of the habits, but she thought herself rather skilled now. She'd had little to do but practice.

In the stable, she opened the letter, anxious for a taste of home. Now that Jonas could sit, was he considering looking for a job in London?

Her eyes flitted over the letter. No. In fact, he'd written the opposite.

> *No one is going to say they enjoy mucking out stalls, but outside of the stable the air is fresh. Mr. Knight likes me more since I have been able to climb back into a saddle.*
> *I cannot ride for prolonged periods of time, but I can exercise the horses in the countryside. I've found wonderful places to sit and sketch. I'll show them to you when I see you next.*

She couldn't ask him to come—couldn't even hint at it. He sounded content. She wouldn't want him to give that up just because she wasn't. If she asked him to come to London, he'd willingly work in the dankest stable in town to make her life better.

If Jonas were here, he'd tell her she was despondent because the heart truly longed for God and wouldn't be happy until He was its purpose. Maybe there was something to that. After all, six years of trying to regain what she'd lost wasn't leaving her fulfilled.

MRS. CARLTON STOPPED her after dinner that night. "The girls' riding has improved greatly. They look very proper."

Sophia smiled with clenched teeth. "Thank you."

"It does not, however, seem to be taking up a great deal of your time."

"Er, well, no. I'd hoped for a few advanced students, but none has shown an interest."

The headmistress nodded. "We can't have a teacher who doesn't work. Perhaps we need to consider what else you can teach the girls?"

What else could she teach them? If they didn't want to expand their riding skills, she doubted they wanted to learn how to clean a hoof or use a currycomb. Horses were all she knew.

"We'll meet next week," Mrs. Carlton said in the same kind but firm voice that had guided many a young girl into womanhood. "You can present a list of other talents that might be useful."

"Yes, Mrs. Carlton," Sophia said, because she didn't have any other options.

That night she lay in bed, staring at the ceiling. Her normal methods of dealing with problems by either seizing her first available option or allowing Jonas to manage it weren't going to work this time.

Jonas wasn't here, and not a single alternative sat before her.

Perhaps it was time to try something new.

"God," she whispered, eyes fixed on a tiny crack in the plaster. "Where do I belong? What would you have me to do? I don't want this restlessness. Jonas always says to rest in you and know you hold my future. I don't think I've been doing that. I've been chasing what I once had instead of what you want to give me."

Her words turned to nonsensical mumbles as she fell asleep, feeling more at peace than she'd been in weeks, even if she didn't know how God would answer.

TWO DAYS LATER, it came in the strangest form.

"Miss Fitzroy, you have a visitor."

Sophia looked up from the book she'd been reading, searching for inspiration on what she could suggest to Mrs. Carlton. "I do?"

"In the drawing room. In the future, Miss Fitzroy, please restrict your visits to the days you have off."

Since Sophia didn't know who could be visiting her, she didn't know how to tell them when to come, so she gave the headmistress a nod and left the room.

Her feet stumbled to a stop as she entered the drawing room. Miss Hancock stood by the window.

"Hello, Miss Fitzroy, dear." She strode across the room, peered out into the front hall, then shut the door with a decisive *click*. "Now, tell me, have you been here long enough to find it utterly boring?"

"I beg your pardon?"

Miss Hancock sighed. "I attended a school like this, you know. I'm glad I did, but I was also happy to leave it behind."

It was difficult to imagine Miss Hancock in an environment such as Mrs. Carlton's. Her uniqueness would have had the teachers' faces scrunched into permanent frowns.

"I'm going to take your silence as agreement, though I don't blame you for not wanting to say it aloud. Miss Fitzroy, I'm in need of a new companion, and I'd like to offer you the job."

"A companion?"

"Yes. I want one who knows how to travel." She tilted her head in Sophia's direction. "You've certainly done your share of that. I won't have to worry about you shying away from a speck of dirt." She started strolling about the room. "I'd also like to learn to ride better. I live in Newmarket, after all. One should ride well when they live in Newmarket."

"Do you plan to race?"

"Goodness no. You proved the feminine ability there quite nicely. It would take me too long to get decent at it and I haven't got enough interest."

"Oh."

She wanted the job. Badly. Wanted to jump up and scream that she would take it. But Aaron had gone through so much to provide her this opportunity. Wouldn't throwing it away insult him? "Does Mr. Whitworth know you're offering me this job, Miss Hancock?"

"Call me Harriet. I can't abide a companion who doesn't feel comfortable with me. May I call you Sophia? Good."

Sophia bit her lips to hold in a smile. It was possible Miss Hancock—Harriet—liked to talk as much as she did. They would be very noisy companions.

It sounded delightful.

"As for Mr. Whitworth, the man doesn't know what he wants, and even if he did, it wouldn't matter. You can't make your decisions based on him, my dear. You need to think for yourself and see what your future holds."

"He went through a great deal to place me here, Harriet. I value that."

"Yes, I suppose he did." She pressed her lips together and narrowed her dark eyes. "Sophia, we are two willful, smart, and independent women. If we can't determine a way to have everything we want in life, no one can."

Thirty-Seven

As soon as Fitzroy was healed enough to ride again, Aaron subjected himself to the man's extended presence by having him exercise the racehorses. The man had a potential future as a jockey, if he wanted it. He wasn't a natural like his sister, but with a little experience, he would do well.

Fitzroy did not, unfortunately, suffer from the same case of jabber-jaw that Sophia did, so there were no dropped tidbits of news about his sister, even though he got a weekly letter from her.

Aaron kept hoping, though, for some indication of Sophia's well-being. He had to assume that if she ever got into trouble or became truly miserable, her brother would do something about it.

Today, it was just the two of them training. Hopefully having Sweet Fleet running alone with Equinox would push the horse to work harder. Fitzroy sat on the younger racehorse's back, waiting for instructions. Before Aaron could give any, he caught sight of a pair of horses riding along the berm. Unsurprising, since every pale horse running along the Heath caught his eye these days.

The riders were female, their skirts fluttering as the horses ran. One of the mounts was pure white, and the rider's posture looked all too familiar.

"I don't suppose you'd have told me if your sister was coming back to Newmarket."

"No, I don't suppose I would have."

"Is that her?"

"If you have to ask, it doesn't matter."

Aaron gave Fitzroy his best glare. The other man laughed and gave a shrug. "Don't be cross with me if you don't like the truth."

Turning his attention back to the horses, Aaron tore his eyes from the first rider and focused on the second. The tall purple plume coming out of the riding hat could only indicate one person. "It appears Miss Hancock has found her new companion."

"That's the rumor." Fitzroy adjusted his position in the saddle. "She must not pay well, though. The rumors also say the companion has a second job."

Aaron turned Equinox so that he could see both Fitzroy and the distant riders. "Do they say what sort of second job?"

"Only that she'll work it when Miss Hancock takes her twice-yearly trips to London for her three-week shopping excursions."

"That sounds like a convoluted arrangement." The horses turned down the far side of the berm. Soon they'd be out of sight.

Fitzroy cleared his throat and Aaron blinked, realizing he'd been staring at nothing but grass.

"Right." He adjusted his hold on the reins and lined his horse up with Fitzroy's. "Why don't we race back to the stable?"

Aaron had some investigating to do.

"IF YOU NEED your companion to attend a dinner party with you, one can only wonder why you want to attend in the first place." Sophia turned the page in her book, refusing to look up at her employer.

Mrs. Carlton had been relieved by Sophia's proposal to come to the school twice a year for a few weeks of condensed lessons instead of idling about the grounds. Those had been her words. Sophia had chosen not to take them personally.

Though her belongings now fit in a trunk instead of a knapsack, it hadn't taken much to load it up and move to Harriet's home.

322

That had been a week ago.

They'd ridden the Heath, gone shopping in Cambridge, and attended church. Harriet did not attend St. Mary's, so Sophia had thus far been able to easily avoid everyone she knew. Though she'd received a few peculiar looks, no one seemed willing to risk an altercation with Harriet as long as Sophia maintained a quiet presence at her side. Jonas came to visit, but otherwise it had just been Sophia and Harriet.

Until tonight. Harriet was going to a dinner party and insisting Sophia come along.

The dinner was being put on by Lady Adelaide.

Sophia was not amused.

She wasn't ready to see Aaron again, wasn't sure when she *would* be ready to see him, and most certainly didn't want to talk about it. "Isn't that what companions do?" Harriet asked as she stalked into the room and loomed over Sophia's chair. "It's practically in the name that you *accompany* me places."

"If you need my company at a party of friends, you might want to revisit whether or not they're your friends."

"Or perhaps you should remember they are yours as well."

"My name wasn't on the invitation."

Grinning in triumph, Harriet dropped a square of parchment onto Sophia's open book. It was a formally stated invitation to dinner, and her name was scrawled across the top in large, calligraphed letters.

Sophia cleared her throat. "This seems rather elaborate for a small gathering. I've nothing to wear that matches the elegance of the invitation."

"Sophia Fitzroy, I would never have hired you if I'd realized what a coward you are." Harriet crossed her arms over her chest and stuck her nose in the air.

"It is not cowardice to avoid situations that have a significant chance of causing great harm."

"And what harm can come to you at a dinner party? If Lady

Adelaide's cook was inclined to poison people, we'd all be dead by now."

Sophia closed the book and looked up at the woman who would likely always be a mystery to her, no matter the amount of time she spent in her company. "I've no concerns about the cook."

"I can haul my own dining chairs over if you're worried their furniture isn't sound."

"Now you're being ridiculous." Sophia couldn't stop herself from laughing.

"Well, I've always thought the best way to converse with a fool was to be one yourself."

"I'm not a fool."

"Aren't you? You're sitting here, still stewing over what might have been instead of going out and discovering what could be. Seems a useless sort of pain to me."

Sophia stood and crossed to the window. "What if he doesn't want to see me?"

"What was that? I'm afraid if you whisper at a window, the sound doesn't travel far." Fabric rustled behind her and Sophia turned to see Harriet picking up Sophia's discarded book. "What are you reading, anyway?"

"What if he doesn't want to see me?" Sophia asked louder. With the question finally out in the open, all her other thoughts poured forth. "Aaron went through a great deal of trouble to get me that job—"

"You mean the one you still have?"

"Yes, in a way, but he doesn't know the arrangement or why."

"That's why you *tell* him. Though if your brother's worth his beans, he's already dropped a hint or two."

Sophia was not bringing her brother into this. "Aaron doesn't want me here. He didn't even tell me good-bye. He just—"

"He waved to you from the street. Am I not telling people good-bye when I wave?"

"I barely know him, and—"

"The potential of a person can be so enthralling that not exploring it will ruin everyone else you meet in the future."

How did this woman have an answer for everything? She was worse than Jonas. "I have nothing to offer him, so there isn't any reason to explore this so-called potential. It will only—"

"Sugar confections that are built up to look magnificent and elaborate always taste like dirty air. I do hope reality is better than that."

"Would you stop interrupting me?" Sophia's voice cracked as she tried to keep it from becoming a scream.

"No," Harriet said calmly, "because if I wait for you to finish, we'll be here for hours and the coach is coming round for us at three o'clock."

Sophia blinked. "Why so early?"

"Because Lord Stildon is going to propose to Miss Snowley this evening, and I promised to decorate one of the box stalls in his stable with flowers from Adelaide's conservatory. As my companion, you get to help."

"Oh."

Harriet widened her eyes in a look that didn't even begin to appear authentically innocent. "You *do* want Miss Snowley to get a romantic proposal, don't you?"

Sophia shook her head. "Harriet, one of these days you're going to find someone you can't manage."

"I do hope it's a man so we can fall in love and get married." Harriet gave a wicked grin and swept from the room. "Now, let's find you something fabulous to wear."

IT WAS ONLY a matter of time before they ended up in the same drawing room.

Aaron had anticipated the moment, bracing himself for it to be awkward and uncomfortable. Instead, it was the most natural thing in the world to walk up to her and say, "You look lovely, Sophia."

"Thank you." She took in a shaky breath, but her grin looked easy. "I should smell lovely, too. I've been carrying flowers for two hours."

"Decorating Hudson's stable?"

"You know?"

"I had to clear out the horses." He couldn't imagine any other woman finding a proposal in the middle of a horse stall romantic, but it was perfect for Hudson and Bianca. "I doubt they will stay long after dinner. He's rather anxious to make it happen."

The awkwardness he'd dreaded swooped in on the falling silence of unasked questions. If those were given a voice, there would be no going back. The swirl in his gut was like the anticipation he felt before a race.

"I saw you riding with Miss Hancock a few days ago." Though he'd poked and prodded everyone he knew as subtly as he could to learn the details of her new arrangement, he'd rather hear about it in her own words.

No matter how many of them she used.

"Yes." She looked at her toes and then up at him before blurting, "I still have the job you got me."

The wall was breached. Aaron fought to maintain his calm expression even as he anticipated her finally feeling the freedom to speak. "Oh?"

Sure enough, the words started flowing, and soon they were tumbling over one another to get out of her mouth.

"Though I enjoyed teaching the girls, none of them had much interest in anything beyond having a decent seat. Harriet wants to learn how to 'ride fancy,' as she says it. It's about training the horse as much as the rider, though, so we're on the hunt for the perfect mount. I've given her lessons on Rhiannon. Harriet's not very patient, so this could get interesting."

She shared how Lady Rebecca and Bianca had also asked for advanced lessons, and though they might have been pity requests, the opportunities still let her demonstrate her skills.

326

His heart lightened with every notch of excitement that entered her voice as she talked of her plans. As much as he enjoyed hearing her ramble, Aaron couldn't help but want to stop her words in a way that only he had ever done.

There were no horses, no confined spaces, no heightened situations to blame it on, but Aaron wanted to kiss her.

He'd spent his whole life saying he would never marry, but he'd begun to question that resolve. It was an admission that had come far too late. Sophia and Miss Hancock were destined for adventure, chasing experiences Aaron could never provide. But he could be here for her to tell her tales to when she came home.

In the meantime, he could show her that he was no longer a man whose life was predetermined by circumstances out of his control. And the moment she tired of following Miss Hancock around, he would give her another option.

"Aren't you glad I made you go to dinner last night?"

Sophia set down her morning coffee with a sigh. "My admission that it wasn't as bad as I'd feared is not permission for you to gloat for the next hundred years."

"I won't gloat on this for a hundred years." Harriet waved a hand through the air. "I'm sure I'll do something else worth crowing about by noon. Until then, indulge me."

"No."

"You're a terrible companion."

"If you wanted someone who always agreed with you, you could have put a plant on wheels and toted it around."

Harriet pursed her lips and her eyes went unfocused.

"That was not meant to give you ideas, Harriet."

"You're right. That would go a little beyond eccentric."

If it got Harriet to drop the discussion of last night's dinner, Sophia would carry around a plant herself. "What are we doing today?"

"First, I want to check in on the happy couple."

"We're paying a call on Miss Snowley, then?"

"Goodness no. I can't stand her stepmother. Besides, she'll be at Hawksworth. We'll go there straightaway after breakfast."

"You're not the least bit subtle, you know."

Harriet grinned. "Doesn't make me any less effective."

Two hours later, they were riding up the drive to Hawksworth. When both Jonas and Aaron stepped out to greet them, she gave serious consideration to turning around and riding away.

If Jonas knew she'd spent a great deal of time staring at the ceiling and thinking about Aaron instead of sleeping, he'd shake his head and tell her . . . Well, she didn't know what he'd tell her or she'd have told it to herself.

Jonas looked from her to Aaron before casting his eyes heavenward, shaking his head, and stomping back into the stable. It would seem he had an idea of her dilemma even without her telling him.

She and Aaron only had time to exchange pleasantries before Miss Snowley pulled her and Harriet into the still-decorated stall to hear the story of Lord Stildon's proposal.

While pretending to admire the flowers she'd helped put in place, Sophia snuck a glance at Aaron, only to find him looking back at her. He caught her eye, gave her a slight smile and a nod, then went about his business. What was she supposed to make of that? Either she had to learn to ignore that man, or he had to learn how to talk.

Thirty-Eight

Eight. Weeks.

Eight very long weeks, which included forty-two dinners, thirty-six rides—twelve of which had been just the two of them—and five fabricated deliveries to Miss Hancock's house. That was how Aaron marked time now. Instead of days or hours, races or training schedules, he framed his life by when he saw Sophia and what they did together.

He'd even written her a letter while he'd gone to look at a horse. He'd had to deliver it himself, since he'd been away all of three days. The embarrassment of handing it over faded when she blushed and produced a letter of her own. Hers had, naturally, been five times longer than his, but he still liked the idea that neither of them wanted to go long without sharing their thoughts with the other.

Aaron's ability to stand by his early November resolve to wait for her to have her adventures was feeling as wan and thin as the December sunlight. Only his nightly conversations with his Bible gave him the strength to keep his mouth shut about his feelings while opening up about his life.

Today, Sophia had joined him in observing the horses training on the Heath. Aaron positioned them on the berm overlooking the area where the horses were doing their brush runs, so they would have a modicum of privacy.

"You'll be very proud of me," Sophia said, eyes trained on the horses below. "I told Harriet no this morning."

It was a skill she had to learn if she was going to live with Miss Hancock. "Impressive. What about?"

"Feathers. She wanted to get us matching hair plumes."

Aaron didn't try to hide his laughter. "There are going to be feathers on your dressing table when you get back."

"And they'll look lovely as part of the maid's duster. I thought about sticking them on her horse's bridle, but I'm afraid that might give her ideas."

The ensuing silence was a comfortable one, free of tension and anticipation. Eventually one of them would speak again—probably her—and the conversation would continue. It was the rhythm between them now.

"Have you seen Lord Rigsby lately?"

Aaron nodded. "I had dinner with him last night."

"He's settled in? That's rather quick, isn't it?"

Another nod. "Yes, but he had everything ready. He was just waiting to find the right place to make his home."

That had been just one more in the growing number of revelations he was having about himself. Returning to his one-room cottage after hearing Rigsby's plans to make his new house a home had reinforced to Aaron that it was time to move on. The cottage was just one more testament to his past that needed to be let go.

He didn't want to bring a wife home to that cottage. Nor was it a place he wanted for himself. He wanted more.

Just one more reason to wait.

That didn't make it any easier.

What had been a glimmer of hope, an opportunity for more, had taken root and grown. Now he had to wait for the right time to let it bloom.

"My request was approved today."

She turned to him, smiling in delight. "That's wonderful! You're an officially licensed trainer now, hmm?"

He nodded. Being a horse trainer was a step down the social ladder from being a stable manager, but he no longer cared. What he loved was working with the horses. Rigsby had given Aaron the idea by asking him to consider coming on as his trainer. The notion had niggled at him until he'd accepted it was what he truly wanted.

Hudson was more than capable of overseeing his own stable. Oliver had developed a genuine interest in running his. Both men wanted Aaron as their trainer as well, so he was going to be just as busy, if not more so, than he'd been before.

Now he just needed his own yard. He could look into renting space near everyone else, but he was tired of hearing whispers and getting dirty looks.

He glanced at Sophia, her head tipped back to feel the sun.

He loved her. He'd known for certain two weeks ago when she'd fallen off her horse and lay in the grass, laughing for five minutes. His dismount had been clumsy as he'd rushed to her side, but when she'd opened her eyes and looked up at him, he'd known.

"I'm buying a corner of Hudson's land." The words came out brusquer than he'd intended, but her reaction to this news was going to tell him a lot about whether she would ever be satisfied with what he could offer.

She brought her chin down and looked at him. "You are?"

"There's an old stable there they used for farm animals before the land around the house was turned into horse pasture. I'm going to build my yard there." He took a deep breath. "And a house."

Saying it out loud, hearing the statement in his own voice, crashed through him and nearly had him falling off his horse. If he could guarantee it would give Sophia the same clarity he'd gained when she'd fallen, he'd have happily tumbled to the ground.

He plunged on, afraid to look at her and see her reaction. "It will take a while. I'll refurbish and expand the old stable first. I'll work from Hawksworth until it's done."

"That's wonderful." Rhiannon pranced halfway around Shadow in a circle. Sophia started laughing. "I'm so excited I tried to come in and hug you. It doesn't work well on a horse."

Before she'd stopped speaking, Aaron was on the ground. "We can remedy that."

It would be the first time they'd touched since her return from London, unless one counted the times their hands would connect when exchanging items. Her wide eyes indicated she was as aware of that fact as he was.

"Yes, I suppose we can," she said quietly.

He reached up. She kicked her foot free of the stirrup and leaned over to place her hands on his shoulders. He grasped her waist and lowered her to the ground, leaving them standing in relative privacy between the two horses.

Then she was wrapped in his arms.

She held him tight and whispered, "Aaron, I'm so happy for you." She eased back but didn't lower her arms.

He looked down at her, taking in the fire of her hair, the emerald jewels of her eyes, the smoothness of her skin.

Patience. He needed patience.

And to remember they were standing atop a hill where anyone could look over and see them.

He stepped back and threaded his fingers together to give her a leg up onto her horse.

As he remounted, he rejoiced in her excitement about his plans. That brought him one step closer to making her a part of them.

SOPHIA WAS AN idiot.

Or Aaron Whitworth was an idiot.

Possibly the idiocy could be equally divided between the two of them.

Whatever way it fell, she was in agony.

"We should take a trip after Christmas," Harriet said over breakfast, two days after what Sophia's brain was fixating on as *The Hug*. Capital letters and dramatic emphasis included.

"Tomorrow is Christmas Eve," Sophia reminded her.

"It's not as if we've anyone to answer to."

"What about your father?" She wouldn't have dared ask about Harriet's parents when she first started working, but she could no longer suppress her growing curiosity.

"He doesn't have anyone to answer to either." Harriet looked up, her eyes unfocused, seemingly lost in another world. Then she blinked. "Where should we go?"

Seeing as Sophia had no desire to go anywhere, she wasn't about to offer an opinion. As much as she adored Harriet and enjoyed living here, she didn't want to leave Aaron.

Even if he seemed perfectly happy with the way things were.

"London is pretty at Christmas," Harriet mused.

"London?" Sophia's cup rattled as she nearly dropped it on the table. "That's . . . so close." What had happened to touring the Continent or seeing the islands?

"We don't want to go too far," Harriet said with a wave of her hand. "Mr. Whitworth is a busy man. I'm sure he'd be willing to let it all slide in order to come fetch you, but there's no reason to go through an excessive amount of trouble just to make a point."

"He's not going to come fetch me." She was just north of town now, and he hadn't made an effort.

"Does he know you'd like him to?"

Sophia opened her mouth and then snapped it shut. That was a rather excellent question. As much as they talked now, and it was still her far more than him, neither of them had ever mentioned wanting more.

Did he want more? Was he waiting on her? It wasn't really fair of her to expect him to read her mind. Not when she knew how impossible it was for her to read his.

She wasn't bold enough to say it. If he said no, it would shred her heart to pieces. But maybe she could show him.

Though Harriet was insistent that a trip to London was the best solution, she didn't balk when Sophia suggested a dinner party. Whether she guessed Sophia's plan or simply liked the idea of demonstrating her new riding skills didn't matter. Including horse-related entertainment in the Christmas Eve gathering would provide the chance Sophia needed.

Harriet presented first, surprising the guests with her ability to take Rhiannon through a series of basic steps. All too soon she was handing the reins to Sophia. "Now you can show us how it's really done."

Sophia mounted, feeling more than a little self-conscious. She was in the evening dress her friends had given her months ago, only this time she had the matching trousers on underneath and her feet were bare.

She took a deep breath and guided the horse forward. What if Aaron didn't understand what she was trying to say?

She wouldn't know if she didn't try. It was the safest declaration a girl could make. If Aaron thought of her the same way she thought of him, he would see this as her saying she was willing to embrace all the past had made them and forge a new future.

Hopefully.

Sophia didn't concern herself with a routine as she sent Rhiannon prancing about the small section of lawn. Only one trick was going to matter tonight. After a few pirouettes, a couple *piaffes*, and an extended trot, she steered Rhiannon in a large circle and nudged her into a run.

One more deep breath.

Then she pulled her leg beneath her.

SHE WAS STANDING.

On a horse.

While everyone around him cheered and clapped, Aaron sat frozen. She'd been too adamant about never doing any of her circus tricks again for this exhibition not to mean something.

He just wished he knew what it was.

He held his breath until she lowered herself down onto the horse's back, then looked around for Fitzroy. Her brother had been invited to all forty-three dinner parties. He always came but stayed on the edge of the group. Aaron finally found him leaning against the side of the house.

Staring right back at Aaron.

"She's wonderful," Miss Hancock said as the cheering subsided.

"Yes."

"We're leaving the day after Christmas. Could you send someone to check in on the horses while we're gone?"

Air rushed out of Aaron's lungs. She'd been making a declaration, but it hadn't been about him. He was thankful she'd accepted that part of herself, but it made him sad that the realization hadn't brought her to him.

Instead she was leaving town. She was going off on an adventure. Without him.

"That won't be a problem." Aaron would keep an eye on the horses himself. That way he'd know the minute they returned.

Then he was coming after her. No more waiting.

"Speaking of horses," he said, "I'm going to go help with Rhiannon."

He rose and rounded the mingling group to wait for Sophia at the mounting block next to the stable.

Sophia's smile was enormous, and her eyes were bright as she rode up to him. "I'd forgotten how fun that is."

"I'm glad you remembered." He glanced at her toes but didn't allow his gaze to linger. "Where are your shoes?"

"In the stable."

He nodded and took Rhiannon's reins to lead her into the warmth of the stable. Did he imagine that Sophia hesitated to pull away after he helped her down?

While she retrieved her footwear, he took Rhiannon to a stall, handed the saddle and bridle to a groom, and checked food and water levels. Sophia stepped into the stall to check for herself and give her horse a pat on the neck.

And once again it was her, him, and the horse in a confined space. The urge to pull her into his arms was strong.

Instead, he grabbed two currycombs and thrust one in her direction.

She took it and turned it over in her hands as if she'd never seen one before. Then she gave him a tight smile. "I think I'll let Harriet's grooms take care of Rhiannon tonight. I wouldn't want them to wait dinner on us."

What had dimmed her light so quickly? Was it something he'd done? Hadn't done?

He followed her to the house, praying God would hold whatever they had until she came back to him.

And if God felt like granting Aaron a little understanding of the female mind in the meantime, that would be welcome too.

Thirty-Nine

She'd been gone for two days and already Newmarket felt colder. Granted, it was almost January and there was a good chance they'd see snow soon, but Aaron had lived through enough winters to know the difference.

Sophia was the sunshine in his days, and now he had to make it without her. Possibly for a very long time.

She and Harriet had taken enough luggage to be gone for a year. Aaron had shown up early the day after Christmas and strapped three large, heavy travel cases to the carriage. Those had been bad enough, but the conveyance had been followed by a wagon laden down with at least eight more trunks.

A saddle dropped onto the bench beside him, the jangle of buckles and the slap of leather against wood jarring Aaron from his thoughts.

"London."

"What?" He looked up at Fitzroy.

"London. She's in London."

"What's going on in here?" Hudson asked, poking his head around the corner from the stalls.

Aaron ignored him and stood, staring down the redheaded groom who looked . . . angry? "Why is she in London?"

"Because that meddlesome woman thinks true love will make you run after her. She doesn't understand love doesn't demand

337

what it wants. Instead, it will sacrifice itself to give the other person what they need."

Aaron stood there dumbfounded, putting together the pieces.

It must have come together for Hudson at about the same time because he suddenly started laughing. "Let me get this straight. Harriet took Sophia to London hoping Aaron would come running after them but didn't tell Aaron where they would be, so even if he was of a mind to do that, he wouldn't have been able to do so without your intervention?"

Both men turned to Hudson, who shrugged. "I just want to make sure I know the story before I go share it with my *wife*."

"You aren't tired of saying that yet?" Aaron asked.

"Not at all."

A ripple of laughter sounded from the row of stalls.

Hudson grinned. "Never mind. She's already heard. Never try to keep secrets in this stable."

Bianca came running around the corner. Unfortunately, she wasn't alone. Oliver and Graham were on her bootheels. Why had no one told these people that aristocrats were not supposed to tarry in stables? Collect the horse, drop off the horse, stay out of the horse trainer's business.

"You're going to London, aren't you?" She clapped her hands. "Should we all come?"

"No," Aaron said firmly.

Her face fell. "You aren't going to London?"

"Oh, I'm going to London, but *you* aren't coming with me." He turned to Fitzroy. "Tell me what you know."

"They're staying at Clarendon Hotel."

Aaron nodded and turned back to his friends, all of whom were smiling like lunatics. He sighed. "You are enjoying this, aren't you?"

"Immensely." Oliver grinned. "I just wish Fitzroy had told me instead of you so that I could drag *you* off by the ear like you did me."

"The situations are completely different."

"The lady loves you, you love the lady but think she wants more than you can offer, so she runs off to supposedly get it, and if you don't follow her, you might lose her forever?" Oliver shrugged. "You're right. I don't see the similarities at all."

"You win the award for most irritating." Aaron looked to Graham. "How is your wife?"

The question surprised him. "I . . . believe she's doing well?"

"Good. You can come with me. I still feel strange going to your parents' home without you."

"You know Oliver's coming too, right? It's always been the three of us. Just because we have wives doesn't change that."

Aaron opened his mouth.

Graham cut in. "Nor does the fact that you currently find him annoying."

Aaron sighed.

Oliver clapped him on the shoulder. "What was it you told me?"

"Stop being a chub and fight for the woman you love."

"Ah yes," Oliver said. "I remember now. Is it my turn to say that to you?"

As Aaron considered the ramifications of hitting a man who would one day be an earl, Oliver scampered away, laughing.

"You know," Graham mused, "Father knows the archbishop. We might be able to make a case that Miss Fitzroy doesn't have a parish and get you a special license."

"If you get married without me, Aaron Whitworth, I'll be very upset." Bianca crossed her arms and frowned.

"And I'll be upset if you make my *wife* upset." The grin on Hudson's face took the threat out of his statement.

Not that Aaron cared. His mind was stuck on the idea that he could come home from London with a wife and not just the promise of one.

He looked at Fitzroy. "I won't have anything but a one-room cottage for at least a year."

"She spent two years sleeping under a wagon. I don't think she'll mind."

"Am I to assume, then, that I have your blessing?"

"I wouldn't have told you where she was if you didn't. But if you think to marry her without me there, I'll retract it."

He looked at the group of people surrounding him. There were varied qualities of clothing, varied levels of stable grime, and an absurd conglomeration of pasts that never should have brought them together, yet here they were. With him. Including him. Supporting him.

"Gentlemen," he said, his chest feeling warm and full for the first time in days, "load up every carriage we have. We're going to London."

SOPHIA STOOD AT the window, staring down at the street. By her calculations, today was the day. If he didn't arrive today . . . well, then she'd be at this window again tomorrow and every day after that, until Jonas wrote her and told her he wasn't coming.

Behind her, Harriet was happily scribbling away on a letter to the new Lady Stildon, detailing her decision to stay in London instead of go on a grand adventure. Harriet was depending upon her ladyship's gossiping about that news so the information would filter down to Aaron. "Just you wait," she'd said as she pulled out her pen, "he'll be here shortly after the new year."

Sophia wasn't waiting that long.

On Christmas morning, it had occurred to her that she was taking advice from someone who was not married and had not, as far as she knew, ever been close. Harriet had never even claimed to be in love.

Counting on her plan seemed foolish, and Sophia no longer wanted to be a fool. So, she'd gone to her brother, who had also never been married or in love but was, at least, a man, and they'd made a plan.

It was a version of Harriet's plan, in that it still gave Aaron a way to reject her gently and maintain the friendship. It did not, however, rely on speculation and gossip.

Jonas was to give her two days to get to London, then mention to Aaron that was where they'd gone.

Coming after her was then Aaron's choice to make.

If he'd come on the mail coach, he could have been here two days ago. If he rode his own horse or took a carriage, the earliest arrival would be today.

What would she do if he didn't show?

What would she do if he did?

The day dragged on with a visit to the museum, a cold walk through the park, a stop in to see Mrs. Carlton at the school, and a visit to an old friend of Harriet's. When they returned to the hotel, there were no messages.

WHEN A FOOTMAN delivered a letter the next morning, Sophia's heart both jumped and plummeted. Was it from Aaron? Or Jonas?

Neither, as it turned out. It wasn't even for Sophia. Harriet was being invited to tea with Lady Grableton.

Graham's mother.

The woman Aaron had gone to for assistance.

Hope once more sent her stomach simultaneously up into her throat and down into her shoes.

"She must have heard we were in town from Mrs. Carlton," Harriet said as she dressed for the day.

Sophia would rather the headmistress had nothing to do with it. She put on her nicest dress and trembled the entire way to Mayfair.

They were shown to Lady Grableton's drawing room, where the woman was not alone. Lady Wharton, Lady Farnsworth, and Lady Stildon were all in attendance and smiling like loons.

Sophia's knees threatened to give way.

"Oh!" Harriet said from the entrance. "All of you are . . . here?"

"Miss Fitzroy, dear, I wonder if you wouldn't mind going to the—"

"Yes!" Sophia's teeth snapped together, and she cleared her throat. "I mean, I would be happy to." They'd be sending her to Aaron, wouldn't they? They wouldn't all be here if Aaron hadn't come for her.

Would they?

Although why Aaron had brought them all she couldn't fathom.

"Good, good." Lady Grableton handed Sophia a piece of paper. "Please give this to my coachman. Ask him for the package in the coach earlier today."

Harriet frowned. "Shouldn't you send a foot—"

"Right away." Sophia scampered out of the drawing room, even though she hadn't a clue where the lady's coachman would be. The mews? Those should be at the back of the house. The hardest part was going to be finding a door that led out that way.

Knowing it was rude, but desperate for a clue, she unfolded the paper.

It was blank.

Her heart pounded faster.

She wandered the floor until she found a door leading to the small back garden. The mews was only a short run farther. Accustomed as she was to the large stables of Newmarket, the city version felt cramped as she stepped inside.

There wasn't a coachman waiting, or a groom. There was, however, a man.

"I don't think you're the coachman," Sophia said breathlessly as she edged toward him until they stood face-to-face in an empty stall.

Aaron ran a hand over his face. "I'm not." He took a step closer and slid his hand down her arm until his fingers could wrap around hers. "I don't have much yet. Won't ever have a lot, really."

Sophia frowned. He did remember all her belongings fit in a knapsack when they met, didn't he?

Aaron sighed. "I'm making a muck of this. Words have never been good for me."

"Then don't use them." Sophia grinned and stepped a little closer. He had come for her, dragged all their friends here from Newmarket, and was stumbling through an ill-prepared speech in the middle of a small, smelly stable. If that wasn't a sign that he loved her, she didn't know what was.

One of his arms wrapped low around her back. "I'm trying to be a gentleman."

"Aaron Whitworth, do you know how many times I thought you were going to kiss me in the past eight weeks?"

"One hundred twelve? That's at least how many times I've thought of doing it."

Sophia tried not to laugh but failed. "Given that I have already kissed you twice, I could hardly do it again and remain a lady. As a gentleman, it is your duty to initiate the next one."

"Yes, ma'am." Aaron grinned and lowered his head.

After several moments, he eased back, resting his forehead against hers as they worked to calm their hearts and catch their breath. "You know," he said, "a gentleman should never kiss a lady like that unless he's completely in love with her."

"I suppose it's a good thing you're a gentleman, then." Sophia smiled up at him. "And I love you too."

His eyes were bright, even in the dimness of the stable. "Would this be an appropriate time to tell you that, as a gentleman, I didn't want to wait to marry you and obtained a special license this morning?"

Sophia pursed her lips and pretended to think about it. "I believe that news can wait until we've evened up the number of kisses, don't you?"

"Absolutely," he said and kissed her again.

Epilogue

Aaron was tying his cravat in preparation for walking up to Trenton Hall for dinner when the door burst open and Sophia stumbled in, laughing so hard she nearly fell over. He leaned one shoulder against the wall and smiled, knowing his wife of three months would eventually get around to sharing the humor. Then she'd tell him about her day while she changed clothes. Chances were he wouldn't say more than *yes* and *mm-hmm* until they were walking toward the large house for dinner.

His lack of a real kitchen had been one of his concerns when they'd married, but Sophia declared it would be nice to put off learning to cook for another year.

Her practicality was just one more thing to love about her.

She dropped her head back against the door and pulled in a shaky breath. "Harriet . . ." Then she collapsed into giggles again.

The way she enjoyed every single moment of life was another thing he loved. The list grew every day, and while he still wasn't good at telling her, he always made sure she knew it.

Aaron crossed the floor and scooped her up in his arms, feeling her shake against his chest as she laughed. He settled onto the sofa and just held her. If he was going to have to wait for her to speak—an uncommon occurrence to be sure—he was going to enjoy it.

Finally, the laughter stopped and she sat up in his lap, wiping tears from her eyes. After another shaky breath, she said, "Harriet wanted to show me something today."

Aaron lifted his brows. At least once a week Sophia and Harriet went riding together. They visited at other times as well, since Harriet enjoyed lingering about the ring where Sophia gave several local women riding lessons. Harriet didn't do anything except talk to the ladies before and after the lessons, but it seemed to keep everyone happy.

Sophia folded her hands in her lap. "Harriet, as you know, has a good deal of land. Aside from the corner the house sits on, she rents the rest out to a farmer. She likes her privacy and didn't want crops growing close to the house, so there's quite a large border around the house portion."

Aaron didn't care, but he liked how much she enjoyed stringing out whatever story she was telling him, so he nodded encouragingly.

"She lets most of it grow wild because she thinks it's pretty and it makes her feel like she's living somewhere exotic and undiscovered instead of a mile out of Newmarket."

Aaron settled further into the cushion behind him. It was a good thing he liked hearing his wife talk.

"Last week she decided to wander her property, and today she took me to her discovery. It seems she inadvertently became a patron of the arts."

Aaron frowned. How did one inadvertently sponsor anyone?

Sophia giggled again and Aaron smiled. Harriet could accidentally drop her money wherever she wished if it amused his wife so.

"She took me to an abandoned cottage. Half falling down, with trees and plants growing right up to the door—which was no longer on its hinges."

Aaron's eyes widened. "Her property extends that far?" And then more besides? He'd known Harriet was wealthy, but he was beginning to realize he had no idea just how wealthy.

"It does."

"Did you tell her it was Jonas?"

Sophia scoffed. "Of course not. It would ruin the mystery for her." She laid her head on Aaron's shoulder. "It was nice to see it again and remember how far I've come. I thought we were alone that day, Jonas and me against the world. Looking back, I'm amazed at the path God was laying. Living it was difficult, but I wouldn't change who I became or where I am."

She sat up. "I love you, Aaron Whitworth."

"I love you, Sophia Whitworth."

"Thank you for being my home." Then she leaned in with a smile and gave him a kiss.

As they prepared to leave their little cottage, he glanced at the Bible, still in a place of honor in the center of the table. Yes, the road to get here had been painful, but he wouldn't trade where he was now for anything.

He took Sophia's arm and nestled it in the crook of his elbow, a gentleman escorting his lady to dinner, walking into the future together.

Acknowledgments

My love of horses started as a child, and my parents willingly fed the obsession by allowing me to plaster my walls in horse posters, own a plethora of My Little Ponies, and fill the bookcase with books featuring the animal. For a brief time, they even let me take riding lessons. Thank you, Mom and Dad, for supporting my fascination.

If you've read my other acknowledgments, you know the people who made this book possible: my husband, my children, the makers of State Fair corndogs and Totino's frozen pizzas.

Also my Voxer Girls, who help my brainstorming and my brain in general and insisted that my books needed more kissing. My beta readers, who point out the plot holes I need to fix—particularly Regina Jennings, who spent hours on the phone helping me change a section when I refused to believe everyone who told me I needed to cut it. (I did eventually cut it, because sometimes the editors are right.) Thanks to Debb Hackett for combing through the manuscript to find any lurking Americanisms, particularly around the word *mad*.

Thank you to the team at Bethany House Publishers and my fantastic agent, Natasha Kern. It truly takes a village to keep my professional life straight.

Finally, my utmost gratitude to all the horse experts who were ever so patient with my ignorance, particularly Charlotte Osborne, who shared her vast knowledge of dressage and horse care. Your insight brought this book to life.

Kristi Ann Hunter is the author of the HAWTHORNE HOUSE and HAVEN MANOR series, and a 2016 RITA Award winner, a Christy Award finalist, and a Georgia Romance Writers Maggie Award for Excellence winner. She lives with her husband and three children in Georgia. Find her online at www.kristiannhunter.com.

Sign Up for Kristi's Newsletter

Keep up to date with Kristi's news on book releases and events by signing up for her email list at kristiannhunter.com.

Also from Kristi Ann Hunter

When a strange man appears to be stealing horses at the neighboring estate, Bianca Snowley jumps to their rescue. And when she discovers he's the new owner, she can't help but be intrigued—but romance is unfeasible when he proposes they help secure spouses for each other. Will they see everything they've wanted has been there all along before it's too late?

Vying for the Viscount
HEARTS ON THE HEATH

You May Also Like . . .

Forced to run for her life, Kit FitzGilbert finds herself in the very place she swore never to return to—a London ballroom. There she encounters Graham, Lord Wharton, who believes Kit holds the key to a mystery he's trying to solve. As much as she wishes that she could tell him everything, she can't reveal the truth without endangering those she loves.

A Defense of Honor by Kristi Ann Hunter
HAVEN MANOR #1
kristiannhunter.com

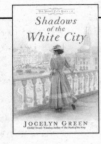

When Sylvie Townsend's Polish ward, Rose, goes missing at the World's Fair, her life unravels. Brushed off by the authorities, Sylvie turns to her boarder and Rose's violin instructor, Kristof Bartok, for help searching the immigrant communities. When the unexpected happens, will Sylvie be able to accept the change that comes her way?

Shadows of the White City by Jocelyn Green
THE WINDY CITY SAGA #2
jocelyngreen.com

After receiving word that her sweetheart has been lost during a raid on a Yankee vessel, Cordelia Owens clings to hope. But Phineas Dunn finds nothing redemptive in the horrors of war, and when he returns, sure that he is not the hero Cordelia sees, they both must decide where the dreams of a new America will take them, and if they will go there together.

Dreams of Savannah by Roseanna M. White
roseannamwhite.com

◊ BETHANYHOUSE

More from Bethany House

Haunted by painful memories, Olivia Rosetti is singularly focused on running her maternity home for troubled women. Darius Reed is determined to protect his daughter from the prejudice that killed his wife by marrying a society darling. But when he's suddenly drawn to Olivia, they will learn if love can prove stronger than the secrets and hurts of the past.

A Haven for Her Heart by Susan Anne Mason
REDEMPTION'S LIGHT #1
susanannemason.net

Luke Delacroix's hidden past as a spy has him carrying out an ambitious agenda—thwarting the reelection of his only real enemy. But trouble begins when he falls for Marianne Magruder, the congressman's daughter. Can their newfound love survive a political firestorm, or will three generations of family rivalry drive them apart forever?

The Prince of Spies by Elizabeth Camden
HOPE AND GLORY #3
elizabethcamden.com

When a stranger appears in India with news that Ottilie Russell's brother must travel to England to take his place as a nobleman, she is shattered by the secrets that come to light. But betrayal and loss lurk in England too, and soon Ottilie must fight to ensure her brother doesn't forget who he is, as well as stitch a place for herself in this foreign land.

A Tapestry of Light by Kimberly Duffy
kimberlyduffy.com

◆ BETHANY HOUSE